FRACKING DINOSAURS

DINOSAURS

THE CAYUGA LAKE DISASTER

DALTON MIRE

◆ FriesenPress

Suite 300 - 990 Fort St
Victoria, BC, V8V 3K2
Canada

www.friesenpress.com

ISBN
978-1-4602-2150-1 (Hardcover)
978-1-4602-2149-5 (Paperback)
978-1-4602-2151-8 (eBook)

1. FICTION, THRILLERS

Distributed to the trade by The Ingram Book Company

To
Pat—Thanks

PROLOGUE

Thousands of years ago a Pleistocene glacier slid into New York State gouging out a series of rivers with its icy tentacles. When this mountain of ice retreated, it blocked the rivers with debris forming a chain of lakes. The original inhabitants of these lakes believed the Great Spirit touched this land with his hand carving these beautiful fingers of water out of mother earth. The Finger Lakes still bear the names of these Native Americans who loved and preserved their homeland. Like the migrating birds resting on these blue waves, tourists and residents flock to these azure ribbons for water sports and wine, but in centuries past, natural beauty and salt lured natives and settlers to these shores

Cayuga and Seneca compete for the title of the largest lake with Cayuga being longer and Seneca the deepest. At the southern end of Cayuga Lake is Ithaca. This central New York town is famous for education with Cornell University resting high above Cayuga's waters and Ithaca College on an opposing hill. For many years, knowledge and salt have been the dominate commodities of this region, but now gas companies have invaded the area eager to fill the Marcellus Shale with fracking fluid to push the valuable gas to the surface. Then they the pump waste water produced by this process back into the earth to get rid of it. This new entry in the competition for the natural resources hidden far beneath the lake provides another challenge for the ecology of the lake to endure.

Throughout history few minerals have been as highly valued as salt. The salt beds under Cayuga Lake were created millions of years ago when a salton sea evaporated and left layers of salt thousands of feet thick. This extinct sea stretched from New York to Michigan and over eons of time was covered with sediments that turned into sedimentary rock capturing the remains of many creatures within its layers. The Iroquois discovered the salt springs and shared this knowledge and their legends of the lake with the Europeans who flooded their land.

Today the deepest salt mine in North America is located far below Cayuga's waters. Miners remove over a million tons of salt each year from this ever growing hole under the lake. Miles of roads and vast empty caverns are honeycombed beneath the lake to keep this profitable industry flourishing. While boats with

5

bikini clad beauties cavort above, gas companies and salt miners compete below for the valuable resources hidden deep under this beautiful lake. This epic battle between industry and environmentalists will decide the fate of the Finger Lakes.

****

BOOK ONE

I shall vanish and be no more.
But the land over which I now roam
Shall remain
And change not.

Song of the Hethushka Warrior Society

CHAPTER 1

He left his cabin early in the morning strolling along the Cayuga waterfront of Camp Minnechaug. Stopping at the water's edge, he looked out at the marshmallow clouds covering the lake. Checking his diver's watch, he had twenty minutes to spare before his friends arrived for their morning jog. Just enough time for a quick Jet Ski ride through the fog. Pushing the jet-ski into deeper water, he discovered that Cayuga Lake had not warmed during the night. Shivering as he climbed aboard his ride, he powered away from the shore.

Racing through the moist puffy white just touching the cold water, a prickly feeling suddenly ran down his back. He wasn't alone. He slowed and looked behind him, nothing. Laughing at his childish fear, he powered the ski ahead.

Lurching forward, the wind blew his curly blonde mane from his eyes. With the mist caressing his face, something big crossed just in front of him. *Wow, I almost caught breakfast,* he thought. *That was big. Must have been a fish. What a fish.*

Slowing down to enjoy his lonely sojourn across the fog shrouded lake, he felt that chill run down his back again. Plowing slowly through the water, he glanced behind him and stopped. Something was there. He could not see it, but could feel it.

Ripples in the water rolled under the fog toward him. Something was behind him hidden in the white mist. Suddenly a huge dark green almost black triangular head with flashing teeth tore through the low flying clouds. The Spector of this beast froze him in place. The thing hit the water with a splash just behind his ski. For a moment, this lake creature lingered on the surface glaring at him. As the flying cold water sprayed over his body, he couldn't help staring at the huge rough skinned body as it disappeared below the dark water. Shaken out of his trance by the cold water, he gunned his ski forward to escape.

Skimming over the lake, he glanced over his shoulder when the mist parted. There, behind him, he spotted it. It was following him. He slowed for a better look. *What was it? An alligator? Couldn't be, not this far North. Bigger too.* As his mind cried out for an explanation, the terrible thing dove under the shimmering water. Ripples flowing on top of the water told him the creature was heading directly toward him just below the surface. He was scared, but questioned what he had just seen. Was this a dream? Could it be real? The thing looked like a dinosaur. Lost in the fog, none of this made sense. Suddenly the beast lurched out of the water soaring right over the back of his ride. With snapping jaws, it tried to bite his shoulder. Dodging out of the way, he knew this was no dream. This nightmare was real and this monster was trying to kill him.

Terrified as the ugly head just missed his body, claws flashing from a flipper ripped red stripes in his leg. With a scream of pain, he twisted his wrist to let his jet-ski jump away from the beast. Flying through the sudsy white foam, there was no slowing down this time. He's seen enough. At this speed he had to be leaving this, this monster behind. As he burst through a hole in the fog bank, two more of these things were there in front of him. These creatures were smaller and casually turned their heads to look at him with water dripping from their glistening saber like teeth. He was too close to them to turn. He squeezed more power out of his machine and tore between them. *Thank God,* they dove into the water as he rammed passed them.

Lost in the mist, he turned hoping to find the safety of the shore. As the fog parted, the biggest creature yet lurched out of the mist. This horrible fiend stretched out of the water with open jaws straining to rip off his head. He could feel the hot moist breath of this creature on his neck as he ducked under the flashing teeth. His nostrils were assaulted by a dead fish smell as he plowed into the safety of the fog. Enveloped by the white mist again, he kept the power on high hoping to leave these devils far behind. Suddenly, the mountains of mist parted as he darted toward dry land. Finally, he was free of them. Or was he? He didn't dare look back to see.

He didn't slow down until he reached the shore running the ski up on the beach. Jumping off, he ran across the flat stones of the shale beach until he felt he was a safe distance from the water. Only then did he turn to scan the fog for evidence of his foe. As his eyes searched the clouds hovering over the lake, he could feel them staring back at him. The terrifying creatures were out there mocking his fear. He shook his head trying to lose the images of prehistoric beasts that were descending into the deep recesses of his soul.

He turned toward his cabin shivering from the visons now locked in his memory. Doubt flooded his mind. With every step, he questioned what he had seen. *Were they real? What had just happened?* He wondered if he had actually seen something or if his imagination was the only thing chasing him. Ramming around in that fog does crazy things to your mind. His hand slid down to the scratches still bleeding on his leg. He nodded his head, the blood was real and so were those things in the lake.

Shouts of "Steve" turned his head. Jogging up to him were his running buddies—Lea, Link and Billy. Sitting on his cabin steps pulling on his running shoes, Steve was still spooked by his encounter with the unknown. As he pulled the laces of his Nikes tight, he explained to his friends in an excited voice, "I…I was just out on the lake and saw these…ah…creatures. Like monster things. One actually chased me. Another tried to bite off my head."

He was surprised when his friends laughed. Trying to make them believe, he argued, "No, honest. They were big, like gators or crocs only with bigger teeth and a shorter snout. I mean really big teeth."

Dressed in her old worn red numbered white cross-country shirt, red running shorts and the latest orange glow Nike running shoes, Lea, a tall slim athletic brunette shook her head making her pony tail dance, laughed, "You have to watch out for freshwater sharks too."

Still haunted by the beasts, Steve tried to convince his friends that something really scary was out there. Alive, in the lake. When he pointed to the blood on his leg, his running partners laughed accusing him of having one beer too many last night. He hoped they were right, but the images of flashing teeth running through his mind made him shudder. With a swipe of his hand, he brushed the blood off his leg. As he ran along with his companions, he wiped his hand off on his running shorts. Steve tried to describe what he'd seen out in the lake as they jogged along, but his friends weren't buying it.

Turning to cross the dirt road running along the waterfront, an old rusty red pick-up stopped in front of them. The caretaker leaned out the window, "It's good to see young braves out running this early in the morning."

Wanting to tap into the driver's Iroquois heritage, Steve shouted at him louder and with more excitement in his voice than he intended. "Shanty, I saw something big out on the lake this morning. I mean really big. A bunch of them. Don't know what they were. Might have been gators or something, but with bigger longer teeth. What are those things?"

Shanty pulled off an old worn red baseball cap with a threadbare bill. *Mohawk Pride* was embroidered in faded gold on the front. After wiping his brow with his forearm, he pulled his cap back down over his long black hair. "You musta seen Apotamkon and his friends. In our legends, he's a serpent that lives in the lake."

Billy chimed in, "In my ghost stories, I call him Appysaurus. He's the Cayuga Lake dinosaur. Now the campers just call him, "Appy.""

His friends laughed and waved good-bye to Shanty as they ran across the road in front of his pick-up. Only half raising his arm to wave good-bye, Steve nodded to the caretaker as he said under his breath, "Maybe that's what I saw." Trailing after his friends, Steve said to himself, "Sure don't want to see them again."

Shanty watched them run off. *Better running through the hills surrounding this ancient lake than through the mountains of Afghanistan,* he thought as he rubbed his thigh kneading a scar hidden beneath his faded denim jeans.

Wounds can heal, but the memory of pain lasts forever. He sighed, *Warriors never cry. Well, at least not on the outside.*

After pumping down on the clutch throwing his old truck in gear, he floored it spitting out stones behind him. As he sped off, he wondered. *If not from the eyes, do a warrior's tears fall from your heart or your soul?*

Driving toward his cabin, Shanty's thoughts turned to the lake monster he knew so well. In the Iroquois legend, Apotamkon was a huge sea serpent with giant teeth who lived in ancient times. After a good life in the great salt waters beyond the land, each year Apotamkon swam up a great river with his mate to raise their young. Later with their children, these creatures would swim out to the ocean to continue the cycle of life. Then a great winter turned the world white. Apotamkon and his children found their river cut off by mountains of ice.

Trapped in the cold waters, Apotamkon's children were torn from the sea and Cayuga Lake became their home. Normally they ate fish, but occasionally when they were very hungry they ate the things swimming on top of their watery home. For them these creatures splashing on the surface weren't people just food that was easy to catch.

Shanty laughed, Billy told the campers *Appy* still prowled the lake and ate campers who swam beyond ropes defining the limits of the swimming area. For Billy, the legend was just a story to entertain campers, but he knew it was more than that. One of Apotamkon's children had visited him once when he was fishing with his father off the old pier. Driving with one hand, he reached down with his other hand and rubbed the scar Appy left on his calf. Yes, he knew Appy was very real.

As his camp friends ran up the steep path through the woods around the perimeter of the camp, Billy looked back as Shanty's pickup drove away. Getting to know Shanty had been an unexpected bonus of his summer job. As the caretaker, Shanty was the only permanent resident of the camp. Joe, or Shanty to his friends, lived in a small cabin on the far side of the camp hidden by a strip of forest. Billy's cabin was next to Joe's just a short walk from the lake.

Billy knew Shanty was proud to be a full blooded Mohawk or as he explained it, as pure as you can be after years of family members breeding with questionable members of other gene pools. Shanty had explained to Billy that he didn't like being called *Indian* because that name was imposed on his people by Europeans. He felt the same way about being called *Native American*. Native was the white man's way of calling his people poor and ignorant. American was another name imposed on his people by their *conquerors*. He didn't hate white men, but fiercely defended his Iroquois pride. Yes, Shanty explained that he was both Mohawk and Iroquois. Mohawks were part of the Iroquois Confederacy. Tribal Americans called this confederacy Hodenosaunee. It was a unified government of tribes long before the Europeans showed up.

Shanty told Billy that he often wondered how long Americans could claim they discovered this land. His people didn't need to be discovered? We were not lost. The explorers were the ones who were lost. Yes, those men thought they were in India. Then the Europeans destroyed a way of life they never tried to understand or accept. A lifestyle that had existed long before they set foot on our land.

With some reluctance, Joe told Billy that he would accept being called a *Tribal American*. At least the title Tribal Americans pointed out that we not all the same people. Each tribe was fiercely independent with different languages and beliefs. If you had to call him anything, Shanty told Billy to call him Mohawk or Iroquois. That was his ancestry.

Circling the camp was a long demanding course. Running up to Billy's rappelling cliff, this small group of dedicated athletes ran along the edge of the gorge and then splashed through the stream above the falls. From the top of the camp, they descended in a wild downhill race along a narrow path through the woods to the lake. Their rule was that each runner had to splash both feet in the lake then sprint from the water up the road between the athletic fields to the dining hall. The first one to sit down on the steps won their morning training run.

With images of lake monsters chasing him, Steve Swenson with his long swimmers body won today's race. Using the kick she had learned on her Cross Country high school team, Lea Avery came in second with Billy Barton close behind.

As Billy slammed down on the step next to her, between breaths, he told her, "I beat you. You, you...cheated."

Breathless, Lea disagreed, "No way...I, I was three strides ahead of you."

Billy held up his finger, "Ah...but you didn't step in the lake."

"Of course not, these are brand new shoes."

"Hey, rules are rules."

"Yeah right." Lea surrendered with a laugh, "Okay, today victory is yours shell boy. Tomorrow, I'll wear my old Adidas and beat your butt."

Trailing behind just his friends, Link Jefferson staggered in gasping for air wondering why his buddies liked to run more than the length of a basketball court. With his hands on his hips sucking in large gasps of air to recuperate, Link, a tall slim African-American, bid his friends good-bye as he slowly walked back to the boys' cabins where he was the lead counselor.

As Steve stood up, Lea slid her hands up his sweaty body and leaned against him. She had to stand on her toes to whisper in his ear, "Nice race big guy. I'm always proud of you, but watch out for those lake monsters. I don't want anything to happen to you." Then she kissed his cheek.

From the porch of the dining hall, the Camp Director's sister, Hilda, yelled, "Stop that." Dressed in her traditional black sweat suit jacket, camp T-shirt and black Bermuda shorts, she shouted, "No fraternizing between counselors."

Just to upset Hilda, Lea gave Steve a quick but sensuous kiss on the lips as she hugged his neck. Before Hilda could tell her to stop, Lea ran off to the girls' cabins with a smile.

Billy Barton put his head down trying not to laugh as Hilda lectured Steve about public displays of affection. After she stomped off, Billy told Steve that he'd see him at breakfast before turning to jog down to his cabin near the lake.

As Billy ran away, he thought about how lucky he was to land a job at this camp. Usually camp jobs went to Cornell athletes, the director's alma mater. Billy was the exception due to his scouting experience. His empire included obstacle and ropes courses, but his favorite camp activity was teaching kids how to rappel off a cliff. Once campers learned to overcome their initial reluctance to go over a cliff with only a thin line to prevent them from plummeting to their death, they gained the confidence they needed to confront the obstacles they would face in life.

Billy smiled. *How cool is a camp with its own cliff?*

After Billy grabbed a bar of soap and a towel off the railing of his cabin porch, he passed the caretaker's cabin as he walked to the edge of the lake and slipped off his khaki shorts and camo T-shirt. Then he threw his undershorts on the pile and waded naked into the cold lake to wash off.

Billy was the odd man out. He attended the other school at the end of the lake, Ithaca College. He was the lead man on their championship Varsity 8 crew team. At five foot seven, he was shorter than Steve and Link, but much more muscular with bulging arms and thighs. His short unruly mop of twisted brown hair was no competition for Steve's golden locks, but was longer than Link's Obama cut.

After soaping up, Billy dove beneath the chilly waters to rinse off.

CHAPTER 2

After the fog burned off, Jacob walked out on his flimsy dock resting on old barrels. As the bright rays of sun bounced off the glistening waves, he had to stagger to keep his balance as the dock swayed back and forth. He surveyed the lake noticing a little wind kicking up from the North before stepping into his heavy old rowboat. After sliding his tackle box under the middle seat, he carefully laid his fishing pole down so it dangled over the end of the boat. After untying his craft, he shoved off. As the boat slipped away from the dock, a momma mallard and her brood scurried out of his way. He watched them for a moment before pulling back on the oars.

As his oars dipped into the water, Jacob remembered building this old boat with his dad. When his dad left quarter-inch gaps between the boards on the bottom, Jacob thought the old thing would never float, but dad was right. After sitting in the lake for three days, the boards on the bottom swelled and it never leaked again. Leaning back pulling hard on the oars, his old tub surged toward the middle of the lake.

Jacob was excited to try his expensive new rod with its oversized reel and high test line. *With this baby*, he thought, *I have enough line to fish down deep where the big ones are hiding and nothing will break this heavy line.*

When he reached the deep center of the lake, he put the oars up on the end of the boat and rubbed his muscled arms. Good for the arms, back and legs, rowing was his only fitness program. He noticed an oil film on the ends of his oars and wondered if it was from the motorboat folks who didn't maintain their craft or from those new gas wells at the North end of the lake.

He pulled an old lure his father had carved from his tackle box and baited his line with it. After adding plenty of lead weights to take it all the way to the bottom, he cast out his line. Sitting down on the middle seat, he opened his thermos and poured his first cup of coffee of the morning. Sipping the bitter liquid, no sugar for him, he sighed as he surveyed the beautiful lake waiting for a bite.

Waiting is the best part of fishing, he thought. *Most people don't realize that. Floating on the lake with my boat rising and falling with the waves is a great way to start this day or any day.*

Suddenly Jacob's line yanked taut. Dropping his coffee, he grabbed his pole just before it was pulled out of the boat. Jumping up, he pumped his pole up and down pulling in his catch. Jacob kept reeling in his line until he could feel something big pulling hard against it. A strong fish that didn't want to surrender was fighting back.

After a half an hour struggle, *the fish seems to be tiring.* Jacob thought. *With aching arms, so am I.* He had never fought such a powerful fish.

A shadow of a huge black fish swim under his boat. It was bigger than anything he'd ever seen in the lake. When his line went slack, he kept reeling it in.

Have I lost my fish? Near the back of the boat a black fin appeared. *No, what was it? Maybe the back of a big turtle. No, a triangular black head. God Almighty, big teeth. Fangs.* As the creature surfaced behind his boat, he was scared. No terrified.

The creature rose up out of the water with Jacob's line caught between its huge ugly teeth. Its mouth was bigger than a Great White Shark with much longer yellowish teeth. Images of the old scrimshawed whale's teeth he had seen in museums flashed through Jacob's mind. Terrified by the creature emerging from the water, Jacob threw his new pole at its gaping mouth hoping to chase it away. The beast caught his pole between his jaws crushing it in one bite. It seemed to be smiling at Jacob with the ends of his fishing rod sticking out of each side of its mouth.

Jacob slammed down on the rowboat's middle seat dipping his oars deep into the water pulling hard to escape. As he pulled away, he kept his eyes on the beast as he left it behind. At first the beast just watched him go, but soon it began to follow him. Then suddenly it was gone. When Jacob was close enough to the shore to feel safe, he let his oars dip in the lake and leaned over exhausted breathing hard in great gasps. Suddenly the huge black monster rose out of the water at the end of his boat.

Wondering how he was launched into this nightmare, Jacob tried to grab his oars. As the terrible creature bit into the back of his boat, he jerked Jacob's hands off them. Ripping off a piece of the old lumber, the thing shook the hunk of wood like a dog with a bone. The monster seemed to be toying with him. Jacob finally grasped the oars and leaned back as he thrust them into the water hoping to escape from this monster beast. His back ached as he pulled, but no pain could not stop him now. The creature easily caught up with him and clinched his powerful jaws into the side of the boat whipping it back and forth like a toy.

"Jesus" Jacob screamed as a curse and a prayer. For a moment he thought his prayer was answered. The creature let go and submerged. Jacob watched as the ripples as the rushed away from his boat. *Thank god, it's leaving. I'm saved.*

No such luck. Soon the ripples turned around gaining speed as they raced back towards him. This time the thing shot out of the water. With flashing teeth, this mammoth beast landed half in and out of his boat throwing Jacob up into the air. When he landed, Jacob almost went overboard. *Man, this thing is huge,* Jacob thought as he tried to keep his balance.

Scared, Jacob wondered what to do. Quickly, he pulled an oar out of its socket and stood up using it as a spear. Aiming for the creature's eyes, he hit it just below the right eye with a quick jab. The thing screeched at him and slipped back into the water.

Panting, trying to catch his breath, Jacob wondered, *What the hell is this thing? It looks like some sort of dinosaur.*

Suddenly a great force pounded up under Jacob's boat lifting it out of the water knocking him over the side. After landing in the water, Jacob surfaced swimming for his life. All he had to do was reach a dock about thirty feet away. His clothes slowed him down, but the adrenalin coursing through his body pushed him forward. Just as he ducked under a buoyed rope stretched across a swimming area, huge teeth tore into his leg ripping it off. His last sensation was being tossed into the air like a rag doll.

****

That afternoon, Terry Neal drove much too fast down the road to his parents' lakeside home in his big black Ford F-150 with chrome wheels. This four wheel drive triumph of mechanical ingenuity was a present from his dad after he returned from the war. He squealed the tires of his pickup as he slid into their gravel driveway. Slamming on his brakes, he jumped out leaving the pickup door open as he ran to the back door of his home. He flew through the kitchen where his mother was preparing supper and skipped down the stairs to the basement where he and his wife had been living for almost a year. As he thundered down the steps, *Mighty Mite,* his son Tommy, stopped chewing on the chocolate lab's tail to smile up at his dad. His lovely red-headed wife, Brianna, turned to her husband and shouted, "Well?"

Terry looked back and saw his parents standing at the top of the stairs and shouted out so everyone could hear, "I got it. I got the job. I'm a salt miner."

Brianna ran to him in a faded cotton print dress with a hole in the sleeve under her left arm. Terry thought. *Maybe now I can afford to buy my wife a decent dress.*

Kona, his big dog, ran to him jumping up on his waist. "Mighty Mite" followed his dog crawling as fast as he could move. After Bri filled his arms, Terry twirled her around while Kona chased her feet barking at their new game. Feeling left out, Tommy sat down on his diapered bottom and cried. Terry put his wife down and went to his knees. First, he hugged his dog who slurped his long tongue across Terry's cheeks. After Terry grabbed his son, Tommy's tears quickly changed to squeals of laughter as daddy twirled him so high over his head that Bri had to warn Terry to be careful.

On the stairs, his mother crossed herself and uttered a quick prayer. His father put a reassuring hand on his wife's shoulder while glancing up toward the ceiling whispering a quiet thank you. Bri threw her arms around her husband and son kissing them both. Then she sat down on their ratty old couch, "Sit down and tell us all about it."

As Terry dropped into his broken recliner, Bri waved to Terry's parents to join them. As he put Tommy on the floor, his parents each grabbed a chair from the small kitchen table to sit across from their son and his family. Understanding something important was happening, Kona sat down next to his master hoping for a treat to celebrate his master's good fortune.

With his dog at his feet, Terry patted Kona's head gently pulling his silky ears. "I've been gone all day because in addition to the interview, they put me through a test. I had to fix a piece of machinery with the tools they gave me. Wait, wait let me go back to the beginning. First, when I got to the salt mine they shuffled me into a warehouse with maybe a fifty or sixty guys waiting for an interview. I didn't think I had a chance. Remember the job announcement? It said they were only hiring a dozen guys."

Terry took a breath to add a dramatic pause. This was quite a moment. He had been trying to get a job since leaving the Army. Two years of failure had created a discouraging journey for him and his family. He was embarrassed when he had to move back home with his mom and dad because he couldn't scrap together enough to pay the rent for their crappy little apartment.

Bri poked his shoulder, "C'mon. Tell us what happened."

Proudly, Terry smiled. "After my interview, I had to wait for the rest of the guys to get their interviews. Everyone paced around. Some sat on equipment and others on the floor. I went from group to group talking about how hard it was to get a job. Finally an old guy in a tin hat kinda like a World War I military helmet 'cept it was silver with a light on it came out to talk to us. Anyway, he told us to quiet down while he read the names of the twenty-five finalists who would compete for ten positions. That upset all of us because the announcement said they had twelve jobs. Since complaining wouldn't help, we shut-up. Each name the old man read made me more depressed. I wanted so much to hear my name. Just before he finished, there it was. He called my name. I couldn't believe my luck."

Terry stopped and turned to Bri, "I've gotta have a beer. I haven't had anything to drink all day."

Terry rubbed Kona's neck and then reached down to mess up Mighty Mite's fine blonde hair. After receiving a smile from his boy, Terry took the beer from his wife and leaned back into his chair looking at his parents. "Man dad, it was something. Out of all those guys, they picked me. I couldn't believe it. Finally being a tank mechanic in the U. S. Army has paid off."

He popped the top, took a long slug and then let out a proud burp that made his mother wince.

"Where was I? Oh yeah. The ones of us who got our names called waited for the others to leave. Then we were separated into two groups. Twenty on one side and I was with five guys in the other group. The old man announced that after a two week try-out period, the best ten out of the twenty laborers would get the jobs. As those guys were marched off for physicals, I wondered what would happen to our group."

Terry stopped for a moment. This was great. He hadn't been the center of attention for a long time. Chugging his beer, but without a burp this time to show deference to his mom's delicate nature, Terry resumed his story. "Now there was five of us."

His mother corrected him, "That's were five of us."

Terry sighed, "Okay, there were five of us. Whatever. Anyway, they took us out to a yard with broken equipment. Each of us was, ah…were told to fix the machine in front of us. We all had broken conveyer belts. The other guys tried to start up the belts and ground up the gears worse than before. Just like I learned in the Army, I went around my belt and looked for the problem without turning it on. I didn't spot a problem on top so I got on the ground and slid under it. I saw a broken gear wheel and knew exactly what was wrong. I don't know how many times I had the same problem with tank treads. I fixed the problem in twelve minutes before anyone else finished. When I finally turned on my belt, it ran like it was brand new. In fact, only one other guy was able to fix his belt. Me and this other guy, ah… Fred, eh…Fred Drath, I think that was his name. I talked to him earlier when we was waiting for the names to be called. He was in the military too. Anyway, we were the only two told to come back tonight for the final test."

"You have to go back tonight?" Bri asked.

"Yeah, no celebrating tonight."

His dad asked, "What's this final test?"

"The old guy, I think his name was Charley. Yeah, Charley. Anyway, he explained that not everyone is cut out to be a salt miner. Evidently quite a few guys freak out once they go down a half mile under the surface of the earth. That's what he told us. The elevator shaft alone goes down the height of two Empire State buildings."

Concerned, Bri asked, "Do you think you can go that far under the earth day after day?" His mother nodded wondering the same thing.

"Honestly, I don't think it will bother me. I've crawled around inside and under tanks without getting claustrophobic so I think I'll be okay. The old guy told us the openings in the salt mines are pretty big, but, yeah, they're still way underground. This old guy looked like someone who had escaped from an Alaskan gold rush. He had a long scraggly white beard and a pot belly. He had on a dirty red shirt and worn blue jeans with old black boots. He *sorta* looked like a dirty Santa Claus, but seemed like a good guy."

His mother clasped her hands and fingers together holding them to her breast, "Are you sure you want to be a miner? That seems like a very hard life. Dangerous too."

"It won't be easy, but it's good honest work. I don't mind working in a dark hole at the center of the earth as long as they pay me. Besides, I'll be working with the salt of the earth." Smiling at his joke, Terry added, "If I can keep from panicking tonight, I'll have a job earning good money. How great is that? We can move out of your cellar. Get a real home."

His mom blurted out, "It's a basement not a cellar."

Terry sighed, "Whatever."

Terry's dad added, "That sounds great. I'm proud of you son."

Glowing from his dad's praise, Terry smiled at his mom "This old guy told us part of our job would be taking apart equipment so the pieces could be taken down in the elevator. Then we'll put them back together down in the mine. My other job will be keeping the equipment down there working. Taking tons of salt out of the earth every day and night is tough on machinery."

After pausing a moment to hug his dog, Terry continued, "This guy told us the history of the mine. Let me think, yeah, he said they used to have battery powered small railroad engines on tracks, but after the International Salt Combine took over…that's the ISC for those of us in the know, they have brought in new equipment that I will get to work on."

Proud of his new job, he stopped for a moment and sipped his beer before continuing, "Anyway, now the miners use big front end loaders and conveyor belts. Charley said he had worked in the mine so long he could remember when they used shovels to load the salt into the cars. He also told us that ISC has made a lot of improvements in the mine. They've put in new lighting and ventilators that have really improved the work environment."

Stopping to finish his beer, Terry crushed the empty can in his hand and then he threw it toward the waste paper basket way across the room. He shouted "Yes" as it fell in for three points. With a smile, he thought, *no way I can miss today.*

Then Terry started to show off telling them everything he could remember from a video Charley made them watch and explained to his captive audience, "I'll be working in the deepest salt mine in the western hemisphere. It has eight different levels that go really deep. There are like miles and miles of roads down there. The goal is to produce ten thousand tons of salt each shift. Do you believe that? Ten thousand tons."

His mother questioned her son's memory. "You must mean ten tons a day not ten thousand."

"No mom, I'm sure that's right. Ten thousand tons per shift. In fact, this one mine produces over, oh what did they say? Like over a million tons of salt each year."

Finding it hard to believe his mother asked, "What would anyone do with that much salt?"

"Road salt, mom. The stuff they spread on the highways during the winter comes from my salt mine."

His mother continued to worry, "All those holes under the lake, isn't that dangerous."

"Mom, they've been digging under the lake for over a hundred years and nothing has happened yet. These guys are professionals. They know what they're doing. You worry about everything."

"Someone has to worry about my baby."

Terry sighed and decided to tease her, "Get this. They blast out salt three times a day with dynamite."

His mother put her hands to her cheeks, "Oh dear."

"Don't worry, mom. They do it between shifts, but there are still some guys down there when it goes off. That must be a blast."

Smiling at his pun, Terry continued, "I don't think I want to be down there when they blow that shit up, but it can't be much worse than sitting in a tank when a shell goes off. I've done that more than a couple times."

"Watch your language, dear. You don't want Tommy saying that." His mother cautioned.

Bri added, "You don't want that to be his first word."

"Are you sure you want this job? It sounds awfully dangerous to me."

"Mom, this is a good job. I have everything covered. Don't worry."

After a brief silence, Kona looked up when Bri asked, "If you pass your test this evening when will you go to work."

"Charley told us the mine goes twenty-four-seven with three shifts. I will be working the night shift with him. The only uniform is work pants and a T-shirt."

"What about the winter?" His dad asked.

"Doesn't matter. The temperature in the mine is the same all year round. I think he told us it stays around sixty-eight or seventy degrees. Something like that. Besides, I'll be working hard enough to keep warm. Bri, another beer."

His mom shook her head, "No more beer for you if you're working tonight. We'll have an early dinner upstairs and send you off together. Tonight we celebrate with a good meal. As soon as you get an evening free, your dad and I will take you and your bride out to dinner at a good restaurant. It'll be on us. We're both very proud of you son."

CHAPTER 3

With the sun just hiding behind the hills, Carol Powell looked in the mirror and admired her body. *Not bad for a fifty-one year old*, she thought. She turned to look at her firm butt and strong muscular legs. *Yes, not bad at all.* A lifetime of long distance swimming had kept her 5' 10" frame trim. At her last Triathlon, she had to show proof that she was over fifty to register in the right age group. Even then they didn't believe her. One of the young men at the table claimed she didn't look over thirty-five. Her husband, bless his heart, would have enjoyed that comment. Ray had worked hard to make his millions before forty and then cancer stole him away from her.

Ray had insisted that his wife could not work. Her job was to keep house and direct his charities. Alone so many days at home, Carol turned to the swimming she enjoyed as a member of the Cornell swim team. With their big house and dock on Cayuga Lake, it was easy to make the lake her personal training pool.

As Carol pulled on her new age tank suit, she wondered at the new materials they had for swim suits that let you glide through the water. Then she rubbed her special body oil on her legs admiring her rock hard muscles. With part of her husband's money, she marketed the oil and now it was sold throughout the world. It was especially popular with long distance swimmers. It was much better than that grease swimmers used to smear on their bodies and lasted longer too. Her husband had often kidded her that he liked the looks of her glistening body before a swim.

Carol had some renown in the Finger Lakes region and in international swimming circles. For the last five years she had hosted events that drew many of the best swimmers from around the world to swim the Finger Lakes for her husband's charities. Hundreds of swimmers joined her effort to conquer the lakes. Her proudest swimming achievement was last year when she became the fastest woman over fifty to swim across the English Channel and back again. She would always remember that quick glass of champagne in France before she started back.

This morning she warmed up by swimming ten miles. Then under the scrutiny of her trainer she did sprints until her body could do no more. What a work out. Stretching, sit-ups and weights were also part of her regimen. She shook her head, enough dreaming. She had to get in the water. As she left her bedroom, she pulled a fluffy white robe over her high-tech suit and picked up a towel.

It was getting late. If she was going to get in another six miles before sunset she needed to hurry. At the end of the dock, she carefully folded her robe and laid it down with her towel on top so they would be there to welcome her return. Next she slipped on the harness of the buoy that she would drag behind her as she swam. Swimming in any body of water without a spotter was dangerous, but she liked to swim alone. Her concession to safety was dragging this buoy with its flashing LED lights and a bright orange flag on a three foot whip antenna. Hopefully this would keep the motorboats zooming around the lake from running over her.

She tucked the buoy under her arm and did a standing flip off the dock landing on her feet in the water. She was proud of her athleticism. Cayuga Lake was always cold, but her high-tech suit and oily body lotion moderated the chill. Her goal for this swim was to head down to Taughannock State Park just 3.2 miles up the lake. After adjusting her buoy and line, she started off for the park using powerful over-hand freestyle strokes and driving her legs to glide through the water. The water surrounding her body felt good.

She loved swimming because the rhythm of her body freed her mind to think about life. On every third stroke she would turn her head to the left to breathe and check out the lake around her. After three more stokes, she would do the same thing to the right. When she noticed the state park on her left, she was surprised she was already there. She felt fresh after swimming over three miles. As she treaded water, she thought it must be her training regimen. Hard to believe, but at fifty, well fifty-one, she might be in the best shape of her life. With a smile, she headed back. On her return trip, she decided to pick up the pace to increase the training effect she hoped to get from this swim.

On the way back when she looked to her left toward the expanse of the lake, she spotted a big black fish swimming right next to her. *That's neat,* she thought. On the next breath when she looked toward the shore, there was another large black body swimming beside her on that side. She slowed to lift her head out of the water. The body of the fish next to her was big and greenish black. Suddenly, a big head with terrible teeth poked out of the water and dove under again. Scared, she stopped swimming.

Her instinct was to turn toward shore, but one of these things was blocking that escape. Frightened, she did what she did best. She put down her head and swam. By increasing her speed, she hoped whatever they were would get bored and swim away. As she glanced to each side, she saw that they were still swimming next to her almost like dolphins following a boat. They were scary looking beasts, but seemed to be leaving her alone. After a half mile of increased speed, Carol began to tire. Finally, she decided to stop to see what would happen. Hoping these creatures would swim away, she stopped suddenly and treaded water. The things kept swimming leaving her behind. *Good*, she hoped, *they're going away.*

The beasts surfaced and seemed to be looking for her. They spotted her and swam back toward her. When they reached her, for a moment, they all just stared at each other. All she could think of was dinosaurs as they started to swim circles around her. Their bodies were about five feet long with big heads on short necks. Their snouts were about half the length of an alligator, but their heads were bigger and wider. Their heads were black with dark green stripes on each side of their nostrils. They had flippers with claws coming out of them. She didn't want to make the comparison, but they looked kind of like the raptors in a Spielberg movie only with bigger teeth and a blunter nose. They seemed interested in her, but stayed about ten feet away. They were so close she could smell their foul breath stinking of dead fish. They were ugly, but didn't seem to be threatening her.

When she saw an opening, she sprinted away from them toward shore. Looking over her shoulder, she stroked away hoping to leave them behind. Stroke after stroke and kick after kick she pulled toward land. Unfortunately, these beasts were good swimmers. They easily caught up with her, but still kept their distance. Encouraged, she hoped she would be free of them once she reached shallow water.

Carol had no way of knowing that mother dinosaurs had the same instincts of a *momma grizzly* when it comes to protecting her young. When the female Appysaurus saw one of those things swimming between her twins, she thought her offspring were in danger. She dropped the large lake trout she had just caught and headed toward the surface ready to protect her young. On her way up, she decided ramming the thing would be a good start. Her twelve foot body sped through the water as she retracted her claws to increase speed as her flippers propelled her forward.

Frightened by these creatures swimming next to her, Carol pulled deeper with each stroke and drove hard with her legs to reach the safety of shallow water. Suddenly a terrific force hit her just above her hips lifting her out of the water. The collision knocked the air out of her lungs and threw her almost ten feet in the air.

* * * *

Earlier that day, Bob Fletcher pushed back from his huge antique English Partners' Desk putting his feet up on it. He didn't really like the desk, but his wife assured him that it set him apart from other CEOs. The desk certainly cost a bundle. On top of that he had to pay to ship it over from England. *God, the Brits,* he thought. *Lousy food and even worse weather.*

Surveying his office, he was proud of the atmosphere his wife had created. He didn't like the original Impressionist art, but it was as good as money if you wanted to sell it. His prize was a Van something or other. *You know, that crazy artist that cut off his ear.* He smiled. *Winning the bid in that snobby London auction house was fun. The kind of fun you can have if you have lots and lots of money. He loved the looks on the faces of the other bidders when he kept raising his paddle.*

Decorating my office. At least my wife is good for something. She certainly wasn't much in bed. She spends more time pleasing our kids than me. What a life goal. How could anyone be happy being a soccer mom for two children? If she wasn't the daughter of a real Texas oil baron, I would have dumped her long ago. No, love was not an issue in marrying her. Marrying the boss's daughter was my ticket into the world of the one percent. The wonderful world of the ultra-rich.

Ah...the gift of wealth, he thought with a smile. Joining the rich had exceeded all his expectations. A mom for his kids and hungry women on the side to attend to his more basic needs. Still, giving his wife some credit, his office did look impressive. She had created a business environment that showed everyone who entered that he was a wealthy man to be admired and yes, feared. As President and CEO of RealAirGas, he could make or break careers. R.A.G. was a branch of Anergize, his father-in-law's Texas based corporation.

On their trip abroad, his wife insisted he buy something expensive in every country they hit. Image, she told him, was important for an executive with his power. Glancing at his platinum Patek-Philippe, Bob wondered where the hell Herman Douglas was. *God, a frog watch on my wrist,* he thought. *Hell, it's probably Swiss, but I bought it just outside the Disney frogland. Those bastards in France outlawed fracking. God how I hated spending money to support their anti-fracking economy.*

Bob knew that fracking was the greatest technological achievement of the twenty-first century. Fracking made it possible for man to inject a secret blend of fluids into rock far below the earth and push gas to the surface to make him rich.

Bob was getting mad. *If Herm wants to keep his job as Vice President, he'd better show up on time for a meeting with his boss. Boss hell, his superior in every way.*

Bob stood up and straightened his red silk power tie. He smoothed it over his starched white Armani shirt before grabbing his jacket off an antique clothes tree. *Supposedly that stick of painted black and gold wood had once belonged to some king or other. No, maybe it was Napoleon. Who the hell cares? It cost a bundle.*

Wondering where Herm was, he opened his closet door and primped in front of his full length mirror. *Ah, I do look good today. Today? Hell, every day,* he thought with a smirk.

Herm, Bob thought, *was the perfect empty suit.* Good-looking with a great smile, but dumb as a post. The slightest breeze made his hair look like he had just come in off the range, but after running his fingers through it, every hair would fall back into place. *A real talent,* Bob thought. *Yes, Herm was the Wall Street image of a Texas oilman. Tall, slim and good-looking, he was one of the few people I know that can wear a cowboy hat without looking stupid. Herm was also believer. He was smart like a parrot. Reward him with a cracker, in his case an exorbitant salary, and he would preach the gospel of gas greed to anyone who listened.*

Bob shook his head and sighed. *Greed was truly a misunderstood concept in today's society. Darwin was right. The fittest survived and being rich made you fit. Of course, I'm a Christian first, but except for his evolution crap, Darwin was right on the money. Ah...money, what a lovely thought.*

As images of his big house and expensive cars flashed through Bob's mind, a knock on his door brought him back to reality. He pushed his closet door shut before assuming the power position behind his huge desk. When Louise stuck in her pretty head to announce Herm had finally decided to show up, Bob waved her in. Not really to talk to her, but to admire her assets. He laughed to himself. *This woman certainly has plenty of assets to admire. Why hasn't she surrendered to me yet?*

Louise approached his desk and leaned forward putting both hands on it displaying the cleavage she knew Bob enjoyed so much. She winked at him and announced, "Herm's here, darlin.'"

Finding it hard to concentrate with this vision of well-endowed womanhood leaning in front of him, Bob finally spit out, "He's almost ten minutes late. Make him sit out there fifteen minutes. Then get him in here."

Leaving him with a smile, Louise turned and left knowing Bob's eyes were glued to the fluid movement of her hips. Sighing again as she disappeared behind the door, Bob picked up the production report on his Cayuga Lake gas wells to review the figures to find something to complain about. That was a challenge. His operation was going great. Production was exceeding all predictions.

Except for a small group of environmentalists, the whole operation had a very low profile in the community. When Herm's time in the penalty box was up, Louise opened the door for him. Running his fingers through his tousled hair until every hair fell into place, Herm strode in on his bowed legs adorned with his standard alligator cowboy boots. With the confidence of a sheriff that had just gunned down Jessie James, he went to Bob's desk.

Bob made his flunky stand in front of his desk. *You only get to sit down with me when you get here on time,* he thought. Arriving late for a meeting with your boss wasn't to be tolerated and Bob knew how to deliver that message. "Well Herm." Bob used his nickname on purpose because he knew Herman didn't like it. *Herman is such a stupid name,* Bob thought. He enjoyed making this underling feel uncomfortable. "Why the hell were you late? Herm. Herm, my time is money. You just threw a shitload of dollars down the outhouse one holer."

Herman winced at the use of his nickname, but lowered his eyes in a show of deference to placate his boss. "I was on the phone with Hager, you know, that salt mine bitch. Jesus, she's a pain in the ass. Evidently, they never had to, you know, deal with environmentalists before we got here. They think a few protesters are, you know, a big damn deal and blame it all on us."

"Don't let her bully you. Christ, that big hole under the lake is a hell of a lot more dangerous to the environment than our little wells. An open sore compared to pin pricks. Tell that bitch we're all in this together. Yeah, tell her she needs to shape up and support us or we'll get the protesters to focus on them. On the abuses of salt mining."

"How would we do that?"

Flustered by his question, Bob stopped a moment to think. Then he threw his hands in the air, "Hell, I don't know. Threaten her with a negative advertising campaign or something. Earn your damn salary for once. And before you leave, understand that in the future tell her you've got a meeting with your boss and will call back. Has she given us a map of her damn mine yet?"

After Herman nodded no, Bob shook his head. "Course not. All we need to do is drill into one of their shafts and have the whole damn lake empty into their mine. You know that happened to Texaco in Louisiana. I want to make damn sure it doesn't happen here."

"That's what she called about. Says, you know, that we almost drilled into her mine. Threatened to sue us. Said that we have to get permission to drill through their salt beds."

"Bull shit, we bought the gas and oil rights from the land owners. We don't have to get anyone's okay to drill. Get our lawyers on it. They'll create such a storm these backwoods salt moles will beg us to forgive them. Now sit your ass down and tell me why Well 4 is producing about half as much as the other wells."

Relieved that his boss had forgiven him, Herman finally sat down. "The short answer is that the engineers don't know. The drill may have hit a fissure."

"What? In English."

"Ah….a fissure is a crack that, ah…that, you know, could be draining off our fracking fluid. That can happen. The fluid we pump into the ground is under high pressure to force the gas out. If the fluid finds a fissure, ah… crack, the pressure is reduced and we can't force up as much gas. No big deal, the other wells are doing better than expected. We may have to shut that well down and you know, drill a bit further down toward the lake."

"Jesus, when are you going to get it? Not down by the lake. I've gone to great lengths to hide our operation from the road and the lake. Right now no one even notices we're here."

"Boss, hiding our operation behind a barrier of trees was a brilliant idea. You're right. Most people don't even know we're here. And the sound barriers you put around each well, you know, cut down the noise. The wind here is great. It almost always blows the methane out over the lake before anyone can smell it. You made the sign at the front gate so small no one notices it."

Bob nodded with a smug look on his face, "Mark my word. One day, my precautions will shape the whole fracking industry. We need to camouflage all our operations. When people can't see or smell us, they don't complain."

"That's brilliant boss. Oh, last night my daughter dragged her liberal boyfriend home from Cornell. God, the kook has long hair, nose ring and everything. I hate sending her to that freaky school. She belongs in a good school like the University of Texas where girls are cheerleaders and boys play football as God intended, but her mother wants her here with us. Anyway, I went into my media room and found them watching MSNBC. Before I made them switch to FOX, I saw an interesting segment. Did you know that Rex Tillerson, the CEO of Exxon Mobil, has filed a lawsuit against fracking? On the TV program, they said Tillerson claimed in the lawsuit that he lived in an upscale community and didn't want an ugly fracking tower in his neighborhood."

"Upscale? I've been to his place. Believe me, upscale is modest description," Bob added with a smile.

"I wrote down a quote from his lawsuit. I thought, you know, you...you might be interested. They went on to say that in his lawsuit, Rex said he 'wanted to live in a community free from industrial properties, tall commercial buildings and other structures that might impact the rural lifestyle he sought to enjoy.' Do you believe that?"

"Yeah, I do. Had a conversation with my daddy-in-law this morning. The man who owns our little enterprise is madder than hell. After the millions we've spent lobbying Congress and advertising on TV to get people to support gas injection wells, a man on the inside files a suit against his own people. Our Board of Directors wants to destroy the bastard. They're already organizing the lawyers to fight his lawsuit. What was he thinking? You wait. His lawyers will have him changing his story right soon. I've always respected him, but he's hurt us."

Bob took a moment and looked around his desk then shouted, "Louise, bring me some damn coffee."

Then he looked at Herm, "That lawsuit lists every reason that every rural bumpkin next to a fracking site in Texas has been complaining about for years. Trucks, 24/7 noise, smells and of course, quakes. Christ, he could have given any of us a call and we would have quashed that fracking tower in a minute. But no, one of our own files a lawsuit that clearly outlines the problems with fracking. His lawsuit supports those crazy folks ten miles down the road in Denton who want to ban fracking from the town limits. Can you believe it, a town in Texas? I can't believe a leader of our industry can do something this stupid. Well, at least now he's gone political. As Trump's Secretary of State, he'll leave us alone here at home and maybe get us some gas rights in Russia."

Finally, Louise brought in a steaming cup of coffee in a delicate English bone China cup with the RealAirGas seal emblazoned on the side. Bob ordered them in England and shipped them back with his desk.

Tired of listening to Herm say, "You know", Bob dismissed him. "Louise, get this guy out of here and put him to work. Make damn sure everything is ready for tonight's cruise." Once again, Bob's eyes followed her out.

****

That evening, Bob Fletcher stood on the deck of his yacht on Cayuga Lake with a three olive Bombay-Safire martini in his hand watching his guests arrive for a voyage out on the lake. Tonight his guests were some of his fellow industrialists, and a few state senators and their wives looking forward to a late night cruise.

Standing in his expensive slacks and a Tommy Bahama flowered Hawaiian shirt, he was proud that his yacht was the largest on the lake. He knew it was the biggest because he hired an agent to investigate the size of all the other yachts on the lake before he purchased this monster with company funds. He felt the Operations President for R.A.G. couldn't be seen on anything smaller. He needed to dominate the land and the water just like the TV commercials that touted his environmentally friendly industry.

Tax laws are great, he thought. Dredging out a berth for the *LuvGas* and building a dock to handle this behemoth had all been written off as business expenses. On paper, RAG needed the dock for boats that would inspect the lake to make sure their operations weren't polluting it. In reality, he wanted a place to tie up his hobby craft without having to pay a Marina fee.

Tonight, one of his crew members would take three water samples by dipping small glass test tubes in the lake and putting in black rubber corks. This arduous task would be conducted to make this a business trip rather than a pleasure cruise. Those samples would make it possible for him to write the cost of the excursion, including the catering, as a business expense.

In fact, the *LuvGas* was written up as an environmental vehicle each year on their tax forms. Through environmental incentives, this *Titan of the Lake* had cost him and his company nothing. Instead, the government paid him money for buying his pride and joy. Raising his glass to the LuvGas, he saluted the best tax write off on the lake.

Bob Fletcher loved entertaining on his yacht. He liked to watch the *little people* who were cowed by his wealth and power. He spotted *Handsome Herm* striding down the dock ready to make sure all the wives had a good time. All the women liked Herm. It was part of his job to relish his attention on them, even the ugly ones. Bob shuddered. He didn't know how Herm did it. *Now and then,* Bob thought, *he did get a pretty one.*

Herm's seduction of clients had a long and checkered history. Before he left work today, Bob made it clear to Herm that he was to entertain the wives without taking any of them to one of the plush bedroom suites. He smiled when he thought of the time Herm got caught on top of a rather attractive wife by a husband looking for a toilet. Being a wise business man, the cuckold kept his investment in RealAirGas and got rid of his wife.

Louise, his secretary, had done a good job supervising the caterer. She was flitting here and there making sure everything was just right. Trying not to be too obvious, Bob checked her out. He had to be careful, his wife was around here somewhere. Louise looked great in a silky pink dress that complimented her blonde hair. He liked the way the fabric was clinging to her butt. Jealous of the other rich guys with their trophy wives, he knew his wife was too valuable to divorce. As President and Chairman of the Board, her daddy wouldn't hesitate to end Bob's career if he left his precious daughter for a looker. Bob sighed, *if I can't have a looker at least I can have hooker.* Bob smiled at his jest just as his wife slid up next to him grabbing his bicep.

"Darling, I like these evenings. With a full moon, this will be a romantic night. I know this is a business trip, but save some time for me. I need a little romance too."

Bob smiled down at Lydia. "Of course you do. Count on it." As he kissed her on the forehead, he looked over her shoulder at Louise's ass. Smiling at his wife, he thought. *Tonight you look as good as you can.* In her defense, she was attractive enough to entertain men without trophy wives and keep them interested. *Hell, if you weren't my wife,* he thought, *I might even want to do you once or twice myself.*

Bob sighed. *That was the problem with Lydia or any wife. Once you gave her that ring, you had to do the same woman over and over again for the rest of your life. That was just wrong. Hell, he could afford a harem so why shouldn't he have one?* He squeezed his wife around the waist and told her to be a good hostess. He knew he had no problem there 'cause her daddy had *brung* her up right. She knew how to work a party. As she walked off to welcome the guests, Bob sighed. *She was good everywhere except in the bedroom.*

As his tax write-off slipped out into the lake, the band started playing soothing background music. Bob stood back and surveyed the main deck. The senators and their wives looked like starving peasants as they attacked his giant mountain of shrimp. He didn't mind entertaining his rich friends, but tolerating these hack politicians and their frumpy wives was a real pain-in-the-ass. With alcohol flowing freely, his guests started to explore his floating palace. While everyone else was enjoying the cruise, it was his job to convince these dolt politicians to join his fracking team.

No more drinking for him. In Texas, a generous contribution to a politician's campaign fund was all you needed to secure his allegiance. These New Yorkers wanted to be wined, dined and paid under the table. Even then you couldn't depend on their vote.

Getting rid of the Governor of New York State, that ass, had cost the gas companies' tons of money, but it was worth it. Getting the legislature to pass new laws that allowed fracking back into New York State cost another ton of gold. Now New York had laws supporting fracking and the profit was rolling in. His thoughts were interrupted when he spotted a troublesome Senator approaching. Raising his glass to salute the man as he approached, he put on his best smile.

"I'm Carl Lewis. We met when you came to Albany to talk to my legislative environmental committee about fracking. After you left, I thought of a few questions."

"Senator Lewis, of course, Carl. So glad you could join me tonight. I want you on our team. Gas exploration in New York needs your support. The new technology we use to extract gas will bring jobs to your constituents without harming the environment."

"Yes, yes. I remember what you told my committee. I don't want to ruin your party tonight, but I would like to ask you a few questions if you have the time."

"Time. That's why you're here. Ask away. If I can't answer a question tonight, I'll have my people send you answers tomorrow."

"On TV, I heard a lady say that somewhere in Oklahoma they had over a hundred earthquakes in one week."

"I bet you weren't watching FOX news. Shame on you."

Puzzled with the non-answer, Carl tried again. "I'm not sure what network it was. I find a hundred earthquakes disturbing. I don't want that to happen in New York."

Bob wondered if this was guy for real, "You and I know you can't trust what you hear on TV. The lame-stream media has always been against the gas industry. Attacks us all the time even though we pay half their salaries with our ads." With a hic-up laugh, Bob added, "Cars will never run on solar driven fans."

Put off by this tycoon's refusal to give him a direct answer, Carl continued to press the point. "My constituents don't want their homes reduced to rubble from fracking induced earthquakes. They had pictures on TV of home owners showing cracks in the walls of their homes."

Bob raised his glass to get Louise's attention. It was a signal that she needed to drag this imbecile away from him before he threw him overboard. *Okay*, Bob thought, *what's the company line here?* "First, earthquake is the wrong term for the small tremors sometimes found near fracking sites. Slight movements in the earth should not be called earthquakes. No one even feels them."

Refusing to be put off, the Senator told Bob, "I saw pictures of walls cracking in a house."

"As home owners, you and I know cracks in a house can be caused by many things. Let's see, poor construction, shoddy maintenance, roof leaks and a thousand other problems. As soon as gas companies move in, home owners near our wells blame us for every defect they can find in their home hoping we will pay to fix them. These problems existed long before we showed up. We shouldn't have to repair every house around our wells. Hell, sometimes homeowners want us to build them new ones. Do you know that not one scientist has ever proved a direct connection between fracking, what we in the industry call gas extraction, and what you call earthquakes."

Lewis had come prepared and had not swallowed a drop of alcohol. Taking several index cards out of the inside pocket of his dark blue sports coat, he studied them for a moment. While Carl studied his notes, Bob looked for Louise. Where the hell was she? He wanted her to get rid of this guy.

Louise saw Bob raise his glass, but was tired of saving her boss every time he called. This would be her third save of the evening. Hiding from Bob in the crowd, she grabbed her purse and headed to a restroom for a toke.

Looking up from his cards, Senator Lewis announced, "Yes here it is. A Rick Summers called the link between fracking and quakes probable."

"Exactly my point. Look at what he said. Probable? Really, that's nothing. No proof. These are tiny tremors. They say quakes. I say shakes. Nothing to them."

"What about the Texas couple that won almost 3 million dollars in a suit against Aruba Petroleum? They lived near 22 fracking sites. Their daughter woke-up every night crying covered in blood from nose bleeds caused by the methane gas you guys pump into the air. I don't want the families in my district to have to go through that kind of suffering."

"You know some kids are very delicate. They react to the smallest changes in their environment. Why blame gas companies. It might have been pollen or a hundred other things. For every sick kid near an injection site, there are hundreds of healthy ones."

"Isn't it more serious than that? That case was the first monetary judgment against the fracking industry. The settlement included money for loss of property value, and the pain and suffering of the family."

Bob raised his glass again...*where the hell was Louise*. He was so upset, he forgot to deliver a politically correct response, "Our lawyers will crush it on appeal. Count on that."

"Did you know that Beverly Hills, California has banned fracking?"

"I'm well aware of that, but that's just California. Kooks coming out of the woodwork. They won't have any impact on the gas industry. Crazy environmentalists subverting local politics. That's all."

Bob took a short breath to calm down hoping his agile mind would come up with a better response. "If you are serious about knowing the effect of fracking in California research the California Department of Conservation. You will discover a completely different view of gas injection wells. That august body has stated that hydraulic fracturing has been used for more than 30 years in California with no reported damage to the environment.

My advice to you is to research both sides of the debate before you start blaming us."

"But California has a drought and fracking uses a tremendous amount of water?"

"Ah, so you believe in the myth of global warming. The gas industry has as much right to use the water in California as farmers and toilet flushers. Remember, corporations are people too."

"I have looked at both sides of fracking. It's not just TV or the Internet. Look at what happened at the Dallas-Fort Worth Airport. The airport Board of Directors let a gas company drill fracking wells on their land and then pump the wastewater back into the ground to get rid of it. The fracking or maybe the disposal of the waste water caused so many earthquakes that their terminals shook and the runways were declared unsafe. It got so bad the airport managers had to ask the company to stop drilling. Guess what, when the drilling stopped, the earthquakes stopped. What about that?"

Checking his note cards again, Carl added, "Dave Magana, the Senior Manager at Dallas-Fort Worth said the connection between fracking and earthquakes was an accurate assessment of the problem."

"What does an airport manager know about geology?"

"Science, you want science?"

Getting irritated, Bob spit out, "Yes, as a matter of fact I do. Science is on our side."

"Brian Stump, a seismologist at SMU, said that based on the timing and location of the earthquakes there was a plausible linkage."

"Weasel words. There you have it. A plausible linkage. What the hell does that mean? Think about it. Nobody knows what happens underground. Tomorrow, I'll send you a dozen articles from our geologists that will demonstrate this guy doesn't know what he's talking about."

"Of course your scientists would disagree. How can I trust them? They work for you, a gas company."

"You can trust them because they actually work in the field not some god-damned Ivory Tower hidden on a campus surrounded by hippie environmentalists."

"A Cliff Frohlich from the University of Texas says basically the same thing."

"Another liberal professor. Let me assure you there won't be an earthquake in New York."

Just as the words left his mouth, Bob felt his boat sway up and down. *This baby is too big to rock from the wake of a passing boat*, he thought. Suddenly the sloshing turned into big waves that violently tossed even his big yacht back and forth. He had to spread his feet and grab the ship's railing to keep standing. As he tried to keep his balance, he looked around and saw people slipping and falling down from the rough water. As his boat rode up each wave and fell into the next trough, his guests fell, rolled and skidded across the dance floor. Others grabbed each other to keep from falling. Soon even these folks went down joining the others sliding across the deck.

The legs of the buffet table crumpled under the strain. What was left of the shrimp and other tasty treats slid dangerously close to the edge of the table and then cascaded across the deck. This sliding food slopped through the bodies of his guests as they rolled back and forth on the deck. The pyramid of champagne glasses was the next casualty of the quake-induced waves. The grand stack of crystal swayed once and then crashed off its table. Broken glass, ice and bubbly liquid joined the mess of food and guests already polishing the deck with their backsides.

That crash was soon joined by the tipping chocolate fountain where guests could dip their strawberries. The sweet fruit spread across the floor in a sticky wave of brown sludge. The bar tender tried to grab his glasses and bottles as they fell off his bar. Women in beautiful silk dresses rolled through the mess coming up covered with goo. Hair coiffured long hours in expensive salons now stuck out at weird angles. Many women couldn't see through the chocolate and champagne dripping from their tresses. As men tried to stand, they just swore as they fell back into the slippery mess often landing on broken glass.

The risers holding the band joined the collapse. Musicians stumbled and tumbled to the floor as their chairs folded beneath them. Music stands, pages of music and instruments joined the crowd riding the muck covered rolling deck. The conductor of Mitchum's Bitchin' Band skated for a moment, but finally slipped and fell into the goo still holding his baton high trying to maintain some small degree of dignity.

In one of the plush bedroom suites, the waves were so bad Herm was thrown off a Senator's wife landing unceremoniously on the mahogany deck. Damn silk sheets, he thought as he fell. Soon the not unattractive, but neglected wife plopped on top of him wanting to continue their tryst hoping the waves would enhance their pleasure. With a smile, Herm ran his hand through his hair and, you know, picked up where they left off.

Sitting on a toilet in an unobtrusive bathroom, Louise finished a long drag on her joint and stared at the smoke wafting up from the end of her hand-rolled fag thinking,

God, this is some good shit. My whole world is rocking.

With his feet slipping, Senator Lewis held on tightly to the rail trying not to fall. Nodding toward light poles swinging wildly on a nearby dock, he just managed to squeeze out a single word in a high-pitched squeal before he fell, "Earthquake." Bob just glared at him as he joined his guests in the sticky goo.

CHAPTER 4

E arlier that evening just before the quake, Laura McGinn stabbed her cell phone with her boney finger and looked up at her husband. "I don't know why my mother won't answer. I've called three times. Now it's dark out. I don't know how many times I've told her not to go swimming at the end of the day. When the sun goes down, it's really hard to see her in the water."

Without looking up from his laptop computer, Jim reminded her in a gentle tone, "Your mother has been swimming in that lake for years without even a close call. You know she drags that light thing behind her. Wait awhile and call her again."

Laura stared at her cell phone and began stabbing at it again. She held the thing to her ear and waited, but there was no answer. Her eyes flashed back to husband, "Let's go over there and see if she's all right."

"Babe, we just got Patty to sleep. We shouldn't wake her up just to drag her over to your mother's."

"Then I'll go by myself."

"It's a forty minute drive. By the time you get there your mother will be sipping Merlot and watching the news. Wait half an hour and give her another call."

"No, I can feel it. Something is wrong. I'm leaving. You stay and babysit."

Laura lifted her car keys off the kitchen rack and grabbed her large black purse. It was a nice evening so she left the house in her red Bermuda shorts, her gray Cornell T-shirt and flip-flops. Quickly backing out of the driveway without looking, she had to slam on the brakes to avoid hitting a car passing behind her. Sighing after just missing a collision, she started again after warning herself to be more careful. This time she looked both ways and slowly backed out of her driveway.

She loved her mother, but wondered if she would ever grow up and stop swimming. Since dad died that was all she did. *What about growing old gracefully?* Forgetting her promise to drive safely, Laura stomped down on the gas pedal hoping to get there as fast as possible.

When Laura pulled into the circular drive of her parent's big white pillared lake front mansion, the first thing she noticed was that there were no lights on. That had to mean her mom wasn't home or was still out on the lake. She didn't bother trying the front door, mom always kept that locked. She walked around to the back of the house on the paver pathway. As she crossed the patio, Laura noticed that the sliding glass doors were open. She stepped through them and called out to her mom, but there was no answer. After flipping on a wall switch, she saw that everything looked normal except for no mom. With the rest of the house dark, she decided going upstairs was a waste of time and headed down to the dock.

At the end of the dock, Laura spotted what she was hoping not to see. Her mom's robe and towel were sitting neatly folded waiting for her return. Mom was still out there somewhere in this damn lake. Shaking her head she stepped back and sat down on a white wooden bench looking out at the dark lake. Worried, she watched the waves roll under the dock as the wind picked up. She wondered what to do. *I'll just sit here and give mom hell when she finally shows up. That's what I'll do. She shouldn't be swimming this late.*

Laura kept checking the time on her cell phone. Five minutes, ten. After waiting fourteen long terrifying minutes, her imagination went wild. Finally, she decided she had to do something. She punched in the numbers for the local police. After a long wait listening to elevator music, someone finally answered and she explained she was worried that her mother was lost in the lake. The policewoman was not particularly helpful until Laura mentioned her mom's name. *Carol Powell* was all she needed to say to be immediately forwarded to another line.

Now, she was talking to the Captain of the Cayuga Lake Police Patrol. He explained everybody knew her mother and asked if there was anything he could do to help. Laura explained that her mother was still out in the lake. It was dark and she was worried. The officer understood and promised to grab his crew, and run out to Ms. Powell's dock. He knew where it was because he helped Mrs. Powell's plan her charity swims.

Still worried, Laura couldn't sit down. Pacing up and down the dock, she would occasionally yell out "Mom." Waiting for an answer, all she heard was the steady flapping of the waves as they hit the pilings below the dock. She didn't really expect an answer, but shouting gave her a chance to blow off some steam. Ten minutes turned into twenty and then half an hour… *Where the hell are the friendly Lake Police?* At the forty-minute mark, she saw a spot light swinging back and forth approaching from the South. As the light grew bigger, she was pretty sure the police were finally on their way.

"God", she said under her breath. *What's taking them so long?* Their boat was hardly moving. When they actually pulled into the dock, another seventeen minutes had passed. The boat had three members of the Lake Patrol onboard. One jumped off and introduced himself as Captain Homan. He explained that once they were within a couple miles of the dock, they had slowed down to look for her mother along the way. To speed up the search, Laura explained as fast as her tongue would let her that her mom was still out there somewhere.

Homan understood and tried to get her to calm down. "Your mom knows this lake better than anyone, but she should be in by now. We'll find her and give her a ride back."

"If mom had a long swim this morning, she liked to finish the day with a swim up to the state park and back at the end of the day."

Captain Homan told her that he knew her mom usually swam around four hundred yards from shore and promised to search that line tonight. He added that whether or not they find her, he'd stop back to report to her before going in for the night.

Laura folded her arms as she watched the police boat pull away with the man on the bow slowly sweeping the spot light back and forth. As it disappeared into the dark night, she hit the number for home on her cell and waited impatiently for Jim to answer. When he finally picked-up, she explained what was happening and told him to stay at home when he volunteered to drive over.

The Lake Patrol Captain looked to the right as the spotlight beam crossed his way and his deputy, Tony, watched the beam when it headed toward shore. Chugging slowly along almost halfway to the state park, Larry noticed something flashing in the water just as the cone of light flashed back in the other direction. He slowed to a stop and had Ed, the guy on the bow, shine his search light out toward the middle of the lake. Sure enough, there was a light flashing under the water. After Homan maneuvered the boat next to the blinking light flashing up through the green water, Tony used a long grappling pole with a hook on the end to grab a rope floating on the water.

After Tony snagged the object, he yelled out, "It's a buoy with a strobe light."

Larry called back from the cabin, "That's her, I helped her design that rig so she'd be safe."

Tony tried to pull the buoy up, but it was caught on something. While Tony held out the line attached to the buoy, Larry reached down and grabbed it. Together they pulled up the weight on the end of the rope. Slowly something rose to the surface. Finally a headless torso popped up on top of the water.

In unison, Tony and Larry shouted "Jesus." Ed came down from the bow dressed in his Horseheads T-shirt and knee length swimming trunks. He jumped over the side and helped Larry and Tony pull the body into the boat. As they looked at what was left of Carol's body still encased in her slashed high tech swim suit, Larry shook his head. "God, some boat really cut her to pieces. Could one boat do this much damage? Put an anchor buoy in the lake so we can find this spot in the morning. Now, all we have to do is tell her daughter."

****

Not long before the quake, Lea strolled down the hill from the girl's camp for a meeting with the Director hoping to run into Steve coming up from the waterfront. This summer she had enjoyed every muscle on his rippled body. He had been awarded the title of the camp *Adonis* by the female campers and counselors. With his curly blonde hair and swimmers body, he looked more like an escapee from the California surf than the Camp Water Front Director. His chiseled Scandinavian features and confidence made him a magnet for every female in the camp. This living *David* was also the envy of every male in the camp who had ever wanted to look good on the beach in swimming trunks.

With her lustrous brown hair, cute face and slim athletic figure, Lea looked like she had jumped off the cover of a fitness magazine. As the number two female tennis player on the Cornell team, her goal was to become *Number One* next year as a senior. Her *girl-next-door* looks and personality made her popular with the both campers and counselors. Lea ran the camp soccer and tennis programs, and on rainy days, she helped the camp director's wife with the craft programs. For her, the camp provided time in the sun and plenty of time to practice her serve. Her summer romance with Steve had turned out to be an unanticipated bonus.

Suddenly her best friend and buddy, Lincoln Jefferson, *The Third* came up behind her and grabbed her waist. After a screech of surprise, Lea threw an arm around Link's waist and jumped up to kiss his cheek. Link, as he was called by his fans, was the starting point guard on the *Big Red* basketball team. He was proud to have been named after two Presidents and was a direct descendent of Thomas Jefferson. He often pointed out that before Obama, his family were the only African-Americans directly related to a President of the United States.

His family had participated in a DNA project in 1998 which proved they were direct descendants of Sally Hemings, Thomas Jefferson's mistress. The Lincoln part of his name had been a family tradition since the Civil War.

Or as his family remembered it, "The War of Liberation." There was no rebel flag in their home. The first male of each generation was named after the man who literally freed their family. Link's standard camp dress was long red Cornell basketball shorts, a gray camp T-shirt and red high top basketball shoes. Link taught basketball skills to eager campers.

****

Billy Barton decided to take the shortcut to the dining hall by using the rope bridge across the stream next to Shanty's cabin. He taught the campers how to build it and was proud of their work. As Billy Barton started up the stairs of the Camp Minnechaug Dining Hall, he heard a familiar call, "Hey BB wait up."

He turned knowing Steve Swenson was behind him and wasn't surprised to see Lea emerge from the darkness with one arm around Steve's waist and the other thrown around Link's. Tonight, they were all dressed in matching camp T-shirts and khaki shorts. The happy Cornell trio pushed passed Billy, "Out of our way, Ithaca College boy." Smiling, Billy bowed to his august Ivy League friends.

As he entered the dining hall behind them, he glanced up at the Camp Minnechaug motto above the door, *Wild Blossoms Bear Fruit.* Shanty Brandt explained to Billy that the motto was a loose translation of the Algonquin word *Minnechaug.* The original meaning, Shanty told him, was *Berryland,* but insisted the Director had added a bit of manure to help the meaning grow.

The building was actually a dining hall on one end with a covered basketball court on the other. Between them was a kitchen, restrooms and shower rooms. The basketball court was used for camp league games and rainy day activities. As Billy pushed through the double swinging doors, he found the Cornell threesome waiting for him. When Billy caught up, Link put his arm across Billy's shoulders as they followed Steve and Lea passed the Camp Director.

Dressed in his usual camp T-shirt and long khaki cargo shorts, Director Harold Grayson was testing the mike and sending a squeal radiating throughout the dining hall. When the Director saw Steve, he called him over. Steve left Lea and joined the Director who put his arm around Steve's shoulders and walked him away from the microphone. Quietly he told Steve, "My sister told me you were interacting inappropriately with our attractive tennis instructor this morning. Were you doing something like that?"

Steve answered in a hushed tone, "No sir. Ms. Avery was just congratulating me after I won our early morning race. That's all. Ms. Grayson took the moment out of context."

The Director nodded, "She said you were hugging and kissing."

"Sir, it was an innocent moment. Honest, that's all there was to it."

"That's all I need to know. Just a word to the wise. Try to avoid displays of affection in front of my sister. Unfortunately, she's adopted the role of camp chaperone. I'll tell her to leave you two alone, but that probably won't stop her."

Trying not to smile, Steve answered, "Thank you sir. She embarrassed both of us. I hope it won't happen again."

"Yes, yes I understand. We need to get started now. Go join your friends."

With a large smile on his face, Steve joined his buddies sitting on a picnic table in the last row of tables near the back of the hall. Lea sat between Steve and Link on top of the picnic table, and Billy sat on the table bench next to their feet. As Billy sat down, he noticed that Shanty Joe was sitting on the table bench across from him.

Billy smiled and nodded to Joe as he sat down. He noticed Shanty was dressed in his old jeans and a worn red sweatshirt with the sleeves cut off showing his massive arms. His long black hair cascaded down his back falling over the top of his shoulders. *With a headband,* Billy thought, *Shanty would look just like an Apache scout from the old west. Only this Apache had replaced his headband with his old grease stained red baseball cap.* His solid body made Shanty look more like an escapee from a professional wrestling arena than a camp caretaker.

Shanty watched Billy as he interacted with his friends. He liked Mr. Barton. The others were all right, but there was something special about Billy. When he heard Billy's friends kidding him about being from the *other school,* Shanty could tell that while Billy laughed at their jokes he cried inside. Shanty knew it always hurt when people treated you as something less than you are.

Shanty knew about pride and was proud of his heritage. He had descended from greatness. His grandmother told him his forefather was Thayendanegea. How easily that name had flowed off her tongue. Thayendanegea had tried to build a bridge between the newcomers to his land and the Iroquois nations before there was a United States or even an America. After a war the white man called the "American Revolution", they came after Thayendanegea because he fought on the wrong side. He had to escape to Canada where he died in exile in 1806 far from his boyhood home. Today, Shanty was proud to have his famous ancestor's English name, Joseph Brandt.

Ursula Grayson, the Director's wife, had been watching Steve as he talked to her husband and made his way back to his friends. She liked what she saw. Ursula had noticed Steve in those skimpy racing briefs he wore on the waterfront. Her plan was to enjoy a romp with the camp stud before the summer was over.

She noticed that when his little girlfriend wasn't looking, Steve would glance at her. Ursula smiled and gave him a very indiscreet wink when she caught him staring at her. She knew by his reaction, he had noticed her too.

Ursula was the most popular crafts teacher that Camp Minnechaug had ever seen. At least, she was the favorite of all the boys. Her popularity didn't come from her knowledge of crafts, but from her beauty. Her classic Nordic features and talent for displaying them enthralled all the males in the camp. Ursula was a cross between a beauty pageant contestant and Victoria's Secret model. She was naturally blonde with alluring curves attached to a slim waist. A trophy wife, she was bought and paid for by Director Grayson.

Ursula's wink made Lea mad. Steve belonged to her. Steve was a summer romance, but she still expected some loyalty. For Lea, Steve was every girl's dream. He was handsome by any movie star's standard with just enough rebel to make him irresistible. Lea knew that when you walked into a room with Steve on your arm, you enjoyed the heady feeling of being envied by every female in the room. Lea enjoyed his body almost as much as Steve liked to show it off.

Confidence was the secret of his appeal. Steve was never afraid to approach a woman and always knew just the right thing to say. As the self-crowned King of the Waterfront, his domain was a half mile of lake shore with canoes, rowboats, small sailboats, two whale boats and a jet ski. With him at the helm, every camper learned how to swim. As the reigning back-stroker on the Cornell swim team, Steve was proud of his talent and his athletic frame.

Camp Director Harold Grayson, was a 'barrel-chested' nice guy six older than his wife. Plump and out of shape, he lived a sedentary life with his computers. He had been very successful with a variety of dot-coms and sold them for millions that he turned into billions. While creating his technology empire, he had little time for women and they had even less time for him. Once he gained billionaire status, beautiful women suddenly seemed more interested in him. Ursula was a gift Harold had purchased for himself.

When Ursula appeared at a Paris party, he picked her as his prize. She was absolutely gorgeous. Every time he looked at her, he couldn't believe his luck. Harold was not naïve enough to believe she actually loved him, but he knew she needed him. She liked being rich and the lifestyle it provided. Their pre-nuptial agreement would leave her quite rich, but not rich enough to continue the life style he had created for her. She tolerated summer camp because it was Harold's passion. Since he held the keys to the life of the ultra-rich, two months at camp was a small price for Ursula to pay for access to his wealth.

Along with computers, helping children was Harold's true passion. He was too busy for fatherhood, but used his fortune to help children who could benefit from his wealth. He knew about kids needing help. As a child Harold led a privileged, but lonely existence. His parents made it clear he was a leftover from a marriage they wanted to forget. Neither of them wanted to be with him or even see him. During the school year when he was young, they sent him off to military school where a gentle boy was tortured by his classmates and instructors. He hated every minute of military life and found that his computer was his only escape. His retreat into the solitary world of technology led to his fortune.

His only positive memories of human contact as a child were from summer camp. At camp, he discovered counselors who enjoyed children and found the time to give him the confidence he needed to navigate through life. As an adult he wanted to provide the same experience to other lonely children. When he found an old Boy Scout camp for sale on the shores of Cayuga Lake, he bought it with the goal to create a camp where lonely girls and boys could find the love and caring they seldom found at home.

The camp was free and open to a mixture of students from near-by towns and inner city New York, Hartford and Boston. The final ten percent he called, "Harold's Kids." He had a research group go to private military schools to find young *Harolds*. They approached the families of these lonely rich kids to offer them a free summer camp which the parents greedily accepted. Harold personally led a camp team that helped these kids. Privately, Harold felt his greatest gift to education was buying his old military school, tearing down every trace of it and building a park for children over the site.

After graduation from high school, his parents sent Harold off to Cornell and he loved it. Cornell introduced him to the beauty of the Finger Lakes and friends without uniforms. To salute his Cornell experience, he provided summer employment for Cornell athletes and jobs for the best and brightest after graduation.

As Harold stepped up to the mike, he cleared his throat. "Ah, uhm...I want to thank you all for doing a great job with the parents this weekend. The summer is off to a fine start. After the campers are tested on the ropes courses and qualify for swimming, we will implement the schedule my sister is handing out." As Harold talked on and on, everyone feigned attention while dreaming of being somewhere else.

Link saw Mrs. Grayson wink at Steve and looked at him in awe after thinking. *That woman is certainly some of God's better work.* As Harold droned on, most of the male contingent watched Ursula cross and uncross her legs. Once when she dropped the pen she was using to take notes and leaned over to pick it up, every male leaned forward to catch a glimpse of her perfect chest.

Harold noticed the sudden lull in attention and looked down at his wife as she sat back up smiling at him. He coughed several times before continuing with the weekly assignments.

Link leaned behind Lea and whispered to Steve to check-out the Camp Director's sister, Hilda who was frowning at Ursula. Harold didn't know he had a half-sister until she introduced herself to him at Cornell. She was another lonely outcast of their wealthy father. Harold and Hilda had become friends in college and now she supervised Harold's child searches. As the Assistant Camp Director, she felt she was more important than the sports directors because she was a year round employee and they only worked for the summer. She dismissed Steve and his friends as mere college students.

Hilda was wearing her signature black frame glasses. You know the ones that are clear inside and turn dark when you went out into the sun. That way she didn't have to lug around two sets of glasses. She wore no make-up and always pulled her hair back in a severe bun. If she tried, she could have been attractive, but she never tried. She may have had a personality, but no one could tell because she seldom talked except to criticize or order people around. Dark clothes always adorned her solid, but trim body. With toned arms, square shoulders and short strong legs, she was a force of nature.

Hilda was fit from many hours of lifting weights and running on her tread mill inside the indoor basketball court. She preferred running on the treadmill in the gym to jogging along the beautiful lakeshore or nature paths through the woods. Nature was dirty and she didn't like dirt. She was the self-appointed camp chaperone dedicated to keeping the sexes apart. She was especially hard on the camp counselors because she felt they needed to be good role models for the campers. She wanted to be feared and used her brother's authority to intimidate others.

As Harold finally approached the end of his monologue, the lights flickered and the cafeteria floor began to roll up and down. After a large shock, the heavy picnic tables danced across the floor as the shaking continued. Quiet descended in the hall as everyone wondered what was happening. The realization they were experiencing an earthquake finally dawned on them. But wait, this was the East Coast not California. As the shaking increased, the lights went out causing audible groans from the people now riding out a quake in the dark on trembling picnic tables.

With rumblin' tumblin' noises coming from beneath them and darkness surrounding them, the directors and senior camp counselors remembered their flashlights. Since the camp didn't have street lights, everyone carried flashlights at night to move around the camp. Soon the dining room was swarming with beams of light shooting in every direction.

Harold shouted for everyone to run out to the fields. Without panicking, everyone pushed quickly through the swinging double doors, down the wide steps and ran out to the soccer field. Pointing the flashlights back at the dining hall, everyone could see the building sway back and forth. An eve trough broke off and swung near the corner of the roof.

Finally, the ground stopped shaking. Harold shouted to get the attention of his camp leaders. Soon the flashlights focused on his face. Shading his eyes to filter out the beams shining into them, he told everyone to get back to their cabins and check on the campers. He insisted that as soon as they checked every cabin, he wanted them to send a runner back to report to him. If anyone needed assistance, he would send help.

Just before Harold sent his leaders off to their cabins, the earth trembled and shook again. An aftershock? The low rumble seemed to be coming from the area of the girls' cabins up the road. The noise ended with an explosion of dust that rose above the trees momentarily stamping out the moonlight. Everyone started running up the road toward the cabins with Harold doing his best to jog slowly behind. Billy was in the lead with Steve, Link, and Lea close behind. After running together each morning, this hill was no challenge for them. Always cool in an emergency, Shanty Joe followed the group in his pickup.

As the camp counselors ran up the hill, the moonlight was filtered through the cloud of dust settling around the girls' cabins. Billy sprinted between the cabins to the end of the row. Following the beam of his flashlight, he almost ran off the edge of a huge deep hole. Just in time, he slid to a stop a few feet from the cliff of this new sinkhole. Billy shined his flashlight over the edge into the bottom of the pit and spotted a cabin upside down at least thirty feet below him. It seemed to be in one piece. He hoped that was a good sign.

His friends joined him as Shanty Joe pulled up behind them in his pickup. Billy flashed his light to the left where a second cabin was teetering over the edge of the new cliff ready to slide into the crater.

At that moment, Billy Barton discovered he was a natural leader and immediately took charge of the situation. First, he pushed people back from the edge. When the Camp Director wheezed to a stop, Billy told him to call 911. He added they needed the fire department rescue unit more than the police. Then Billy ran to the second cabin that was teetering over the chasm. As he jumped up on the cabin porch, he motioned for Shanty to drive his pickup up on the porch.

When Shanty hesitated, Billy yelled, "Your truck up on the steps." When Shanty caught on, he drove the front wheels up on the porch. The weight of the truck tipped the small cabin back from the cliff and pinned it down on solid ground.

Billy ripped open the door and found the girls scattered across the floor. Some were huddled together while others were holding on to their beds. He rushed inside telling the girls to get out of the cabin. He helped one girl off the floor then guided her toward the door. As the girl stepped out on the porch, she stepped off the porch into the pit. Billy caught her by the arm and to keep both of them from falling into the pit, he grabbed the corner post supporting the roof swinging them both back on the porch. When her feet hit the porch, he helped her down the steps passed Shanty's pickup to safety.

Lea jumped on the porch to guide the other girls off the porch away from the huge hole. When the cabin was empty, Billy jumped off the porch motioning for Shanty to back the truck down the steps. When the front wheels of the pick-up hit the ground, the cabin tipped toward the hole and slowly slid into the crater flipping over twice before it hit the bottom of the pit.

After Steve helped Lea get the girls off the porch, he felt a hand on his shoulder. In the moonlight, he turned and found Ursula Grayson staring into his eyes. She stood on her toes and whispered in his ear, "You are much too valuable to this camp to risk staying here in danger. I'll save you." Then she took his hand and guided him into the woods away from the crowd intently focused on the rescue.

With the first challenge solved, Billy ran to the edge of the hole. When he couldn't see the bottom, he told everyone to shine their flashlights down at the other cabin which was on its side near the bottom of the sinkhole. As they did, one girl with a bloody face waved for help from a broken window. Billy shouted for her to stay where she was and yelled down that someone would come down to get her.

Billy looked down the side of the hole wondering what to do. The side dropped straight down. He shouted to Shanty, "Drive down to my cabin and get my climbing ropes."

To his surprise Shanty went to the bed of his pick-up and returned with two rappelling ropes. Holding them up, he yelled, "Will these do?"

Billy didn't know why Shanty had ropes in the back of his truck, but thanked God that he did. He motioned for Shanty to drive his pick-up close to the chasm. Shanty made sure the emergency break was set and left it in gear. Then he lifted a big white painted rock from in front of a cabin and placed it under his truck's front wheel and then put another stone under the other tire. With the truck well anchored, Billy and Shanty each tied a rope to the bumper of the truck before rappelling over the edge. As they went down, everyone shined the flashlights on them to light the way.

Shanty yelled up, "Not in my eyes."

When Billy and Shanty reached the cabin, they found it on its side balanced on a pile of debris about thirty feet down just waiting to drop another twenty feet to the bottom.

Steve let Ursula lead him into the woods away from the rescue. As they passed a big tree, she pushed him against it and put her arms around his neck. With her shapely body plastered against his, their lips met in a passionate kiss.

Shanty knocked out the broken glass and helped a girl out the window. Rappelling down a slope takes skill, but climbing up a cliff is an entirely different challenge. He told the girl to lay against his chest and put her arms around his neck. Shanty's strong legs and arms gave him the power to walk up the cliff carrying this young girl with him. With the other counselors pulling from above, Shanty carried this first girl safely to the top of the cliff. As they were helped over the edge, everyone yelled in triumph. The girl was ushered away from the hole by Lea as Shanty rappelled down for another.

Steve smiled when he heard the cheer come from the cabins. *They must be cheering for me,* he thought. Here he was kissing the Camp Director's wife who was fondling his body as his hands traced her curves.

As Shanty was climbing down for another girl, Billy climbed in the cabin window and found the girls in pretty bad shape. After being tossed from the floor to the ceiling and back again, they were hurt, bruised and confused. He told the girls if they could move, they should to go to the window and climb out. He grabbed a dazed girl and carried her over to the window. After helping her out, he handed her off to Shanty. Then Billy made another trip back across the cabin to rescue another injured girl. He had to carry this one across the cabin rafters to the upside down window. As he gently helped her out the window, he looked up and spotted Shanty taking the second girl to the top.

Once everyone was outside, Billy helped Shanty carry the girls up the cliff. Billy's strong arms and legs from rowing crew came in handy that night. He and Shanty climbed the cliff face a half a dozen times each as they carried the girls to the top. Link and Lea had organized the counselors into two lines to help pull Shanty, Billy and the girls up the side of the crater to safety. As Billy went down for another girl, Lea looked around. *Where the hell is Steve,* she thought. *He should be helping us.*

Steve couldn't believe his luck. This tempting *Cougar* was his. He was surprised when she leaned back, "Steve, right?"

He smiled with a wicked grin, "Yep, Steve." Then they continued their silent, but passionate exploration of each other's bodies.

A bit later Ursula whispered into his ear, "I noticed your skimpy racing briefs at the waterfront. I'd been hoping for a chance to find out what you had tucked in them."

"Believe me, your bikini is hard to miss. But now, you've got to get back to the crowd at the cabins. Act like you never left. I've got something to do." He gave her a quick kiss on her beautiful full red lips before he walked away with her scent still lingering in his nostrils.

Ursula was amazed. This was the first time a man had ever walked away from her. Stunned, she thought. *Am I getting old?*

While the camp nurses and doctor examined the girls, Lea looked around again for Steve. He wasn't anywhere in the crowd. She noticed Ursula standing at the edge of the crowd of campers near the tree line and thought at least he's not with her. Lea told the counselors to wrap the girls in blankets and find bunks for them in other cabins.

Harold rushed up to Shanty and Billy exclaiming, "I can't tell you how much I appreciate what you've done. Both of you were magnificent." He slapped them both on their shoulders and promised that when the camp returned to normal, he would make it clear how much he appreciated their efforts.

Blaring sirens drew the attention of the crowd to red and blue lights flashing through the trees. A police car drove up the road with a fire truck and two ambulances following close behind. With flashing lights, the police car roared between the cabins almost hitting several campers who had to jump out of the way. Steve jumped out of the backseat and led the policemen to the Camp Director who explained what had happened. Billy and Lea directed the medics to the girls who had been injured. The camp nurse identified three campers that she thought should be taken to the hospital. Soon after the first responders agreed, both ambulances were tearing down the hill taking these girls to the Cayuga Medical Center.

CHAPTER 5

The afternoon before the quake, Ruth Hager looked up from a thick black binder on the conference table in her office with a frown. She'd just told her secretary to hold all calls and give her at least an hour with no interruptions. She needed time alone to concentrate. The shifts weren't meeting their quotas and she hoped by combing the figures she could find a way to increase salt production in the mine.

There it was again. A faint timid knock of her soon to be ex-secretary. "What part of time alone don't you understand? Take message for God's sake."

After that response, she couldn't believe her secretary had the nerve to knock again. "All right, what is it?" Ruth yelled.

With great trepidation, Melinda Bower cracked open the door and announced just above a whisper, "Your lead engineer and Shift Foreman are here. They say they need to talk to you right now."

"Fine, fine, I can't get anything done with you pounding on my door. Give me five minutes, then show them in."

Ruth stood up, stretched and went to her desk to put on the jacket that was hanging on the back of her chair. Ruth was worried. She was part of the transition team for the new owners. Along with Albert Olson, they were the only two American managers that had survived the takeover by the International Salt Combine from the Netherlands. Albert's position as Vice President was a permanent position, but ISC only gave Ruth a three year contract and with a year and a half of that contract already gone her future wasn't looking good. She hadn't been able to meet the new production quota of 14,000 tons of salt every shift. After reviewing the production analysis for this month, she knew the shifts were averaging just below 11,000 tons per shift. Although it was her responsibility, she couldn't figure out how to squeeze out the additional 3,000. Morgan's shift, one of the employees waiting for her, came closest to this achieving her goal by averaging 13,000 tons per shift. *What does he know that I don't?* She wondered.

Throughout the mine, Ruth was known simply as "The Bitch." She knew what others called her and accepted the title with pride. Mining was a man's world, and she made it to the top by being tougher than any man. The only physical activity she enjoyed was climbing over the bodies of the men who dismissed her as just a woman. She was ruthless. Ready to take any gamble that gave her a chance to move up the executive ladder. If she lost this job, she knew it would be the end of her career in mining. Women didn't get a second chance in mining or life. Her only outlet was work.

Her job gave her a big condo overlooking the lake, but her life was dedicated to the mine. She could afford a house, but wasn't into mowing grass. Pets? She's rather run over a dog or cat than let one in her condo. Her black Porsche was her only pleasure. That small sports car saved her time traveling to and from her work, and gave her the only sense of freedom she found in her day.

Ruth was business attractive with short closely cropped mousey brown hair. Blessed with a metabolism that kept her thin, she didn't have to waste time exercising. Her suits were three colors; dark grey, dark blue and black. And she was always searching for a darker shade of black. She was the first employee to arrive in the morning and the last to leave at night. Her married colleagues from the Netherlands could divide their attention between work and their family. Ah, they were Dutch from the homeland and didn't have to worry about their jobs.

Ruth couldn't allow such a career threatening distraction as a partner. She didn't have a significant other and wasn't looking for one. Besides, with the end of her contract in sight, she couldn't afford the time. She hoped her remarkable mind that could store information and retrieve data with ease would save her once again. Ruth's only talent for humor was cutting down her colleagues with sarcastic comments.

When exactly five minutes were up, Melinda entered Ruth's office followed by an attractive woman dressed in dark green coveralls and an old man with long scraggly hair, dirty work clothes and a terrible untamed beard.

When Melinda hesitated, Ruth saw her confusion and yelled, "At the table. The table. All of you, that side."

As the two sat down across from Ruth, Melinda sat at the end and pulled out her notebook. Ruth told them with a frown, "Well, I'm waiting."

Jean Rogers knew Ms. Hager didn't like bad news and quickly deferred to Mr. Morgan hoping he would explain why they were there. Morgan didn't feel he should even be at this meeting. He was a miner not a *Suit*. For him all activities above ground were best left to the bosses in expensive suits.

Time for you to earn your money, Ms. Engineer, he thought. *After all, I work for a living.*

Ruth waited almost three seconds, "You are wasting my time. Get on with it or get out."

Jean looked at Charley, "You found it. Tell her."

Morgan sighed, "I canceled blowing the north wall today. I..."

"You what? That will cut down the product available for the next shift. Why would you do something that stupid? What possessed you? You don't have the authority to do that. You're..."

This time Jean interrupted Ruth, "Don't say it. You can't fire him, he just saved the mine."

Exasperated, Ruth shouted, "Will one of you get to the point."

As Charley stared at the ceiling, Jean knew she had to break the bad news. "The mine is seldom quiet, but between shifts there is less noise when the machinery shuts down. It was as quiet as it can get in the mine and Mr. Morgan called me down to listen to the north wall."

"Listen to the wall. Have you two been drinking? Drugs?"

Wanting to escape this unpleasant woman, Charley barked, "Hey, I'm on my own time here. I should be at a bar drinking by now. When we were about to blow the north face, I heard a strange noise. I closed everything down to listen to it. The north face is pretty close to those RAG gas wells. One of their drills almost hit our mine. If they had hit it, ground water or maybe the whole damn lake could leak into the mine closing it down forever."

"Never. A leak wouldn't shut down this mine."

Jean stepped in, "Yeah, it could. The same thing happened when a salt mine was breached under Lake Peigneur in Louisiana. Peigneur was a beautiful lake that was used for recreation just like Cayuga. It was smaller and not as deep, but like Cayuga, it had a big salt mine under it. When Texaco was searching for oil under the lake, they drilled into the salt mine. Their drill punched a hole in the top of the mine that drained the whole lake."

"When Texaco made that hole, it was like they had pulled the plug in a bathtub. The water and muck swirled down into the mine filling every inch of the enormous hole under the lake that we call a mine. The water disappeared so quickly, a giant whirlpool was created that sucked down the drilling platform, a bunch of barges, boats and trees. The water flowed into the mine so fast it needed a way out. The pressure from the falling water caused geysers to shoot out of the mine shafts. Oh, a couple islands disappeared into the hole and waves washed away about seventy acres of land around the lake. The same thing could happen to Cayuga if a RAG drill had punctured our mine."

The shocked look on Ruth's face let Jean know she now had the full attention of the *Salt Bitch*. "The good news at Lake Peigneur was that all the miners escaped by using their well-rehearsed evacuation drills. Even the workers on the drilling platform got off just before it sank into the whirlpool. But the mine, the mine was gone. Totally lost and the freshwater ecosystem was destroyed. It was replaced with a dead saltwater lake. That lake had about 3.5 billion gallons of water. Cayuga has approximately 2.5 trillion gallons of water. That's trillion with a capital 'T.' Think what would happen if that much water flooded into our mine. There would be no stopping it. Now can you see the problem? It would be the end of the mine. Hell it would be the end of the lake."

"Are you serious?"

"Very." Rogers answered.

Charley entered the fray, "That's why we're here. Do your job. Get on the phone and tell those gas fanatics to stop drilling near our mine. ISC owns the rights to all the salt under the lake. For God's sake, it's illegal for them to drill through our salt bed without our permission."

Jean jumped in, "You've got to get them to stop drilling near out mine before they hit us."

"I'll call their Vice-President. Everything below Cayuga is ours. Now, get out of here, you've made me late for a meeting."

****

Leaving the thick black binders behind in her office, Ruth watched from the back of the conference room as Albert Olson, the Vice President in charge of the Cayuga salt mining operation, finished a meeting with the management group from the Netherlands that was making their first visit to the mine. "Let me summarize the presentations you just heard. First and foremost under my leadership your investment is safe. I am pleased to be part of the International Salt Combine. Together we will reap significant profits from under this lake. The previous owners were plagued with unscheduled breakdowns and the maintenance costs were sky-rocketing. With the new Chinese equipment you have provided, there will be fewer interruptions in production which will increase efficiency. Your predecessors outsourced maintenance. By hiring our own maintenance crews, downtime for repairs will be drastically reduced. The mine will operate using only state-of-the-art technology. These changes will save you money and more importantly increase your profits."

Albert stopped to survey the group. After a moment, he asked if there were any questions.

One of the directors asked, "How long will it take to complete these changes?

Albert didn't hesitate, "We're almost done. We scheduled two years for the changeover and are seven months ahead of schedule." Albert noticed the Chairman of ISC, William Ryskamp, making discreet circles with his finger indicating for Albert to move on. Albert thought. *Evidently the chairman is ready for his martinis.*

"One other thing before I close. This mine will continue to use *room and pillar* extraction. Salt is extracted to form rooms that are supported by pillars to keep the ceiling of the mine from collapsing. The former owners used large pillars of salt to maintain the integrity of the mine and prevent cave-ins. This large pillar method of mining salt is old-fashioned. We have switched to small pillar mining. This method provides easier access for the larger machinery you purchased and it will mean increased salt extraction on each shift every day."

Chairman Ryskamp frowned when a member of his team asked, "Is this new method safe?"

Albert nodded and answered, "Large pillar mining has been used for almost a hundred years. It was put into use when miners had to guess the size of the pillars necessary to support the ceilings. This small pillar method was developed by our engineers. At the same time, we paid for an independent study conducted by Cornell professors to determine the optimum size for pillars. Both groups came up with almost the exact same sized pillars. Our engineers arrived at a slightly smaller diameter for the pillars so we are using their figures. After all they work in the field not a university classroom. We have been using this new method at the lower levels for over a year and a half, and have found it is safe and efficient. The small pillars are designed to survive a 4.0 to 5.0 earthquake. In recorded history, there has never been a quake that big in this area of upstate New York."

Albert noticed the chairman waving his hand once more and this time other members of the team saw his gestures, too. Following his lead, when Albert asked for more questions everyone kept quiet. After surveying the group, Olson finished, "Thank you for your attention. Be assured that every day, I will focus on increasing ISC profits."

CHAPTER 6

hile the ISC executives held their martini glasses high toasting to the success of their salt mine, Terry Neal with his belly full of his mom's cooking and a second piece of pie kissed his wife good-bye thru the window of his Ford. She wished him good luck as she stepped back from his pickup blowing him a kiss. As he backed out of the driveway, he waved to his mom who was waving Tommy's little arm up and down. His dad waved politely as Kona howled and everyone laughed. They were all excited for him.

As Terry drove to the mine, he felt confident about passing this last test. He knew one day his military experience would serve him well and this was the day. He was so excited that when he reached the gate to the mine, he had to search his pockets for the temporary pass. After finding it in his shirt pocket, he handed it to the guard. The man in uniform smiled and told Terry to park in the lot on the left.

"Then go to the first door of the large building at the end of that lot. Inside you'll find the elevator that will take you to the middle of the earth."

Charley Morgan sat at his desk in his surface office looking through his glass wall at the rookies assembling in the warehouse as he pulled on his beard. His assistant was getting their names, having them fill out address cards and insurance waivers. After wiping his nose on the sleeve of his dirty ole' red shirt, he remembered going down in the mine for the first time. *I had to ride in a small elevator that was so crowded I felt like a sardine trapped in a can. For some reason it never bothered me. Now thirty-one years later, God had it been that long?* Charley sighed, he had spent more than half of his adult life underground.

As Terry handed the foreman his address card, he saw the dirty Santa Claus come out of his office. Now they would get to go down into the mine. He was ready. In his wildest dreams, he had never considered being a miner. Actually, a mine mechanic to be exact. He knew this was going to be the start of a grand new career.

The old guy motioned for the group to follow him as he led them to the elevator. Charley waited for the group to catch up before he began his spiel. "There are three shafts. One for ventilation. One for product removal. In the mine, we call salt *product*. And this last shaft is for people and equipment. You are about to enter the deepest twelve foot hole ever drilled in the earth's crust. The elevator you are about to ride is called a "hoist." This hoist is longer than any elevator on the face of the earth. The engineering going into this hoist separates it from the up and down elevators you find in a mall. The hoist goes down through the first three levels of the mine. From there you have to ride electric pick-up trucks to reach the bottom. Product is blown out of the mine wall, ground up and carried to conveyor belts. These belts take the product to the buckets that haul the salt to the surface."

After taking a deep breath, Charley continued in a bored monotone, "This hoist isn't exactly what you find in a fancy hotel. We call it a man cage. It's got no music or lights. The only light will be on your safety helmet. Turn on your helmet light before you enter and keep it on until you get back to the surface. After six minutes of descending into the bowels of the earth, you may smell fumes from the blasting as you exit the hoist. This is normal. Don't be alarmed. Blasting takes place at the end of each shift. The fumes linger around for the beginning of the next shift. Soon after the shift starts, the ventilators will suck most of the remaining fumes out, but count on a small residue hanging around to stink up the place."

Charley knew descending under the earth was a test. The different reactions of people always amazed him. Down in the mine, there was a small variance in air pressure that affected some people. This small change forced some rookie miners to get right back on the hoist and ride back up never to return. Some rookies didn't like the darkness. Compared to the old days, the rooms and roads were well lighted, but some folks still felt closed in and claustrophobic. These guys usually quit after a week or two. Several members of his shift were ex-submariners who thought the mine was spacious compared to the confines of a nuclear submarine, safer too.

For some rookies, it was that trace smell of nitrate left over from the blasting wafting through the air that ended their careers. For Charley that smell made him feel at home. When he was young, it used to smell a lot worse. Now with the new ventilators, it was like breathing fresh lake air. Well not really, but it was better. *These young guys sure have it easy.* When his assistant waved the insurance cards, he knew it was literally time to take them down.

Charley looked into their eyes. *No fear yet,* he thought. "Any questions? Okay, next your equipment. For now grab a tin hat with a cute little light on the top out of that crate. Turn the light on. Make sure it works. Next, take a package of ear plugs from this bin. Normally you'd put them in as you go down, but since I'm giving you a tour of the mine today, just keep them in your pocket until I tell you to put them in. Finally, get an emergency gas mask over there. They hook on to your belt like this. Once you pick up all this crap get on the hoist. Next stop, the center of the earth."

When everyone was on the elevator, Charley yelled, "All aboard. This cage is going down. Way down." After he pushed the button, the elevator dropped beneath the surface of the earth.

Terry felt funny standing in a miner's helmet that came down around his ears. Whoever wore it before him must have had a much bigger head. During the ride down everyone was very quiet. Terry remembered once when he was a kid, he played a game with his friends where you had to close your eyes and guess the length of a full minute. A minute seemed to last forever. *Multiply this game by six*, he thought, as his silent journey into darkness continued. Down and down it went. Creaking and clattering further and further under the earth. When the hoist jolted to a stop, Terry was eager to get off.

As Terry stepped out of the elevator, he noticed the mine was dark. Near the hoist, there was light, but the light was definitely below the intensity of a room in your house at night. Long tunnels disappeared into darkness. His group piled into the back of modified Chevy pick-up trucks with benches in the back. They sat on the benches with their knees almost touching. Terry's nose was keen enough to smell the trace scent of fuel oil and nitrates from the blast that Charley had warned them about.

As the truck traveled down long roads at what Terry guessed was about fifteen miles per hour, he looked around at his new environment. The road they were traveling had power cables running along the ceiling with lights spaced pretty far apart. The tunnel was about the width of a country road. Terry guessed the ceiling was about 12 to 15 feet high. All sorts of broken rusted equipment littered the sides of the tunnel. In caverns along the side, they passed containers being used as storage sheds. The empty caverns seemed to have an impenetrable darkness. Terry noticed there was a constant mechanical noise like a bunch of neighborhood guys mowing the lawn at the same time on a weekend morning. To him, it seemed like riding through a large underground parking garage.

Suddenly, the guy next to the cab two men away from Terry coughed and cried out in a weak sickly voice, "Get me out of here. Take me back now. I mean it. I've got to get out of here now."

Sitting across from him, Charley told him, "You ain't going back right now sonny. Close your eyes. Bend over and put your head between your legs. As soon as we get to where we're going, I'll have one of these here vehicles take you back to the hoist ta get ya out of here."

"I gotta go now." The man pleaded.

"No ya don't. Head over and close those eyes."

Terry watched the guy bend over with his eyes shut tight. He could actually see him trembling. *This isn't the greatest work environment, Terry thought, but it wasn't that bad. In some ways it was kind of neat. A new life experience. That's what it is, a new experience. I'd rather be here than riding a hummer down a road in Afghanistan waiting to run over an IED. At least here the explosives are in the walls of salt not under your ass.*

When the trucks finally stopped, Charley motioned for everybody to get off. Terry was surprised how far they had driven. Checking his watch, he was surprised to discover they had been on the road for twenty minutes. Everyone jumped off the back of the trucks except for the rookie near the cab who was now sobbing. As they stood in front of a wall of salt, Charley continued his lecture. "You don't have to worry about losing your job. There are around four trillion metric tons of salt under this here lake. This mine only covers about 18,000 acres." Charley stopped a moment to let those figures sink in. *Not many people,* he thought, *understood the massive nature of this mine.*

When everyone seemed ready for more, he started up again, "This a salt face. You'd call it a wall. We call it a face because this is an area we are going to work. Notice this section is about 30 feet long and 10 feet high. To start a production cycle, the machine over there scales the tunnel roof to knock off any loose material. See, it's using that flat pick on the boom to scrap off the ceiling. Next, that machine over there will drive in bolts to secure the roof. Different length bolts are used depending on the condition of the roof. Sometimes we don't need them at all. The face is then undercut to provide a new place to drill the holes for blasting. Twenty-four holes are drilled into the face. These are filled with a mixture of ammonium nitrate and fuel oil. Electric blasting caps are placed in each hole and set off by remote control."

Charley took a deep breath, "If you sniff the air you'll pick up this scent of ammonia and gas. Next the front end loaders over there scoop up the broken salt from the blast. They take it to a breaker that grinds it up. The salt goes through a series of crushers to reduce the size of the chunks. After this process the salt rides conveyor belts to surge bins that carry it to the surface."

"Now most of you will stay here with my assistant, your foreman, Steve Schrupp. Terry you and this poor bastard will go back with me to the hoist. Terry, when we get there, I've got a surprise for you."

As they walked towards the truck, Terry felt the earth move beneath his feet. He spread his feet to steady himself not knowing if this was normal or if something bad was happening. It felt kind of bad.

The lights along the tunnel flickered and then went out. A deep unreal darkness descended in the mine. Now the mine floor was rolling and the walls were shaking. Bits of salt fell from above. When Charley shouted, "Brace yourselves", Terry bent his knees and grabbed his oversized helmet to steady the light. It was the only thing he had to chase away the darkness.

The guy in the truck started shouting, "We're going to die. We're all going to die."

As the salt mine shook, Terry paid no attention to the guy yelling in the truck. Holding his helmet tight, he didn't want to lose his only light. With the mine floor rippling under his feet, it was all he could do to ride out the quake on his feet. Terry was determined to show Charley he wasn't afraid. He needed this job.

When the back-up generators kicked in, the lights flickered on, but not as brightly as before. Charley wasn't sure what to do. As shift manager, he had the responsibility to evacuate the mine in an emergency. He had weathered the occasional tremor, but never a quake like this. When another even bigger tremor hit, he had had enough. By remote control, he pushed his evacuation button which turned off all the lights in the mine. Turning off the lights was the quickest way to tell every miner it was time to get out. Miners at all levels stopped what they were doing to move toward the hoist as quickly as possible. Wondering what had happened, Terry found his little helmet light reassuring as he shined it on his hands to make sure he was still there, alive.

After climbing on the back of the truck, Charley slapped the guy shouting out doom on the top of his helmet and at the same time growled, "Shut the hell up."

Terry saw the heavy equipment operators running toward two other pickups parked nearby. All the trucks raced toward the hoist. As the pickup bounced along the dark salt road, he was glad it was going faster than it had on his descent. Terry had to hold on to the bench with one hand and his hat with the other. When they reached the hoist, it had already carried several loads of workers to the surface. They were next. By then the shaking had subsided, but nothing stopped an evacuation once it was underway.

When the elevator clanked to a stop at the surface, Charley looked at his watch, forty-four minutes. Not the best time, but pretty good for an unannounced evacuation. The goal was to get everyone out in less than an hour. With everyone back on top of the earth, he told the miners to take a break and added that no one would return to work until the mine was inspected.

He immediately gathered his inspection teams together and headed back down into the mine to look for damage from the earthquake.

After letting off teams on the first two levels, on the third level the men divided into pick-ups without being told what to do. They had practiced this drill many times. They'd even done it for real a couple times. Each group left to check their assigned level. Charley and his team headed down the slope to the bottom level. The inspectors on the older top levels with the bigger pillars found nothing wrong and reported back to Charley using the Wi-Fi system ISC had just installed in each level of the mine. When his team reached the bottom of the mine, Charley got out of his truck to inspect the new thin pillars.

Some of these small pillars near the West face of the mine had cracks in them and a couple were broken. Charley and his crew checked every pillar spraying an orange ring around every defective column. The damage seemed to be confined to the bottom three levels of the mine where the new small pillar technique was being used.

These new pillars pissed Charley off. He thought the pillars should be getting bigger as you drilled deeper into the mine not thinner. After all, the further down you went the more the pillars had to hold up. Ah, but that was common sense. Unfortunately, the engineers armed with their computers kept making the pillars thinner. Charley frowned, *engineers don't live down here. If they are wrong, the miners will be digging our own graves.*

On the ride back to the hoist, Charley declared the mine safe. He called the shift operator up top to get everyone back down to finish the shift. Standing next to the elevator as the cage opened, Charley saw Terry, "What happened to the guy who cracked up?"

Terry shook his head, "He sort of staggered toward the parking lot. I don't think you'll see him again."

"Well, you showed me you can handle it. Never saw you flinch. How you doing? This is quite a baptism for your first time down under."

"I was worried about losing my light. You know, sort of like a nightlight. Made me feel safe. Is it always like this?"

"Sonny, you just went through the worst earthquake I've felt in thirty years of mining. I've got to find out why the east coast had a son-of-a-bitch like this. Before I call my friend at the college seismic center, let me show you your surprise."

Charley strode away from the hoist making Terry run to keep up with him. As they rounded a corner, Charley pointed towards some big equipment explaining, "You mechanics have a great deal with this company. The shafts aren't big enough to take broken equipment up and down so we have a complete garage down here."

Terry was surprised to find a stock room, rebuild shops, electrical shops, machine rooms and even a hydraulic shop. "Everything we have on top, you have down here. If a machine breaks down here, it gets fixed down here. Those god-damned conveyor belts break all the time. Most of the time you'll work over here."

Charley pointed to a man under a truck across the bay. "You'll be working for that guy. He's Bud Rump. A bit of a hard ass, but if you do your job you shouldn't have a problem with him. You won't be the only rookie for long. We'll be hiring a truck load of mechanics. By the time they arrive, you'll be an old hand. Don't be afraid to be a leader. Help the new guys adjust. Leaders get promoted in this corporation. Always be ready to help. This ain't the military. Volunteer here, you get more money. By the way, you'll get paid for two shifts today. One for the interview and one for tonight. Might give you a little pocket change to celebrate the new job. The union got that benefit for you. Oh, I suggest you join. Miners who don't join the union seem to have more accidents."

CHAPTER 7

During a romantic dinner the evening of the quake, Shelley Olson looked between the candles on her small dining room table at her mentor and lover, Dr. Dan Cooper. In a moment of serene silence, she noticed ripples rolling across the wine in her glass. At first they made her think of a quote from Percy Bysshe Shelley that her mother used to tell her, "I have drunken deep of joy, and I will trust no other wine tonight."

Tonight, the joy of being with Dan was better than the wine. I guess that was what Percy was talking about, she thought. Dan looked like he had been selected by central casting for his job as a geology professor at Ithaca College. He was tall and fit with just the right amount of gray in his temples to look distinguished. Right now, he was ignoring the wine to drink in her beauty as he stared at her with a cute smile on his face.

Shelley noticed the ripples on the wine were growing bigger and left the thoughts of her man to point them out to Dan. "Look at your glass. Are we having an earthquake?"

Dan shook his head to end his thoughts of the woman of his dreams. Smugly he answered, "No it's just me. I rock your world."

Shelley laughed and pointed to her wine glass, "No, look at the wine. It's moving."

Focusing on the wine as the quake grew in intensity, Dan told her, "I think you're right."

As the table continued to shake, he added, "We need to get over to the college right now to find out what's happening. If it's a quake, Bob Jacobi at Buffalo will be all over it. He's the expert on upstate New York earthquakes. I'll give him a call when we get there. From the ripples in the wine, I would guess the quake is coming from the West which could mean the Linden fault near Batavia is acting up."

Dan knew the sensitive equipment in his seismic center would be recording every aspect of the quake. The equipment in his lab was so sensitive it could record a small earthquake as far away as New Zealand. With this one so close, he was sure his machines would be going crazy capturing every detail. He left the table while Shelley was still sitting there. Without stopping, he yelled back to her, "Let's go."

Dan loved the idea of Shelley tagging along with him. Last year Shelley had been an undergraduate in one of his classes. Unfortunately, the school had rules against fraternization with students. Dan found it a difficult rule to obey after seeing her smile at him during each lecture. Often she would look up at him with those beautiful eyes with a strand or two of her blonde hair caught at the side of her mouth. He would never forget those images. *God, she's beautiful.*

Back then he didn't dare start a relationship, but after graduation, she became fair game. Dan was pretty sure the college rule only applied to undergraduates. From his perspective, graduate students were free and independent. When Shelley answered his ad for a grad assistant, he was quick to make her a member of his team. This summer, she had been a great help planning his geology field trips. More important, their relationship had blossomed each day they worked together. If she would have him, he wanted her to be his wife, but so far he hadn't found the right moment to broach that topic with her.

Shelley grabbed her purse, "Will anybody be in the lab this late?"

Dan called back over his shoulder, "Rahul has night duty. Hell, he's always there. It's a good place for him to study while he gets paid. Usually there's not much action, but tonight he's got some."

As she passed the mirror by the door, Shelley brushed her blonde locks into place with her fingers. Noticing that her light yellow sweater looked pretty good on her, she pulled the back of it down over the top of her jeans. She liked the way she looked. The only thing she didn't like about herself was her name. Her mother's love for that English poet, Shelley, had damned her forever.

In his old jeep, Dan was excited about the earthquake and spouted off like a professor just gaining his stride midway through a freshman lecture. "I bet it's the Linden fault. Remember when we took pictures of it on the thruway bank just a few weeks ago."

"I remember you found it hard to stay in your own hotel room that night."

Dismissing the image of making love with Shelley that flashed across his mind, Dan concentrated on the quake. "This quake may be something. I tell you the East coast is coming alive. You have a 5.8 quake near Mineral, Virginia in 2011 and a 2.4 one at almost the same place in 2012. Then you have a 4.6 quake in Hollis Center only twenty miles from Portland, Maine in '12. We recorded each of them right here in the Finger Lakes. We've had some in New York, too. In the Adirondacks in '83, there was a 5.1 quake in Newcomb that was followed in 2002 by a 3.8 quake at almost the same place. Do you realize what all this seismic activity means?"

Shelly enjoyed her man's enthusiasm. All this energy from the Director of the new Ithaca College Seismic Center was exciting. To tease him, she asked in a very serious voice, "No Doctor Director, what does it mean?"

"It means we may be living through a rebirth of earthquake activity on the East coast. When you run a seismic center it doesn't get much better than that."

Still mocking her lover, Shelley switched to a Southern accent. "*Muh* dear *Daator* Cooper are *ya'all* sure this here quake was caused by natural forces?"

Completely missing her taunt, Dan answered, "I think this one was a real earthquake, but you never know. We'll find out at the center. I hope it isn't a *fracking* quake created by the drilling up at the north end of the lake. There's been enough of them around here lately. They have fracking quakes all the time in Texas and the Midwest, and now it's happening here. Hell, Pennsylvania too. Fracking quakes have been migrating East with the fracking industry. They also have them in Europe. Fracking is so dangerous it's against the law in France."

Trying to provoke some sort of personal response, Shelley continued with her *Gone With The Wind* accent. "Oh *muh* dear Cooper. I do declare. This innocent damsel of the Confederacy needs to know, whatever is fracking, dear sir? Are you are insulting *muh* ears with a dirty word? When I was a young child in the old South, unwashed boys used that word as a substitute for, pardon *muh* French, fucking, sir."

Finally Dan realized he was being teased and played along. "Well Missy, I'm so glad you asked. It is a true pleasure having such a delicate flower of the 'ole' south under my personal supervision. Fracking, my dear young girl may have meant sexual intercourse to your filthy mouthed boyhood friends, but I'm talking about drilling for gas. This fracking, my dear is the hydraulic fracturing of rock to get out gas. Gas companies pump unsavory liquids under great pressure into rock formations far beneath the earth. This smelly sludge pushes the gas to the surface for companies to sell and make tons of money. Unfortunately, then they pump the waste water back into the ground. This polluted brine tends to migrate along fissures to faults deep in the earth. Many theorize these solvents grease unknown faults in the earth and generate earthquakes. Fracking has caused a swarm of small quakes in Texas, Oklahoma and a 4.0 quake in Ohio."

"Oh my. Is there no end to your genius? I do believe I'm getting the vapors. Is there more?"

"Ah...yes my dear Charlotte there is. I have so much to teach you. An earthquake swarm is when you have many earthquakes in a small localized area."

"Oh my, dear Rhett, I do believe I'm glowing. My palms are positively damp."

"My belle, recently these swarms have been attributed to fracking and the disposal of waste water in Texas and Oklahoma."

"Oh my, Texas, the pride of the Confederacy, is being fracked. Tell me it's not so. I bet it's those Yanks. Someone must defend *muh* 'ole' south."

"It is I, your knight in denim armor. I will defeat the frackers. In the Northeast, the fracking is in the Marcellus Shale. This is a layer of strata far below the earth in Pennsylvania and upstate New York filled with gas. It even stretches under the Finger Lakes."

"Ah, but that's up north with those damned Yankees. Does anyone really care?"

"Yes, along with many others, I do. This is the environmental crusade of this generation."

"My, my, a crusade. *Muh* rebel friends will finally get even with you *Yankee* bastards. These Texans will ruin your homeland the same way you did to my 'ole' South. Oh...Tell me more, tell me more."

"That muh dear is from *Grease* not *Gone With The Wind*." Dan told her. "You're mixing musicals with your movie."

"Oh sir, please do forgive *muh* literary ignorance. Do tell me what will happen when the frackers arrive. Glory be, will I be fracked? I so want to save my virginity until you return from the battles. How can I save *muh* heritage?"

"*Muh* dear, my theory is that fracking in the Marcellus Shale is lubricating the deep old tectonic plates of the Northeast which will make them active again. If my theory is correct, there will be more quakes in the east. For a seismologist it's great, but not so great for the people living around here. I'm going to have lots of wiggly lines to analyze. The folks living here will have cracks in their houses and roads. Hell, the East coast may fall into the ocean before California."

"Thank God, when it does the south will rise again. Just for me, do say tectonic one more time. It truly rings in my ears."

"Tectonic."

"Oh my, I do believe *muh* face is flushed."

Dan smiled, "One last time, just for you. Tectonic."

"My God, this talk of fracking is truly making me wilt."

"Frankly my dear, I do give a damn. Having a sexy blonde southern belle such as yourself talking dirty to me makes me sure my ole Confederacy rise again."

****

Sitting in his white lab coat, Rahul Sati was studying when the quake rescued him from his boring text. He hit the touch pad on his computer to analyze the streams of data flowing from the teleseismoneters and accelerographs. These machines were spitting out data that appeared by magic on his computer screen. The array of interconnected seismometers and other state-of-the-art equipment in the lab let him determine the intensity of the ground motion and pinpoint the source. In this new facility, they could even get sub-surface images of the quake. By the end of his shift, he would have a good summary for Dr. Cooper.

Rushing into his seismic lab, Cooper threw his dark blue blazer into his office. It landed in a crumpled pile just short of his couch. Dan rolled up his shirtsleeves as he ran to Rahul and his computer.

Rahul pointed to the screen as he explained what happened. Rahul cleared his throat, but his first words came out sort of squeaky. "Et…ita… was a 5.3 quake centered just below Batavia on the Linden fault."

As Rahul cleared his throat, Dan yelled, "I knew it, I knew it. Man, show me the data." Rahul hit his computer keys to make the data flash across his screen pausing only long enough for Dan to scan each page and grunt for the next.

As they watched the screen, the office began shaking again. All their instruments swung into action recording the aftershock. Dan braced himself as the trembling continued. As soon as it stopped, they ran to different machines to check the new results.

"Aftershock, 4.3." Dan shouted out.

Rahul shouted back, "Linden fault again."

Rahul was excited and asked Dan, "Does this support you theory that fracking is causing earthquakes around here?"

"I'm not sure I can prove that fracking fluid has reached the Linden fault. This data might help. That's the problem. How do you prove that fracking is causing manmade earthquakes? That, of course, is considered fact by most independent scientists, but is violently disputed by scientists hired by gas companies. The dangers of injecting liquid under great pressure into fault areas is known to cause earthquakes. This phenomena was known long before fracking became an issue. In 1965, Dave Evans, a geologist out of Denver connected a series of earthquakes to the Army's disposal of waste fluids in a 12,000 foot well. The Army injected pressurized fluid into preexisting fractures causing the strata to move. Do you know what happened to him? I do. No one paid any attention to him."

Sitting next to Dan, Rahul nodded. This exchange of ideas was what he had hoped for when he took this low paying position as lab assistant. He wanted to learn from Cooper. He was one of the best. Rahul nodded again to encourage Dan to continue.

Finding an attentive audience, Dan told him, "Then Bill Rubley and King Hubbert, two oil company geologists, entered the equation. Because they worked for money making oil companies, people paid attention to them. Anyway, they confirmed Evan's analysis. They found that elevated liquid pressure reduced the friction between layers of fractured rocks making it easier for them to slide apart. It wasn't hard to figure out this slippage caused earthquakes. When you lubricate faults with high pressure waste water or fracking fluid, the plates slide and you get quakes. Who would have guessed?"

Dan paused and asked, "Do you have any coffee?"

Standing behind them watching the action, Shelley volunteered to get it for him. After grabbing a mug from the sink, she ran to the coffee maker and tried to pour the sludge out of the bottom of the pot still cooking on a hot plate. It came out as more of a solid than a liquid. At least it's hot, she thought, as she ran back to Dan.

Dan had to chew the bitter sludge to squeeze out a bit of caffeine. "Unfortunately, we still don't know exactly what happens when you drill a well and inject fluid deep into the earth. Sometimes you get quakes and other times you don't. I think the key issue is injecting this fluid into fissures that you don't know are there. It doesn't take a brain surgeon, or in this case a geologist, to figure out injecting high pressured fluid between fault plates allows them to slide with less effort. Causing, you guessed it, earthquakes."

Daring to take another sip of the brown liquid sticking to the bottom of his mug, Dan continued. "You know that the Richter scale measures the amount of energy released at the epicenter of a quake. Most fracking quakes are relatively small. About 3 or less on the Richter. Usually quakes of this sort aren't noticed by people living above the wells. People will feel a 4 or 5 quake depending on how close they are to the source. Quakes of this intensity don't usually cause much damage above ground. When you get to 6 or 7, these quakes are considered major. People will be aware of them and they may cause considerable damage above ground. Above 7, the quake can kill people and destroy infrastructure."

With his mini-lecture drying his throat, Dan took a long slug of the toxic brew. He winced as the vile liquid slid down his throat in one piece.

He coughed it up and spit it back into his mug. After clearing his throat, he asked Shelley, "Please make some real coffee. Rahul doesn't know how much to put in that dam machine."

As Shelley ran away, Dan continued. "The problem is worse on the East coast because the underground geologic structure is denser and allows seismic waves to travel farther without weakening. That quake in August, 2011 near Richmond caused $200 million dollars' worth of damage. That was the one that cracked the Washington monument in D.C. and broke open cracks in the National Cathedral. That was only 5.8 on the Richter scale. On the West coast that might interrupt your lunch, but not much more."

"My theory is that fracking lubricates the faults causing earthquakes. If gas companies keep pumping their fluid into the ground around here, the quakes will keep getting larger and more devastating."

After Shelley delivered a freshly brewed cup of coffee, she went to Dan's office leaving Dan and Rahul to their data. After picking up Dan's jacket and draping it over his desk chair, she went to his couch for a nap.

Rahul looked up and asked, "How long was this quake?"

"You mean the duration of the quake? That's difficult to answer. For a geologist it means the length of the fault rupture. The length of time the earth is actually being ripped apart. For people in a building on the surface it's how long their world shakes. Fault rupture can spread very quickly and even a short quake can cause a lot of shaking when it reaches the surface. Let me see."

Dan traced his finger across his screen looking for the right data. "The fault rupture of this quake lasted 53.6 seconds. That's a long quake. The area of the fault rupture must have been quite large. A quake this long could shake the ground your house is on for 3 to 4 minutes depending how close you are to the epicenter, the nature of the strata under your house and how well your home was built. A wood frame home is going to shake longer than a reinforced concrete building. The shock waves making these buildings shake are called tremors and they can be really scary."

Dan looked up from his computer at Rahul, "In 2004 in Sumatra, there was a fault rupture of 900 miles that lasted for almost 10 minutes. That's the longest quake in recorded history. The 1994 Northridge Quake in California that caused so much damage had a fault rupture of 12 miles and only lasted for 15 seconds. As we get to the bottom of this data, I'll bet we'll find the length of the rupture for our quake today is 18 to 20 miles along the Linden fault. Something big is happening around here."

CHAPTER 8

T he morning after the quake, Steve wandered out on his cabin porch. Today there was no fog. Shivering at the thought of those things chasing him, he surveyed his domain. His boats had made it through the night without being damaged by the big waves from the quake. Then he spotted an old wooden row boat with only one oar drifting near shore. Shaking his head, he wondered if the quake had pulled it off a dock.

Must have drifted in here, he thought. *Last night there was a lot of really big waves.* He waded into the water up to his chest to grab a rope hanging from the bow of this derelict. Dragging the old boat to shore, he noticed a board on the stern had been ripped off and spun the heavy old boat around to look at the damage.

It was a fresh tear. The wood was bright and jagged. Then he noticed an odd object embedded in the wood. He tried to pull it out, but it had been driven deep into the board. Wiggling it back and forth, he finally popped it out. It reminded him of the teeth on the creature that had chased him. He shuddered and tossed it away. After looking around to make sure the tooth's owner wasn't lurking behind him, Steve pulled the boat up on the shore. *Someone,* he thought, *would show up during the day to claim it.* He noticed a tackle box under the middle seat. *Yes, some fisherman will be looking for his boat.* As he strolled back to his cabin to shave, images of the old boat were quickly replaced with thoughts of Mrs. Grayson.

After the morning jog with his friends, Billy Barton grabbed a piece of soap and a towel from his cabin before heading to the lake to clean off with a quick dip. This area of the beach next to Shanty's cabin was hidden from the rest of the camp. Washing off in the lake was easier than trudging up to the dining hall for a hot shower. When he got to the shore, he slipped off his undershorts and dropped his towel next to them. Naked, he waded knee deep into the lake. After a quick dip in the cold water, he started soaping up. While he was scrubbing his chest looking out at the lake, he heard a laugh, sort of a giggle, come from Shanty's cabin. He turned around to find a very attractive young woman with long black hair laughing at him from the rocking chair on Shanty's porch. He quickly dropped down into the water, but it wasn't deep enough to hide much so he dove backwards swimming to deeper water.

When Billy poked his head above the surface, he heard two people laughing at him. After wiping water from his eyes, Billy saw that Shanty had joined the fun as he stood next to this beautiful female creature. Standing up in waist deep water not sure what to say or do, Billy couldn't think of a *cool* response. Shanty wasn't much help, "You're turning blue. You'd better get out of there. Don't worry about my sister. From here there doesn't look like you have much to hide."

After debating what to say, Billy finally shouted back, "I didn't know you had a sister."

The girl was wearing a red sweatshirt over jean shorts that couldn't hide the curves of her sculptured body. Her oval face was a touch Asian. It gave her a mysterious air. She had dark eyes and a slim yet enticing figure. She definitely was the total package. Then the vision spoke, "I think you should finish bathing and get out of the cold water. I'll get you some hot coffee. You need something to warm up."

As the girl disappeared, Shanty laughed as Billy scurried out of the lake. Just as Billy was picking up his towel, Shanty's sister poked her head out the door, "Do you like it black or with milk? Sugar?"

Quickly covering himself, Billy answered, "Black's fine. No sugar."

When the beauty disappeared, Billy had a chance to pull up his underwear. As he passed the porch, he told Shanty, "You never mentioned a sister."

Still laughing, Shanty called back. "You never asked."

"Tell uh...your sister..."

"Annie."

Tell Annie I'll be right back."

Just after Billy ran off to his cabin with a smile, Annie came out carrying two steaming mugs of coffee, "So that's your Billy Barton?"

"What do you think?"

"He's a good looking boy. Sure is muscular and trim. Probably a bit rough around the edges."

"Do you like him?"

"Yeah, after thirty seconds I'm deeply in love."

"You certainly saw enough of him."

"From what I saw, all I could tell was that the water's cold."

"I don't mean that. It's just that you spend all your time in that dusty museum. You need to get out more. You should have a man in your life."

"First, the museum is not dusty. It's state of the art. A good place to work or visit. Second, when did you become my matchmaker? And last, but not forgotten, I thought you only wanted me to date Mohawk boys."

"Billy's special. A neat kid. I like him. He has a good soul. Sometimes marrying outside our tribe is acceptable if it's a move up. This guy would add to any bloodline. I bet somewhere in his past, he has a bit of Iroquois blood in him."

"Is he Hispanic? With his brown hair it's hard to tell."

"You noticed he is a bit of mixed breed. From what he tells me, his great grandfather was a British civil servant who served in India where he found his true love. When they returned to England, his family didn't accept his new dusky-skinned wife. Then his great grand-dad left for the states never looking back."

"A mixed breed like us. Welcome to the family." Annie added with a smile.

"About time we actually get some real *Injun* blood in us." Shanty answered with an even wider grin.

After pulling on a clean t-shirt and pulling on his shorts, Billy looked in his mirror. He quickly brushed his hair, but it didn't do much good. His shaggy brown mop stuck out at odd angles and flipped up in the back. *I need a haircut*, he thought. He couldn't believe how it was poking out in every direction. *Maybe this beautiful girl will see it as a fashion statement. Hope so.*

Spitting on his comb, he tried again and again to tame his tangles. When he looked almost acceptable, he left his cabin porch by grabbing the post and swinging down over the steps to the ground. He hit the ground running. Time to officially meet Shanty's sister with clothes on. *That beautiful apparition had laughed at him while he was naked. Not a good start,* he thought.

Billy found Shanty sitting in the rocking chair on the porch holding a mug of coffee with his sister sitting on a bench on the other side of the cabin doorway with her mug. On a small table in front of her on the bench sat another mug of coffee. Billy climbed the stairs to pick up his steaming drink and nodded thanks to this beautiful young woman. The only place to sit was on the bench next to her, but he thought that might be a bit forward. Besides he wanted a place where he could get a good look at her. He sat down on the porch steps leaning against the post with one foot on the porch and the other on the next step down trying to look as cool as possible.

As he leaned back, he spilled the coffee on his T-shirt. "Yeow", it was hot. He jumped up trying to brush the scalding liquid off his chest spilling more of the hot brew on his shorts. As Shanty laughed, Billy couldn't believe what he'd done. He looked down and saw that his front looked like he had just wet his pants. Trying to get them to focus on something other than his soggy shorts and wet T-shirt, he asked, "Did Shanty tell you about the excitement last night?"

This attractive girl ran into the cabin and returned throwing him a towel. As Billy wiped off, she answered, "Yes. He told me you were quite the hero. I can see why you needed to wash off this morning. Now, you might have to clean off again."

"Sorry about that. I run with my friends every morning. I didn't know Shanty would have a sister ogling me this early in the morning."

"Hey, I wasn't ogling. I just thought you were part of the entertainment. Besides, couldn't see much from here."

Shanty added with a laugh, "Wasn't much to see."

Billy grimaced, "That's what every growing boy wants to hear from a beautiful girl who just saw him naked."

"Hey, hey. Remember she's my sister. Annie, officially meet Billy Barton. I have to admit he did a *helleva* job last night. You should have seen him carry those girls up the cliff in the dark. Anyone can rappel down a cliff, it's climbing back up that's hard. Last night, he proved he was strong enough to climb up again and again rescuing a damsel in distress each time."

"I'm impressed. Joey, let me get to know this guy."

"Joey?" Billy questioned with a smirk on his face.

"Don't you go there. Only my family calls me that."

"Annie, where did you come from?"

"Connecticut, I work for the Mashantucket Pequot Museum next to the Mohegan Sun Casino. Joey invited me down here to enjoy the lake. I'm an amateur paleontologist and want to look at your new sinkhole. The collapse may have exposed some fossils."

"I'm a fossil hunter, too. Come to my cabin, I'll show you what I've found."

"Hey, don't go inviting my sister to your cabin."

"I'd like to see your collection. Pay no attention to my brother."

"You'll need to rappel to get down into the sinkhole. I'll be happy to teach you."

"Billy, she can out rappel both of us."

"Then you'll need a spotter. I've got campers on the obstacle course this morning, but I'm free after that."

Shanty spoke up. "I'm busy this morning, but I want to see that sinkhole in the daylight. How about an afternoon rappelling party?"

Billy turned to Shanty, "Come to think of it. Where did you learn to rappel? You surprised me last night. I've never seen you rappel around camp."

"Uncle Sam taught me for free. That's all you need to know."

"Fine, but I've been wondering why you had the rappelling ropes in your truck last night. That saved us."

"Remember you asked me to whip the ends of your ropes so they wouldn't fray. I drove by your cabin yesterday afternoon and saw those old lines on your porch. I remembered you wanted them fixed so I threw them in the back of my truck. I planned to do the ends last night before we got distracted."

When the dining hall bell ring, they put their mugs on the small porch table before heading for breakfast. Shanty walked ahead while Billy and Annie lagged behind deep in conversation.

Outside the dining hall, Billy introduced Annie to Lea, Link and Steve. Inside, they went to their assigned tables to eat with the campers. Shanty started to take Annie to the back where he usually ate when the Director called to him. "Mr. Brandt, please join me at my table. Is this attractive young girl your sister?"

Shanty introduced his sister as they joined the Director at his table. This table wasn't much more than a longer picnic table centered at the end of the dining hall so the Director could see all the campers and they could see him. The meals at this head table were served while the campers and counselors stood in a cafeteria line off to the side.

The Director was still handing out invitations. He went to the cafeteria line and asked Billy Barton to join him at his table. Billy shrugged his shoulders as he followed the Director back to his table. Before they sat down, Grayson introduced Billy to Annie and told him, "Of course you know everybody else."

Billy was pleased to get a warm welcome from everyone except Hilda Grayson who snorted at him. He nodded politely to her trying not to smile at her less than cordial greeting. *It never hurt to be nice to the Director's sister even though she is a bitch,* he thought. He did notice that the Director's wife gave him an unusually bright smile. He nodded at her as he sat down. Billy didn't think it was necessary to tell the director he'd already met Annie, especially after the circumstances of their first encounter. Hilda and Harold might not approve of him washing off in the lake.

The Director spent the first part of the meal recounting the previous night's rescue heaping praise on Billy and Joe. When he finished his accolades, he promised to demonstrate his real appreciation for their actions later in the summer. Billy and Shanty looked at each other wondering what that meant.

After Steve went through the cafeteria line, he sat down at his table with campers so he faced the front of the dining hall and could stare at Mrs. Grayson. He hoped to get her attention and finally he got the reaction he was hoping for. Her eyes found his with a wink. Checking that Lea wasn't watching, Steve smiled back. He knew that last night's encounter in the woods would not be their last. *Yes, I have a plan for you,* Steve thought with a smile.

Involved in a discussion of tennis strategy, Lea sat across the dining hall from Steve and missed the exchange.

Near the end of the breakfast the Director stood up to talk to the campers. "First I want to publicly thank Mr. Barton and Mr. Brandt for their heroism last night." The campers responded with cheers, hoots, whistles and applause.

"I have talked to the hospital and the three campers injured last night will be retuning this afternoon."

After more applause, he quieted the multitude, "Last night the camp endured an earthquake which resulted in what I believe was the collapse of a sinkhole next to the girl's cabins. Today a geology professor from Ithaca College will visit us to look at it. He will be able to tell us what happened. We want to make sure the camp is safe for everyone."

Thinking of the beautiful girl next to him, Billy paid more attention to Annie than the Director. The Director finished by announcing, "We will follow the same schedule handed out last Friday. The obstacle course and swimming tests will be held today."

As everyone got up and started to leave, Steve let the campers go in front of him making sure Lea left the dining hall before him. Then he waited by the door for Ms. Grayson to pass by. When Ursula saw Steve standing to her left, she drifted over to him. After Steve whispered something to her, Ursula nodded and left the dining hall with a smile on her face.

Billy planned his escape from breakfast so he could walk out with Annie, but just as he caught up to her the director called him back and asked him to stay for a moment. Reluctantly, Billy sat down as the Director asked him to wait for Mr. Brandt to join them. Shanty showed up with a pot of coffee to refresh their cups. When Shanty sat down, the Director told them, "I have asked Dr. Cooper from Ithaca College to inspect our sink hole. He will need to rappel into the hole to inspect it. Billy, I noticed you don't have anything scheduled this afternoon. I would like you to escort him around the camp and help him get down into our new pit. Joe, could you to arrange your schedule to go with them?"

"You bet Mr. Grayson. My sister can help too. She's a great climber."

"That's settles it then. Thank you both again for last night. I also appreciate your assistance with the professor." Finished, the director left the table after excusing himself.

As Joe stood up, he slapped Billy on the back, "Watch out for Mrs. Grayson. I saw her watching you during breakfast. She's hit on me a more than a couple times. Don't go there. Too dangerous if you value your job. Besides, Grayson is a good guy."

As Shanty started to leave, Billy called to him, "Wait. Don't go. What's your sister's story?"

Nodding with a smile, Shanty straddled the picnic table bench and sat down, "Well, you should know she's smart."

"Okay."

"No, I mean really smart. My family first noticed it when she was reading books at four without anyone teaching her how. By five, she was telling the stories she read to the other kids on the reservation. I don't mean just telling the stories, but repeating them word for word. By seven, she was reading adult books. Mostly ones about our people. When she was ten or eleven, an anthropologist from Columbia came to study our tribe. He was surprised to learn she had read all his books on our culture and could recall everything in them. She blew him away."

"Wow."

"Wait, wait. That's just half of it. This guy called her a "prodigy." By twelve, she was attending classes at Columbia in New York City. She could have gotten a degree there, but wanted to return to the reservation to teach our children about their heritage." Shanty picked up a cup of coffee, took a sip and grimaced. It was cold. "Then the Director of the Mashantucket Pequot Museum and Research Center heard about her. I guess she was, maybe, fifteen. Anyway, she's been working there ever since. Once she reads a book, she's keeps it all right there in her head. She has helped researchers publish articles about our tribe because she can tell them what's already been written about our people. And she's good at telling them when they misquote something. She likes to do that. She's published a few articles herself, and I think she's writing a book. I'm real proud of her. She's a real treasure for our people."

"Will she be here all summer?"

"I hope. For all her smarts, she's socially retarded. Don't think she's ever had a boyfriend or even a date."

"Maybe I can be the first."

"Yeah, maybe, but go slow. I don't think she's discovered she has a heart."

CHAPTER 9

Hoping to flop on his bed after a difficult shift, Charley Morgan looked up as the elevator slowly climbed to the surface. He was impatient to get out of this man-cage and head for home. Getting everyone back to work after inspecting the columns made for a demanding shift. As soon as he left the hoist, he spotted two Suits. Vice President Olson and the female Suit, Hager, were waiting for him in his office. *Jesus,* he thought, *having Hager the Horrible waiting for you at the end of a shift isn't good news.*

As he walked toward his office, he wondered why this woman dressed like a man. *Hell, if she tried,* he thought, *she might be good looking.* With a smile on his face, he asked, "What can I do for you folks this fine morning?"

Hager asked in sarcastic tone, "Did you call an evacuation last night?"

"I did."

"Why."

"You may not have felt it up here, but we sure did down there. There was one helleva of an earthquake last night."

"Yes, I know. It was all over the morning news."

"My understanding is that we've had other quakes and never evacuated," Olson told him.

"In over thirty years, I've never felt an earthquake this bad. Besides, there's never been one so close. You're lucky to have a mine left."

Ruth challenged him, "I bet your shift will be short at least 3,000 tons."

Trying to keep calm and not to raise his voice, Charley answered, "That's right. We had an earthquake. It forced us to evacuate, inspect the mine for damage and then go back to work. Clearing the mine then getting everyone back down there cut three hours out of the shift. That's why we will be short."

In a condescending tone, this…this female asked, "Well, did you find anything wrong?"

Charley found it difficult to retain his cheerful demeanor with this woman treating him like he was stupid. "Matter of fact we did find some problems. First, your engineers better get back to their computers. Those tiny pillars aren't working. Sure, everything is fine when they just have to stand there, but throw in a good quake and they crack. I've got thirteen columns down on the bottom level with orange rings around them. Thirteen is not a good number. Most are just cracked, but two are completely gone. I've got six cracked pillars right above them on the next level up. Those levels hold up all the other levels of the mine for Christ-sakes. Take it from me, the deeper we go the pillars should be getting larger not smaller. They have more to hold up. Your fancy engineers may not have thought about that."

"With the damage to these small pillars, you may have to close that section of the mine. Hopefully more bolts in the roof around the cracked pillars will keep the ceiling from caving in, but they might not do the trick. We may have to shore up the mine the old-fashioned way with timbers. Well, today we don't use timbers, but you know what I mean. I don't want my people to work in the bottom levels until I'm sure they're stabilized. Did your engineers figure quakes into their calculations?"

Controlling her temper, Ruth told him, "If your shift doesn't meet its goals you won't have to worry about working in that section or any section."

"Lady, my shift has the highest product numbers every month and you know it. We'll do it again this month. Wait for it. But while you're checking things out, you'd better get your college educated engineers out of their offices and down in the mine checking those pillars. While they're at it, tell them there's water in the mine."

"Probably just drainage from the surface." Vice President Olson suggested.

"It didn't rain last night. The water is at the bottom of the mine not the first or second level. I waded through a big puddle. There isn't supposed to be water in a salt mine. It might not be water. Smells kinda like gasoline to me. Believe me something is wrong down there. Your experts better figure out the problem before this liquid crap, whatever it is, melts away the rest of their tiny little pillars causing the whole mine to collapse. Guaranteed that won't increase production. I also noticed a bump in the hoist coming up. It wasn't there yesterday so the quake may have shifted the shaft."

"That shaft is carved through bedrock. Now you're inventing problems." Hager told him.

Unbelievable, Charley thought, this woman just won't quit. Won't give me a break. "That shaft is my lifeline lady. Every miner depends on it. The bump was about a third of the way up. It might be the hoist, but my bet is on the shaft. Add that to the list for your engineers to check. My shift report will include the cracked pillars, the water and the hoist. Now they're your problems."

****

Still upset from her encounter with that dirty uncouth miner, Ruth Hager stabbed her finger into her secretary's desk. "Call the engineers. Tell them to check out the problems that old guy reported. I want results by noon."

At 11:59, the engineers gathered around Ms. Hager's secretary ready to report to their boss. After exactly a minute's wait, Melinda took them into Ruth's office. Without saying hello or offering them something to drink, Ruth motioned for them to sit on the far side of her conference table. She was surprised when Vice-President Olson followed them in and sat next to her.

Olson waited for her typical assault on the engineers. He couldn't wait until her contract was up. Until then he had to put up with her.

Ruth stared at the mine engineers, "Did you find anything that will hurt production?"

Jean Rogers, the lead engineer, explained that the earthquake had caused some serious damage. "In the bottom levels, the new small pillars are under stress. We found cracks that are visibly widening. Your foreman was right. Some pillars are completely broken. We directed the current shift to add more bolts to the ceiling around the cracked pillars to see if that will reduce the stress on them. If the bolts don't solve the problem that section of the mine will have to be abandoned until we can erect more traditional steel supports. As you know, that will be costly."

Upset by this news, Hager spit out, "Are you kidding me? You're the ones who said those small pillars would stand up. What did you get wrong?"

"Our calculations designed the new pillars to withstand a 4.0 earthquake. This earthquake had an intensity of 5.3 It's that simple."

"So you're telling us your previous calculations were wrong. Now we have a real problem because you guys screwed up. This is a mess. You'd better get on top of this pillar thing real quick or pack up and get out. I'll find some bright young graduates from down the lake who can do a better job than you worn out professionals. Anything else broken down there? If there is, you'd better know how to fix it?"

Trying to keep her temper, Jean was careful to answer in a calm tone. Hopefully one that would quiet this bitch down. "Our calculations were right, but we had not anticipated an earthquake that big…"

Ruth interrupted. "That big. It's your job to anticipate."

Jean ignored her boss's outburst, "I called Dr. Cooper at the Ithaca College. This quake was just 200 miles away. That's so close there was little time for the intensity of this quake to wear down."

Excuses, excuses, I want to know what you're going to do."

"We checked the hoist. Your shift manger was right. The elevator does have a jolt every time it goes up and down. There was a shift of about a half inch in the strata at the bottom of the lake as a result of this quake. The problem exists in all three shafts. The good news is that the shafts can be ground down and sealed. They don't represent a long term problem."

"What about the water?"

"We haven't solved that problem yet. We have determined that it's not water. It definitely smells like gas or at least some sort of petroleum product. We took samples for analysis. There are no visible fractures, but it seems to be seeping in from the bottom of the mine. This percolating fluid will be extracted with pumps. As we speak, there is a crew down there setting up pumps to remove the water and keep it controlled. The problem seems to be manageable. It shouldn't interfere with production. However, if it is coming from the lake, we would have a major problem."

"What the hell does that mean?" Ruth asked in a sarcastic tone.

"If it's lake water, the leak could grow as the water dissolves the salt. This could result in the mine flooding. Ultimately, that could result in a complete collapse of the mine."

"You mean flooding the bottom level." Olson quickly questioned hoping to reduce the impact of what he just heard.

"No. I'm talking about the whole mine."

"You've got to be kidding. That can't happen. You can't let that happen." Ruth said with a worried look on her face.

"We don't want it to happen, but it could. Collapsing salt mines are not news. We've had this discussion before. Remember when we talked about the collapse of the Akzo-Nobel salt mine in 1994. That was in the Genesee Valley just West of us right here in New York state. Our mine is a lot like that mine. They were expanding to new areas under a lake just like we are. Unfortunately just like them, we don't know the structural geology until we dig out the salt. We could find a structural anomaly that might cause the mine to collapse."

Jean hesitated a moment and wondered how she could get Ruth to grasp the seriousness of this problem. She decided to stay with the facts. "Richard Young, a professor at SUNY Geneseo, warned that using smaller pillars to support that mine or any mine was a gamble. He called this process *Pillar Robbing*. He pointed to the collapse of the Akzo mine as evidence. That was one of the largest salt mines in the world. It flooded because the supports collapsed in two sections of the mine. Caverns collapse naturally all the time, they're called sinkholes. We create caverns we call rooms. They, too, can collapse for a variety of reasons. Our rooms could go down from natural settling, water seepage, quakes and a myriad of other reasons. The quality...

"Get to the point," Ruth growled, "What's the bottom line?"

Without acknowledging her boss's interruption, Jean continued, "As I was saying, the supports will determine if our mine stands or collapses. This last quake demonstrated smaller pillars are good for profit, but aren't safe. If you tell me to make the mine safe enough to withstand a larger quake, I can do it. Understand that will reduce production. Let me make it clear, it would cut into your profits. It's your decision. What do you want me to do? Which is it, safety or money?"

Exasperated, Ruth told her, "It's your job to give us both."

Deciding to take another tact, Jean asked, "Do you know the game of *Jinga*?"

Albert shook his head in recognition, "I used to play it with my daughter."

Ruth frowned at the mention of children and told her, "Get to the point."

"*Jinga* is a children's game where you stack a tower of wooden pieces up and then you pull out the pieces of the tower until it collapses."

"Yes, yes, I know that game."

"Salt mining is a lot like that game. To increase production, we have been using smaller pillars and larger rooms each year hoping the tower won't fall down."

Albert asked a question in such a meek manner that it upset Ruth, "Is there anything we can do to keep the tower from falling?"

Jean nodded, "Of course, there are several options. First, this recent earthquake has demonstrated the girth of the pillars we use to support the mine are inadequate. We need to increase the pillar size. My engineers are already working out the size necessary to survive a 6.0 quake. The second problem is more difficult. The new Chinese equipment is bigger than the equipment we used before. This means we have to blast out larger rooms for them to operate. We can't reduce the size of the machinery so the room size we excavate has to be increased. Making the chambers larger is like pulling out a couple more pieces of wood out of the *Jinga* tower. We make the whole structure weaker hoping it won't fall down."

Just as she finished, the windows and furniture rattled from an aftershock. Ruth frowned as she held on to the edge of her large conference table waiting for the shaking to stop. She hated to make changes, but realized Mother Nature wasn't cooperating. When the shaking stopped, she announced, "Enlarge the pillar size and beef up the small ones. That should keep the mine safe. We're through here."

CHAPTER 10

O n a bright sunny afternoon with Cayuga stretching out behind him, Steve walked out on the dock followed by five lifeguards. The dock was shaped like a "T." The top of the "T" ran along the swimming area with a diving board on each end. During a swim, one lifeguard sat in each elevated chair near each the diving board and a third stood in the middle of the T with a rescue cane to extend to any swimmer having trouble. The fourth guard watched the students on the shallow side of the dock in the non-swimmers area. An additional guard was in the water with the non-swimmers. During a swim, Steve patrolled the swimming area on his jet ski just outside the ropes ready to respond to a distressed swimmer in deeper water. The director insisted on water safety and Steve knew how to deliver.

Steve explained to the campers lining the dock, "To become a swimmer you must dive under the water. When you come up, you can use any over-hand stroke to swim to the boundary ropes where you will tread water for half a minute. Then you must use the backstroke to swim back to the dock."

Two sets of buddies lined up on the dock and dove in when Steve, standing in the middle of the dock, blew his whistle. The two on the left end came up swimming toward the rope. When the other set surfaced, both of them turned to the dock coughing and splashing. One boy, who was choking, managed to yell out, "There's...there's a body down here." His buddy started swimming in panic back to the dock. When he reached it, he climbed out shouting, "A...a dead guy." Gasping for breath he added, "Only one leg. I...I went right over him."

Steve blew his whistle and motioned for all the swimmers to leave the dock while his lifeguards called the other swimmers back. When these campers returned to the dock, the guards helped pull them up. When the swimmers were safe, Steve took his swimming goggles from around his neck, put them on and dove into the water to find out what had scared them.

As the cold waters of Cayuga enveloped his body, Steve saw something with a sort of yellow-green tint on the bottom of the swimming area. Swimming toward it, a truly gruesome sight welcomed him. He gulped water and pulled back. They were right. There was a body. A dead man with only one leg. Recovering, Steve swam toward the dreadful sight. The man's eyes were open. He seemed to be staring up at Steve. The corpse's left leg had been torn off. His leg had been ripped off just below the hip and shreds of his skin waved to Steve as they floated in the water below him. A great hunk of his right side had been ripped away. Strings of flesh and some of his bowels were floating up from his body like snakes trying to reach the surface moving with the action of the water.

Exhaling and swallowing water, Steve jerked back from the mutilated body. He surfaced quickly to get away from the lost soul haunting the bottom of his swimming area. For some reason, the image of the creature that had chased him in the fog flashed through his mind as he pulled himself up on the dock.

He motioned for his lifeguards to join him. As they gathered around, he confirmed what the young swimmers had seen. He canceled the swimming tests and told the counselors to take the kids back to their cabins to get dressed. Still unnerved by the horrendous image of the dead man, he went to his towel and picked up his cellphone to report the body to the director so he could call the police.

****

Up from the camp on the main road that went around the lake, Shanty was sitting in the cab waiting for the geologist to show up. Billy and Annie sat in the bed of his pickup looking at the green hillsides that stretched along the great blue ribbon of lake. On this bright sunny day, Billy was pointing out landmarks across the lake to Annie. He finished by telling her about the ISC salt mine complex near Lansing not far from the airport. He told her that during World War II some of the great museums in New York City stored some of their most valuable artwork in that salt mine to protect them from bombs. He explained that salt mines provide the perfect dry environment. With no water, humidity or heat, they are a great place to store precious art. After he finished his verbal tour of the lake, they sat together quietly enjoying the pristine beauty of this lakescape.

As they shared a moment of peace gazing at the lake, they were startled from their revelry when an old rusted silver jeep pulled up next to the pickup. A good-looking man, wearing a light blue denim work shirt with his shirt sleeves rolled up, leaned out the driver's window and shouted hello to

Shanty. As they talked, Billy and Annie jumped down from the back of the pickup to join Shanty in the cab. Shanty motioned for the guy to follow him down the road to the camp.

Driving through the camp, Shanty turned up the road between the fields toward the dining hall and noticed police cars at the waterfront with their lights flashing.

"What's that all about?" Billy asked.

Shaking his head, Shanty told him he didn't know. As they drove up the hill, Shanty stopped to let a large group of campers run in front of his pickup. When they got to sinkhole, their visitor jumped out of his jeep to shake Shanty's hand.

A tall blonde girl came around the front of the jeep at the same time that Annie and Billy got out of the pickup. When the blonde saw them, she stopped shaking her head in disbelief, "Billy?"

Dumbfounded, Billy stared at the blonde, "Shelley?" For a moment they both stood still looking at each other without saying a word. Stumbling forward, Billy reached out his hand. Shelley brushed passed it and hugged him. For Billy, it was awkward. It was obvious to everyone that Shelley was very glad to see him and that Billy wasn't sure what to do. Embarrassed, he stepped back without saying a word.

Everyone stood silently looking at each other until Dr. Cooper stepped forward and extended his hand to this young man, "I'm Dan Cooper. Here to look at your new sinkhole."

Still staring at Shelley, he unconsciously shook Dan's hand muttering, "Billy Barton, sir."

Shanty rescued Billy by introducing Annie to Dr. Cooper and the blonde. When he finished, Shanty turned to Billy, "I guess you two know each other."

By now, both Shelley and Billy had recovered from their surprise. When they both started to explain at the same time, they laughed. Billy surrendered, "Ladies first."

Shelley stuttered, "Bill...Billy and I took some of the same classes together when I was an undergraduate."

I bet you did more than that together, Annie thought.

Billy added, "That's right. Classes together. I borrowed her notes. Good to see you again."

He held out his hand to Shelley who after a moment finally shook it.

Wondering what was going on between these two, Dan focused on why he had driven out here. "Let's see what you've got for me."

He led the group over to the edge of the new crater making sure to position himself between Shelley and this *Billy* guy. Annie stood next to Billy while Shanty stood just behind them.

Looking over the edge, Dr. Cooper examined the sinkhole. The sides went straight down about fifty feet to the floor of the collapse. He was surprised to see two cabins at the bottom of the hole. After Shanty explained what happened, Dan pointed to mounds of rubble dotting the floor of the hole at regular intervals. He told them that was unusual and that he had an idea what had happened, but to be sure he would have to go down into crater.

Dan asked Shanty the best way to anchor the ropes to rappel down. Shanty drove his truck to the edge of the crater. After putting on the emergency brake and leaving it in gear, Shanty picked up the same rock he used the night before to wedge under his tire. Then he asked Dan to park his jeep next to his pickup. While Dan was moving his jeep to the crater's edge, Shanty picked up another rock to put under the jeep's front tire. As soon as Dan stopped, Shanty slid the rock in place after telling Dan to make sure he left in in park and set the emergency brake.

While Billy pulled two rappelling ropes out of the back of the pickup and tied them to the tow loops of the jeep, Shanty grabbed two other lines and tied them to the bumper of his pickup. Shanty suggested Dan and Shelley could use the ropes on the jeep while he and Billy used the ropes on the pickup.

Shelley laughed, "I don't do cliffs. And don't want to learn."

Shanty told Dan that Annie knew how to rappel and would like to explore the cliff face for fossils if he didn't mind. Dan declared, "Sure. She won't bother me. The more the merrier." Turning to Annie, he told her, "Call me if you find something interesting."

When the others were ready to descend, Dan scrambled down the cliff with ease and when he reached the bottom, he held up his fists in triumph yelling, "Yes." Billy and Shanty were impressed with his skill and followed him down.

Stepping back from the edge of the cliff while she watched the men walk across the crater, Annie turned to Shelley. "How long did you go out with Billy?"

Surprised, Shelley asked, "How did you know?"

"Wasn't hard from your reaction."

"We dated last year and were pretty involved. He's younger and our relationship wasn't strong enough to survive the age difference."

"Who broke it off?"

"I guess, it was mutual. Billy was pretty upset. Are you Billy's new girl?"

"Oh no. We just met today. I'm visiting my brother. Billy seems like a nice boy."

"He is. He's a nice guy. Maybe too nice. Are you sure you just met? He seems to look at you with ah…I don't know, some interest."

"You think? That would be nice. I could teach you how to rappel. We both could look for fossils together."

"No, no, I'm an indoor kind of girl."

I bet you are, Annie thought. "Well, nice to meet you. I'm off to hunt fossils." Annie smiled at Shelley as she went over the cliff and descended slowly examining each layer of rock searching for elusive fossils. About half way down, she swung from side to side to examine a larger section of the new rock face.

As Dan, Shanty and Billy climbed over the debris, Billy wasn't paying much attention to the erudite pronouncements emanating from the professor. He was thinking about Shelley. He spent most of a year with her. It was good, but not great. He was surprised that seeing her today brought back those old feelings. He hadn't seen her for months and wasn't sure how he felt about her sudden appearance.

Hearing rocks fall behind him, Billy turned to see Annie going over the edge. He stopped to watch her as she swung back and forth looking for fossils. She looked like a spider running across a wall. *Not only can she rappel,* he thought, *she's damn good at it. I bet if there's a fossil up there, she'll find it.*

Watching Annie, Billy didn't notice that Dan and Shanty had stopped and ran into Dan knocking him to the ground on his hands and knees. At first, Dan assumed Billy had done it on purpose and jumped up glaring at him. Billy held up his hands with his palms up toward Dan and quickly apologized. Billy tried to help Dan brush off his jeans, but Dan pushed him away.

Trying to recover, Billy explained that he had been watching Annie and pointed to her swinging back and forth on her line. For a moment, they all watched her.

As Dan focused on her, he too was impressed. Then he remembered he might need help on the way up. "Don't worry about it. I just hope you can get me out of here when we have to climb back up."

Billy guaranteed he and Shanty could pull him up if necessary.

Dan led them up to the top of a mound in the crater. Then he pointed out three similar ones spaced at regular intervals. He added that the crater seemed to be more of a rectangle than an oval. "This is a very unusual shape for a sinkhole. I'm not sure what we have here."

Dan quickly started off to inspect the next mound without telling his entourage to follow. Shanty and Billy had to hustle to keep up. When they reached the next mound, Dan started looking very carefully around the base. Seeing something he liked, Dan took his mountaineering pick to break a few samples off a grayish white rock. Then he took a couple of plastic bags out of his knapsack and carefully put small pieces in each bag.

With a sharpie from his pocket, he wrote something on each label. Taking a small digital camera from his belt, he stepped back to take a couple of pictures of the mound. When he finished, he knocked off another sample and tasted it. Then he tossed it to Billy who tasted it before handing it to Shanty. Together, they all said, "Salt."

Dan asked Billy and Shanty to go to the top of the next mound. When they reached the top, Dan threw Shanty a tape measure. While Billy held one end, Shanty pulled the tape out as he walked to the bottom of the mound. As Shanty yelled out the measurements, Dan wrote them down in a small notebook. When they finished, Dan pointed his pick toward the next mound and shouted dramatically, "To our next mountain."

Annie was disappointed with her search and climbed back up the cliff. As she unhooked her rope to explore another section of the cliff, Shelley offered to help. "Can I help you?"

"Thanks, but I like to check my own lines and knots."

After attaching the line to a tree, Annie disappeared over the edge to explore a new section of the exposed wall. Dropping straight down the cliff, the fossils continued to elude her. Swinging left and right, she was disappointed again. She repeated her efforts at different levels, but still no luck. Enjoying the climb, she started running back and forth on the cliff face just for fun. Bouncing over the cliff, she enjoyed the thrill of swinging on her line. Noticing a promising site just beyond her reach, she hustled up the cliff to change the position of her line to get to the new spot.

Dan led his companions through the same process at the next mound. The new measurements roughly matched the first mound. After writing down the dimensions, Dan and his crew headed to the next one.

Annie secured her rope to another tree. This time she was more animated as she dropped over the cliff directly above the spot she was eager to explore. Almost halfway down the slope, there was a ledge where a slab of rock had broken off the cliff face. Waiting for her was part of a big skeleton of an animal about the size of a cow. It was spectacular. Gingerly, she reached out to touch it. Here were the remains of an animal that had lived long before even her people had lived on the shores of this lake.

Only the back half of the skeleton was there, but what a find. Carefully she traced the bones with her fingers. She could see the back bone and ribs. One rear foot stuck out from the wall and was shaped like a 'V'. The rest of the body was still entombed in the stone of the cliff.

The foot looks more like a flipper than a foot, she thought. This wasn't a small trilobite or brachiopod. No, this was a full sized fossil that looked like something she had seen at the Peabody Museum at Yale in the dinosaur section. Suddenly she had an idea and quickly rappelled down the cliff to the bottom of the crater.

After measuring the third mound, Dan found the measurements similar to the first two. Standing on the top of the mound, Dan slowly turned in a full circle pointing the end of his pick axe out as he turned. Finally, he stopped, "This isn't a sinkhole. It's a collapsed salt mine. It's my guess that if we look around the perimeter we'll find the mine shaft. Let's see, our rectangle is basically running from the west to the east toward the lake. Let's keep going toward the lake and see what we find."

After reaching the bottom of the crater, Annie looked for the slab that had fallen from her ledge. She flipped over flat rocks to see what was on the other side. None of them were the piece she wanted. Looking up at her ledge, Annie tried to estimate where the piece she was looking for might have fallen. *Maybe I should looking be closer to the cliff,* she thought.

Annie extended her search by approaching a pile of large rocks near the cliff face. In front of her was a medium sized flat stone. With a heave, she turned it over discovering another piece of her fossil. *That's better,* she thought. She knelt down beside the rock slab. Before her was a vertebrate from the back of her ancient animal. She stood and looked around. Nearby was a larger slab resting on a bank of dirt. She tried to lift it up, but it was too heavy for her to move. Instead, she lay down on her back so she could slowly slide under part of the rock that was sticking out from the bank. With sharp stones digging into her back, she had images of the stone tipping forward and crushing her skull. Very carefully, Annie maneuvered her body under the slab trying not to disturb it. When she spotted the rest of her fossils, she squealed with delight.

The three salt mine explorers went to the debris at the east wall of the crater to look for a way into the old mine. Dan climbed up the slope and sunk his pick into the rubble. After a couple of swipes, he couldn't find anything. Billy and Shanty joined him stomping around on the debris sloping away from the cliff. After a short discussion, Billy went left while Shanty and Dan went to the right stomping on the pile of dirt along the rim of the hole to find an entrance to the mine. Billy jumped up and down on the rocks thinking this was a stupid idea. A complete were a waste of time. He'd rather be looking for fossils with Annie. After a couple of jumps in a new place, the earth suddenly collapsed beneath him swallowing him whole.

Out of the corner of his eye, Shanty saw Billy disappear under the bottom of the cliff.

CHAPTER 11

After pushing out from under the slab, Annie tried to lift it again. Nope, much too heavy. She stood on a pile of debris and spotted the intrepid explorers on the other side of the crater. Dan and Shanty were on their hands and knees looking into a hole in the debris next to the cliff. Thinking they had found more fossils, she yelled loud enough for Shanty to stand up and then she motioned for him to join her.

Shanty waved his arms wildly, "Hurry. Billy's gone. Get a rope."

Hearing the tension in Shanty's voice, Annie forgot her fossil and ran to the cliff wall calling up to Shelley. Shelley had been watching the three men and saw Billy disappear under the cliff face. When she heard Annie call, she looked down as Annie shouted to untie her rappelling rope and throw it down to her. Shelley ran to the tree and began pulling at the knots. *Boy, they're tied tight*, she thought as she broke a nail trying to untie them. After a stream of profanity celebrating her lost fingernail, the knot finally pulled loose. She yanked the rope from around the tree and dragged it the edge of the crater.

Waiting at the bottom, Annie wondered what was taking so long. Finally Shelley appeared at the edge and threw the rope over the cliff. Annie caught it and starting running to her brother.

Surrounded by darkness, Billy shook his head as he opened his eyes. Slowly he wondered where he was. What had happened? He hurt all over. Looking around his new ink black home, he tried to focus his eyes. Something warm made his left eye blink. He wiped it away with his fingers. Finally, he spotted a light above him. Someone was shouting down at him. He shook his head not sure any of this made sense. When he tried to get up, he fell backwards hitting his head on the floor of this hole with a painful thump.

Up top, Annie arrived with the rope. Shanty pushed Dan aside as he anchored the rope over his shoulder and around his waist. He braced his legs as Annie took the line ready to slip into the dark pit to rescue Billy. Before she started into the hole, Dan told her to wait. He opened the top of his knapsack and pawed through its contents. Pulling out a flashlight, he handed it to her. She tucked it in the pocket of her cutoff jeans as she thanked him.

After Annie ducked through the hole into the dark cavern, Shanty slowly lowered her down. At first Annie dangled in the air, but soon her feet hit a pile of rubble. Climbing over the broken rock in the dark was a challenge. When her foot slipped on the loose rocks, she twisted her ankle and then tenderly stepped down on it. It hurt, but not too much. She worked her way down the rubble to the floor of the old mine and fished the flashlight out of her pocket. Watching the beam of the light penetrate the dark, she spotted Billy about ten feet away.

Running to him, she found him on his back. She shined the flashlight on his blood covered face. There was a long gash from his forehead that ran up into his hairline. She placed the flashlight on a nearby rock to illuminate the area and pulled off her sweatshirt revealing her black sports bra. After using the front of it to wipe the blood off his face, she pulled a small knife out of her pocket and cut off both sleeves.

Billy moaned as he looked up in the dim light and thanked her for dropping in.

After wiping most of the blood was off his face, Annie tied the wrists of the sleeves together to make a bandage for his head. Billy winced as she tied her makeshift bandage tight.

As Annie flashed the light across his eyes. Billy turned his head away asking, "Where are we?"

Annie put the flashlight back on the rock. "Shanty says you fell into an old mine shaft." Annie carefully lifted his head and put it in her lap asking, "Where do you hurt?"

Blinking his eyes still confused, Billy asked again, "Where am I?"

"Looks like you fell into an old salt mine. You hit your head when you fell. How are your legs and arms?"

Billy slowly moved his legs. He winced with pain as he moved his right leg. His knee hurt like hell. He moved his arms, they hurt, but seemed to be okay.

"We've got to get out of here. Besides you need help. You're 'kinda' bloody, smelly and dirty." Annie slipped her now sleeveless sweatshirt back over her head. "Time to get you out of here."

"How do we do that?"

"A rope over there. Shanty's ready to pull up us up as soon as you feel okay."

Annie helped Billy up. After standing up, he felt dizzy. With his mind spinning, he had to lean over to clear his head while Annie held his waist.

Slowly he stretched backward to regain his balance, but still felt unsteady. After picking up the flashlight and shining it on the rope, Annie put his arm over her shoulder to help him limp to it.

Even with his back and knee shouting out with pain, Billy enjoyed being close to her and told Annie, "I hurt all over."

Suddenly they heard something roar in the dark cavern behind them. It was loud enough to make them stop. Chills ran up their backs as Annie shined the flashlight at the sound. The beam of the light was lost in the darkness without revealing the source of the frightening scream. Not able to see anything, they could hear something moving in the dark. It seemed to be coming towards them sloshing through water.

A worried Shanty shouted down from above, "Did you find him? Is he okay?"

"Got him. He's shaky, but we're ready. Billy's coming up first."

As they climbed the pile of debris, Annie shined the flashlight back toward the sound. Another roar echoed through the shaft. Their minds tried to make sense of the unknown beast threatening them from the dark. Their imaginations ran wild. This was not a friendly roar. Now, they heard a slither like sound. Like something was being dragged along the floor of the mine.

Annie flashed the light around searching for the monster hiding in the black just beyond the beam of her light. In front of them was a shaft descending into darkness. Off to their right was a large open room that extended well beyond the beam of the flashlight. Yes, the sound came from that cavern. She could see a couple of large pillars that had been carved into the salt to hold up the roof of the old mine. As Annie moved the flashlight, a dark form moved from behind one pillar to another.

As the shadowed black body crawled before them, they weren't sure if they had seen something or if their eyes were playing tricks on them. Were their imaginations craving black images out of this dark hole? Whatever it was or if it was, this apparition was big.

Shanty called down again, "What's going on? Do you need help?"

Annie yelled back, "We're coming, Joey."

To make sure he was ready, Annie shined the light on Billy's face. Her bandage was working. Only a trickle of blood was running down the side of his nose. She blotted that up with the dangling arm of her sweatshirt bandage. Annie wasn't concerned because she knew head wounds tended to bleed a lot.

Looking at Billy, she asked, "You set?"

Billy carefully shook his head, "As ready as I'll ever be. Let's get out of here."

Suddenly another loud scream roared out of the cavern. As the sound echoed off the walls around them, they were scared. Neither of them had heard anything like it before. It was definitely getting closer. Without thinking Annie flashed the light toward the sound. A dark form emerged from between the pillars. Searching their minds for an answer, they wondered what they were seeing. Was the dark bulky creature really there? When it roared again, they were sure that it was and turned to the rope to escape.

Annie shut off the flashlight. She didn't want to attract the thing. With terror chilling their bodies, Annie and Billy struggled up the mound in the dark with just a single beam of light shining down from the hole. They could see the dangling rope hanging from the glow above. Annie grabbed it and helped Billy secure it around his waist. "He's ready. Pull him up."

Shanty shouted back, "Hold on."

With the line tied securely around his waist and his hands holding the rope, Billy lifted off as Shanty and Cooper pulled him up towards the light. Alone, Annie took a chance and pointed the beam of the flashlight on Billy to make sure he was all right.

Angered by the light shining in his world, the thing roared again. It was right behind her.

Annie didn't dare look around. She quickly switched off the light hoping to disappear again in the dark. Her only hope was to get out of this place as soon as possible.

Through the light from the hole, she saw them pull Billy through it. Annie hugged the pile of rocks to hide from this monster hiding in the dark. Something was moving near her. A dead fish smell assaulted her nostrils. A dark terrifying form appeared at the edge of the light shining from above. She kept motionless just out of the glow hoping to escape its glare. The shape of its body reminded her of the fossil she had just found. There was another roar at the bottom of the pile. The monster near her turned and looked down the pile. For a long torturous moment, everything was quiet. There was more than one of these things. Suddenly, the creature was swallowed up by the darkness again.

In the stillness, curiosity overcame fear. Annie flashed her light where she had just seen the animal. In the quick flood of light, she saw the back of the beast. It had massive legs with flippers instead of feet. It reminded her of a giant rough skinned Sea Lion sliding away from her. A head with large fangs turned slowly and looked back at her. Frightened, Annie quickly turned off her light and hid on the pile of rubble hoping this creature would keep walking away.

Shanty found it hard to pull Billy up the last five feet, Billy was quite a load. With Dan's help, they finally pulled Billy from the collapsed mine.

Shanty and Dan were surprised by the bandage and blood. After helping Billy crawl through the hole, they dragged him to a nearby boulder. Feeling weak, Billy waved Shanty off, "Get Annie. There's something down there. Maybe a bear. Get her out now."

As Annie flattened her body against the rumble to hide, she hoped they hadn't forgotten her. She needed to get out. There was movement below her on the pile and she couldn't tell if the creature was getting closer or going away. She flashed on the light to find out. This time there was nothing there. *No, maybe something off to the right.* She thought. *Damn flashlight. C'mon light up what I want to see.*

Then the thing cried again. This scream was joined by others. Now she was sure she wasn't creating images of things that go bump in the dark. This cacophony of terrifying roars was real.

Shanty threw the rope down hitting her in the back. The shock of it made her jump. Quickly, Annie tied the rope around her waist and yelled up that she was ready. As Shanty pulled her up out of the hole, she flashed the light below her. As she swung back and forth on the rope, she followed the light as it moved across the pile of rubble where she had just been standing. There it was. A black form. In the beam of the flashlight, she saw its giant mouth with yellow-white fangs slashing up for her legs.

Shanty found pulling Annie's feather light body up much easier than pulling up Billy's solid athletic frame. In no time, she was crawling out of the hole. When Dan and Shanty saw the blood on her sweatshirt, they were both alarmed.

In a panic, Dan pointed at the blood on her sweatshirt, "Are you okay?"

Looking down at her front, she told them, "It's not mine. It all came from Billy's head. Man, there's something big down there. It came after us. You pulled me out just in time. I saw its teeth. I mean big teeth. I don't know, maybe it was a bear. But it looked more like an angry Sea Lion. It was scary."

Billy looked up from the rock he was sitting on, "We could hear it, but couldn't see it. Whatever it was, it sure scared me."

Dan laughed, "It was dark down there. That does tricky things to your mind."

Shanty chimed in, "If you fell into the old mine something else might have fallen in it too. Might be a bear. They're coming back around here."

"Whatever it was it was coming after me. You pulled me out just in time. God, I saw its teeth. Believe me, you saved my life."

As Shanty coiled up the rope, he told them, "We've had enough fun for one day. Let's get out of here."

Annie went over to Billy to see if he was all right. He told her he was shaky, but was coming around. As everyone started for the cliff to get out of the crater, Annie suddenly yelled for them to stop. She insisted that she needed their help before they left the crater. Suddenly her excitement made her forget the monsters she saw in the dark as she started to walk off without telling them to follow her. Then she stopped and turned back to them, "C'mon, you've got to see this before we leave."

Thinking of Billy, she asked, "Are you up for one more adventure?"

Wondering what she had in mind, he answered, "Sure. I guess."

They all trailed after her as she led them across the crater with a new spring in her step. Billy was surprised when Annie stopped only to point excitedly at a plain old slab of rock that had broken off from above. He wondered why she had dragged them this far to see a hunk of stone. The way he felt, he wanted to get back to his cabin and collapse. His head and knee were aching.

When everyone reached her, Annie told them she wanted them to carefully tip this rock slab over. Tired, they didn't ask why. Mindlessly, they lined up to do her bidding. Dan and Annie got on each end and Shanty took the middle. With his bad knee, Billy stood back and watched. They heaved and flipped the rock over amazed with the spectacle they revealed. They carefully laid the slab down before they stepped back to stare at it.

Without a word, they savored Annie's discovery. Breaking the stunned silence, Shanty told them in a reverent voice, "Apotamkon."

Staring at the huge fossil without looking up, Dan asked, "What?"

Annie was first to reply. "Apotamkon is a legendary sea monster that Iroquois stories tell us once lived in Cayuga Lake. This fossil just confirmed that legend. This is the animal the old ones were talking about."

Dan got down on his knees to look at the unbelievable object before him. He reached out to touch it as Shanty and Annie joined him on the ground next to it. For Shanty this was a sacred moment. Here was the creature his grandmother had told him about so many times as a boy. Annie quietly chanted a Mohawk song. Soon Shanty joined her. For Dan and Billy, it added solemnity to this moment of discovery. Forgetting his pain, Billy stepped closer as he looked in awe at the fossil.

After Shanty and Annie finished their chant, Dan pointed out the features, "Look at that snout. Kinda' like a crocodile, but shorter with a bigger more triangular head. Look at those teeth. Much bigger than a crock. T. Rex would be proud of them. The neck is thick and short." Tracing its front leg with his finger, "It definitely was aquatic. Look at this flipper. Wow, it has claws too. Unfortunately, it's only the front half of the animal. Too bad the rest is missing."

Annie squealed as she pointed up the cliff face, "It's not. It's up there still in the wall. See that cut. Like a cave about half way up."

Everyone looked up, but couldn't find the feature she was pointing too. Dan asked, "Where is it?"

Annie tried again, "Look half way up the face. Then come down to that brown layer. Just below that you can see the top of the opening. From here it looks like a slit."

Billy spotted it and tried to point it out to Shanty. After Shanty picked it out, they all tried to help Dan. Dan shaded his eyes, but still couldn't find it.

Dan told them what counted was that it was up there. He turned his attention back to the fossil in front of them. Kneeling down he told them, "This looks like a plesiosaur. That would put him anywhere from 65 to 250 million years old. These guys swam in the ocean the same time the dinosaurs were wandering around the land. They are called aquatic carnivores not dinosaurs. They found one like this in an oil sand mine in Canada around, let me think, 1994. It took the paleontologists there several years to get it out of the sandstone, but look at this guy. The shale split so neatly we have the bones of this aquasaur right in front of us. He looks like he's still swimming through primeval seas. Do you realize how rare this is?"

Shanty wanted to know, "Doc, could something like this be alive in the lake today?"

Dan shook his head, "No, you'd need a breeding population. There is no way you could have a breeding population without people seeing them." Dan noticed the crushed look on Shanty's face and added, "You know the long nosed gar still swims in this lake. He goes back 136 million years to the Upper Cretaceous period so it's remotely possible. We know the gar has a breeding population, but no one has ever spotted one of these guys."

Shanty answered, "I have." He pulled up his pant leg revealing a long scar on his calf. "Apotamkon did this. He tasted my blood. I know his wrath. Believe me, he's still out there."

Billy speculated, "Maybe that's what we saw down in the old mine. They're about the same shape. I'm sorry, but I'm going to fall over if I don't get out of here. I'm not even sure I can climb up the cliff."

Annie agreed it was time to go and turned slowly, "I know it's hard to believe, but this looks like what I just saw in the old mine."

No one responded as they started walking toward the rappelling lines. Suddenly Dr. Cooper stopped them, "Wait, we can't leave this great fossil exposed like this."

Shanty nodded his approval telling him, "I can fix that." He called up to Shelley who was watching them from above, "Go to my pickup. Look behind the seat. There's a big blue tarp there. Grab it and toss it down."

Shelley quickly retrieved the tarp and heaved it over the cliff. It fell toward Billy who was just able to limp out of the way before it landed on top of him. Dan took some quick pictures before they stretched the tarp over the fossil. As he pulled the tarp tight, Shanty saw a fossil tooth that looked loose. He quickly looked around. No one was watching. Surreptitiously, he reached down and pulled it out. Unseen, he slipped it in his pocket as the others put rocks around the edge of the tarp so it wouldn't blow away.

Apotamkon, you tasted my blood as a boy, he thought. *Now I'm even. I have a piece of your ancestor.*

CHAPTER 12

Shanty drove Billy and Annie to the camp infirmary leaving Dan and the blonde at the collapsed mine. After the nurse cleaned off Billy's head, the doctor threaded six stitches into his scalp. Billy tried not to react to the pain in an effort to convince Annie he was a man. When this torture was over, Billy felt weak. When he stood up slowly, he became so dizzy he had to sit back down. After a moment when he felt his was ready, Annie helped him up and slowly walked him to the porch where they sat together on a bench.

Annie apologized for making him stay so long in the crater to look at her fossil, but Billy dismissed her concerns, "I'm just glad I got the chance to share that moment of discovery with you."

Annie reached into her pocket and showed him a piece of the vertebrate from the fossil she found. "This piece of back bone led me to slab with the rest of the fossil. You will never know what this means to me. When I was a little girl my grandmother would tell Joey and me the stories of our people. Apotamkon was one of our favorites. She told us that in the past our people would make fires out on the lake to feed Apotamkon's children when they were drawn to the flames. She always insisted his children were still out in the lake. Today I met one of his ancestors. I even have a piece of him to cherish. I'm sure Apotamkon's spirit guided me there today. It's too mystical for you to understand, but that's how I feel." Embarrassed as tears rolled down her cheeks, she covered her face with her hands, "Don't laugh."

Billy put his arm around her shoulders, "I can't begin to understand how you feel, but I'm excited for you. I feel privileged to be with you on a day you will always remember. I'm just happy to be a part of your discovery."

Annie couldn't hold back her tears. As she clasped the bone of her legend in her hand, she held it to her chest. Billy gently rocked her back and forth.

After a minute, she laughed and pushed him away, "You must think I'm a real head case. I'm sorry to be such a baby."

After sitting quietly for a moment, Annie talked about her family. "Joey is the third generation of our family to work on this piece of land. My grandfather fished off a large pier that went out into the lake near Shanty's cabin. A steamboat used to dock there. My mother went out on it as a little girl. Tourists used to tour the lake on that old boat. After a storm, it sank just off that pier."

"If you dive down off the pilings, you can find the boat. Grandpa helped build the hotel you use for crafts. My father did odd jobs at the old hotel and then became the caretaker when it became a scout camp. Now Shanty has his job. In many ways this is our home. That's why I came here this summer. I wanted to be close to the spirits of my ancestors."

"You called him Shanty. I've tried not to call him that. Isn't that sort of an insult?"

"No, but I'm not surprised that's what you think. It's not an insult. Before I tell you that story, let me ask you a question. Did you know Shanty went to college?"

"No."

"I'll bet you didn't know he was in Special Forces."

"Right again."

"Let me tell you about my brother. Your friends are very proud of their Ivy League education. What they don't know is that Shanty is one of them. He graduated from Dartmouth with honors. He's a great athlete. Jim Thorpe was his idol as a boy. When Dartmouth offered him a scholarship for lacrosse, he went there because that school was originally intended to be a school for Indians. The Indian school started in Columbia, Connecticut. When the good citizens there didn't want that many Indians hanging around their town, the founder, Eleazer Wheelock, moved his school up the Connecticut River to Hanover, New Hampshire. One of the first graduates of Wheelock's school was a member of the Mohegan tribe, Sammy Occom. He was the son of a great grandmother of mine. Shanty went to Dartmouth to honor his heritage."

Annie wiped away a tear. "Shanty could have had a very comfortable life with his degree in architecture. Instead he chose to serve his country. He could have gone into any branch of the armed services as an officer, but he enlisted in the Army. He told me he needed to find his inner warrior. Joey is very spiritual. As a member of Special Ops, he can't or won't tell me what he did in the service. One time a friend from the army visited him at my home in Connecticut. Shanty wasn't there so I spent the afternoon talking to his buddy. He was eager to tell me that Shanty had saved his life. For the first time, I learned how Joey got that nickname."

Annie stopped a moment to wipe a single tear off her cheek. "In Afghanistan, Joey learned the local language. He showed great respect for the homes they had to search. In the mountains near their camp, they passed a home each day on the way up the mountain to an observation post. He and his men called this little stone hut, *The Shanty*. It wasn't much more than a stone hovel, but was still a family's home. Joey got to know the family. Each time his platoon crossed their land, he would drop off a couple of MRE packaged meals."

"One night, Al Qaeda killed the family. The next morning, they ambushed Joey and his men as they walked passed the stone hovel. They killed two of Joey's men and wounded three others including the man who told me this story."

"I believe that was the day Joey found his inner warrior. With his men pinned down, he attacked the hut by himself killing all the Al Qaeda warriors. As he rushed them, he was hit once in the thigh, once in his side and in his shoulder. Before he was evacuated, he limped over to the shanty and blew it up it up so it could never be used for an ambush again. After that everyone called him, *Shanty*. When he came home, that's what he wanted to be called, but he never told us why."

Billy nodded, "I always felt there was something beneath the surface that he never talked about. I attributed it to his Mohawk upbringing. I'm just glad he shared his Mohawk stories with me."

"He likes you. You're important to him because you listen. Let me tell you a bit more. Being a warrior, or a soldier as we call the troops in the military today, is in our blood. I bet you were never taught that there was a full blooded Seneca Union officer at Appomattox when Lee surrendered to Grant at the end of the Civil War."

Billy nodded his head, no.

"Well, there was. His Seneca name was Hasanowanda, but he adopted the American name of Ely Parker. Our great, great, great grandmother was Seneca. I think that's right number of greats. Anyway, we feel a connection to him.

"Ely grew up on the Towanda Indian Reservation in Western New York. He met Grant in Glena, Ohio and became part of Grant's staff. His penmanship was so good, he actually drafted the surrender documents in the McLean House that both generals signed. Some of the Confederate officers were upset because Ely was there. They thought he was a Black man and thought Grant had included him in the surrender party to embarrass General Lee."

"Your family is full of surprises. I was amazed when Shanty rappelled down the side of the old mine collapse to save the girls. I didn't even know he could use a rope. Now that I think of it, he liked to watch me teach the campers how to rappel and once he told me I was doing a good job. I had no idea he was the real expert."

"He taught me on the same cliff you use with the campers. He likes this job because for two thirds of the year, he's alone here. The director doesn't know it, but he uses the camp in the off-season to work with boys and girls from the Onondaga reservation. He teaches them outdoor skills and gets them in shape. He says he helps them discover their Iroquois spirit. I know you run with your friends each morning. I've been trying to get Joey to join you. He's suffering from PTSD. I can't convince him to get help. He needs help to come out of his shell and make friends.

"Post-Traumatic Stress Disorder? Really?" Billy asked. "He seems so squared away."

"No, he seldom leaves the camp and always keeps to himself. He is reluctant to make friends and often tells me that friends just die. That's why you're so important. You're the first person outside of the reservation who has penetrated his shield. I'd like you to help me get him back into the more balanced life he had before he learned how to kill."

****

Dan walked Shelley to the jeep. As soon as they were in the cab, he asked, "What's with *Billy the Kid?*"

"We went together for a while. I was shocked when I saw him. That's all. It's over."

"Didn't look over to me."

"You're jealous? That's good."

"Of course, I love you."

"Love, really? That's a surprise. I thought sex with your Grad. Assistant was part of the job."

"No, not at all. Being my assistant doesn't have anything to do with us. You're much more important to me than your job. I respect your work, but I have loved you since you smiled at me when you walked into my *Basic Geology* class."

Surprised Shelley didn't answer. Dan looked straight ahead concentrating on the road down the hill from the old collapsed mine. Amazed at this new turn in their relationship, Shelley tried to digest what she'd just heard. She needed to weigh her feelings toward both men.

****

When Annie finished her stories about Shanty, Billy felt tired. "I'm beat. Walk me to my cabin."

Annie helped him up and put his arm over her shoulder as she helped him down the steps of the infirmary. Billy thought having an attractive woman help him walk was a new experience. It felt good. He liked it.

"Who's the blonde?"

"An old girlfriend."

"She still cares for you. When she saw you at the pickup, she forgot to hide her feelings."

"That's her problem. I'm over it."

"Are you?"

"I guess. We were together for a long time. Breaking up was hard."

"She still cares for you. You could always go back."

"That's not in the cards. Maybe a friend. Nothing more. Anything we had is gone. I wish her the best. That's all."

"Are you sure you're ready to move on?"

He squeezed her hand, "I wasn't so sure until I washed off in the lake this morning. Then I heard a diminutive Mohawk girl laughing at me. One who can swing across the walls of a cliff like a hummingbird?"

"A hummingbird?"

"Yeah, that's good, a compliment."

"My Mohawk name means Hummingbird."

"Really? Unbelievable."

Annie laughed, "No, but I had you for a second."

"You can have me for longer than that if you want."

****

Steve Swenson was not pleased with his waterfront. There were police cars, rescue vehicles and an ambulance making ruts in his shale stone beach. Earlier when they arrived, he took the rescue teams out on the dock and pointed to the body. Then they had to wait for the police dive team. After the scuba divers arrived, they finally pulled out the body that was now out there on his dock in a black body bag. The divers were still in the water searching for the guy's missing leg. When the police Chief, Wayne Rogers, took Steve out on the dock to view the body and unzipped the bag, Steve told him he didn't recognize the dead guy and assured him he wasn't from the camp. When Harold Grayson showed, he told Chief Rogers the same thing.

As the director was leaving the dock, a diver came up holding a grim piece of leg above his head. The boot and sock were still on the foot of the bloody stump. The leg looked like it had been chewed off.

Harold and the Chief joined Steve at the end of the dock. Talking to himself, Chief Rogers wondered, "What the hell happened to this guy. Getting hit by a boat wouldn't rip a guy apart like that. But what is more amazing is that this is the second body in less than twelve hours that I've seen torn apart like this."

The Chief stood looking back at the body on the dock. "Last night my Lake Patrol found the body of Carol Powell and her remains looked...

Steve interrupted, "Carol Powell is dead. My God, she's a Cornell legend. She gives the swim team a motivational speech each year. I swim in her events. The whole team does." Steve kicked the stones on his beach not believing this legend was dead.

The Chief nodded, "Yeah she was a good one. I have no idea what killed her. My Lake Patrol officers think a boat must have hit her. Maybe more than one. I don't see how a boat could rip her apart like that. This poor bastard out on the dock certainly wasn't killed by a boat."

Still digging his foot into the shale, Steve muttered, "Carol Powell, I don't believe it. Carol Powell gone?"

The Chief asked them both, "Has anything unusual happened around here lately? Anything that might explain this?"

Both Harold and Steve nodded no, but then Steve remembered, "This morning I found an old boat on the other side of the dock. It only has one oar. I think the big waves from the quake last night pulled it off a dock and it drifted in here."

The Chief was interested. "Let's take a look. Might be something."

Steve led them across the waterfront to where he had beached the old derelict. "Come to think of it, the boat did have a piece ripped off the back."

Now the Chief seemed more interested. When they reached the boat, Steve showed him the broken board. The Chief agreed with Steve that it was a recent tear. Inspecting the boat, the Chief looked inside and noticed a tackle box tucked under the middle seat. After putting on rubber gloves, he set the box on the middle seat.

Flipping open the catch on each side, the trays unfolded as Rogers pulled up the top revealing an array of hooks and small fishing gear. The Chief looked under the trays and spotted a light brown wallet and held it up. Waving it at Steve, he smiled and added, "This may help." He opened the wallet and slid out a driver's license. Looking at the picture, he nodded, "This is our guy. Our dead fisherman is Jacob Brooks from up the lake. Probably out for a day of fishing. What the hell happened to this poor bastard?"

CHAPTER 13

Early the next morning, Lea, Link and Steve were waiting at the bottom of the soccer field for Billy to join them for their morning run. Link looked at his running watch, Billy was almost five minutes late. Ready to leave without him, they spotted Billy limping toward them with Annie and Shanty walking beside him. When he reached his friends, Billy announced, "My knee is hurting, I can't run today. Annie and Shanty will take my place."

Annie stepped forward, "If you want to try it, I've convinced my brother to lead you on what our people call a *Chase*. The object is not to win, but to follow. Because you don't know the trail, this time Joey will lead for the whole run. When he raises a hand like this…" Annie demonstrated by putting her arm straight out from her shoulder with her forearm pointing toward the sky forming a right angle. "The front runner moves to the side to let the others to go by. Then that runner takes a position in the back with everyone following the new leader."

Shanty took over, "I've watched you run, but today we'll run a different course. It will be more of a steeplechase than a cross country run. Ya want ta try it?"

The three friends looked at each other and nodded. They were pretty confident they could keep up with an older guy in a faded kaki T-shirt, an old pair of Army camo pants and muddy combat boots. Shanty started out slowly running up the hill with Annie right behind him. The runners filed in behind them smiling at how easy this was going to be.

Annie ran backwards for a minute motioning for the others to stay in single file and close up the gaps. The pace steadily increased. By the time they reached the top of the hill all the runners were breathing hard except for Shanty and Annie. Shanty kept running and raised his hand. Annie stepped aside allowing Lea to become the first runner behind Shanty. Then Annie waited for the others to pass before she fell in at the end of the line.

This was a new trail for the other runners, but she had run this course in Shanty's Iroquois winter boot camp. She knew that the runners would be severely tested this morning following a course that kept zig-zagging up and down the mountain. Every time Shanty raised his hand, another runner would step aside to let the others move up.

The line of braves jumped over fallen trees and ducked under branches. When Shanty ran into the rushing stream everyone followed. The runners found it hard to stay on their feet as they splashed through the cold water. Shanty put his hand in the air again dropping Link to the back. As they ran through the woods, Lea moved up behind Shanty again. Running through the stream again, her foot slipped on a rock throwing her into the water. When Shanty heard the splash, he turned as she went under and jumped into the swift current to catch her as the rushing water swept her to him. As Shanty pulled her from the water, Lea coughed as he helped her up the bank. Link peeled off his sweatshirt and let her use it to wipe off. While Lea was recovering from her spill, Annie whispered to Shanty to stay out of the water on the way back to the soccer field.

When Lea nodded that she was ready, Shanty started off again. Running along the edge of the stream, suddenly Shanty raised both his hands in the air and stopped. As the others ran up behind him, they saw a dead stag at his feet. The bloody body of the deer had been ripped into pieces. Shanty grabbed its antlers and dragged what was left of the front half of the poor animal out of the stream. Then he waded into the stream to grab a hind leg sticking out of the water at a weird angle.

As Shanty dragged the back part of the carcass out of the stream, Lea was shocked by the gruesome remains. "What could do something like this to a poor deer?"

Before Shanty could answer, Link told them his money was on a bear. Steve thought it looked like the cattle mutilations out west. Shanty shook his head, "Saw something like this once with my father when I was a kid. No way a bear did this. There's no tracks on the bank. Something else is living around here going up and down this stream."

Shanty went to one knee to look closely at the ragged tears in the skin. "The rips in the skin are too big for a bear. See here." As he pointed at the torn hide, he was about to tell them that only Apotamkon could rip apart a deer like this when he saw Annie nodding her head, *no*. Instead, he told them, "Let's finish the run. I'll come back and get rid of this poor guy later."

With the image of the great dead stag with its eight point rack still in their minds, everyone ran faster to get away from it. By the time they joined Billy at the dining room steps, everyone even Annie and Shanty were exhausted. With their hands on their knees gasping for air, all the runners agreed that Shanty had to come back tomorrow. When Steve told Billy about the dead deer, his blood and guts description made Lea turn her head, bend down and toss up.

As part of her plan to socialize Shanty, Annie invited the college kids to a campfire at Shanty's cabin after the campers were tucked in for the night.

As Link left, he told the group, "First, I have to run after crazy white kids running up and down hills and now I'm chasing a wild Indian, sorry Native American, through the forest. This is not my idea of summer fun." Laughing with Link, everyone agreed to get together that night.

As the others left, Steve started to go up the steps to the dining room when Lea grabbed his arm, "We have time to go to your cabin."

"Not today babe. That run beat me up. I'm going to take a hot shower and wait up here until breakfast."

Lea gave him a shove, "You usually soap up in the lake. Why shower today?"

"Heat, I need to soak my body under hot water."

Rejected and dejected, Lea told him, "Get rested. I'm coming to your cabin tonight."

"We'll go to the campfire together. Okay?"

"Good. I'll make sure you have fun afterwards too."

Steve smiled. *Life. Could it get any better?* After he was sure Lea was on her way back to her cabin, he went around the dining hall to the shower room. He pulled off his running shirt as he walked to the last stall. When he saw it was empty, he was surprised. He scratched his head trying to think of the last time a woman stood him up. Disgusted he threw his shirt on the floor, pulled off his shoes and stripped down his shorts.

As his shorts hit the floor, Steve heard the locker room door squeak open. Naked, he stepped into the aisle between the showers, folded his arms across his chest and casually leaned against the wall. Ursula shed her clothes as she approached him with a big smile on her face, "Just the way I like my men; sweaty, twenty and hard." When she reached him, Steve wrapped his arms around her pulling her to him. In a husky passionate voice, Ursula told him, "You young guys are great."

Fully involved in their lovemaking something in Steve's primal brain heard the door to the shower room squeak open. Holding his finger to Ursula's lips, he whispered, "Quiet."

They could hear footsteps tracking down the wet aisle between the showers. Steve whispered again, "Stay here. I'll take care of this."

Tip-toeing toward the one shower that was running, Hilda was hoping to catch the two counselors together. She was sure Lea and Steve had sex in here. As the Camp Director's sister, she felt it was her duty to catch them and put an end to it.

Suddenly Steve stepped out of the shower stall standing naked in front of her at full mast.

As Hilda looked away, she told him, "My God, cover that thing up."

Smiling, Steve asked her, "What are you doing in the Men's Locker Room?"

"You're having sex. I heard the sounds."

"Sorry, just entertaining myself. Is that why you came in here? To watch?"

"No...no of course not. That's gross." With that retort, Hilda spun on her heels making a fast get-a-way.

When the door squeaked shut, Steve turned to Ursula. "Where were we?"

Ursula smiled as she threw her arms around him and jumped up putting her long legs around his waist.

****

Tired after a long shift, Charley Morgan left the hoist ready to go home for a date with his pillow. He rolled his eyes and sighed when he saw the woman *Suit* waiting for him in his office again. He got a quick chill thinking, *she might be here to fire me. Hell with her. She'll never find a replacement with my experience. Let her try to reach her production quotas without me.*

Smiling to himself as he entered the office, he told her in an impatient tone, "Make it quick. I'm on my time. I really need to hit the sheets. I work for a living."

Ruth Hager bristled, but forced herself not to react to his impertinence. She needed him more than he needed her. "Mr. Morgan, your shift has the highest average tonnage of any shift. I want to know why. How do you outperform the others on a consistent basis?"

"Show up tomorrow with a big cup of Starbuck's. Then I might tell you."

"You'll have Starbuck's for a week if you tell me now."

"No matter what I say?"

"I want to know. Now."

"Honestly, I don't have a clue. I've never worked the other shifts."

"Really?"

"That's right. My guess is that I've got a better team, but I don't know that."

"I'll let you observe each shift then report back to me."

"Not my job. You get the big bucks. Figure it out yourself."

"I'll have you rotate through each shift. Then you can see the other shifts at work."

"Not a good idea. Then you just mess up my shift and the other ones. Besides, I wouldn't get to see the other shift managers in action. It's your job to watch us and figure out the difference."

"I don't know enough about running a shift to tell the difference."

Charley hesitated and looked her squarely in the eyes, "Lady that's the first honest thing I've ever heard a *Suit* say. Tell you what. I'll work an extra half shift this summer rotating between the shifts. You pay me overtime for a full second shift each day. When I finish, you personally have to bring me a cup of Starbucks down to the center of the earth where I work. If you do that, I will share whatever I learned."

Ruth held out her hand, "Deal."

Ruth went back to her office with something unusual on her face, a smile. But not everything in her world was going her way that day. In her office, her secretary showed her a copy of one of her private company memorandums that had been mailed to her. It had a smiley face drawn in green ink at the bottom with a signature saying, "Thanks, Your friendly neighborhood Green Peace Alliance."

Ruth was upset and wondered how her inter-office memo could have been leaked. She tried to control her temper as she questioned her secretary. With Melinda sitting in a chair at the side of her desk, Ruth asked in an angry voice, "How did an environmentalist group get this? It's my private memo."

Melinda snatched it off her desk. Two years older than Ruth, she was wearing her typical dark gray blouse and black skirt to mimic her boss's taste for the unexciting. Very loyal to Ruth, Melinda was just as upset as Ruth. "When I opened your mail this morning, I read this. I checked your private file. Your copy is still there. I don't have a copy in the outside file. I only sent this memo to the Vice President and the directors. Mr. Morgan and the shift manager have this information, but did not receive a copy."

"Could a copy get stuck in the machine or an extra copy get thrown away?"

"No, I'm much too careful for that. No one else has access to that machine and I do not make extra copies. I only sent out copies to the people on your list."

"Does that mean one of the directors is suspect?" Ruth wondered with a puzzled look on her face. "Let's send out another memo. Say in this one the water damage at the bottom of the mine is more serious than anticipated. Say the water is dissolving the supports in the bottom level of the mine."

Looking up at Melinda thinking, Ruth added, "I want you to change a word, spacing or font so you can identify each letter. Record each difference and keep a list of who received each one. That way if this rag-tag environmental group sends us another copy, we can find out who gave it to them. Understand?"

"Got it. Do you want me to give a special copy of the new memo to Vice-President Olson?"

"Anyone who got the last one."

About an hour later, Ruth looked up from the production reports strewn across her desk as Melinda entered her office. Melinda handed Ruth a stack of letters and challenged her to spot the difference. After a cursory examination, they all looked the same to her. Melinda told her to try again. Tired of the game, Ruth told her to cut to the chase. Melinda took the stack of letters and proudly circled one word in the third paragraph. When Ruth still didn't see any difference, Melinda pointed to the *e* in that word and told her each *e* had a different font. While it would be very hard for someone reading the letter to spot the difference, she could identify each memo from that one letter. Melinda challenged Ruth to test her.

After mixing up the letters, Ruth gave one to Melinda. After Melinda located the *e*, she easily identified it as the one sent to Director Shaver. Ruth liked the game. From the middle of the pack, she pulled out one more. Melinda grabbed it from her with a flourish announcing, "That letter is going to Vice President Olson." Impressed with Melinda's effort, she reminded her send them out in *Eyes Only* envelopes.

****

In his lab, Dan Cooper stood waiting for his printer to spit out the article he had just finished. When it finally hit the tray, he grabbed it and turned back to his desk to read it. Circling two corrections, he turned to his computer to make them. When he finished, he hit print again. Waiting for the printer to spit out the new copy, Shelley crossed his mind. He wondered how he rated with her compared to this camp boy. Shaking his head, he hit another key to send Shelley the final copy.

When Shelley leaned in the door, he told her, "Send that article to the *New York Times* with pictures of the fossil. Then with a devilish grin on his face, he added, "If you're interested, Annie Brandt. You remember her that Indian girl. Called to invite us to come to a campfire at Minnechaug tonight. Ya *wanna* go?"

"If you want too, ah…sure, it might be fun. You can show them this article."

"It's settled then. We'll need to leave early to get there. How about a trip to my bedroom before we go?"

"I've got some personal errands. Pick me up about quarter to ten at my place?"

"What about 9:30."

"Fine. I'll be ready."

Upset, Dan wondered why Shelley didn't want to run over to his place before they left. *Last week,* he thought, *she would have jumped at the chance. Now she has errands. She's changed since this Billy guy showed up.* He vowed to watch them closely at the campfire to see if any sparks passed between them.

★★★★

Disregarding the pain in his knee, Billy limped up the path to the top of the falls with Annie at his side. Sure that it would be worth the effort, he wanted to share his special place with her. Following a narrow trail, the hike to the top of the falls took them through pine and cedar woods scattered under a canopy of deciduous trees with green leaves that would turn to bright golden hues in autumn. Now and then wind blowing through the branches revealed the silvery bottoms of the leaves. As they climbed, they caught glimpses of the lake stretching off below them in an endless ribbon of blue.

When they finally reached the summit, Billy led her to a moss covered clearing surrounded by cedars at the top of the falls. He sat down on the bank of the stream only a few yards from the foamy white water cascading eighty feet to the pool below.

Billy rubbed his knee as Annie sat down beside him. After admiring the beauty of Mother Nature's spectacle, she told him, "This is lovely. I can see why you brought me here."

"It's my special place. In my spare time, I come up here to think about life. I wanted to share it with you."

"I'm glad you did, but I bet I'm not the only girl you've brought up here."

"Yeah, there have been others, but I know it means more to you then it meant to them. Believe me, it means more to me to have you here."

As Annie leaned back on the blanket of moss to look up at the sky, Billy gently leaned over her. First he kissed her cheek and then their lips met. Not wanting to be aggressive, after a tender kiss he lay next to her looking up at the blue as a Golden eagle glided overhead riding the wind. Annie sat up to watch it fly over the lake. Drinking in nature's vistas, she sighed as she listened to the water at their feet rush over the falls with its quiet roar. Her eyes followed the green stream below the falls as it snaked toward the blue lake under the shroud of tall trees swaying gently in a warm summer breeze.

In a state of bliss, she turned to Billy and kissed him gently. She lowered her head to his chest to feel the beat of his heart. Lost in the closeness of their bodies, after a long soulful kiss, she rolled off him as the eagle floated back over them hoping to spot a careless fish swimming near the surface. Tired of riding the thermals, the eagle landed in an old dead tree across the stream from them. They sat up together to watch him preen his feathers. Finally with a screech, he soared over the speckled green limbs reaching out to touch the cloud sprinkled blue sky.

Billy slipped his arm around Annie's back. Before they kissed, Annie put her hand on the back of his neck drawing him to her. Their lips met with a passion he had not anticipated. It was as if she had an inner need to be with him. His feelings were mixed. That surprised him. After a shared moment of passion, suddenly Billy stopped, "I'm not ready for this. I can't do this."

Lost in lust not yet love, Annie simply questioned, "Why."

"You're Shanty's sister. I can't betray him."

"My brother wanted me to meet you. I'm glad I did. He set us up. He would never deny us a chance to share this moment."

"But you haven't gone out much. Been with men."

"Where did you hear that?"

"Shanty told me you never really dated."

"My brother is a wise man, but only sees me as his little sister. Believe me, four semesters at Columbia taught me more about men and lecherous professors than I wanted to know."

"If it's not him, then it's me. I'm not ready for this. Don't get me wrong, I desperately want you. I have since I stood naked before you in a freezing lake, but before I'm your lover, I want to be your friend. Does that make sense?"

"Of course."

"There is something else I've been trying to figure out about you."

"What is it? Tell me."

"When I first saw you."

"Standing in the lake?"

"Yeah, you were on the porch. When I looked up, I knew I'd seen you before."

"I don't think so. That was the first time we met."

Billy shook his head, "I'm not so sure. All my life I've had visions of the woman I'd marry. My life companion. She has always haunted my dreams, but I could never see her face. I've seen her silhouette and the back of her head a thousand times in my dreams. Sometime I'd catch a glimpse of her profile, but never her face. When I saw you for the first time, I knew it was her face."

Annie didn't know how to respond. Finally she quizzed him, "Is that a line Billy Barton? If it is, it's a good one. No, not good, beyond good."

"Honest, no line. Just a feeling I can't explain. It's been haunting me since I saw you swinging around the cliff face. I wasn't surprised. I'd seen you do it before. Dreamed it. I feel weird even talking about it."

"The spiritual world is mysterious. I'm not sure what to tell you. My people feel the Gods are always trying to communicate with us. Only special people listen. When I saw you go into the lake, it was like watching a baptism. Not a boy washing in a lake. More of a purification ritual. I knew immediately that there was something special about you."

"Special that's it. I felt that way too. I've been trying to figure it...err... you out. You are a very special person. For now, just having you in my life is enough."

As they lay back on the moss looking up through the branches holding the clouds above them, their hands touched. Silence enveloped them as they shared their feelings without words.

As the setting sun colored the sky, Annie sat up to watch as orange and pink rays reflected off the waves setting the water ablaze. Billy sat up next to her with his arm around her waist. As she leaned against him, the splendor of the sun bouncing off the silver ribbons foaming across the lake created an enchanted world. As Mother Nature painted the lakescape below them, Annie hugged Billy. He had touched her soul. Marveling at the miracle of colors radiating from the lake, Annie looked up at him, "That's what the ancients told us."

"What?"

"In many of our creation stories, our ancestors tell tales of the lake burning. This is what they were describing. You have revealed a truth of my people to me. This is special. You're special, thank you." As Annie kissed him on the cheek, the mystery of Cayuga's grandeur unfolded before their eyes. She was sure that *Taronkiawagon*, the *Sky Holder*, had summoned them here today as his messenger returned floating high above them. With a screech, the Golden Eagle delivered the Sky Holder's welcome.

As the sun disappeared behind the trees, the lake waters overcame the fire demons from above. It was time to descend from heaven back to life. Before they left, Billy walked to the edge of the cliff to stare at the white water as it fell to the green pool far below. As nature shared her beauty, suddenly he saw a large black animal swim out from under the falls with two smaller ones tagging along behind. As he motioned for Annie to join him, he told her, "Quick, quick." When she hesitated, he waved at her to hurry. Finally when she was standing beside him, he pointed down telling her, "Look."

Annie looked down, "At what?"

Billy studied the pool below the falls. It was empty. Nothing was there. *Had his eyes deceived him?* He explained that there were three big animals swimming down there. "They looked sort of like a mother hippo with two little ones."

Annie kissed his cheek, "Mother Nature has a way of fooling us. Now step carefully back from the edge." She put her hand on his rippled stomach to guide him safely back from the edge. With a laugh, she whispered, "Time to go. That's a long way down."

As Billy stepped back, he shook his head glancing down at the pool one more time. He was sure he'd seen something down there. He told Annie, "Something about them reminded me of the thing we saw in that old mine. The same shivers ran down my spine."

"I don't want to go back down in that mine again. That's for sure. Gives me the creeps just thinking about it."

After walking hand in hand down the forest trail to Billy's cabin, Annie and Billy stopped in front of his porch. Annie turned to Billy, "Tonight at the campfire, you must talk to the blonde girl. End it or start your relationship up again, but make a decision. Find out where you are. I'll keep the professor busy. Just nod your head and I'll distract him. Believe me, your ex-lover is ready to walk down the beach with you. Don't worry about us. You and me. Think only of yourself. Find out tonight if you are still serious about this girl or are ready to continue what we just found up by the falls."

CHAPTER 14

As Dan waited impatiently outside Shelley's apartment, he felt like a high school boy waiting for his first date. In their last call, Shelley told him she would be waiting by the curb. He didn't have to bother coming up to her apartment. To him the message was clear, no sex before they left. *Where the hell was she, he wondered. Ah...there she is.*

As he spotted her running out the door to him, he couldn't stay mad at her. *God, she's beautiful.* Her hair bounced with each stride and her makeup was perfect. He wondered. *Who does she want to impress. Me or Billy the Kid?* Shoving aside his self-doubt as her fragrance filled the jeep, he welcomed her. "You look great."

Shelley slammed the door shut and clapped her hands together. "Thanks, I'm ready. This is going to be fun." As she put her hand on his thigh, he pulled out with a big smile on his face. "Do me a favor. Talk to this Billy guy tonight."

"I told you it's over between us."

"Make sure it's over. I'll keep his girlfriend busy."

****

Shanty piled up the wood for a big fire near the dark water. On a beautiful clear evening with the stars of heaven on full display, a silver disc hanging over the lake created a ribbon of light that ran to the shore over shimmering waves. At first Shanty argued with Annie about having a campfire, but as he split wood for his fire, the spirit of the evening captured a part of his mind that hadn't been tapped in a long time. As he arranged the wood in the form of a teepee, he thought of the morning run with those kids. It reminded him of his carefree days in college when he led his lacrosse team through the forest to get in shape. *Maybe Annie was right, I do need to get out more.* As he walked away from the fire pit, for a moment, he forgot the image of death war had burned in his soul.

When Annie slammed on the brakes of his pickup to skid to a stop on the gravel driveway next to his cabin, Shanty hoped her questionable driving skills hadn't hurt his pickup. He valued that old truck. After inspecting it for damage, he helped her unload the munchies and drinks. Then he made the mistake of complaining there were no Mohawk treats on the menu.

Annie laughed, "What did you want nuts and berries. They didn't have a package of edible roots at the 7-11. Wait, I might have time to dig some up before your guests arrive. No need to wash them. The grit is good for your teeth. Too bad you didn't go hunting today. Then we could roast deer liver on the fire tonight. Damn, they were out of dried buffalo strips. At least we have plenty of firewater to make your friends forget the missing Mohawk delicacies."

Shanty threw a bag of chips at her that Annie caught and threw back. As he dropped the chips back into the cardboard box, she was surprised to see him in such a good mood. He set down the box and grabbed a couple of boards from next to the cabin and carried them to a couple of sawhorses near the fire. After arranging the boards, he smiled as he set the box of salty treats on them. Nodding his head back and forth, he thought. *This make-shift table is all I need to hold the Whiteman's contribution to indigestion.*

Annie continued to tease him, "Great Chief, do you have an ancient Sty-rofoam chest to freeze the firewater."

Shanty pulled one out from under his porch, "Here squaw. Fill this with beans and squash."

Ready for a night of friendship and camaraderie, Lea and Steve were first to arrive. Lea helped Annie lay out the chips and dips while Steve helped Shanty arrange rocks and boards to use as seats around the fire. When they finished, Shanty pointed to the cooler, "Firewater over there." As Steve fetched the beers, Shanty started the fire. After the flames shot up in the air with sparks and smoke, Steve threw Shanty a Coors. They sat next to each other while Shanty poked the fire with a stick. As they sipped their beers, Shanty pumped Steve about the morning run. Steve told him he had been surprised that a guy in combat boots could challenge him.

Billy showed up next carrying a guitar in one hand and a banjo in the other. He leaned the cases against a bench before joining Steve and Shanty near the fire. When Annie saw Billy, she brought him a beer. This simple favor delivered a personal message to Billy and the others. Shanty and Steve smiled at each other as they lifted their beer cans in a quiet salute to Billy who actually blushed.

After making sure his cabin kids were settled, Link left them with the junior counselor and headed off to Shanty Joe's cabin. He didn't like wandering through the camp at night. He looked up at the evening sky and thought. *At least tonight there's some moonlight.* He wondered. *Why don't camps have street lights? Streets in the city might occasionally have a light or two out, but at least you can see where you are going.*

After crossing the soccer field, he was forced to make a decision. He could go through the woods and over the stream on the rope bridge close to Shanty's cabin or take the longer way down to the road and across the concrete bridge. He chose darkness over distance and entered the woods.

Not much of the moonlight penetrated the tall trees above him so Link turned on his flashlight. Flashing the beam around the path, the night noises of the woods spooked him. Things were scurrying around out there in the brush much to close for comfort. When something flew by his head almost hitting him, he ducked involuntarily to get away and wished he had walked down to the road instead of taking this lonely dark path through the wilderness.

When he reached the rope bridge across the stream, he thought about going back to the road where there was a real bridge. He had to convince himself that he was being foolish. After all, he was a modern college student who wasn't afraid of the dark. With creepy crawly things running around him, he sighed as he shined his flashlight on the rope. How was he supposed to walk up the single big rope using the small rope hand rails for balance while holding his flashlight? He hadn't thought of that. Let's see, he had to go up the rope to the two crossed logs that were lashed together forming an *X*. Then cross the stream on the rope suspended over it. During the day this was fun, but tonight it was spooky. He wondered, *how can I hold on to the hand ropes and keep my flashlight shining on the big rope I'm supposed to walk on?*

His flashlight had a clip so he attached it to the neck of his T-shirt. Climbing up the rope to the X-notch, the beam danced all over seldom hitting the rope he had to walk on. As he stood in the notch, he wondered how he could make it across the stream with his flashlight bouncing from his chest. He had to find a better way to hold his light so it would shine on the walking rope. He tried to hold it in his hand and grasp the small hand ropes at the same time. That wouldn't work. Finally, he decided to hold it in his teeth. He might have to visit a dentist, but it seemed like the best idea. He inched out on the rope just able to keep his balance while shining the beam of light on the walking rope.

He didn't dare take a step forward. Instead, he slid along the rope. Moving slowly so the bridge wouldn't swing, he reached the middle where the bridge sagged suspending him just a few feet above the roaring stream. A glimpse of moonlight created an eerie green glow in the rushing water. As he started to slide up to the rope toward the X-notch on the other bank, a scream like a frightened woman came from up the stream. The shrill call created chills that made his body tremble.

He stopped and looked up the stream. Suddenly, a dark object appeared coming down the stream toward him. Concentrating on the rope, he steadied himself as the thing approached. What was it? Glancing quickly at it, he saw that it was large like a rowboat. No, it wasn't a boat, maybe a log. Suddenly, the dark object rose out of the water snarling and hissing. The narrow beam of his flashlight caught a dark head full of flashing teeth the size of sharp bananas. The creature was going for his foot. His light reflected off the terrifying jaws as they snapped shut just below his Nikes. The creature just missed.

It looked like a 'gator' only bigger like an angry giant sea lion with mean looking fangs. His mind rushed to an image of Godzilla floating under him. Link was frozen in place. Whatever it was leaped up again. This time it's head hit the rope causing the bridge to swing wildly from the blow. From the jolt, Link's left foot slipped off the rope.

On one foot, Link swung back and forth trying to regain his balance. As the beam of his flashlight bounced up and down, the black creature rose again from the murky water below him. Jumping up at him, this time its jaws snapped shut just below his foot. Link held on tightly to the hand ropes trying not to fall into its gaping mouth. *God, I can't join this black monster for a swim.*

As Link screamed from the terror below him, he spit out his only light. His eyes followed it as it splashed into the stream. The thing under him seemed tired of the game and swam down the stream, but before Link could relax, a second frightening dark object slashed out of the water illuminated only by the shadows of moon beams filtering through the trees. This one was smaller, but still big enough to frighten an angel. This guy jumped up and tried to eat him too. The poor light added to Link's fright. Just in time, the bridge swung away from this new pair of slashing jaws. The creature fell back into the water with a splash just missing his leg. Surrounded by darkness, Link crouched low on the walking rope desperately praying for the bridge to stop swinging.

Below him, the faint yellow glow of his flashlight at the bottom of the stream was his only friend. Then this friendly beacon winked out. He was alone with monsters waiting for him to fall.

As the wind blew through the trees, a trace of moonlight outlined another monster slipping under him. Its eyes blazed yellow as they caught a moonbeam. Link shut his eyes praying a long prayer. Slowly the rope bridge stopped swinging. Not daring to open his eyes, he was able to get both feet securely back on the rope. After what seemed like an eternity, the rope bridge stopped swaying.

Opening his eyes, Link wondered if the monsters were gone. He wasn't sure as he looked at the dark water rushing below him. Not waiting for an answer, he inched up the rope to the set of crossed logs on the other bank. With his adrenalin spiking, he grabbed one of the logs holding it tighter than a long lost lover. After several minutes, his need to escape overcame his fear. To flee this monster infested stream, he grabbed the hand ropes and slid down the big rope to the ground.

When his feet hit the earth at the end of the bridge, he fell down clutching the ground like a skydiver whose chute opened late. He was still alive, but he could feel those things right behind him. Thinking only of the terrible jaws hiding in the dark, he crawled to his feet. Soon he was crashing through the woods in the general direction of the path. Finally, he spotted a light ahead. Tripping over roots and stones, Link ran toward Shanty's cabin ignoring the branches whipping his face and legs. When Link broke into the clearing, he fell down on the gravel driveway next to Shanty's pick-up gasping for air as the security lights on the corner of Shanty's porch flashed on bathing him with glorious light. His prayers had been answered.

Shanty and Billy saw Link fall out of the woods and ran to him. Soon the others followed as Shanty lifted Link to his feet. With his feet on solid safe ground, Link let out a string of oaths. "God damned bridge. Motherfing monsters. The Son of bitches came out of the dark. The damned trees and bushes tried to grab me. Worse than Central Park at midnight. Why do people put camps out here in the middle of the damn wilderness?"

His friends let him shout and swear as they guided him to the fire trying not to laugh. After Link sat down on a bench, Shanty gave him a beer. He tried to chug it, but his throat hadn't relaxed from his encounter. He choked and poured most of it down the front of his sweaty camp T-shirt. This drenching initiated another round of cussing.

His friends could no longer contain themselves. When they laughed, Link shouted, "It's not funny." After taking several deep breaths, he was able to keep a swig down. The cold liquid running down his throat seemed to calm him. As the adrenalin drained from his body, Link sagged and almost dropped his beer.

Shanty put his arm over his back, "You're safe now. What happened?"

Link sputtered, "Christ, I went through the god-damned dark woods to that shaky damn rope ridge. No way I'll ever do that again. Jesus Billy, did you make that thing just to screw with me? Man, I'm trying to cross your weak ass bridge with the damn flashlight in my mouth. Then these monsters attacked me and I spit it out..."

At that, everyone burst out laughing forcing even Link to smile.

When the laughter died down, Link continued with less profanity. "Hell, I get halfway across that damn bridge when this big monster comes out of the dark. I mean freaking Godzilla. It scared the hell out of me. Jumped up out of the water and tried to bite off my foot. Almost knocked me into the stream. I'm telling you it was a damn hippo-crock. Its yellow eyes popped out at me."

Link took a deep breath and continued, "Then two more escapees from *Jurassic Park* came out of the dark trying to get me. When one tried to bite my leg, I almost fell off the bridge. Man, those monsters almost had me for dinner."

Rubbing the cold can of beer against his forehead, Link shouted, "I was scared. Swinging back and forth holding on for dear life. When the damn rope stopped swinging, they chased me to the end of the bridge. I hit the ground running. I could feel them right behind me. Hell, I must have bumped into every damn tree in your stupid forest. Tripping over roots with bushes whipping my ass. This place really sucks." He exhaled and slumped over as everyone clapped. As his friends crowded around him, he knew his odyssey of terror was over.

Link sounded convincing, but his audience dismissed his story as *night fright*. They assured him there was nothing that big in these woods, but Billy wasn't so sure. After Link had a chance to relax, Billy told everyone about the noise they heard in the old mine and the dark thing hiding down there.

Link jumped up pointing at Billy, "See, see, they are real."

Billy supported Link's claim by telling them what he'd seen from the top of the falls without mentioning that Annie was with him.

Link pointed at Billy and shouted again, "Yeah, see I'm not making this up. There were three of the bastards."

Everyone laughed telling them both that there were no monsters lurking in the lake or under the falls. Steve disagreed and thought about telling his story, but decided not to join the lunatic fringe. Steve shivered as he thought of Link's monster chasing him through the fog. *No, best not join the crazy crowd just yet.*

After an old jeep pulled up along Shanty's pickup, Professor Cooper and his grad assistant joined the group. Dan got Shelley a beer and one for himself. As they popped their cans, Lea told them Link had an encounter with monsters on the way to the campfire. When Billy added that he saw some large animals in the pool under the falls earlier in the day, Dan was intrigued and insisted on hearing their stories.

Link told his story first with more drama and less profanity. By comparison, Billy's tale was tame, but the number of animals matched. A large one with two smaller ones. Deciding to add to the mystery, Steve finally described the attack by his morning monster.

After he finished with it chasing him to shore, Shanty wondered out loud, "Could there be a connection between these creatures and Annie's fossil?"

Dr. Cooper shared his doubts that prehistoric animals could be living in the lake, but kept everyone interested by telling tales of creatures supposedly seen in other lakes. While Dan recited his stories of "Champy" in Lake Champlain and "Ogopogo" in Lake Okanagan, Annie noticed that Shelley was trying to get Billy's attention. Completely missing Shelley's efforts, Billy waited until Dan finished his monster stories to bring out his guitar.

After a classical guitar piece, his banjo appeared leading to an old fashioned campfire sing-a-long. Soon everyone was singing old *Peter, Paul and Mary* songs finishing with a rousing rendition of the Beach Boys' golden hit, *The Sloop John B*. Everyone held up their beers and shouted out when the verse "drinking all night" rolled around. Link stood up singing out "Let me go home" every time this line was repeated in the chorus.

After Billy put his guitar and banjo back in their cases, he grabbed a beer and walked down the beach alone. Shelley was watching him and after he departed, she casually got up to follow him. To disguise her departure, she threw an almost full can of beer away pretending it was empty. She left the campfire in the opposite direction from Billy's exit, but when she reached the water she turned to catch up with him. Annie watched both of them leave and joined the professor to give Billy time to talk to his old girlfriend.

When Billy heard someone calling his name, he turned to find out who wanted him. Shelley was standing behind him with her blonde hair shimmering in the moonlight. He couldn't remember her looking more beautiful. He approached her asking, "Shouldn't you be with the professor?"

"I'm not sure. Should I?"

"You put an end to us before you graduated. I'm still not ready to get married. Besides I've moved on. You should too."

"It wasn't me. It was you. You brought up marriage first. I thought I was taking us where you wanted to go."

"I talked of the future once. You're the one who had to get married after graduation. That was your schedule not mine."

"I suppose now you're ready?"

"I'm closer. We all grow up as we work our way through the world."

"So now you're all grown up."

"Getting there. Certainly not there yet. Your problem was that you never realized it's about the relationship not the ceremony. Caring about each other is the important thing. Not marriage. Everything else falls into place if the relationship grows. Ours didn't."

"Such a philosopher. That Indian girl teaching you to be more spiritual or are you just a squaw woman."

"Ah...there's the mean streak I remember. While you are beautiful and fun, you can be really nasty. You're only fun if you get your way. If someone stands up to you, you go berserk. I couldn't live with it then and won't live with it now. I'm glad we had that fight because it showed me a side of you I'd never seen. You're a beautiful, but still a bitch. It's over. Live with it."

"One fight and you run. If that's all we had then it is over." Shelley turned and steamed back to the fire.

Billy spit and kicked his foot into the shale beach wrenching his knee again. Swearing to himself, he limped back to the campfire making sure he returned from a different direction than Shelley.

When Shelley returned to the campfire, she sat down on the other side of the professor glaring at Annie. Annie acted like she was listening attentively to Dan as he droned on and on about aquatic fossils, but she almost smiled when she noticed the blonde girl's icy stare. While Dr. Cooper was just claiming today's fossil discovery would put Cayuga on the map, Annie was thinking that Shelley's little talk with Billy must not have gone well for her. Annie smiled to herself. *Maybe their talk went well for me.* When Billy returned, she wanted to leave the know-it-all professor, but the blow-hard wouldn't stop talking. She wanted to get Billy alone to learn the details of what just happened down on the shore with his old girlfriend.

When Annie excused herself to get a drink, Dr. Cooper got everyone's attention to make his big announcement, "Tomorrow an article and picture of the fossil will be published in the *New York Times*. I've named the fossil "Annie" after the young lady who found it. This fossil will have a great impact on everyone interested in the history of the lake." He finished by assuring them he had mentioned all of their names and hoped they didn't mind him breaking the news.

Everyone was excited except for Shanty who asked, "What will happen to our new *Annie?* People should see her. Know that she exists. I don't want her shoved in some old dusty box forgotten in a university storage room."

To alleviate Shanty's concern, Dan answered, "She will be studied and recorded in hundreds of photos and documented in many articles. Annie is too important to be forgotten. This fossil will not disappear on my watch."

CHAPTER 15

fter listening to others tell their tales of lake monsters, Shanty decided it was time to share his encounter with Apotamkon. Everyone got a fresh beer and a handful of munchies before settling back for another story.

Shanty took a deep breath, "Early one morning when I was nine, my dad took me fishing on the old pier that went out from the shore at this very spot." He stopped and pointed out to the pilings standing like dark sentinels guarding the shore in the moonlight.

"Right out there, I met Apotamkon on a fog covered lake. I remember my dad let me carry the poles and tackle box as we went out on the dock. I was proud when I sat down next to him. When we threw out our lines, they disappeared in the bank of white riding the waves. I can still hear the bait plunk as it hit the water."

"After a few minutes, my dad and I heard water splash somewhere out in the wet clouds. Soon ripples searching for the shore swam toward us from under the mist. I shivered and my father hugged my shoulders to warm me. He was sure we would have good luck that foggy morning. The fish were out there just waiting for our hooks. He promised that our family would have full bellies that night."

"When I felt a tug on my line, I pulled back hard to set the hook. Suddenly, a roar came out of the fog. A frightening sound that I had never heard before or since. As my line straightened out, I was jerked off the dock into the cold water and towed through the fog not willing to let this family feast get away."

"My dad called to me telling me to drop the pole, but I couldn't. My big fish was going to feed my whole family that evening."

"Lost in the cold water surrounded by the wet misty fog, my line went slack. Treading water, I reeled it in. When the line jerked tight, my families' dinner towed me away again. Through the patches of the fog, I caught glimpses of the large black fish in front of me. At least I thought it was a fish."

"I pulled back on my pole to haul it in, but Mr. Fish pulled harder dragging me further from shore. At first, it was fun. I enjoyed skimming over the water just waiting for this fish to tire so I could take it back to show my father. Finally my line dipped in the water. Treading water with my legs, I pumped my pole up and down to reel in the great fish swimming somewhere out in the low flying clouds. Floating in the water trying to haul in my catch, I noticed ripples of water surrounding me. Hidden in the fog, the great fish was swimming circles around me."

"Suddenly in a shower of raining water, great white teeth slashed out of the fog as a huge black beast surfaced in front of me. Screaming, I shoved my pole down its throat. While it crushed my pole, I swam away hoping to hide in the fog. The monster spit out my pole before chasing me. I could hear its mouth snap open and shut churning the water white behind me. In my desperate attempt to escape, I had lost all sense of direction. I swam as fast as I could hoping I was heading for shore."

Noticing the rapt attention of the group surrounding him, Shanty smiled and continued, "Something swam below me brushing against my chest. I put my feet on its back. For a second, I actually rode the beast. To escape, I dove away from it. Soon waves streaked passed me as the monster's head rose out of the water right in front of me. The creature looked like the dinosaurs I'd seen in a museum. A cross between a swimming T-Rex and a crocodile."

"Long jaws with flashing teeth lunged at me. I ducked under the water to get away. The monster missed my legs, but his rough skin brushed my side as he dove below me. Surfacing, I looked over my shoulder. The beast was following me with glistening water dripping from his fangs. I heard my dad call and turned toward the safety of his voice kicking hard to reach him.

The beast was gaining on me. I stopped, turned and kicked him in the eye. Only a small boy would do something that stupid, but it worked. Swinging its head back and forth, it let out a terrible scream. The thing stared at me while it churned the water frothy white with its teeth. Now he was mad. Scared to my soul, I swam toward my dad's voice. The horrible creature disappeared under the water and then surfaced right behind me. He seemed to be delighted to be between my father and me. Then he rushed at me hoping to end this game."

"I dove to the side to escape its jaws. His fangs pierced my calf pulling me under the water. With my other leg, I kicked his head hard to get loose. As his teeth tore my flesh, I cried out in pain and swallowed water. As I struggled for air, I knew I was about to die. With my last breath, I recited my death song. I prayed to the Great Spirit, Ha-sen-ni-yu. Then the thing towed me to the surface and tossed me into the air. I'm sure Ha-sen-ni-yu saved me that day."

"When I hit the water, I struggled for air as my father's voice penetrated the fog. When the devil surfaced behind me, my dad called again. I kicked away from the terrifying beast toward the safety of the dock. I remember how my leg hurt, but fright overcame my pain. Guided by my father's voice, I was at peace. The Great Spirit was with me. Glancing behind me, I saw the monster just floating on the water watching me go. Then slowly at first then much faster, it chased me. Guided by my father's voice, I swam toward the pier. As I broke from the fog, the monster slowed not wanting to leave the protection of his white world.

Ahead, I could see my father motioning at me with outstretched arms. The sight of him made my arms stronger as I thrashed through the water to reach him. The monster roared out of the cloud bank behind me as my father grabbed my hands. The monster lunged at me trying to get another taste just as my father swung me up to the dock next to him. With a great splash, the creature plunged back into the water. With our eyes swollen wide from fright, my dad hugged me close as we watched the terrible thing disappear back into the fog."

"After my father wrapped his shirt tightly around my wounded leg, he carried me to the bed of his old pickup. The same pickup standing over there in the driveway. As dad was driving the pickup away from the lake, we both heard that wicked scream from deep in the fog. Every time I see fog on the lake, I can still hear that scream."

Shanty nodded, "That day when I tried to feed my family, Apotamkon almost had me for dinner."

Mesmerized by a master story teller, everyone was quiet when he stopped. Soon they recovered shaking their heads trying to forget the image of a monster spitting out a small boy who had tried to catch him. With everyone's attention still on him, Shanty rolled up his pant leg to reveal the long scar on his calf. With a flourish, he told his audience, "This is the present Apotamkon gave me that day. Proof of his attack."

As everyone clapped, Shanty turned and pointed to the dark sentinels of the old pier, "It happened right out there." His audience glanced out at the dark lake wondering if something was still out there watching them just beyond on those dark pilings.

Shanty reached deep into his pants pocket to get the tooth he had pulled from Annie's discovery. As he held it up, he apologized to Dr. Cooper for taking it from the fossil, but insisted that he had earned this keepsake when a descendent of this prehistoric animal tasted his leg as a boy. To illustrate his story, he passed the tooth around the group for everyone to touch and examine.

When Lea handed it to Steve, he shouted, "Oh my God. I've seen one of these before. Not a fossil, but a real one." Without hesitating, he told the story of how he found the derelict boat and pried out a tooth just like this from a torn board in the back. He insisted the tooth from the boat looked just like this fossilized version only it was slightly bigger. He finished by pointing out that his tooth was very real not stone.

Astonished, he said more to himself than his friends, "My God, now I know what killed the guy they found in my swimming area. And what chased me in the fog. I bet the creature ripped apart Ms. Powell too. Shanty, Link, your monster is still out there and alive."

Shanty was first to ask, "What did you do with the tooth?"

"I tossed it into the water behind me. Touching it was creepy."

Dr. Cooper was quick to follow-up, "Is it still there?"

Steve looked at the doctor, "I guess. It should be."

Shanty announced, "Tomorrow morning, we find it."

As the campfire burned down, Steve asked everyone to get together for a picture. After clowning around for the first couple photos, Steve gave them a stern warning forcing his group to consent to one serious picture. After his flash photography, people started to drift away. Link wanted to leave, but didn't want to walk back alone. When Shanty volunteered to drive him to his campsite, Link jumped at the offer thanking him over and over again. Dan and Shelley thanked everyone for a great night before a silent walk back to his jeep. After Lea and Steve thanked Annie and Shanty for the fun, they strolled down the beach holding hands.

Annie sat next to Billy and told him how impressed she was with his musical talent and added that she especially liked his classical guitar piece. After staring at the fire for the longest time hoping Billy would tell her what happened with Shelley, finally Annie couldn't stand it any longer, "Well, how did it go?"

Billy knew exactly what she was talking about, but with a smile he answered, "How did what go?"

"Blondie. You talked to her."

"How did you know?"

"Both of you were gone for almost half an hour. I had to keep the professor busy after you two wandered off. Boy that guy likes to hear himself talk. Especially if he thinks he has an attentive audience. I want you to know I smiled and nodded at all the right places. I sat there enraptured with each word waiting for you to come back."

"Thank you, I'm glad I talked to her."

"I must say Shelley didn't look happy when she returned."

Billy was slow to answer. "I'm not sure what happened. It was over before tonight. It's still over. Nothing has changed except now I'm convinced leaving her was the right thing to do. She is beautiful, smart and a real bitch. We were good together for a while. She certainly taught me about relationships. Leave it at that."

Annie put her arm around his back and rested her head on his muscled shoulder. Holding him tight, she stared at the glowing embers with a smile on her face.

****

The jeep was eerily quiet on the way back to Ithaca. Dan waited for Shelley to say something first. Finally, Dan couldn't stand the silence any longer, "How'd it go with your old boyfriend?"

"He's not my boyfriend."

"Whatever. What happened?"

"Why do you think I talked to him?'

"You were both gone for what, maybe twenty or thirty minutes. I had to keep his girlfriend busy while you were gone. I almost ran out of crap to say. You know that's rare for me."

Shelley responded with a hic-cup laugh as she tried to think what to say. "I ...I thought I was being so clever. I didn't think you would notice that I was gone."

"I care about you. Of course, I missed you."

"I'm not sure what happened. When I saw him yesterday, I was unprepared for the old feelings that came rushing back. I didn't even know they were there. You may have noticed I haven't been my usual self since then."

"I have, but I understand. I've loved and lost in my life."

"Don't worry about him. Tonight closed that door for good. Ended it. Once I admired him. Now, I don't. He took great pleasure in pointing out my flaws tonight. If you don't mind, I want to forget him and move on." After a moment, Shelley added, "I'd like to stay at your place tonight."

Don't mind at all, Dan thought. The jeep was still quiet on the way back to his place, but it was a much warmer quiet full of anticipation.

****

When Lea and Steve stopped in front of his cabin, Steve thought about going in, but then stopped. "Hilda is trying to catch us. Let's take our fun down the beach. Wait here a second."

Steve ran into his bedroom and turned on the light. As he left, he found some romantic music on his radio. Then he grabbed a large beach towel before they headed down the shore to where the canoes were all tipped over on their sides in a line with each one leaning on the other. On the way, Lea asked why he left the light and radio on, and Steve explained that if Hilda showed up nosing around, she'd think they were in his cabin.

When they reached the last canoe in the line, he tipped it over on its bottom. Between the canoes, he spread the towel out on the beach. Together they sank down on it to be close. Just as things were getting passionate, Steve saw a beam of light flash across the ground near them. He quickly put his hand over Lea's mouth.

When Lea nodded that she'd be quiet, Steve silently rolled the last canoe over them so it covered them up by leaning it on the next canoe in line. Hidden under the canoe, they peeked out and discovered Hilda standing on the dock. Then she prowled down the shore line toward the canoes flashing the beam of her flashlight back and forth in front of her. She was sneaking up on his cabin hoping to catch them together. As she passed the canoes, her foot fell right next to their heads. Lea let out a single giggle which Steve cut short quickly by putting his hand over her mouth making her laugh come out as more of a squeak, but Hilda heard it. Stopping inches from their heads, she stood right next to them listening while flashing her light toward the cabin wondering if she had heard something or if it was her imagination.

While Hilda stood next to their heads, Steve put his finger to his mouth for Lea to be quiet. Finally, after the rippling of quiet waves was the only sound she could hear, Hilda continued to creep up on Steve's cabin. After she passed by, Steve carefully tipped the canoe back on its bottom. Then he whispered to Lea that she should hustle back to her cabin. As she silently hurried off, Steve carefully crawled out from between the canoes creeping up behind Hilda matching her step by step as she carefully approached his cabin. When she stopped, he stopped. He got very close behind her without her having a clue he was there.

Creeping up to Steve's bedroom, Hilda found a wooden box next to his cabin and placed it below his window. Stepping up on the crate, she stood on her toes to peek in. As she squinted through the window, Steve took his small digital camera out of the front pocket of his hoodie hoping to capture her pose for prosperity. When his camera flashed, Hilda instantly spun around falling off the box. Blinded by more flashes as she fell, she didn't know what was happening.

Steve caught shots of her in the air before she hit the ground. Her facial expressions looked like those pictures taken by the automatic camera at the end of a wild roller coaster ride. Her mouth was wide open with a look of fear mixed with surprise and awe. Letting out a guttural yelp as she hit the ground, Hilda ended up sitting on her butt staring at the red dots dancing in front of her eyes trying to figure out what had happened as a dark shadow emerged above her.

Finally the dark figure spoke, "Why are you peeking in my cabin at night? Do you want me? Is that it? First, you come in the men's shower to see me naked. Now you invade my privacy by peeking in my bedroom. Are you stalking me?"

"No, no. I know you and that tennis girl are, well, do'in it. I'm here to stop you. It's… it's not right. I just…just left her cabins and the junior counselor says she's been gone all night. I knew she'd be down here with you."

"Madame, I'll show you my cabin. Prove that you're wrong. Then you'd better get out of here and leave me alone. If I find you around my cabin or the men's shower room again, I will file a sexual harassment charge against you. This is my work place. I'm going to show your brother the pictures of you peeking in my cabin window tonight. Stop following me. Get it? If it happens again, you'll be sorry."

Steve grabbed her by the arm jerking her to her feet. Still trying to focus, Hilda struggled to her feet as he marched her around the corner of his cabin up the stairs to the porch and threw open his door. Then he dragged her to his bedroom, "See, no one here. Don't ever come back here again. Stop stalking me."

****

Steve and Lea were sitting on his cabin porch watching the sun rise munching bowls of cereal with bananas and blueberries when Annie, Billy and Shanty showed up. No run today. Finding Steve's tooth was more important. Link appeared next thankful to see the morning sun had chased away his demons.

They all turned when Dr. Cooper pulled up in his jeep. Jumping from the cab, Dan waved and headed toward the group with a new zest for life. Shelley was still in his bed resting from a great night. With a broad smile on his face, Dan joined the group at Steve's porch.

Steve left his bowl on the porch and stood up. After skipping down the steps, he took long strides down the shale beach announcing, "Let's do this."

As the others followed, Steve stopped about fifty feet from his cabin. Pointing out toward the lake, he told his friends, "I pulled the boat out right about here. I was, maybe, waist deep when I noticed the torn up board and pulled out the thing…err…tooth. I threw it behind me into deeper water out towards the dock that way. I didn't throw it very far. It was ivory white with yellowish stains around the bottom. Maybe five or six inches long."

Riding down the dirt road next to the waterfront, Harold saw the group looking out at the lake and slammed on the brakes of his polished black SUV skidding to a stop worried that they had found another body. Harold jumped out the door without shutting it. Winded from his short sprint to them, between gasps for air, he asked why they were here so early in the morning.

Dan sensed his displeasure, "We're here to find a tooth Steve found in the derelict boat. The one the police took. The tooth might be related to the fossil Annie found in the collapsed mine."

When Shanty showed Harold the fossil fang, he became excited and approved of the search. Steve, Link, and Billy lined up along the beach where Steve thought he'd tossed the tooth. Then they waded into the water searching for it.

These intrepid aquanauts waded up to their chests into the water straining their eyes trying to see the bottom through the shaded green water. Soon they all dove under the water to search the bottom, but came up empty. While the boys kept diving, Lea went to Steve's cabin to get two snorkels and masks.

When Steve came up for air, she tossed him one set and put on the other. While the others waded out, Lea and Steve continued to search in deeper water. Waiting on the beach, the group watched Lea surface, squirt water out of the end of her snorkel to get a breath and dive down for another look. When Steve popped up treading water holding up empty hands, he yelled, "Can't find it."

Just behind him, Lea shot to the surface holding something in her hand, "I've got it."

Steve swam to her and confirmed her discovery. Lea waded out of the water waving her treasure and handed it to Dr. Cooper who carefully turned it over in his hand. Shanty then handed the fossil tooth to Dan for the comparison. Cooper couldn't believe it. The teeth matched in size and shape. The wet tooth was a bit longer than the stone one, but the match was amazing.

Dan was at a loss for words and stammered, "Do, do you know, know what, what this means? Is it possible? A...a prehistoric aquatic dinosaur living in this lake? I, I don't believe what I'm seeing."

He passed the teeth around for everyone to see. They all came to the same conclusion except for Link who wouldn't touch either of them. He already knew the creatures were out there waiting for a chance to get him.

Dan forced himself to remain calm. As Harold handed the teeth back to him, Dan began to develop a plan that he explained to the group. "Telling the public about this discovery must be done very carefully. If we tell anyone without more proof, they'll call us bat-crap crazy. I wouldn't blame them because that's how I feel right now." Everyone laughed, but realized he had a point.

"I will take this tooth to the college DNA lab. If they can get a sample from it, they may be able to identify the creature that lost it. Then I'll send Shelley over to video tape each of your stories. If we put all your stories together, we might be able to convince people the beast actually exists. That we aren't crazy. Last night they were just stories, but now. Now with this, wow, they ring true."

Thinking out loud, Dan added, "I'll get a copy of the police report. That might help. I think your poor fisherman was killed by this...this lake creature."

Steve interrupted, "Don't forget Ms. Powell. These things might have gotten her too."

Dan nodded, "Yes, yes this is becoming more of a mystery every minute. My God, what else should we do? Ah...anyway we need to wait until I collect all this info before we break the news. Man, I don't even believe this and I'm holding the evidence right in my hand. I've got to get back to the college. How could these things be living in the lake without anyone seeing them? Oh Link, when you tell your story to Shelley keep the cuss words to a minimum when the camera is on." Everyone laughed as Billy put his arm around Link and hugged him.

Shanty was very pleased with what he was hearing. For him, his boyhood memory now seemed less of a dream and more of a reality. His grandmother's stories ringed true. The Mohawk legends confirmed. Before, Dr. Cooper left, Shanty shared more of his Mohawk lore with him, "I know this may not be scientific, but there is an Iroquois story of our people going out on the lake at night to feed these sea monsters to keep them from eating our children."

Dan looked at him, "An hour ago I would have laughed at that idea, but now I think that might be an interesting experiment. Set it up. I'll get the cameras and lights. But everyone must remember, for now, it's our secret."

CHAPTER 16

When a fellow worker kicked Terry Neal's feet, he slid out from under a piece of heavy equipment for lunch. Actually, midnight snack time. He tried to brush the salt off his work clothes as he walked to the lunchroom, but he just couldn't get the stuff off. He grabbed his brown sack out of the dented refrigerator and sat down at the end of an oversized picnic table.

The lunchroom wasn't really a room. It consisted of four picnic tables placed on a platform that was covered with a rubber mat. Off to one side was a table with an old coffee maker next to the rusty refrigerator. Another table held two microwaves on top of each other with large plastic jars of catsup and mustard on each side ready to be pumped out on any delicacy a miner needed to improve with a squirt or two. A salt encrusted water cooler stood across from the refrigerator next to an old gray metal desk. Over the desk hung on two gray pipes was a bulletin-board full of safety reminders and work announcements. Next to this board was a panel of circuit breakers with electrical lines and cables stretching out in all directions to other parts of the mine. Four large lights over the tables made the lunchroom an oasis of light. Unfortunately, two blue plastic outhouses were located just close enough to allow a faint smell of chemicals and feces to waft through the dining area.

This lunchroom was located between the elevator and machine shop. It was larger than the other ones scattered around the mine. The auxiliary sites kept the miners from having to be transported back and forth for breaks to eat or answer nature's call. This one even had vending machines for coffee and snacks on the other side of the gray desk. All of these lunchrooms and toilets had one thing in common, they were all covered with salt dust. This didn't bother the miners because they were covered with it too. Still each lunchroom was a place to rest, eat and share tales of life above ground.

Charley was the subject of tonight's conversation. Everyone was wondering if he was going to become a *Suit*. His fellow miners had seen him huddling together with that female Suit plotting the demise of ordinary hardworking men and women. They were sure he was about to desert their maze of salty rat holes for a cushy job up top where the sun actually shined.

Charley joined their teasing and told them it was about time someone in management knew what the hell was going on under their feet. He assured his team that when he was in charge they wouldn't be able to spend their days in leisure in these luxurious break-facilities.

The miners continued to tease him by reminding him of all the money he'd have to spend on suits and ties. Oh, and they insisted his beard would have to go.

Another colleague reminded Charley that he would have to start going to health clubs to trim his fat gut. One of the ladies in the crew threw her arm around his shoulder and fluffed up his beard, "Management money isn't worth shaving off this magnificent beard."

Everyone clapped as Charley pushed her away, but she wasn't quite done, "So Charley, you hot for this *Suit*? Is that what's going on here? Romance?"

Much to everyone's surprise, Charley's cheeks flushed red. He looked like the jolly old soul of Christmas fame. Laughter broke out as Charley pushed her away and finally joined the fun laughing with a ho, ho, ho.

After Charley scooted his tormentors back to work, he retreated to his desk. Concentrating on his production report, he added, in the comments section, that the number of cracked pillars was growing and he was worried. This deterioration of the pillars was turning into a real safety problem. He stretched his arms in the air wondering what was causing these cracks. *The new pillars are just too thin hold up what's above them.*

As he stared up at the bright overhead lights trying to deny the truth, he tried to concentrate, but couldn't. Instead, he thought about the years he had lived underground. His life had degenerated into sleep and work.

He was fifty-three years old, divorced and alone. What would it be? God, come October it would be eighteen years without her. His only female contact since then had been one short affair with a neighbor and a couple drunken ladies from a local bar. If it wasn't for frozen dinners he could throw in the microwave, he would have starved to death. No sex and lousy food. Something had to change. Yes, he had to change. It was time for him to get a life. Find a life. Make a life. His buddies were right that *Suit* wasn't a bad looking woman. Still, a *Suit* would never fall for an old mole with a ratty beard.

****

Ruth Hager pushed back from her desk rubbing her eyes wondering if that old man down in the mine would discover anything that would help her. He'd spend the summer visiting each shift and she hoped he would find a way to increase production, but doubted that he could help. *After all, what do miners know about mining?* She smiled, proud of her droll sense of humor.

What was his name? If Charles, no, if Charley did discover something to increase the output of the mine, she would take all the credit and then fire the old bastard. She'd been wanting to do that since she first met him. What a fool he was to do this extra work for a bit of overtime. She would have paid a lot more if he held out. Hiring an efficiency expert to do the same thing would have cost her a fortune. Not to mention what a team of experts would have cost. And to think he almost did it for a cup of coffee.

Funny, he did seem pleasant in a bumbling sort of way. Calling her a *Suit* upset her at first, but soon she understood it was his way of showing respect. She did give him some credit for not drooling when he talked? What kind of person would take a job under the earth? She shuddered just thinking about going down in the mine to see him. She avoided the mine whenever possible. The mine was the last place she wanted to visit.

Still, it wasn't clear if she owed him one cup of Starbucks or a week's worth. Maybe she could buy him off with a pizza and beer. What a fool.

＊＊＊＊

Shelley came in from the student union in jeans and a loose Ithaca College sweatshirt carrying a tray of hot coffee with newspapers tucked under her arm. Rahul rushed over to relieve her of the tray and just as he took it from her, the cardboard tray folded in the center. Rahul almost dropped the cups, but was able to swing the tray low to keep from dropping it and then swoop it up to a lab table. After saving their morning brews from the near disaster, Rahul delivered Dan's cup to him in his office while Shelley sat down in the lab leafing through the *New York Times* sipping her latte. As Shelley got toward the back pages of the front section, she let out a whoop and ran into Dan's office folding the paper.

After barging into his office, she shouted, "They finally printed your article on the fossil." Excited, she handed Dan the paper pointing out a small headline hidden deep in the back pages.

Dan pushed back in his desk chair as he followed her finger to the headline. Quickly scanning article, he started swearing, "No wonder it took so long for them to publish it. They wanted that old coot from Cornell to comment on it. That bastard. You'd think he'd have the professional courtesy to call me before he said something like this to the press."

Wondering what had happened Rahul stood behind Dan scanning the paper for the offending headline. Just below the fold, he caught a glimpse of the title, "Lindenhurst Declares Fossil A Fake."

Dan read the article out loud, adlibbing as he yelled out the words, "Dr. Colby lowlife Lindenhurst the Third of Cornell U-no-versity says the fossil discovered by Dr. Danny Cooper, that pretender from Ithaca College, is a fake. He adds that the animal described as the fossil did not exist during the period when the strata around the lake was formed. That pompous ass." Dan stood up and threw the paper on his desk spilling his coffee.

As Shelley starting pulling tissues from a box on Dan's desk to mop up the spill, Dan screamed "Shit. I've got that old fart's phone number. Let him put up or shut up. I'll dare that sequestered old monk and failed fossil hunter to actually leave his ivy covered monastery to look at the real deal. Then I want to see him claim it doesn't exist. If he refuses, so help me I'll rip the fossil out of the rock and shove it up his wormy old ass."

Innocently Raul inquired, "What does the Third mean?"

Without looking up, Dan shouted over his shoulder, "It means he's the third degenerate in a long line of 'em."

As Dan opened his middle drawer, coffee ran into it and he yelled, "Shit", again.

Shelley rescued him as she damned the flood on his desk with more tissues. Shaking the offensive milky liquid off a damp stack of business cards, Dan pulled off the rubber band, letting it snap to the floor while he sorted through the cards. About halfway through the stack, he threw one on his desk landing it in the puddle of coffee. Seeing it sink into the spill, he yelled, "Shit." One more time.

He picked up the rubber band from the floor, put it around the other cards and threw them back into his damp desk drawer slamming it shut. Using his thumb and fore finger to pick Lindenhurst's card from the puddle, he shook off the dripping coffee as he held it up looking for a number. Bringing the very small phone number into focus, he punched each number into his desk phone hitting each key harder than the last. He was pissed. Waiting through four rings, he was about to hang up when he heard, "Dr. Lindenhurst's office."

"This is Dr. Cooper from Ithaca College. It is imperative I speak to the good professor right now."

Without another word, he was put on hold. Waiting, waiting, waiting, he was about to slam the phone down when he heard, "This is Dr. Lindenhurst. Is this the quack trying to perpetuate a fraud on the science of paleontology? I'm not surprised you called. You are either confused or ignorant. No doubt you are in pursuit of my assistance."

"How can you publish such defamatory statements without examining the fossil first?"

"To which article are you referring? I was published in both the *Ithaca Times* and the *New York Times*. They included essentially the same information, but I digress. Sir, I do not need to see a fake to identify one. When a simple scientist from a non-Ivy League college tries to interpret paleontologic evidence without the proper training, it is my duty to correct you in public. You, sir, are not a paleontologist. You have no business making declarations without consulting an expert, like me, first. You are perpetrating the greatest fraud since the Cardiff Giant and that imposter now rests in disgrace in the Cooperstown Farmers' Museum. By the way, are you related to James Fennimore Cooper? He too dabbled in fiction."

"Did you see the pictures? "

"Young man. With today's technology photo-shopped pictures just add to your deception. They do not justify it."

"Why are you so intent on discrediting this unbelievable discovery?"

"Finally sir, you have it right. Your *Annie* as you call it is just that unbelievable. As a professional, I had to expose you. As a geologist you may be able to tell a rock from a stone, but please leave fossils to the experts."

"Fine, Dr. Paleontologist, this afternoon I'm going to show my discovery to the press. I am man enough to invite you to examine the fossil with them. After you see it, you will be free to talk to the press. You may decide then if you want to be part of the greatest fossil discovery on Cayuga Lake. If you're not there, I will eviscerate you, your reputation and your *Ivy League* condescension in the press. "

"Where is this elusive phantom of yours?"

"Do you know Camp Minnechaug on the west bank of the lake?"

"Of course. Harold Grayson is the proprietor of that institution. I have met him several times. He is an important contributor to the Cornell endowment fund. He has graciously supported my department on several occasions."

"Fine. Two this afternoon. You can explain to the press why you're wrong. Watching you eat crow will make my day." After slamming down the phone, Dan winked at Shelley who was dropping the soggy coffee stained tissues into his wastebasket, "That should get the old bastard to show up."

Shelley nodded, "I take it we're headed back to camp this afternoon. I didn't know you set up a press conference."

"Haven't yet. I needed something to pry that old fart out of his Ivory Tower. He'd never miss a chance to stand in front of a camera or a reporter. It'll do him good to shake off the dust and actually do some field work."

After calling the press and convincing them to show up, Dan realized he needed to start for the lake. Unfortunately, Shelley insisted she had to change before they left. As she ran to her apartment, Dan fretted outside in the Jeep waiting for her return. She was taking forever. Finally, she ran from the building and climbed in. Dan had the tires squealing before she closed her door. As they started down the street, Shelley grabbed his arm and told him she left the Nikon at the lab.

Dan wanted professional photos of the fossil with a couple of Linden-hurst standing next to it. He swore as he whipped his jeep around to head back to the lab. As they entered the lab, Rahul excitedly called him over. Dan wanted to get the hell out of there, but couldn't resist the call of new data. Rahul showed him seven new small earthquakes, all between 2.0 and 3.0, radiating out from the RAG drilling site. Three stretched out toward the Clarendon-Linden fault and the others extended in a line going under the lake. Dan was alarmed. If the fracking fluid or waste water lubricated the Linden fault, there could be a serious quake. He didn't know what was worse. Lubricating the fault or polluting the lake. After making sure Shelley had the right camera, he told Rahul to keep monitoring the quakes as he rushed out.

****

Shanty and Annie stood on the edge of the mine crater staring down at the tarp eager to see Annie's discovery again. After making sure all the ropes were ready for the descent, they were getting impatient. It was almost 2:30. Where were the professors? Would they ever show up? When they heard a car laboring up the hill, they hoped their wait was over.

An old Oldsmobile bumped into the road between the cabins crawling to a stop in front of them. When the driver shut off the engine, it continued to whir and ping until it finally shuddered then died with a cloud of smoke shooting out the exhaust. Harold was first out of the car. The Director nodded to Shanty and Annie with a smile. When the driver's door opened, Colby William Lindenhurst, *The Third*, emerged in all his glory. When Annie saw him, she had to look back at the crater to hide a snicker. Shanty found it difficult, but was able to keep his stoic Mohawk stare without uttering a sound or revealing any emotion.

Colby stood before them with his hands on his hips, "I have arrived. Where is this travesty?"

His feet were adorned with the latest bright green-glow Nike shoes. Sprouting up from them were two spindly legs dressed in long black business socks stretching halfway up his calves. His kaki cargo shorts hung over these thin stalks like lampshades on floor lamps. Under his kaki expedition jacket with its oversized pockets, he wore a gray T-shirt emblazoned with Cornell in red letters across his sunken chest and emaciated frame. Running down his cheeks were two long white sideburns stretching around his chin, but not quite meeting. His skinny six foot three body was topped off with the proverbial pith helmet straight out of a Tarzan movie.

"Dr. Livingston I presume?" Shanty said under his breath.

Annie burped a laugh as she tried to keep from laughing out loud.

Shanty was the first to step forward holding out his hand, "Shanty Brandt, caretaker and all around handyman."

Harold, standing behind Lindenhurst, bent over silently laughing with a big grin on his face. After a moment of quiet delight, Harold stepped forward to introduce Annie. After everyone had shaken Colby's thin boney hand, Harold led him to the edge of the crater with Shanty and Annie trailing behind trying not to laugh.

Lindenhurst was impatient and demanded, "Where is this fake?"

Shanty and Annie were insulted when he called their cherished fossil a fake. Annie spoke up first. "Sir, wait until you see it before you call it a fake."

Colby actually patted Annie on the head, "My dear child, you have been duped. Now where is this...this creation?"

Shanty pointed down at the blue tarp, "Down there."

Astonished, Colby asked, "Why did you put it down there? I don't do cliffs."

Shanty volunteered to create a rope chair used by Swiss mountaineers to lower Lindenhurst into the crater. He explained to the good doctor that he would have to stick out his legs to keep from hitting the wall as they lowered him down, but that was all he would have to do.

"My good man, let us proceed." Lindenhurst enthusiastically shouted out.

"Shouldn't we wait for Dr. Cooper?" Harold asked.

"I'm sure Cooper will decline to show up. After I exposed his fraud in the papers, he has to be embarrassed. No need to wait for a professional rockhound. He'll just hold us up. By the way, where are the reporters?"

****

Dan slammed the steering wheel of his jeep with his fist. The dike of a RAG brine pond had cracked and broken during the earthquake and spilled across the road sending the salty waste water into the lake polluting it. Now, the traffic was backed up and he would be late for his date with Lindenhurst.

CHAPTER 17

Shanty finished the Swiss rope chair by threading a short piece of rope around Colby's waist, looping it under his crotch, crossing it in the back and then tying it around his waist again. Annie rappelled down next to Lindenhurst to help him keep from bumping into the wall as Shanty lowered him into the crater.

Watching Colby go over the edge was painful. At first, he stopped walking backwards and almost turning upside down. Annie caught him just in time to keep him upright. Shanty reminded the revered doctor that he had to hold on to the rope with both hands and use his feet to keep from away from the cliff. When he finished, Annie helped Lindenhurst creep down the side of the crater.

About half-way down, Colby's pith helmet tumbled off his head revealing his bald pate with white hair lining his temples. Trying to catch it, Colby let go of the line and flipped upside down.

It happened so fast, Colby had no time to be scared. It took him a moment to understand why his world had suddenly turned upside down. With the rope tugging at his waist, he suddenly realized he was dangling from the cliff on much too thin a line. He was about to scream for help when the Indian girl rescued him. She helped him plant his feet on the cliff face as the big Indian up on the top of the cliff pulled him upright. He looked down at his pith helmet now resting in the crater.

Suddenly he realized how high he was. Scared, he finally concentrated on what he was doing. *What is the girl saying? I've got to hold on to the rope. Yes, of course*, he thought, *brilliant*.

The professor weighed so little, Annie found it easy to get him right side up again. When she could, Annie kept one hand on his back the rest of the way down. Although Colby was a bit flustered, he finished the descent without further incident. At the bottom with his feet firmly planted on the ground, he concluded, "A bit of a hiccup there. Really quite exhilarating."

Professor Colby Lindenhurst III retrieved his pith helmet before trailing after Shanty and Annie who had started toward the tarp. While his peons cleared away the rocks used to hold down the cover, Colby stood with his feet apart and his hands on his hips supervising his minions.

When Annie and Shanty excitedly pulled off the tarp to reveal Apotamkon, Colby announced, "Just as I thought. A fake."

Annie and Shanty were insulted and hurt as Colby continued, "First, the fossil is too perfect. Seldom do you find a fossil exposed like this. Fossils of this age have to be painstakingly carved out of the stone. Such work often takes years to complete. No, this fraud was clearly planted here. Mind you, it's a good fake. The best I've seen. I can understand why you were fooled."

Not noticing Annie and Shanty's disappointment, Colby continued, "Again, this slab is too perfect. It's just the right size to lower down into this crater for amateur fossil hunters like you and Cooper to find."

In a hopeful tone, Annie reminded the good Doctor of Paleontology that, "In your book, *The Paleontology of the Cayuga Basin*, you wrote that '*While much is known about the fossil history of Cayuga Lake, there is still much to be discovered.*' Why can't you accept this fossil as evidence of a new discovery?"

Taken back, Colby was amazed this little girl had read what he considered a very academic tome. And to boot, she could quote from it. It took him a moment to recover. After clearing his throat, he lectured her. "Yes, my dear you are correct, I did write that, but this illustrates why a little knowledge is the devil's plaything. Certainly there is more to learn, but this fossil contradicts what we already know. In short, this fossil is too old for the strata in which it was found."

Not impressed with his answer, Annie was thankful for her ability to retain every volume she'd ever read. Again, she used Colby's own words against him. "In your book, *Paleontology for Professionals*, you said, '*The future of Paleontology will be defined by exciting new discoveries.*' Why isn't this one of those exciting new discoveries?"

Now Doc Lindenhurst was both impressed with this girl's knowledge and upset with her impudence. How dare this young upstart keep challenging his rejection of this obvious fake? He decided to hit her with the facts she couldn't get from reading a book.

Before he could respond, Shanty spoke up. "There was no time for someone to move this slab down here. The crater caved in at night. Dr. Cooper and the rest of us went down the next day. No one had time to plant it here."

"Young man, there you have it. Cooper is at the bottom of this. He was supposed to be here today, but where is he. He knew this fake couldn't withstand my scrutiny. If this was a real find, he would be here to refute my observations. I tell you he was too embarrassed to show up."

Colby found it difficult to get down on his knees as he pulled a magnifying glass out of a large pocket on his safari jacket. He looked like an old Sherlock Holmes examining a body. Carefully examining each fossil bone locked in the stone, he announced, "They did a marvelous job faking this rock, but this is obviously some kind of concrete. Yes, quite well done. Look here, one of this monster's teeth is missing. A flaw to enhance the deception."

Burning from this quick dismissal of his heritage, Shanty pointed out, "I pulled that fang out. Dr. Cooper has it."

With a dismissive tone, Colby answered, "My point exactly young man. When you've seen as many fossils as I have, you know you don't pull out an embedded tooth from a fossil captured in rock." Colby kept examining the fossil, "The forgers only created half the fossil, the hind quarters are missing. A nice touch."

Shanty took a step toward the creepy old man, but Annie held him back. She looked into Joey's eyes and shook her head no. They continued to listen to this expert as he derided this creature who had confirmed their legends. Together, they became more incensed with every insolent word. Finally he said something that made sense to Annie. The professor pointed out that if this was a real fossil, especially something in such good condition, you would find another slab with the imprint of these bones.

That criticism made sense to Annie. She walked to the end of the slab where it stuck out and noticed a flat stone broken into two pieces that was about the same shape and size of the piece with the fossil in it. She motioned for Shanty to help her. Together, they turned over the first piece.

Challenging the good doctor, she announced in a sarcastic tone, "Here's your imprint. What do you think now?"

Colby stood up slowly with creaking knees and walked stiffly to them as they turned over the second piece.

Colby examined the two slabs. "Yes, an imprint. Another fraud. My, they went to great lengths to create this forgery. Ah, but where is the rest of it? That's the key. That something they can't fake. No hind quarters. With such a perfect fossil, they would have to be here."

Shanty stepped in, "Doc, if you found the hind quarters of this fossil still embedded in the rock would that make it real?"

"Now you're getting it my good man. Yes, if the fossil was embedded in the strata it would be genuine. You can't fake that."

With glee, Annie pointed up at the cliff. "The rest of the fossil is up there still embedded in the rock wall. That doesn't fit your theory does it?"

Colby answered, "Sadly it can't be up there. This beast is the wrong age for this stratum. This creature would have had to survive into the Cretaceous period if that were true. Utterly impossible."

Smiling, Annie answered, "But it's up there. See that opening up there that looks like a small cave. It's there. The rest of this fossil is still up there embedded in the stone. We can show you."

****

Dan pulled his silver jeep into the path between the cabins and parked behind an old car and a press van. There standing in front of a reporter was the old fart himself. Standing erect with his hands on his hips and his pith helmet tilted back for the pictures, Colby Lindenhurst announced to everyone in hearing distance, "I have just made the fossil discovery of a lifetime. Ah…Mr. Cooper. I want to thank you for your assistance. Mr. Grayson has agreed to donate this brilliant new fossil to Cornell University. Now then Cooper, what delayed you? Why didn't you want to defend this fossil?"

When Dan didn't answer, Lindenhurst continued, "Mr. Cooper's identification of the fossil was wrong. Cooper, I expect that you'll claim it was your discovery, but since you did not identify it correctly that renders it my discovery not yours. A plesiosaur does not have the fangs found on this fossil. Besides, plesiosaurs had a much longer neck with a smaller head. The elongated teeth and short neck on my discovery makes this fine fellow a pliosaur. His body is also the right shape, sort of tear shaped. A team from the University of Oslo recently found a pliosaur fossil in Norway. My discovery matches the photos they recently published. His teeth are incredible. They could crush or rip apart anything he wanted to eat. They would make Tyrannosaurus Rex jealous."

Lindenhurst smiled as the photographer snapped another picture of him. "That should enough photos. Really, all you need are the pictures of me next to the fossil slab and imprint. Remember to include the pictures of the rear end of the fossil that is still anchored in the bedrock. Those photos prove it is a genuine fossil and not a fake. Yes, having part of the fossil still embedded in the cliff makes all the difference. No way to fake that."

Dan was so enraged when he heard Lindenhurst claim credit for his discovery he hardly noticed the professor's ramblings, but there was Lindenhurst in front of the press while he was relegated to the background. *Jesus, the old fart has completely outfoxed me and stolen my discovery.*

When Lindenhurst was finished and the reporter was walking to his van, Dan stepped forward, "God, you are a pompous ass. You are on record calling this fossil a fraud. You can't possibly claim this discovery as yours."

"Again my dear Cooper, if you read my article carefully, you'll see I clearly stated it is could not be a plesiosaur and of course, it is not. Only an untrained rock hound like yourself would confuse a plesiosaur with a pliosaur. Really, for your information, the correct name is Pliosaurodea, but today we paleontologists have shortened it to Pliosaur to accommodate the untrained such as yourself. By the way, this class of aquatic carnivore was first named that by Richard Owen in 1841."

"Your arrogance is amazing. Was that the only thing that changed your mind?"

"I must admit I was a bit skeptical at first, but after those Indians dragged me up the cliff to show me the hind quarters still embedded in the shale, I knew it had to be genuine. Not even a geologist could fake that. I say, old boy, why were you so late?"

CHAPTER 18

Later that day, Harold Grayson wasn't looking forward to a meeting with his sister. He wanted to get her to relax and enjoy the camp. And life for that matter. She was always stressed about sex. Not having it, but preventing it. For him, a private moment between counselors over the age of consent was their business not his. He hired her as the as Assistant Camp Director to oversee his budget for the summer, but had no idea she would become the self-appointed camp chaperone.

At night she patrols the road between the boys and girl's camps like a sentry. Woe to any boy or girl she catches trying to sneak away for a late night rendezvous. Watching out for the younger campers is okay, but extending her role as sex policewoman to curtailing the sexual interaction between the college kids working at the camp is unacceptable.

He sighed. Supervising the sexual activities of the campers and staff was about as close to sex as she could get. He couldn't recall if she ever had a boyfriend. She actually fit the profile of a Harold camper, but needed more help than he could provide. Maybe he could send her to some sort of makeover spa to update her severe look. Ursula could give Hilda pointers about relating to men, but unfortunately they didn't get along. Hilda hated Ursula and Ursula couldn't stand Hilda. Keeping those two apart was an ongoing pain-in-ass for him.

Hilda reluctantly entered his office, but refused to sit down, "What did I do wrong this time?"

"Just sit down and talk to me. You're not in trouble. I need to head off a problem before it gets worse."

"When I'm being called on the carpet, I stand. I don't want to make it easy for you."

"Okay." Harold answered. "Have it your way." He threw a picture across his desk, "Is that you."

After snatching the photo from his desk, she told him, "That bastard sent this to you. Now, you've got to fire him."

"Him? He's accusing you of stalking."

"Me stalking him? He's having intercourse with that innocent young tennis girl. I'm trying to stop them. You need to support me. Send them both packing. It would send a good message to the other counselors."

"Did you go into the men's shower room and see this guy naked?"

"It wasn't my fault. I thought he was in there with someone."

"Got a real good look, did you?"

"God, you don't understand. The whole experience was gross."

"What about his cabin. Were you hoping to see him naked again when you peeked in his window?"

"No, I was trying to catch him with that young girl."

"So you wanted to watch them having sex?"

"You're twisting my words. They are having sex in your camp. I would think you'd want someone to stop them."

"Hilda, they're consenting young adults. Who appointed you the sex cop? Certainly not me. As long as the counselors and area directors do their job, I don't care what they do on their own time. What you need to do is leave them alone. My waterfront director has a good harassment case against you for stalking. His job falls under the same sexual harassment regulations as an office job downtown. You, not him, are the one out of line here. You will stop following him now and forever. Understand?"

"Someone has to enforce a moral code around here."

"I will not have a prude enforcing a code that doesn't exist."

"Prude really? What a nice way to put it. You need to be a bit more prudish yourself. You might start by having Ursula dress less like a stripper and wear a tank suit at the waterfront."

"Don't change the subject. This isn't about Ursula. It's about you. I don't want you enforcing your standards at my camp. You will keep away from this kid before he files against you. I don't want to have to pay the legal fees your snooping will cost me. Do you get it?"

"No..."

Harold interrupted her, "No is not an acceptable answer. Leave this kid alone, period. One more incident with him and I'll toss you out of the camp. Not the other way around. This guy is great with campers on the waterfront. By the end of the summer he'll have every kid swimming. What he does with his personal time is entirely his business. If I had a body like his, women would be interested in me too."

"What? Ursula not putting out for you anymore?"

"Boy, you can be mean spirited. Let's switch to another topic. I am relieving you of your job as my summer accountant to give you new duties. I have hired a real accountant to collect the bills, pay them and clean up the mess you've made. You have screwed up my finances for the last time. Your new job is Assistant Caretaker. You will work with Mr. Brandt every day. You will do exactly what he tells you to do. Your new job is to help maintain the buildings and grounds, and help him create a plan for the future of this camp. I want to maintain the environment while expanding the experience we offer to campers. I've been working with Mr. Brandt on this project for some time. Now I want your input."

"Maintenance? Me? Really? With the caretaker? You've got to be kidding."

"Yes you. Do it or start packing. Brandt's waiting for you out in his pickup. Treat him with respect, he's a smart guy. I've found there's much more to him than you think. You might think about making him your friend. That would give you two at this camp…"

"Two?"

"I'm your friend. Just like you, I'm still fighting the demons our wonderful and caring father created for us. I want to help you fight your demons. Working with Mr. Brandt will help. Learn from him. Help him design the camp of the future, but keep away from my Waterfront Director and his girlfriend. I will give you one triumph. I've asked Steve to wear surfer swimming trunks and reserve his racing briefs for water meets. Now get out of here. Go work with Mr. Brant. Sweat a little. It'll do ya good."

As Hilda slammed his door, Harold thought. *Hope Brandt can deal with her. I'm not sure he's tough enough to handle her. Hell, I'm not sure anyone is tough enough to deal with her.*

Harold leaned back in his desk chair staring at the rafters over his head. Brandt's sister, Annie had suggested that her brother and his sister work together. In addition, she had volunteered to help both of them become more socially aware. She seemed like a nice level-headed kid. He'd offered to put her on the payroll if she could help Hilda, but she declined. She told him she would work with both of them for room and board.

****

As June turned into July, Shanty didn't like being shadowed by Hilda, but he was getting used to her. With Annie encouraging him, he dedicated himself to Hilda's rehabilitation. He quickly learned that Hilda came from a different world. She didn't like dirt and to her nature was dirty. She didn't like hiking around the camp because it got her athletic shoes muddy. When you walked through a stream she complained about getting them wet. My god, the mud even stuck to the bottom of her shoes. Branches stuck out on purpose to hit her arms and roots reached up to trip her. Once, a limb actually knocked her sunglasses off letting unfiltered sunlight strike her naked eyes. She complained to Shanty about everything, but he just shook his head and led her through the trees. She worried about cancer. Everywhere they went she was constantly rubbing sun-block on her face, arms, hands and legs. Oh, and don't forget her nose. God, her nose was always covered with white goop.

Hilda even amazed Annie. When Annie accompanied them on a hike to design the new camp, Hilda never stopped complaining. On one excursion, Annie discovered that Hilda couldn't swim and told Hilda that Steve could solve that problem for her, but Hilda immediately dismissed the idea by calling him a pervert. "Besides", she added, "I'll never swim in that dirty water. Fish poo in there."

Repairing buildings and fixing things forced Hilda to climb ladders and of course, she didn't like heights. She didn't like carrying around heavy things, but Shanty enjoyed loading her down with repair equipment and watching her struggle with her burdens. Even though he could carry an extension ladder by himself, he enjoyed making her pick up one end.

Everywhere they went, she complained about her toils. The more she complained, the more he loaded her down. After listening to her complaints about ruining her athletic shoes, Shanty got her some work boots that he plastered with mud and kicked around before making her wear them. Of course, she found them heavy and uncomfortable, but surprisingly, she accepted them as a necessary evil.

When Hilda complained her hands were getting scratched, Shanty gave her tight fitting work gloves to protect them. Unfortunately, before she could use them she had to cut her fingernails and of course, she refused. Shanty took some clippers from his pickup glove box and told her to let the clipping fall on the ground. Hilda shuddered, but turned her back on him while she shortened her beautiful nails.

Hilda was actually relieved by her new job, but worked hard to make sure no one discovered her secret. She had hated office work, but after a day with Shanty, the office started looking good again. Every night every muscle in her body ached, but on the good side, she was too tired to chaperone the road between the cabins. At first, she dismissed Shanty as a well-meaning oaf, but slowly she grew to respect him. She hated walking through the messy woods and worried about getting lost. For her every tree looked the same, but Shanty always knew exactly where they were. She had to admit his knowledge of the wilderness was uncanny, but dismissed this talent. After all, he was a full blooded Indian. They probably had some sort of genetic predisposition for navigating through woods.

Hilda had to admit the gloves saved her hands and the heavy boots rescued her expensive running shoes. She was surprised to discover both were comfortable, but she would never admit that to Shanty. He was the enemy or so she thought at first, but Shanty listened to her ideas about improving the camp. Hilda marveled at his ability to stand on a wooded hillside and paint a picture of the camp he was designing for the future. When Shanty showed her his architectural drawings to expand the camp, she was impressed and had to admit she could no longer dismiss him as a dumb *nail pounder*. He was so much more than a simple handyman. Acknowledging his talent, Hilda slowly realized that other than Harold, Shanty was the only other person in the camp to take a genuine interest in her.

When Shanty forced her to make mundane repairs, she was amazed how patient he was. When she told him she was afraid to climb ladders and crawl around the roof, Shanty taught her how to channel her fear by concentrating on the job and not the circumstances. When she was tired, his sense of humor kept her going. She enjoyed his personal ribbing, but would never admit it.

Each day, his dominating arrogance enraged her. He enjoyed ordering her around. When he told her to do something, he expected her to do it. He was polite, but firm. If she didn't do it, he just waited. Nothing happened until she did what he wanted. How many times had he sat in his truck with that old faded cap pulled over eyes after telling her, "Waiting is easy, call me when you're done." And he expected her to do it right. When she purposely screwed up simple tasks to upset him, he never got mad. Instead, he just treated her like a child. He'd use simpler words to explain the task, demonstrate how to do it and wait for her to finish. Like she was the stupid one.

She could never get an angry word out of him no matter how hard she tried. What really made her mad was his damn truck. He drove his old pickup around the camp and never let her, a mere woman, near the keys. He was stubborn, pig-headed and confident.

Then there was the day Shanty dragged Hilda to Annie insisting that she cut Hilda's hair. Annie, just smiled and combed out Hilda's bun. Then she fashioned it into an attractive short cut that made Hilda look quite attractive. When Hilda returned to her room that night, she had to admit that Annie did a good job. She smiled, even Shanty had complimented her new look. The next day she told Shanty that he was ruining her life.

Shanty forced Hilda to confront nature, paint, oil, grime and dirt. She hated cleaning paint brushes. She tried to convince Shanty to just throw them away and buy new ones. She assured him that Harold could afford new brushes.

Shanty just laughed and told her he'd be napping in his truck until she was done. One day he made her climb up on the dining hall roof to paint the chimney. Being so high scared her so much that she found it hard to concentrate on her job. Once after glancing at the ground below her, she slopped red paint on her leg, socks and work boots. She just couldn't endure the filth any longer. Right there on that steep roof, she sat down and cried.

Shanty found her bawling and pointed out that it was just water based paint. He told her to go down the ladder and wash it off with the hose. Then he expected her get back up on the roof and finish the job.

As she carefully backed down the ladder, she thought. *A hose? Imagine using a hose. Yuck, how can I wash off with water that comes through that dirty old thing?* When Shanty climbed down off the roof to find out what was taking her so long, he found on her sitting on her butt still whimpering.

When she looked up at him, he told her to wipe off her tears and clean up. When she brushed a tear off her cheek, she wiped red paint from her glove under her eye.

When he laughed at her, she threw her paint brush at him hitting him on the cheek.

Shanty just laughed, "Now we're both redskins.

Hilda couldn't believe it when he washed off his face with the hose. *The hose. God, he let water from the hose touch his face.*

When he finished, he looked up at her, "See. All gone."

Then he grabbed her leg with the red boot and held it up in the air. With Hilda tipped her on to her back, he sprayed off her boot.

Even got my sock wet.

When he stepped over her leg with his back toward her to clean off her pant leg, she kicked him in the butt so hard with her other foot that he had to drop her leg and stagger forward to keep from falling.

With a smile, Shanty turned and squirted her in the face with the hose. She wasn't sure what was worse. His insolence at daring to spray her or that she was covered with hose water. She kicked at him again before wiggling away from the spray. As she backed up, Shanty couldn't help but notice she looked pretty good in a wet T-shirt. Shanty called her back promising not to squirt her again. This time he finished cleaning her pant leg, but was careful not to get kicked again.

Hilda was amazed, it worked. The paint had disappeared, but now her boot was wet. She insisted that she couldn't go back to work until it dried.

Shanty, ever the philosopher, told her, "It'll dry faster if you get back to work." Then he insisted she use the hose to wash the paint off her hands and face. She tried it. It wasn't so bad. Sort of cool and refreshing.

When she finished, Shanty totally grossed her out. He drank water right out of the end of the hose.

Yuck. How could anyone do that?

That evening Hilda complained to Harold. She told him working with Shanty was too much and demanded a different job. She made it clear she didn't want to go back to her office job, but emphasized that she really needed to get far away from Joseph Brant.

Before Harold told her Mr. Brandt was her only option, he stopped a moment and looked at his sister. "You hair looks great. You have a bit of a tan. You look healthy and fit."

Hilda was surprised and pleased by the compliment, but tried not to show it.

Then Harold had the nerve to tell her, "Solve your own problems. Quit running to me."

Hilda surrendered and told him as she stood up to leave, "When I fall off the roof or have a tree fall on me, you'll be sorry."

Tired from working with Shanty, Hilda's morning jogs on the treadmill became shorter and shorter. One day returning from a run with Annie and the college kids, Shanty found Hilda in the sweltering gym on her treadmill. He told her to hurry up, they had work to do. She frowned and kept jogging.

"Why do you use that stupid machine in this hot old building? You have this beautiful lake with glorious woods to run through and you come in here. It doesn't make sense."

Hilda punched a button on her treadmill. When it stopped, she put her towel around her neck holding each end with her hands, "I like a controlled environment. Outside there are bugs and other things that bother me, including you. No, especially you."

In her high-tech gym clothes, Shanty noticed her muscle tone and figure. This woman has possibilities, he thought. As she bent over to pick up her gym bag, he noticed assets that he had missed in her loose work clothes.

When she told him to pick her up at the hotel after she showered, Shanty just smiled. "I ain't no taxi service." Then he tossed her a set of one piece orange coveralls, "Wear these. Save the wear and tear on your fancy work outfits."

As she stomped off, he called to her that she'd find him behind the hotel adjusting the water heater. "It'll need fixing after you use up all the hot water." With a laugh, he added, "Why shower when you can rinse off with the hose after a good day's work?"

Hilda snorted and threw the coveralls over her shoulder as she walked away.

When she finally showed up behind the hotel, Shanty pretended to adjust the water heater. After he finished, he pulled on the straps of her coveralls, "That's better."

Hilda asked, "How did you know my size?"

Shanty disappointed her when he answered, "I have no idea what size you are. The coveralls are Annie's idea."

Shanty hopped into his truck and drove off while she was still climbing into the seat next to him. As she slammed the door shut, she frowned at him, but he was just kept staring down the road with his infuriating smile.

****

After a morning of emptying garbage cans, Shanty drove up to the rappelling cliff to deliver some new line to Billy. When they arrived, Billy and Annie were just finishing a class. As they got out of the pickup, he and Hilda saw two campers drop over the cliff. Each camper had two lines. One for rappelling and a safety line held by a counselor in case a camper slipped or had a problem.

Shanty and Hilda joined Billy and Annie at the edge as they watched the kids scamper down the cliff. Watching them descend, Hilda said to no one particular, "This is the stupidest thing in this camp. Campers should not be encouraged to jump off a cliff and risk their lives. This activity is an accident waiting to happen. It will be the first thing to go in our plans for the future of this camp."

Upset by her criticism of his favorite activity, Billy started to tell her off.

Annie waved her hand to stop him. "Do you want to try it? It's quite a thrill."

Hilda looked at her, "Me? Do this? Never, I'm much too smart."

"Or too chicken," Shanty said as he made clucking sounds to support his argument.

Annie shook her head and sighed to get him to shut-up. Then she tried to tempt Hilda. "This skill lets you overcome your fears."

Upset with her failure to try new things, Shanty entered the fray again. "What's the scariest thing you've ever done in your life?"

After thinking a moment, Hilda answered, "When you made me get up on the roof of the dining hall and paint that chimney. That was it. I didn't want to go up there. I couldn't wait to get down. I certainly don't want to do it again."

Shanty continued to challenge her, "Did anything bad happen to you up there?"

"I was lucky. I made it down with my life. I'm not a thrill seeker. I like being safe."

Billy chimed in this time, "Rappelling is not about thrills or safety. It's about confidence. Most of the kids who come to this camp don't have any self-confidence. This worthless exercise, as you call it, does more to instill self-confidence than anything else we do at this camp."

"Risking your life is a high price to pay for confidence."

Trying to be patience, Shanty explained, "It's about learning. Helping someone learn a skill and then apply what they learn to the real world. Overcoming fear is a lesson some people, including you, have never learned."

"I can learn about cancer from a book. I don't have to have cancer to understand it."

"With a book you may understand the disease, but you don't know how it feels to face your own mortality when the doctor tells you, you have it." Shanty said in a harsher tone than he intended.

Annie stepped in to mediate, "I'll bet you don't know you are with three of the best rappelling instructors in the world." Then she added with a wink at Billy, "Or at least the best in this camp."

Surprised, Hilda asked Shanty, "You do this too? Why, you seem so, so normal. Oh yes, of course. The night you saved the girls."

Shanty laughed, "I used to do it professionally out of helicopters so this little cliff isn't much of a challenge."

"You were in the military?"

"For a while. Just a grunt. Nothing special."

Annie looked at both of them thinking. *Maybe these damaged people can help each other.*

"I am not reckless with my life. Good teachers or not, I'd never do that."

Billy challenged her, "Shanty and I could have you going down this cliff before lunch if you'd let us."

Hilda had never been good at resisting social pressure. It was one of the reasons she avoided making friends. For her it was simple, if you don't have friends there is no pressure. Intimidated by this group of thrill seekers, she didn't want to stand close to the edge let alone go over it. Right now, she just wanted to run away, but these people were the closest things to friends she ever had even though she wouldn't admit it to them.

Shanty was maddening, but supportive. He wanted her to succeed. He made her do ugly things, but she didn't think he would let her die or kill herself. Succumbing to the pressure generated by the small group staring at her, she felt forced to tell them, "Oh what the hell. Go ahead. You have about an hour and a half before lunch. If you can't do it by then, you have to promise to leave me alone. Wait, if I go over this cliff and survive. I get to drive Shanty's truck for a week."

Shanty frowned, but the other two quickly agreed for him. Billy took Hilda's arm and led her to the practice rock. He explained that first you always check your equipment by running the line through you hand. Next you check your anchor to make sure everything is attached properly. Then you put on this fancy head gear.

"If this is so safe and easy, why do I have to wear a safety helmet?"

Billy answered, "Proper safety gear and technique makes it safe."

To demonstrate the proper technique, Annie descended halfway down the ten foot boulder as Billy explained what she was doing. Billy told Hilda to notice that Annie's body was at a 60 degree angle from the face of the rock. Then he told Hilda if you get parallel to the face, your feet will slip out like this. Annie went parallel to the rock and let her feet slip out. Then she caught herself with her feet before she bumped back into the rock.

When Annie recovered, she let out more rope until she was leaning perpendicular to the rock. Billy pointed out why this position was dangerous and usually resulted in a fall. He also explained that Annie didn't fall because she was an expert. Then he told Hilda to watch as Annie demonstrated the correct way to move down the rock.

Annie climbed back up to the top of the rock while Billy taught Hilda how to attach and hold the line. Now, with Annie next to her, Billy told her to mimic Annie's movements as they went down the rock together.

Standing at the bottom of the rock, Shanty shouted up, "Nothing to be afraid of. I'm right down here to catch you if you fall."

Hilda was surprised by her first thought. *Humm…falling into his strong arms might not be so bad. Maybe I should fall on purpose?*

Annie interrupted her thoughts of Shanty, "You need to concentrate. Watch me."

Needing to focus on the challenge before her, Hilda wiped thoughts of Shanty from her mind. After looking down the sloping rock, she questioned the size of the line, "Is this rope big enough to hold me?"

Billy told her, "It's called a line. It could hold all of us and then some."

Slowly Hilda inched down the rock slope bent over with butt sticking out and her feet in front of her. Billy called her back. He told her she was thinking about the descent and not about positioning her body correctly. He told her to take small steps backwards and keep her body straight. "Concentrate on the rock face. Remember the angle of your body and trust your line."

This time Annie demonstrated the proper angle. When Annie took a step, Hilda took one. Watching Annie's feet, Hilda carefully let the line slip through her hands and kept inching down the rock following Annie's direction.

Surprised when Shanty's hands touched her waist, she let go tumbling them both to the ground. After rolling down the grassy slope at the bottom of the boulder, they both sat up laughing. When Billy and Annie helped the smiling couple up, Billy apologized for not telling her to hold on until her feet hit the ground. They all laughed as they guided her back to the top of the boulder.

Hilda successfully rappelled down the boulder three more times without any help. Each time she became more competent and confident. After her third descent, Billy looked at Shanty and he nodded. They both pronounced her ready for the cliff.

Her elation at conquering the rock was matched only by her dread of the cliff. After checking her equipment, she arranged the rope, but was not ready to drop over the edge.

Shanty told her to watch him and grabbed another line. He demonstrated each movement she would do in an exaggerated manner to give her confidence. After dropping over the edge, he called up to her when he reached the bottom, "Your turn. Don't worry, I'm down here to catch you. You can fall on me again if you want to."

After a nervous laugh, Hilda let Billy attach a safety line that he would hold. Then he told her she was ready. Hilda wasn't quite so sure.

Before Annie went over the cliff next to her, she told Hilda she'd be waiting for her halfway down. Then Billy reviewed what he wanted Hilda to do. He told her to concentrate on the cliff face when she went over the edge, "Don't look right or left, or up and down until you reach Annie. Then I want you to stop. Hold your line tight and look around. After you enjoy the view, go down the rest of the way with Annie. Oh, and don't forget to breathe."

Stepping back slowly and focusing on the cliff face, Hilda took small steps backwards keeping her body rigid at a 60 degree angle to the cliff. When she realized she was over the edge, she kept her eyes glued on the rock face not daring to look anywhere else. She let the line slip slowly through her hands with each step.

Suddenly Annie told her, "Nice job."

Surprised, Hilda grabbed the line firmly before looking over at Annie, "My God, I'm halfway down."

After Annie told her to look around at her new world, Hilda was amazed at how blue the sky seemed. How it matched the muted azure of the lake. She looked down at the tops of trees. She could see parts of the camp. Finally she looked down. Suddenly, it seemed like she was falling.

As she wavered back and forth, Annie told her in a clam voice, "Concentrate on the cliff face again." When she was steady, Annie added, "Take small steps and start down. I'm right here with you. Remember to breathe. Let the rope slip through your hands as you walk down. Honest, you have to take a breath now and then."

Hilda slid her feet tentatively down the rock face taking very small steps. Annie was on her right encouraging her as she descended. Sooner than she thought possible, Shanty put his hands on her waist. This time she kept going until her left foot hit the ground followed quickly by the right.

She turned and hugged Shanty. He hugged her back and got tangled in her safety line.

After Shanty unclipped her safety line, Hilda shouted, "I did it. I did it. I want to do it again, right now." Annie laughed at her reaction, but was even more excited to see her two projects sharing this moment together.

Shanty grabbed Hilda's hand holding it high like a fighter who had just won the championship. Hilda insisted she had to do it again. When they told her it was lunchtime, she was disappointed, but vowed to do it again.

As the adrenalin of the descent subsided, her reserve came flooding back. First, she smoothed her coveralls and apologized to Shanty for hugging him.

Shanty just shook his head and smiled at her.

Billy showed up in Shanty's pickup and jumped out running. He gave her a big hug lifting her off her feet and telling her, "You did it. You did it."

Hilda shouted in his ear, "I did. I did. You were right. This camp needs to keep this challenge. Thank you, thank you." When he put her down, she held her hand out to Shanty, "Keys please." Reluctantly, he dropped them into her hand as she announced, "Let me drive you all to the dining hall its lunch time."

BOOK
TWO

The ground on which we stand
is sacred ground.
It is the dust and blood of our ancestors.

Plenty Coups, Absaroke

CHAPTER 19

Smitty Doland, Rig Foreman for Well 4, swung up on the derrick wondering when the welders would finish repairing the well head. He had hired the Walter brothers to weld shut a system of valves that were no longer needed. The boss in the office wanted him to hire as many local guys as possible. His only task today was to make sure the welders finished their job so he could get the well back on line. The RAG big-wigs were pushing him to get this work done fast.

Smitty looked through the barrier of trees that led to the lake. What a beautiful day to spend outdoors getting paid for doing nothing. *After seventeen years,* he thought. *Yeah, seventeen years kicking around gas sites with nothing much to show for it, but this place has been good to me.* After working at every dusty well site in West Texas, he liked the cooler weather and forested beauty of upstate New York. After enjoying the summer on the lake, he was looking forward to the bright display of autumn colored leaves that he had never seen.

Things were definitely looking up. He'd met a girl. The right girl, Peggy Sue Simon. Only woman to ever beat him at pool. A wise-ass smiling creature with laughing eyes and a great body. What a body. And she could drink. Put him under the table more than once this summer. He had a steady job, enough money to marry her and she'd said yes. He couldn't wait to see her tonight. Her smile was great, but holding her close was even better.

He stood on the platform above the welders wondering what the hell was taking them so long. He looked over the railing trying to figure out how close they were to being done. When they finished, he was out of here. Hello Peggy Sue.

Most everyone else had already left for the day. He'd never seen two welders poke around so long. He was far enough away from the welding torches that the bright blue flame couldn't hurt his eyes, but he looked away just in case. He didn't see the welding torch ignite the gas that was leaking out of the last valve.

The well head blew off heading directly up at him. It blasted through the platform he was standing on and hit him in the chest. This massive projectile carried him high above the rig. For a moment he didn't know what was happening and had a quick flash of wonder, but before he could realize what had happened his body was ripped apart.

Pieces of Smitty were carried high in the air. No time for one last thought of Peggy Sue, he was gone. When gravity determined Smithy's remains had soared high enough, pieces of him descended through the orange and yellow flames erupting from the explosion. He did not feel his skin burn as pieces of his body were scattered across the drill site and out into the lake.

Carl Walters was still conscious. The explosion had blown him off the drilling platform up through the air until he landed with a thud when he hit the ground. When his pants caught fire from the flames licking out from the explosion, he rolled away from the well to put out the flames on his legs and escape. As he dragged himself away, he learned he had broken his left leg. The pain was excruciating, but he had to get away. Ignoring the pain, fear and adrenalin drove him away from the exploding flames. Through this daze of searing heat and pain, he hoped Kyle, his brother, was okay. Then he heard Kyle's scream.

Kyle Walters, Carl's welding partner, was lifted high in the air by the explosion and landed on a nearby stack of pipes breaking his back. As the flames from the well licked his face and body, he tried to move, but couldn't. His skin started to melt as his clothing burned. His burning legs would not respond when he tried to move. One arm. Yes, he could move his right arm. He put it over his face to shield his eyes from the intense heat and flames, but he was too close to the well. Paralyzed in place, Kyle could not escape the flames charring his body and cried out for God to end his life. The only thing he could do was scream. Paralyzed from his broken back, Kyle was roasted alive twelve feet from the well.

Still crawling away, Carl knew Kyle's last scream was his brother's final plea for salvation.

****

Bob Fletcher watched the small white pebbled ball rolling, rolling across his office floor toward the hole. *Man, its bending toward the hole. It's going in. There is a God.*

As he danced back holding his putter high, he heard a boom followed by a deafening roar. Suddenly his building began to shake changing the trajectory of his ball. He leaned back using *body English* to guide the ball back into the hole. "Damn it", he yelled, as the ball crossed in front of the hole.

When the full impact of the explosion hit the building, Bob was knocked to the floor. Exploding windows blew sharp pieces of glass across his back shredding his Armani shirt as he fell on his thick plush carpet. When the shaking stopped, he climbed up to one knee using his putter as a crutch. Louise ran in from her desk as red spots appeared on the back of his torn white shirt. Rushing to Bob, she helped him to his feet. Together, they staggered to the window. Staring out, they saw soaring flames slicing through ugly thick black smoke fouling the bright blue sky. The dragon's mouth was open and breathing flames that set the pine trees next to his office ablaze. Well 4 was now a tower of horror for everyone to see.

Bob shoved Louise away. "For Christ sakes, call the police. No, no, the fire department. Christ, this is too big for a bunch of volunteer firemen to put out."

Glancing at his frog watch, he yelled, "The last shift has gone home how the hell do we stop this? My God, my boat, my beautiful boat. I've got to save it."

Bob pushed Louise out of the way and ran down the stairs from his office, across the foyer and out the door. As he stepped outside, the superheated wind from the well fire hit him in the face. He almost retreated to the protection of his administrative building, but he needed to save his beautiful big toy. Through smoke and sparks, he stumbled through the flying soot and stinking plumes of black smoke as the trees along the path to the lake exploded in flames. The burst of fire knocked him down. He scrambled up now literally running for his life. Towering flames licked his back as a storm of glowing pines needles floated down burning his face as he ran through them. Holding his arms in front of his face to ward off the floating flames, the intense heat drove him on. He jumped down the steps to the dock and fell to his knees as he landed.

Crawling to his boat, suddenly attractive arms surrounded his shoulders and helped him up. Doris, a tall brunette office assistant, pushed him toward the gangway yelling, "I'll get the lines." As she ran through the dense smoke and sparks to throw off the mooring lines, Bob staggered over the gangway and tripped as he stepped down to the deck. Falling face first, he started to push himself up when he smelled burning flesh. Just a foot from his nose, he spotted Smitty Dolland's charred smoldering leg.

He heaved and threw up. After puking on his beautiful mahogany deck, delicate hands grabbed him under his arms again. After picking Bob up, Doris kicked the burning leg off the deck into the lake. Helping Bob into a chair, she went topside to start the engine. As he leaned back in the chair, he drove the shards of glass deeper into his back. As a flaming tree fell toward the lake, Bob screamed as the LuvGas slipped away from the dock through a shroud of dense smoke and terrible flames.

When the LuvGas was out of danger, Doris ran down to help Bob. When she noticed the blood on his back, she started to lead him to a bathroom to tend to his wounds, but Bob pushed her away and stumbled to the railing to contemplate the disaster unfolding before him. Leaning against the railing, they stared at the dark column of ugly billowing smoke stretching across the water reaching high above them staining the bright blue sky. Only the orange tongues of flame from his well could pierce this dense smoke. The image of the burning leg still haunted Bob. He couldn't shake the smell of disaster that had permeated his nostrils.

The LuvGas was covered with soot, but having it cleaned would just be another tax write-off. The deck was gross, but no permanent damage was done. He had saved his boat. Through the smoke and flames, Bob and Doris watched vehicles rush into the parking lot next to the flaming well. Fire hoses, fire engines, police cars, ambulances and God-damned press vans littered his kingdom. His dream of keeping a low profile in the community had been lost forever. The flashing tongues of flame were burning down the trees that hid his operation from the lake.

Holding his current best girl tightly around the waist, Bob watched the fire crews run down to the shoreline to stop the fire from spreading to homes along the lake. Saving his yacht had given him a place to hide. With this disaster, avoiding the police and press was his best strategy. *Herm earn your salary. You're probably over there right now running your fingers through your hair getting ready to, you know, talk to the rabble.*

Mesmerized by the flames, Bob sighed. *No way these local-yokels can put out a well fire. At best, they might be able to save my beautiful headquarters. By now, Louise should be calling Texas for a crew of well snuffers to put out the flames. Hope she can get "Wild West Well Control" guys,* he thought. *They know how to put out a well fire. They're the best, but the earliest they can get here is tomorrow. Then only God knows how long it will take them to save my precious well.* Bob said a silent prayer thanking God for letting the wind blow the smoke and pollution out into the lake away from the homes of the taxpayers living near his site.

Bob looked at Doris as a tear ran down his face. She gave him a hug and whispered in his ear, "It isn't that bad."

Pushing her away yelling at her, "No, it's a disaster." Then he asked, "How did you beat me to the boat?"

"I was on the LuvGas looking for my cell phone. I left it on board after our last trip out into the lake. I saw you running. You're so brave. I'm so proud of you."

When his cellphone interrupted her words of praise, he ripped the offending noise out of his pocket yelling, "What?"

It was a text from Louise with a video. Running across his palm was a local news show already broadcasting pictures of his flaming well. Near the end, they focused on a charred smoldering body on a pile of pipes with his burning well as a backdrop. It was too much for him to endure. Bob went to the railing and puked again into a lake that used to be crystal clear. After spitting the gross bile out of his mouth, he wondered how the news vans got on his private gas property to broadcast images of his poor well. He nodded his head. *They must have followed the fire trucks in before security could stop them.*

Turning his face toward heaven talking to himself, he asked, "What the hell do I do now?"

Doris brushed some soot off his face and kissed his streaked black cheek.

Before he could reply, his phone squawked again. This time it was his wife. Without asking if he was all right, she reported in a most arrogant tone that her daddy had called and was upset. The "Breaking News" coverage of the Cayuga Lake well fire had already reached Texas. She insisted that Bob call "Daddy", but he just stabbed the phone with his finger and ended her call. He didn't want to talk to his father-in-law now or ever. With a great heave, he threw his cell phone into the lake with disgust. With the problems he was facing, tomorrow would be soon enough to listen to his daddy-in-law ranting and raving over his failure.

Burdened by the weight of the world descending on his shoulders, he turned to Doris, "After you fix my back, it's time for drinks, drugs and mind-numbing sex." She giggled and led him to the main suite ready for a silk sheeted rendezvous.

****

Four days later, Bob stood behind his desk with his back toward Herm with Louise sitting next to his desk taking notes. Throwing up his arms, Bob vented, "How long has it been? How long does it take to put out a God-damned well fire? For Christ sakes they're the experts from Texas. Just look out my God-damned window. The damn smoke and flames are still out there taunting me. Will it ever end? Turn up the air-conditioning, the damn fire has turned my office into a sauna."

Waiting a moment to make sure his boss had finished his tirade, Herm answered, "You know it's not that easy. These fires could go on for, you know, even weeks."

"I'm supposed to accept that answer. Bull-looney."

Offering a sliver of good news, Herm answered, "They say they're making progress. The flames don't look as big. The explosion hasn't, you know, hurt production. All we had to do was increase the output from the other wells."

"Production, what about PR? It's a PR disaster. A nightmare. They keep showing the damn flames on every local news show. National channels too. And they always finish with close-ups of that poor bastard's burned black body next to our burning well. At least his brother is alive in the hospital. Hell, they can't even find the body of the other guy that's missing."

"I've got some news on that front."

"What?'

"This morning a fisherman found parts of the missing guy in the lake."

"Parts?"

"Yeah, parts Not all of him. They think it's him. What they found is burned beyond recognition. I guess they'll do a, you know, DNA or something. Then it gets worse."

"Worse? Is that even possible?"

"The fisherman called the TV news before he called the police. Probably got, you know, some money. Photos of burned pieces of body will soon join the pictures of the body they've been showing over and over again on every channel. Even the national news shows. But that's not all."

"Can there actually be more?"

"I just saw an interview with the missing guy's girlfriend on local news. She's attractive, well-spoken and weeping. Bad news for us. My sources tell me, you know, that she'll be on the national networks tonight."

"Unbelievable."

"Have you talked to your father-in-law?"

"Yeah, but he surprised me."

"Is that good?"

"This time it is. He told me to hang in there. Said shit happens. Told me steel is made strong from impurities. Whatever the hell that means."

Herm added, "One more thing before I go. I hope you don't have a cow when I tell you. And I mean a Texas size long-horned steer. Get ready, I want to tell you what Lou Allstadt, the Ex-Vice President of Mobil Oil, is doing."

"I used to work with him at Mobil until I married the Chairman of the Board's daughter."

Right, he was a VP for Exploration and Development at Mobil. Now he lives here in upstate New York in Cooperstown. You know, the home of the Baseball Hall of Fame. Anyway, now he's working with an environmental group to stop gas companies from fracking near Otsego Lake. It's a pretty little lake in Cooperstown that is, you know, like Cayuga Lake only smaller.

He's calling for an end to the use of fossil fuels and more investments in renewable energy."

"Didn't Benedict Arnold used to call that area home? Now Lou is the same kind of traitor." Bob Fletcher stroked back his hair. He was having a bad day. Since the well explosion, every day seemed to get worse and Herm's daily briefings weren't helping. All he had was bad news.

Pacing behind his desk rubbing his hands together, he kept repeating, "Lou Allstadt, Lou Allstadt." He stopped and looked at Herm Douglas, "Lou Allstadt. Are you sure?"

Sitting on the other side of Bob's antique desk, Herm nodded, "Yep, Lou. He's in Cooperstown telling the world he no longer supports hydraulic fracking."

"I used to work for him at Mobil. Looked up to him. Now he's a traitor. Hard to believe. My God, can it get any worse?"

"Yeah, it can." I found the information you wanted about a guy named Calvin Tillman who was once the Mayor of Dish, Texas. An august position deep in the heart of Texas. Anyway, our air pollution got to his kids. They got so many nosebleeds he moved his family out of town. When the Mayor of a town leaves that town because of fracking that might indicate a problem to the casual observer. Fortunately, the poor fool can't, you know, prove nothing scientifically."

Bob nodded, "In Texas the rural poor have been dominated by oil and gas companies for generations. Now most of them accept it. Hell, half of them work in our industry. In upstate New York, this is a new phenomenon. Of course we will get support from the property owners who want to sell us the gas rights to their land for big money, but the rest of the community, I'm not so sure."

Herm frowned, "You're right. In Texas and Oklahoma most of the gas wells are in rural areas like West Texas. Not many neighbors out there to complain. Here we have a dense population of middle class voters who are likely to notice the problems we bring with us. With this damn fire, they might even rise up against us." Herm cleared his throat, "Unfortunately there is, you know, one more piece of depressing information."

Bob groaned, "Will this ever end. What did I do to deserve this?"

"Do you remember that large earthquakes in Prague, Oklahoma? You know, back in 2011 when they had a 5.6 quake and then another 5.6 in 2016?"

"Of course, everyone tried to blame it on our waste water disposal."

"That's right. A study was published that blames the quake on us. Well, not us, you know, all the gas companies."

"More environmentalist propaganda?" Bob barked back with a growl.

"Not this time. You know. One of the authors works for the U. S. Geological Survey. An Elizabeth Cochran says "small earthquakes can trigger larger more damaging quakes." The report focused on waste water disposal near the Wilzetta Fault in Oklahoma as an example."

Bob interrupted, "Hell that's an old fault. A natural fault. They can go off at any time. How can they blame gas companies for that?"

"That's the problem. Until, you know, we showed up there hadn't been a quake on that fault for years. We come in and after a series of mini-quakes, there are two big ones on that fault. This report suggests that small quakes near a natural fault primes the fault for a bigger quake."

"Is that it? I've got lunch with Senator Lewis again. I can't get that bastard in my pocket. Unfortunately, he was on the cruise from hell. Who can blame him with this damn fire? If he doesn't come across today, I'll shower his opponent with money. Then we'll see how long it takes him to get on board. Is that all?"

Herm smiled, "No, you know, I've got a little good news."

"About time."

"You know Jack Ekstrom?"

"Of course. He works for Whitney Petroleum in Colorado."

"He said he was ready to fight the environmentalists who are trying to get hydraulic injection banned in Colorado. This guy has guts. He stands up for us. He told the press, the gas industry's intent is to grow in Colorado not shrink."

"There's a man I can admire. He's no turncoat. Men like him and me will be laughing in our mansions long after environmentalists are extinct. Now go save the world. I'm late for the golf course. Gotta' do something to get away from this heat."

CHAPTER 20

helly walked into Dan's office announcing, "The DNA lab just called. They say your results are ready, but they want you to come over and personally pick them up." Dreaming at his desk, Dan forgot earthquakes on the Linden fault as images of sea monsters coursed through his head. *These living fossils could be my ticket to the big time,* he thought.

When Shelley asked why they didn't just send the results over, Dan stretched as he stood up, "I don't have a clue."

Dan Cooper hurried over to the DNA lab eager to discover the results. When he entered the lab, his good friend and lab director, Dr. Zelda Konstantinov, challenged him. "Is this a joke? I'm too busy for you to waste my time."

Surprised at his colleague's greeting, Dan didn't notice the lab assistants migrating toward them wanting to eavesdrop on their conversation. "No joke. I'm hoping you could tell me what I've got."

"The good news is we got several good samples from the tooth. Where did you get it? Where did it come from?"

"Right now that's not important. I need to know what you learned from the DNA. What is the damn thing?"

"That's the problem. I don't have a clue. It doesn't match anything in our data base. The DNA is very primitive. I've never seen anything like it. We've searched every university and national data bank. Is this some fake you engineered to test my people? If it is, you certainly did a good job."

Dan noticed the lab assistants surrounding them and motioned toward her office as he explained that they needed privacy before he could tell her more. Zelda nodded and led him into her office eager to hear the story behind this tooth.

Dan made sure the door was closed before he explained, "You aren't going to believe what I'm about to tell you. But first, if I tell you, you must agree not to tell anyone in your lab or let out the information until I say it can be released."

Her curiosity aroused, Zelda answered, "I'll agree to anything to solve the mystery of this tooth. What's going on?"

Dan took a long breath. *How do you tell a rational colleague you think a prehistoric aquatic carnivore is living in Cayuga Lake?*

He started by telling her about the dead man they found at Camp Minnechaug. He described how this poor guy's leg had been ripped off and made it clear the man had been ripped apart to such an extent the police had no idea what happened to him. Then he added that the tooth was found embedded in this poor guy's boat. After telling her that Carol Powell had suffered the same kind of injuries, he finished by telling Zelda, "If that isn't enough, a young woman at the camp just discovered a fossil with teeth just like the one you tested."

"So let me understand what you just told me. You have a fossil with the same teeth as the one you gave me?"

"That's right."

"Okay. You're saying that as far as you know the tooth you gave me came from an animal that is alive in the lake and is a relative of a fossil."

"That's exactly what I'm saying. Believe me you haven't heard anything yet. This is why we have to keep the information to ourselves. We need more proof before we release this news to the public. We don't want to look like a bunch loonies."

Dan then told her Steve's story about being chased in the lake and finished by telling her of Billy and Link's encounters with these dinosaurs. Or creatures, whatever you wanted to call them.

When he finished, Zelda looked around for the camera, "You've got to be kidding me. If this is a hoax, I don't want any part of it."

"Do you really think I could fake the DNA?"

"You could have someone manipulate it for you. Your story is bizarre and unconvincing. I won't let you to use my lab results to justify your fantasies."

"You did the DNA. I thought you could change the narrative for me. Prove that I'm not crazy. The test must have told you something."

"It did. Now that I know, let's call it your theory, it makes some sense. The DNA is primitive. We've never seen anything like it. It's closest to crocodiles and they are an ancient species. Because your sample is similar to crocs, I did some research. There are two professors that have been doing work in this area. There is an Evon Hekkala at Fordham who has been sequencing mitochondrial genomes for the genus Crocodylis. She has proved that the four American types of crocodiles are actually related to African crocs. Evidently, this species split seven million or so years ago when African crocs crossed ancient seas long before Chris Columbus. Oh, and Carl Schmidt from the University of Delaware has been tracing the evolution of crocodiles, alligators and gharials."

"Gharials?"

"They, my dear geologist, are rare crocs from the Indian subcontinent. You need to get out more. Anyway, this Schmidt feels a gharial is a different hereditary branch of the crocodile. I don't want to go out on a limb to connect your sea monster to animals that actually exist, but you might be dealing with an offshoot of the crocodile family. But you want to get more bizarre?"

"Is that even possible?"

"Yes, your sea monster…make that lake monster."

"Come on, please don't call it that? People are going to call me crazy unless I can capture one and put it on display. Unfortunately, I don't have a clue how to do that. Not sure I want to either. They don't seem to be very friendly. Let's call it a new species of freshwater croc."

"Maybe not. Your sample has elements of turtle DNA in it. Your croc is a distant relative of turtles."

"Fine. Maybe it's a turtle-croc. That would be a better name."

"Name it anything you want, but keep me out of it. I just wanted to demonstrate how the world of science can be more bizarre than fiction. But nothing this large, based on the size of the tooth, could exist in Cayuga Lake without people seeing it? How do you explain that?"

"How will I explain that? I don't have a clue." Dan shook his head before arguing that the existence of the tooth proved these new crocs did exist. There had to be a breeding population in the lake. In this case, he insisted conventional science had to be wrong. After sharing the Iroquois legend of feeding monsters in the lake, Dan told her Shanty's story of being attacked as a boy. Dan wondered if people could have seen these things and dismissed them as something else. He theorized that there were enough fish in the lake to keep a breeding population happy without interacting with humans.

Zelda smiled in disbelief before adding a theory of her own. "Your new croc wouldn't be the only prehistoric animal living in the lake. The long nose Gar is a living fossil. In the South they have *Alligator Gars* that get to be maybe 300 pounds or so. But nothing that big has ever been found in Cayuga. Besides the DNA of your guy says reptile not fish. I did find one article that might help you."

"What's that?

Zelda reached across her desk handing him an article she had printed off the internet.

Dan scanned it. A melting glacier in southern Chile had uncovered four different kinds of Ichthyosaurs. He knew that was the archaic Greek term for fish lizards.

As he read it, Zelda added, "Maybe your fossil is a relative of those guys. That would only make your living fossil about 90 million years old. Add that to your press release, but I doubt if it will help."

****

Bob Fletcher lifted his golf bag carefully out of the boot of his car. Since it was a British car, he continued to call it a boot rather than that crass American term, the *trunk*. This car was another thing his wife forced him to buy on their European excursion, but he approved of this purchase. It was a beauty. *What did the English salesman call it? A beautiful road mobile. That was it. A road mobile.* His Bentley set him apart from the cheap Mercedes crowd.

He turned around when he heard Senator Lewis dragging an old golf bag across the parking lot. When the Senator stood next to Bob's car, he started to lean his clubs against it.

Grabbing the cheap clubs just in time, Bob was able to rescue his car before the clubs scratched his finish. "Jesus, watch out. This is a precision road machine not a hitching post."

Senator Carl Lewis hardly noticed the rebuke and let his old clubs fall to the ground. He hadn't played much golf since his election, but had been on the University of Rochester golf team in his younger days. He saw today's invitation to play as another chance to confront this arrogant CEO. "When are your wells going to stop burning? I can't tell you how many calls I've had from my constituents complaining about the smoke and soot in the air, and the crap polluting the lake. When is this disaster going to stop?"

"I've got the best crews working on it now. I hope they'll get it out soon, but I can't tell you exactly when."

"Better be soon or you're looking at the end of fracking around here."

"Please be patience and try to keep your supporters calm. I will appreciate everything you can do. I want to make this accident right for you and your people."

Carl turned to another topic, "Have you heard of the problems the EQT Corporation is having in Finleyville, Pennsylvania?"

Bob gently lowered his golf bag to the ground being careful not to scratch his auto or his titanium clubs. He looked up at the Senator thinking, *if your questions continue on the course, I'll kill you by the second hole and bury you in a sand trap.* Without revealing his true feeling toward this bastard, he greeted Carl with his patented business smile, "I am aware that there are very profitable gas wells near Finleyville."

"This gas company is offering to pay the residents living near their gas wells fifty-thousand dollars to sign a waiver not to sue the company for the problems generated by their wells."

"A very generous, but totally unnecessary offer. That my dear Senator shows how gas companies take responsibility for their actions and reach out to the local communities. Wait, if that's what you want me to do, I'll be glad to make the same offer for the people around the lake to forget the fire and smoke from my well."

Flustered, Senator Lewis sputtered out, "You don't understand. I think this is awful. A bad thing. Just listen to the abuses the company wants the residents to ignore. For a measly $50,000, the company wants to be completely free from all liability from current operations now and in the future."

"If they pay a handsome fee like half a hundred thousand, I would expect that exact language to be part any agreement."

Getting upset, the Senator countered, "They expect blanket protection from all health problems, property damage, noise, vibrations, dust, smog, odors, fumes, soot, air pollution, drilling activity, construction of pipelines and power lines, tanks, ponds, and traffic. This is a laundry list of the abuses that happen around a fracking site. Your, what shall we call it, well accident is one thing. Now, more than ever, I need to make sure the residents of this beautiful lake don't have to endure the other problems produced by fracking. I can't stop your fire, but I can save my people from future tragedies."

As Bob listened to the Senator complain, he wanted to take out his nine iron to beat him until he was bloody. While he listened to the politician rant on, he decided, *the correct club for beating a politician is the driver. It was longer and would keep the blood from spraying on my new golf slacks.*

When the Senator stopped for air, Bob jumped in. "I know the spokeswoman for EQT, Linda Robertson. If you read the papers, you will find that time and time again, she has pointed out her company has worked hard to address the concerns of the residents. If you check closely, you will find that she also released the information from independent consultants that the company hired. These experts proved the company was in complete compliance with all state noise and air quality standards."

"Just listen to what one resident had to say. A Gary Baumgarden told a reporter that he was insulted when the company offered to buy their silence. He had to take down the pictures in his bedroom because they vibrated all night and kept him and his wife awake. Evidently the noise was as bad as the vibrations. He said the noise from the drilling exceeded 75 decibels inside their home. When they complained, the company put up a sound barrier, but it didn't help. His family had to leave their house three times to escape gas fumes. I won't let you subject my constituents to such unacceptable practices."

Bob wanted to golf. Enjoy the day and leave controversy behind. He decided the way to shut this guy up was to surrender. "You're absolutely right. I won't let the people of this fine community suffer from these problems. Now pick up your clubs and play. We can continue this conversation over a beer at the nineteenth hole. For now, let's just golf."

The senator wouldn't quit as they walked to the first tee, "You've already had an explosion, burned down your fracking site and polluted the air. Your guarantees don't mean much."

Bob didn't answer. He just stroked his ball down the fairway and of course he sliced the damn shot. He walked off mumbling to himself as Lewis hit the middle of the fairway.

By the tenth hole, Bob was mad. This creep Senator with his old rusty clubs was three up. The bastard had won over two hundred dollars from him, but if he could sink this chip in he'd win back half his money. He walked up to the hole to study the break in the green. Returning to the ball, he took two practice swings and addressed the ball. He swung softly and popped the ball up and watched it dribble on to the green. The ball rolled curving toward the hole just as he had anticipated. *God, it's heading directly at the hole.* He held his club high over his head in anticipation as the ball rolled slowly to the lip of the cup and...and stopped. After waiting a full second, the ball refuse to drop in the hole. Bob threw his club at his bag in disgust.

As he walked on the green with his putter, he wondered. *Why can't a well explode when I need it? I'm not asking for much,* he thought. *Just a small act of nature.*

As he approached his ball, he prayed for a gust of wind and *Mother Nature* answered his call. As the first tremor rocked the green, his ball fell into the cup. *One under par,* he thought as he threw his arms up in triumph. When he reached down to retrieve his ball, the next shock dropped him to his knees.

Lewis joined him on the green shaking his putter at him and yelling, "When you frack, you get quakes. More and more quakes."

****

After a yogurt at her desk, Ruth Hager braced for her trip below the earth. She hated going down in the mine, but Charley insisted it was the only place he'd meet her. During July he had pulled double shifts for vacationing shift managers and now he was ready to report. It was more convenient for her to meet with him during the day rather than wait until his evening shift. She avoided the mine whenever possible and dreaded the long dark cage ride down.

With a tall cup of Starbuck's coffee in each hand, her descent into hell was as unpleasant as she expected. She tried to leave the stupid construction hat behind, but they wouldn't let her on the hoist without it. Carrying the cups down wasn't a good idea. The coffee cups were hot and by the time the elevator landed, she wanted to drop both of them. When the damn cage hit the bottom, it surprised her and the sudden bump almost tore the cups from her hands. Swearing as the hot liquid sloshed out of the cups and burned her hands, two miners shoved passed her wondering what was wrong with this lady. Why wasn't she getting off?

As Ruth carefully stepped out of what she considered a sliding coffin, she asked one of the miners where the lunchroom was. He pointed toward a lighted area as he climbed in a truck with his buddy. After watching them disappear down a long dark tunnel, she walked toward the light wondering. *How does anyone stand it down here?*

After stepping up on the lunch platform, she passed a man sitting at a grey desk and asked a young man wearing a *Grateful Dead* T-shirt sitting at a picnic table if he knew where she could find Mr. Morgan.

He pointed behind her, "You just walked right passed him ma'am."

As Ruth turned around, the man turned in his desk chair and jumped up to help her with the coffee cups. In front of her was a clean shaven guy with a short good-looking haircut wearing a new blue and white plaid shirt and clean jeans.

Who is this guy? She wondered. *This certainly isn't the old man I'm looking for.*

As this apparition stepped forward reaching out for a cup of coffee, it spoke, "I finally get my Starbucks. Thanks for joining me down here. I'm more comfortable down in this mine than up on the surface. You *Suits* need to come down now and then just to find out what we're doing."

Ruth handed this unfamiliar man the coffee as she walked to the chair next to the desk. This *new age* Charley stopped her and after setting down his coffee, walked across the break area to grab some paper towels that he laid down on the chair seat saying, "There's a lot of salt dust down here. You don't want you to mess up that expensive suit."

Ruth looked at him, "What happened to your ugly beard? You no longer look like a Neanderthal."

Charley chuckled, "Thanks, I think. For the coffee at least. I decided if I'm going to do a *Suit* job, I needed to clean up my act. Wait…"

Charley reached into the top drawer of his desk and pulled out a red, white and blue striped clip-on tie. He buttoned his collar, snapped it on and held out his hands. "Ta, da. Just for you."

Ruth wasn't sure he was being complimentary or sarcastic, but didn't care. She was here to pump his brain and find out if he had learned anything that would increase production. Only then could she escape this horrible underground dungeon.

"Well? You've got the coffee and overtime. Now, it's my turn to get something in return."

Deciding to tease her, Charley answered, "I did find out one thing. I've been thinking I didn't bargain hard enough. I should at least get a meal out of this. My price has gone up."

Tired of his rhetoric, Ruth responded, "Do you like Italian food?"

"Sure."

"Done. One diner at Ithaca's finest Italian restaurant, Zaza's Cocina. Now spill it. What did you learn?"

"You pick me up in your fancy little sports car?"

"Yes, yes, get on with it."

Pleased with his new deal Charley started his story. "I watched all the shifts and paid more attention to mine, but couldn't find any differences. I asked the other foremen to come watch my shift to see if they could spot the difference. By the way, I promised you'd give them an extra day of overtime if they helped. Okay?"

"Just give me their names. Get on with it."

"I'm not sure of their names."

"You don't know their names?"

"Their first names. I don't know every miner and his social security number."

"You knew my name."

"Don't feel bad. I had to look it up after we talked."

"Welcome to my world. The foreman, right? I'll get their names. Now, for God's sake, did you find anything?"

"One more thing, I had to bring some of my people along with me to get a good feel for each shift. One man can't cover the whole operation. I promised them overtime pay."

"Yes, yes. More names. This time I'll need list from you. Get to the point."

Smiling Charley leaned back, "After watching all the shifts, I noticed their shifts cleaned up earlier than mine. My guys work the full shift and leave product on the floor for the next shift. Now, let me get this straight. No matter what I tell you, you promise not to fire me, right?"

"I'll fire you if you don't get to the point."

"Okay, I stayed down and watched the blasting between each shift. Evidently your engineers issued a directive limiting the depth the explosive material could be put in a face before we blow it up. I completely missed it. My shift places the explosive three feet deeper than the other shifts so we get more product when we blast. We haven't been following your safety regulations, but we get more product. By making the holes four feet deeper, I think all the shifts can meet your quota."

"You mean I haven't been meeting my production goals because the engineers told you not to drill the holes deep enough?"

"That's the only difference I spotted."

"Have you had any trouble with the deeper holes or the extra explosives?"

"No. Am I in trouble?"

"God no. If anyone asks, you were acting under my directions as a trial. You know, a test case. I can't believe we haven't been meeting quotas because the stupid holes aren't deep enough. Damn engineers."

"Believe me, I've said the same thing many times. Damn engineers. Has a ring to it, doesn't it? Okay, I say it was an experiment, right."

"We can do it on all shifts?"

"Sure."

"As a result of your tests, I will issue a directive to increase the depth for explosives on each shift. Will that let us reach our goals?"

"It will be close, but I think so. If you have all the shifts drill a bit deeper you should meet your monthly goals."

"My God, I'll send out a memo today." *I can save my job,* she thought. "Now get me out of this underground hell. I hate it down here."

As Charley escorted her to the elevator, the ground began to shake. The lights flickered as the shaking was followed by serious tremors. As salt dust fell from the ceiling, the whole underground world started to move. The rippling floor of the mine knocked Ruth off her feet.

Charley spread his feet and kept his knees bent to keep standing and caught her. Remaining upright was difficult as the shaking grew in intensity. Holding her in his arms, he noticed she smelled pretty good.

As the trembling continued, she put her arms around him and buried her head on his chest. As she hugged him tight, she started to whimper.

As Charley tried to comfort her, the intensity of the quake grew throwing them both to the floor of the mine. As the floor continued to roll and shake, Charley reached into his pocket to find his remote. *God, being this far under the earth during a quake is...* He never finished that thought as he switched off the lights with a single finger to start the evacuation.

Ruth cried out when the lights went out. As they lay together in the blackest dark she had ever seen, the mine kept shaking below them. The walls trembled around them and pieces of salt fell from above. They could do nothing, but ride out the quake in the dark.

Charley tried to calm her down and told her not to worry, but he was scared too. Then he noticed by the light from his helmet that she hadn't turned on the light on her helmet. Charley knew that a light on your head was a source of comfort when the other lights went off. He reached over to Ruth's hat and turned on her light.

This tiny beam of light, stopped her whimpering as she focused on the new beam of light that she could control. Suddenly helmets in mines made a lot more sense.

After a minute or so that seemed much longer, Charley helped Ruth stagger to her feet when the shaking stopped. As he loaded her into the truck, Ruth started to cry, "Its dark. Too dark."

Charley assured Ruth this was normal and that everything was all right even though he wasn't sure he was telling her the truth. This quake had been shorter than the previous quake, but much stronger. He wasn't sure the mine could withstand a quake this severe and wanted to get this woman and his people out of this death trap as quickly as possible.

In the light from his helmet, he saw that Ruth's panty hose had been ripped at her knees and her expensive suit was covered in salt.

Ruth pleaded, "Oh God. My God, get me out of here."

Charley left Ruth in truck while he waited for the man cage to appear from above. As other men arrived, they all sighed when the hoist cage door finally opened. Everyone rushed in packing the hoist without any regard for personal space. Charley was just able to jam Ruth between two miners before he pulled the door shut.

Ruth felt the walls closing in around her. Sweaty people were touching her all over. She didn't know what was worse, the lack of privacy or the dark, dark smelly cage.

Charley stayed behind to direct the evacuation. With the hoist packed full, he pushed the button to send it to the surface just as an aftershock rocked the mine. The hoist rose slowly and jerked to a stop about halfway up the entrance. Grabbing the back of a truck to ride out this tremor on his feet, several miners near Charley fell to the salt surface. As the shaking rolled through, everyone wondered if the mine would survive.

With the elevator stuck above him, Charley knew he had a problem. He could see the knees of the people inside the hoist. *This might be a blessing.* He thought. *At least they aren't stuck in the middle of the shaft. I think we can get them out of there.*

An audible groan came from the miners stuck inside the elevator as the cage rattled back and forth. Sounds of astonishment and fear came from the people trapped inside.

With pieces of salt still dropping from the ceiling, Charley knew it might confuse the issue, but turned the lights back on and quickly gathered the more experienced miners around him. With this elevator stuck, he told his foremen to lead the other miners to the product elevator and use the buckets as an emergency lift. The miners had practiced this exit before and knew it would be a wild ride, but now, it was the only way out.

Charley kept a few men with him to get the miners out of the stuck cage and maybe get it going again. He told a couple to get some ladders and they hurried off. He grabbed the new mechanic that he had brought with him from the night shift by the shoulder and told him to help him push open the door to the hoist.

Terry helped Charley push and pry open the wire mesh elevator doors and then shined their hat lights under the elevator to see if they could spot the problem.

The elevator was still in its tracks. Charley wasn't sure what was wrong. He pointed to an access ladder on the side of the shaft and told Terry to use it to get on the top of the elevator. Maybe he could spot the problem.

Terry didn't like standing under a stuck elevator when at any moment another tremor could shake it down on top of him and he didn't want to go up the access ladder. Drawing on his military experience coupled with his innate courage, he ran under the elevator. He had to squeeze between the elevator and the shaft to climb the rungs of the metal ladder running up the shaft. Just as he got on top of the hoist an aftershock hit the mine.

With the mine shaking, Terry wondered. *What the hell is the difference between an earthquake and an aftershock? Both scare the hell out of you.* He had to grab on to the cable on top of the hoist to keep from falling. With a quick prayer, he thanked God for not trapping him between the cage and the shaft when he climbed up the ladder.

Below him, Charley and his crew were trying to get everyone out of the hoist. It was so crowded it was hard to pull people out. The people trapped inside had to get down on their knees with their butt toward the opening and lay on their stomach so men standing on ladders could pull them out one at a time. Once they were out, the escapees used a ladder in the middle to get to the floor of the mine.

While Charley watched the miners as they struggled out of the man-cage, he called the folks on the surface to find out if the problem was on their end.

A moment later, Terry ducked out from under elevator. "The problem is on our end. The cable jumped off the wheel."

Terry explained that with the tension still on the cable there was no way to get it back on the wheel and suggested, "If they can reverse the direction of the hoist, it might reduce the tension just enough to let me slip it back on." Terry told Charley to wait until he could grab a long pry bar and get back on top of the hoist before he tried to move it.

As Terry ran to the shop, Charley saw the men on the ladders pulling Ruth Hager out of the elevator. Her plight demonstrated why miners didn't wear skirts. As two men grabbed her legs to pull her out of the cage, her skirt hiked up around her waist. As they dragged her out, Ruth's pantyhose was chewed up.

Charley hung up the phone and helped Ms. Hager place her feet on the ladder. Before helping her down, he pulled down her skirt. When Hager reached the ground, Charley saw streaks from tears running down her salt covered cheeks.

Ruth adjusted her skirt and jacket to recover some degree of modesty. Remembering her position, she forced herself to be brave wondering. *God, will I get out of here alive?*

While Charley tried to comfort Ruth, Terry ran up with a long six-foot pry bar and told Charley he needed help to get it on top of the hoist. Charley took the pry bar and ducked under the hoist with Terry and let him hustle up the access ladder. After handing the crowbar up to Terry, Charley was very happy to make it out from under the cage before another aftershock dropped the damned thing down on him.

Terry put the long pry bar under the cable and braced it against his shoulder. Using his legs, he heaved against the cable just able to slip it back on the pulley wheel. Terry checked the cable. *Yep, it's on there.*

He called to Charley, "Take it up a few inches. See if it works."

As soon as Charley pushed the elevator button, it jerked up and the cable popped off. Terry spotted the problem. The cable guide had broken off. After a struggle, he finally got the cable back into position. Terry slid down the ladder and ducked under the cage. He explained to Charley that if he rode up on the top of the hoist he could keep the cable from slipping off the wheel with the pry bar. If they had the part up top, he could replace it and get the hoist back on line.

Charley was nervous about him riding on top of the cage, but Terry convinced him he could do it. Terry hustled back on top and yelled to Charley that he was ready.

Charley pushed the button and the hoist dropped slowly to the mine floor. When Charley pushed the up button, the cage started up the shaft.

When he saw the hoist was working, he pushed stop and yelled up to Terry. "How you doing?"

Terry shouted back. "Bring it back down and load'em in."

Charley lowered the hoist back into the loading position and yelled, "All aboard." When no one stepped forward, he was surprised. As some left for the product shaft, he realized others were afraid. After shaking his head, Charley gave them a choice, "Get in now or go to the buckets."

No one moved until Ruth Hager stepped forward. She wanted to get to the surface so badly she was willing to try anything. *I sure as hell don't want to ride in a bucket.*

Slowly others filed in after her. This time they gave her a little room. When the lift was full, Charley said a quick prayer before he pushed the button. After the hoist lifted off and continued up the shaft, Charley heard a cheer from inside the cage as it filtered down the shaft.

Terry was glad he had his helmet. Its solitary beam was the only light in the dark shaft. He braced the crowbar on his shoulder to keep the cable on the pulley wheel as the elevator slowly climbed up the shaft toward a small dot of light at the top. Keeping the crowbar braced against the running cable began to hurt his shoulder. He held the bar with both hands to relieve the pressure.

It was hard keeping his helmet light pointed at the cable wheel as the cage jerked its way up. Keeping the cable on the wheel tested his endurance. The trip up seemed to be taking forever. He wasn't sure he could make it. As he glanced up, the dot of light at the top of the shaft seemed to be slowly growing bigger. He gritted his teeth as the ride up became more of a test of will than muscle.

Charley told the men waiting in front of him to count off for the next ride. Then he heard a low rumbling coming from the interior of the mine as the mine shook again. The mine shrieked with creaks and groans as everyone realized it wasn't an aftershock. As the mine shuddered, the intensity of the roar increased. The miners braced as new waves of energy radiated through the mine.

Terry felt the elevator shake and saw the cable slip while he tried to keep his balance on the swinging cage. He shoved the pry bar forward just in time. The shaking hoist flipped off his helmet when the bill hit the cable. His only light hit the top of the hoist and bounced down into the shaft. *God, I can't see the cable.*

He kept pushing on the cable hoping he could keep it on the wheel. He felt like he was spinning on a circus ride. If the cable slipped, he would either be stranded in the middle of the shaft or plunge to his death. This dark shaft was now an underworld hell. With thoughts of Afghanistan flashing through his head, Terry knew that if he could keep the pressure on the cable, he might cheat death one more time.

Down below as the shaking subsided, an ungodly thud rose up from the bottom of the mine. Down the tunnel leading to the hoist, a rolling cloud of salt dust shot up from the lower levels. Loose sections of ceiling crashed down at all levels of the mine. Pillars snapped. Charley heard the hoist stall and stop. He pushed the up button again to see what would happen.

The frightened riders heard the cable grind to a stop as they were jostled back and forth. For a moment, they were trapped between heaven and hell. When the elevator started again, they all let out an audible sigh. As the man cage bumped its way to the top, no one could fall because they were so tightly packed in. Crushed between smelly dirty miners, Ruth stayed on her feet. Not being a particularly religious person, she still recited a silent prayer. After saying amen, she doubted that many miners were atheists.

Surrounded by darkness, Terry hung on to the bar as it cut into his shoulder. As they climbed, sunlight from above provided just enough light for him to see the cable again. Pushing hard to keep the cable from jumping off the wheel, he wondered if this nightmare would ever end. Suddenly the elevator jerked to a stop knocking him down to his knees as the cable jumped off the wheel, but it was too late. Bathed in sunlight, he knew they made it to the top.

When the elevator shuddered to a stop, a cheer erupted from the passengers. Terry stood up and looked around. The sunshine had never looked so good. Not sure if he ever wanted to go down in that hole again, Terry wondered if his mining career had just ended.

As he stepped off the elevator to the access ladder, he slid down ladder without touching the rungs. Now to find a cable guide and replace it. *Damn,* he thought. *I'll have to ride down on this damn thing to test it. Better do a good job.*

Ruth wanted to fall to her knees and thank God for getting her out of the tomb beneath the lake. The crush of miners carried her out as everyone poured out afraid the elevator would fall back into the abyss. The sun's rays made Ruth shade her eyes, but its warmth made her appreciate just being alive. She had survived and now knew the secret to increase production. Life was good.

CHAPTER 21

Entering the lab, Dan found Rahul running from machine to machine scribbling notes on a clipboard. Rahul spotted Dan and took him to a white board where he had summarized the data. After examining it, Dan asked, "It was the Linden fault, right?"

Disappointed by not being able to break the news to his mentor, Rahul nodded without saying a word.

Dan sensed his disappointment, "The shock came from the West. Had to be the Linden. With all this fracking fluid moving around under the ground, it was overdue."

Rahul took Dan to his computer and showed him where the quake started and pointed out that the shockwaves from this second quake of the summer were running across the whole state.

Shelley called them over to a flat screen as she grabbed the remote to turn on the sound. The TV images showed cracks in the capitol building in Albany and cities around them were reporting damage. Roads had cracks and fires from broken gas lines filled the screen.

Dan told Shelley, "Mute it, we have serious work to do."

★★★★

Charley told the nearest miner to take charge of loading the hoist and jumped in the truck and drove through the miners crowding around the hoist slowing only to let two of his crew chiefs jump in the back. He drove to the center of the first level in the direction of the crash. Rounding a corner, he slammed on the breaks.

There it was. A collapse. A gigantic hole in the floor. A huge piece had fallen from the roof and crashed through the first level leaving a great cavern right in front of them. Climbing out of the truck, Charley and the others carefully approached the hole that had been torn through the floor of this level of the mine. With some trepidation, they peered over the edge and discovered that the hole went down through all the levels to the very bottom of the mine. It was a scary deep dark hole, but seemed to be stable.

The collapse had torn away part of an open area, but left the road passed it in place.

The hole was more or less circular with a diameter of about eighty feet. Above the breach, they could see that a chunk of the ceiling that had fallen forming an irregular dome. After carefully walking around the hole, they agreed the rest of the mine seemed to be okay. This collapse was serious, but they all felt that they had escaped a disaster. The mine might survive this quake induced accident after all.

Everyone piled back into the truck as they headed down to inspect the other levels. At the very bottom of the mine, they entered a section that wasn't lighted. Only the truck lights penetrated the darkness. When they reached the collapse, Charley pulled three high-powered yellow electric lanterns out from behind the truck seat. Taking one, he handed the others to his crew chiefs. Walking around the pile of rubble, they were impressed by the size of the huge slab of salt that had crashed through all the levels of the mine creating the giant hole above them. Looking up through the hole they could not see the top of the mine, although they could see lights still shining on four of the levels above them.

Sandwiched between the blocks of salt was a crushed front-end loader. Luckily the man operating it had already left for the hoist. The fallen chunks of salt from each level were stacked on each other like a deck of thick cards and looked like pieces of a giant jig-saw puzzle. After putting the pieces together in his mind, Charley figured out what had contributed to the collapse. Beyond the quake, the new Chinese loaders were larger so they had to carve out higher ceilings between the levels and this had weakened the floors at each level. Taking off his helmet to wipe off the sweat on his brow, Charley thought. *Man, the higher ceilings and thin pillars are a disaster waiting to happen. Of course, the engineers will have the final say. Fat chance of that working out. The deeper you go the pillars should be getting larger.*

When another aftershock rattled through the mine, the large slabs of broken salt teetered above them. Without Charley saying a word, they all hustled to the truck to escape before a chunk fell on them. As they pulled away, they all agreed the absence of water was a good sign. The lake bottom hadn't been breached. *It could have been worse,* Charley thought, as he drove away.

****

Following his foremen, Charley finally boarded the empty elevator ready for the long trip to the top. As the hoist creaked to the surface, he realized how tired he was. As the adrenalin drained from his body, he sat down on the floor of the cage resting his back against the cage fencing. He took off his tin hat and wiped his forehead with the sleeve of his new shirt. *This will teach me to wear a new shirt to work.* An image of Hager crawling out of the hoist flashed across his mind. *This was tough on her. She was really scared. Hell, so was I. She'll probably fire me for evacuating the mine twice in a month. This quake ended any chance she has of meeting her production quotas for the month.*

When the elevator whined to a stop, his crew chiefs grabbed his hands and pulled him up. He told them he'd try to get them some combat pay for staying down in the mine with him to inspect the damage. They told him not to bother, it was part of the job. As they left the elevator, he cautioned them not to talk about the extent of the damage until he talked to the engineers.

Charley felt old and tired. He shuddered when he saw Miss Hager running up to him. Now he'd get the bad news. Surprised by the big hug she gave him, he hugged her back.

Ruth stepped back holding his biceps with each hand, "I was so worried when you didn't come up with the last group. You had no business staying down there."

"Sorry about the evacuation, but we had to get out of there. That was some quake. Worse than the last one. And, and there was some damage."

"I was never so scared in my life. You were amazing. So calm and in control. Your example kept the other miners from panicking and saved lives today including mine."

"How long did it take to get everyone out?"

"I heard someone say it took almost two hours to clear the mine."

"That's lousy. Has to be much faster than that. The jammed elevator was the problem. By the way, the kid who freed up the elevator and the two guys who stayed down there with me to inspect the mines should get a little something extra in their paychecks. They had what we needed when it counted. Maybe an hour or two of overtime for helping during the emergency."

"Get me their names. I'll take care of it."

★★★★

After the quake, a beautiful sunny day surrounded Cayuga. Walking along the shore inspecting his boats with the director, Steve told Grayson, "I don't think the quake did any damage to your fleet, but when I took my canoeing class out in the lake, we ran into the biggest oil slick I've ever seen.

Definitely not a spill from a poorly maintained boat. Maybe the quake let something loose."

Steve bent down to a canoe turned over on its side and ran his finger along the bottom. After Steve held them up to his nose and sniffed, Harold did the same thing.

Smelling his fingers, Harold agreed with Steve, "This definitely smells like a petroleum product."

"Yeah, something like gasoline, but not quite. I'd like to take you out to see it. Maybe you can call your friends at Cornell and report it. Something has changed out there. It could be from the quake, but my bet is the gas wells up at the end of the lake. Maybe both. I can take you out on my jet-ski right now. It'll only take a couple minutes."

Harold slipped off his sandals and waded out to the jet-ski in his shorts and camp T-shirt. Steve helped him climb aboard behind him and told him to hold on to his waist so he wouldn't fall off. Accelerating slowly so he wouldn't dump the director in the water, Steve headed toward the middle of the lake.

When they reached the slick, Steve slowed down and pointed to it. Harold had already spotted the shimmering water reflecting purple, orange and black circles and stripes ahead of them. As they plowed slowly through the gunk, the oily slime stuck to their feet and legs. Steve headed up the lake following the path of the large slick as it spread out before them. When Harold noticed that the long stain seemed to be blowing down from the North end of the lake, he agreed with Steve that in might be coming from the gas wells.

Harold asked Steve to stop in the slick so he could take pictures with his waterproof *Galaxy* S7. He discovered that if he held phone at the right angle, he could get a good reflection of the stain that revealed even more colors than his eyes could distinguish in the bright sun.

Harold was about to tell Steve to head back to the shore when his cell played his ring tone, *Chariots of Fire*. When Harold answered his phone, Steve eavesdropped.

"Dr. Lindenhurst. "You're right, the large fossil is really quite dramatic. Looks like it came right out of a museum."

"You want it for Cornell. I think that's appropriate, but Dr. Cooper has some claim to the fossil. Maybe Ithaca College should get it."

"Yes, yes. Let's meet his afternoon. Call Cooper and bring him along. We need to decide just where this fossil belongs. Besides, we need to salute this discovery with a few Long Island ice teas...I'll be waiting for you on the hotel porch...Fine, see you at quarter to two."

"Oh wait. Could you do me a favor? I'd appreciate it if you could bring someone from the university Environmental Studies Department with you? My waterfront director found a slick in the lake that looks like a gas spill. I'd like someone to test it for me. My director can take your colleague out for samples while we decide the fate of the fossil. If the Department Head is reluctant to send someone, remind him I made a substantial contribution to his department last year."

"You don't think that will be a problem...Fine...Fine...Yes, the hotel at two."

As Harold carefully tucked his cell back in his shorts pocket, he asked Steve if he could drop him off near Shanty's cabin. "I'll pick my sandals up later."

After speeding back to the shore, Steve stopped in the shallow water near Joe's cabin and let Harold slide off. Before Steve left, Harold asked him to meet him at the hotel at two to pick up the scientist from Cornell. He explained that he wanted Steve to take this guy out in the lake for samples. After Steve guaranteed him he'd be there, he roared off.

Harold was surprised to find Hilda sitting on the cabin steps with Shanty, Billy and Annie drinking a beer. From a bottle, no less. As he joined them, he noticed that her hair was still down and attractive. *My God, she even has on a bit of make-up. First time she's ever looked feminine. I'll have to ask Brant how he achieved this miracle.*

When Shanty offered Harold a beer, he declined until his uptight sister challenged him to "Loosen up." He took a sip and leaned back in the rocking chair enjoying a rare moment of calm in his life with his sister and her friends.

****

Enjoying the glorious day, Harold and Steve spotted an old ramshackle Oldsmobile crawling down the lake road before it turned up toward them. Harold said as he stood up, "That will be our professor."

They left the porch and waited on the road until the old car stopped in front of them. With his car still pinging, Lindenhurst got out of the driver's seat dressed in his safari outfit and green glow Nikes, but his pith helmet had remained back in his office. Today, his bald scalp was graced with a gray ball cap with a red Cornell C gracing the front.

Dr. Cooper had trouble opening the passenger side door, but finally pushed his way out of the old car. In his light blue knit shirt and denim jeans, Cooper opened the car door behind him. Out jumped an attractive short Cornell lab assistant with curly blonde hair. Dressed in a plaid shirt, jeans and cowboy boots, she looked like an escapee from a honky-tonk. Not failing to notice her Dolly Parton breastworks, Steve decided she was definitely a cowgirl. The only thing missing from her outfit was a ten gallon hat or in her case maybe five gallons would do.

As this honky-tonk beauty reached into the old clunker to grab a black leather satchel from the back seat, Steve noticed an alluring bottom squeezed into very tight jeans. Slamming the door shut, she strode confidently forward introducing herself as Gloria.

Harold grabbed her hand first before introducing her to Steve and told her Steve would take her out to the slick so she could get her samples.

Gloria pointed to the lake, "I'll bet we're going that way." Spinning on her high heels boots, she started walking off down the hill toward the waterfront. As the three men watched Steve run after her, they all wished they were younger and had his athletic body. With a sigh, Harold put his arms around each man's shoulders and escorted them to his office.

****

Once he caught up with her, Steve enjoyed his walk to the waterfront with this Cornell assistant straight out of the pages of a Louis L'Amour novel. Gloria was excited about getting out of her lab and explained that she loved the lake, but her job didn't give her much time to enjoy it. After Steve explained they could go out to the slick on his jet-ski, a canoe or a rowboat, Gloria told him she'd like to try the jet-ski, but was afraid it wouldn't accommodate her sample case. When Steve told her he was an excellent canoeist, she answered with a wink, "Canoes are romantic."

Steve and Gloria explored the slick that seemed to stretch even farther than he had estimated. His paddle was already slimy as he pushed the canoe to the center of the floating grease. Very professional, Gloria captured the worst of the spill in her test tubes.

After pushing the final black rubber cork in a test tube, she announced, "I've got all the samples I need. The professor told me he won't be finished for a couple of hours. What ever can we do until then? If I push my bag under the seat at this end, I bet we could lie down together and get some sun."

After she hid her black bag away, she unbuttoned her plaid shirt revealing what Steve thought was a deliciously lacy black bra straining to keep its treasures under control.

Steve smiled and pulled out a tube of sun screen from a small bag he had stashed in his end of the canoe. "I have enough lotion to protect your beautiful skin. Just keep peeling off those clothes so I can rub it in."

Gloria was glad she left her boots on the shore, but still encountered some difficulty shedding her tight jeans in the bottom of the canoe. In panties that matched her bra, Gloria turned over on her stomach in the bottom of the canoe to let Steve apply sunscreen to her silky bikini clad body. After the rubdown Steve lay down next to her relishing her glistening smooth skin.

Soon they were rolling around on the bottom of the canoe almost tipping it over several times. While the canoe was rocking, Steve heard a motorboat pull up beside them and stuck up his head. Teenagers in a sleek high powered motorboat were slowly circling around them.

Seeing his head, the kids shouted over and asked if he was in trouble. Steve yelled back that everything was okay. When Gloria's sat up in her black bra, the kids in the boat, two boys and two girls, shouted their approval and roared off.

Steve wanted to return to the bottom of the canoe after the kids powered off, but Gloria announced it was time to go swimming. With several powerful strokes, Steve guided the canoe to clear unpolluted water.

Agreeing that a quick swim was a good way to cool off, Steve half dove and half fell into the cold water as the canoe slipped out from under him. Gloria followed with a cannonball that almost swamped the canoe as she jumped out. Frolicking in the pristine water, Steve threw Gloria up in the air and as she splashed down, he saw a black beast about ten feet into the slick about fifty feet from them. The head of this jagged toothed creature was moving closer.

God, that's my morning monster. Scared, but calm, he told Gloria to get back into the canoe without warning her of the danger. He dipped under the canoe and balanced the opposite side while she climbed in. As soon as she was in, he told her to lean toward the other side so he could slip over the side. As soon as he was in, Steve picked his paddle up from the bottom of the canoe and encouraged her to get dressed as he stroked hard to escape the black menace lurking behind them.

Glancing over his shoulder, Steve saw that the black hulk was following them. He dug his paddle in deeper to pull away. On the bottom of the canoe squirming into her skin tight jeans, Gloria hadn't spotted it yet. Watching it over his shoulder, Steve saw the head of the creature come out of the water.

This frightening Spector was attached to a huge black body. The mouth was full of long ugly yellow-white teeth. *It looks like a swimming T-Rex. It sure as hell isn't an alligator.*

Paddling as fast as he could, Steve remembered Link's description of his monster and knew this was the same creature. Steve felt like he'd been cast in a Spielberg movie as the hopeless victim who was about to be gobbled up.

Buttoning her blouse, Gloria spotted it, pointed at it and screamed.

With all the strength his long arms could muster, Steve shot the canoe forward. As he finished a stroke, Gloria yelled that it was gaining on them. As the huge beast dove under the water just behind the canoe, she saw its intense yellow-black eyes staring at her as it disappeared.

Suddenly the thing came up under their canoe bashing it with its back almost tipping it over. Gloria screamed and grabbed the sides of the canoe as it almost tipped over as it slid off the beast's back.

Steve drove his paddle into the beast's side to push away. The thing whipped its tail at the side of the canoe splashing water on Steve and Gloria. As Steve pulled away, it surfaced and swam after the canoe. Steve realized they couldn't escape and stood up ready to use the paddle as a spear. In a flash, it dove under the water and was gone. For a moment, the water was still around them.

Just as Steve started to paddle away, the beast suddenly rose out of the water inches behind the canoe. This time it didn't miss as its giant jaws tore into end of the canoe. The weight of the beast pulled Steve's end of the canoe down as the other end shot up out of the water. Shelley grabbed the gunwales and tried not to slide down into Steve.

Standing inches from the flashing teeth, Steve struggled to keep his balance as the canoe rocked up and down from the monster's savage jaws. Gloria slid down the canoe toward Steve as the monster was now shaking the canoe back and forth. Terrified, Steve stabbed the thing in the eye with his paddle, but the creature didn't react to his blow.

When the monster ripped off the pointed top of the end of the canoe, the canoe scooted away leaving the creature behind. For a second, Steve watched the creature shake the piece of the canoe like a dog with a new toy. Trying to take advantage of the monster's fascination with the torn piece of canoe, Steve dug his paddle in deep. When the monster saw its prey getting away, it spit out the piece of canoe and started after them.

As he pulled his paddle up after a deep stroke, Steve glanced behind him in time to see the thing rising up out of the water ready to snatch him out of the canoe. He knew he was about to be torn apart. As the wide open jaws descended toward him, there was nothing he could do. He ducked low, but knew he was about to die.

Out of nowhere, the teenage kids returned in their streamlined speed boat and rammed the loathsome creature. Crashing over its back, the speedboat lifted out of the water like it had a hit a ramp. The kids yelled as they flew through the air bouncing on the water as they landed. Speeding away, they swung the boat in a tight circle to head back to the canoe.

Given a new chance at life, Steve dipped in his paddle and headed for the shore. As the canoe knifed through the waves, the teenagers returned in their powerboat crossing back and forth behind the canoe looking for the monster. Literally paddling for his life, Steve kept the canoe surging ahead with each stroke.

The teenagers slowed their sweptback Hustler and pulled in beside the canoe. The kid at the helm yelled, "What the hell was that thing? Jesus that was a big mother."

Steve lifted his paddle over his head and let out a primal scream that came from deep within his soul. Releasing his adrenalin, he shouted, "You saved us."

The girl in the power boat shouted, "What was that? Those teeth were totally awesome."

Steve put his paddle on the gunwales of the canoe leaning forward to rest and yelled back, "I have no idea. God, it was big. Can you circle around us 'til we get to shore? You scared him off. I don't think it'll come back if you stay with us. Maybe the noise from your motors will keep him away. At least I hope it will."

As the kids circled the canoe gunning their twin motors now and then, Steve pulled for the shore. Finally when he was in knee deep water, he waved good-bye to their motorboat saviors as he hopped out and pulled a shocked Gloria and the damaged canoe up on dry land.

CHAPTER 22

fter taking a long swig of Long Island ice tea, Dr. Lindenhurst finished a soliloquy trying to convince Harold to give the fossil skeleton to Cornell. Suddenly Steve and Gloria burst through the office door. As the men looked up, Gloria shouted, "We saw it. It almost got us. It was huge with terrible teeth."

Colby stood up and looked down at Gloria, "Dear girl, get a hold of yourself. Really, whatever are you saying? It's only a fossil."

Steve shook his head, "No, no. You don't understand. It's alive. We saw it. It tried to kill us."

With the men staring at them questioning their sanity, Steve realized he had to calm down before he could describe their encounter with a real live sea monster. Slowly he explained, "We have to tell you what we saw. What happened to us?"

Lindenhurst interjected, "But you've interrupted us. Is it important?"

"Oh, it's important." Steve told him. "Believe me it's important. You've got to hear this."

Upset by the interruption as he pleaded his case for the fossil to go to Cornell, Colby Lindenhurst waved his hand at Steve, "Then get on with it. My time is valuable."

As Steve turned to Dr. Cooper, Gloria squealed, "Tell them. Tell them."

Steve held up his hands, "We were just attacked by a relative of the fossil Annie found."

Colby interrupted, "Really? Attacked by a fossil. Gentleman these young people are wasting our time. That's enough, we have better things to do."

Harold reminded Colby, "Doctor if you want that fossil for your university, you'll hear them out."

With great reluctance, Colby put his hands on his hips and turned to Steve and Gloria, "Well."

Excited at the chance to finally tell their story, Steve shared their account of the attack trying to include every lurid detail.

Even Colby was impressed with his animation, but at the end he insisted, "Next you'll want me believe that Champ is alive in Lake Champlain and

Nessie is swimming with children in Loch Ness. If you'll excuse us, we have a serious scientific discovery to discuss."

Harold was doubtful too, but then Gloria squealed, "But wait, you haven't seen the evidence."

Caught by just a twinge of curiosity, Colby turned to Gloria with an unpleasant expression on his face as Gloria reached into her black satchel and pulled out her I-phone. Forwarding through the part of them swimming, Gloria stopped the video and asked everyone to gather around her so they could see the small screen. When they were in position with Colby standing in the back peering over the others, she touched the play arrow.

The first image they saw was Steve straining to propel the canoe forward. As he took a second stroke, a black object rose out of the water behind him. As the beast came into focus, it had a wide triangular head with large fangs. Steve turned to hit the creature with his paddle as it grabbed the canoe. Then the camera began to shake as the monster shook the canoe.

From the next images, it was obvious that Gloria had dropped her phone in the bottom of the canoe. First, you saw images of the sky and the side of the canoe. There was a quick shot of Gloria's legs as she slid along the bottom of the canoe toward Steve as the terrifying creature pulled down the end of the canoe. Another flash of the sky was followed by a glimpse of Steve stabbing at the creature's eye with his paddle. Then the I-phone became wedged in the end of the canoe pointing up. Huge dirty yellow fangs flashed across the screen. You could see huge teeth ripping off the end of the canoe. Then Gloria stopped the video. For a moment everyone was too astonished to comment.

The quiet ended with sighs of disbelief as heads shook trying to comprehend what they had just witnessed. Dan and Harold sat down while Colby paced around the office. Everyone's eyes were very animated as they stared at each other, but no one spoke.

Gloria and Steve waited for someone to break the silence and were relieved when Dan finally spoke up, "My God that is proof. I mean...did you see that? I...I never expected to see anything like that. How did you get away from it?"

Steve described again how the teenagers saved them by running over the thing with their boat and finished by declaring, "If they hadn't shown up, we wouldn't be here to share our stories and that I-phone would be at the bottom of the lake. You'd think we died in a boating accident. You'd never guess a prehistoric beast killed us."

Dan tried to analyze the video. "What did we just see? We need to put it in terms that we can understand. To me it looked like it was maybe two or three times the size of a manatee with a head something like a crocodile.

No, blunter and wider. Definitely not a croc or gator. In one of the frames, I caught a glimpse of a flipper with claws extending from it. God, it reminds me of a drawing I saw in the natural history museum…"

Standing next to him, Colby interrupted, "No, no what you saw was a living pliosaur. They have filmed a relative of the fossil I found in the crater. What an incredible moment to be alive. This would answer how the fossil could be found in strata that formed after these animals supposedly died off. Evidently not all of them died. Coupled with Cooper's DNA, this animal is clearly a living relative of my fossil. We have proof that prehistoric aquatic carnivores have survived in Cayuga Lake. But before we are dismissed as the psycho fringe, we need to put it all together. Formulate a plan."

On a hunch, Colby asked, "Gloria, my dear girl, what did you think of the slick you saw today?"

Surprised by his question, Gloria found it difficult to switch off her emotions and return to the mundane. "I took the samples you wanted. I won't know what it is until I get back to the lab."

Impatient with her answer, Colby pressed for something more definitive. "Dear girl, you have been testing water from the lake in your lab for months. Surely you must be able to make a prediction about what you saw today based on your research."

Gloria understood he wanted an educated guess, but she had always been intimidated by Lindenhurst and found it difficult to think with him staring down at her. Finally she gathered up enough courage to say, "This is certainly preliminary and may not be proven correct by the results…

Colby interrupted, "To the point, girl."

"As I was about to say, the good doctor is correct. I have been testing drinking water for environmental groups worried that the fracking at the north end is polluting the lake. So far I have found traces of what I believe is fracking fluid. Not enough to be detected by the citizens drinking it yet, but still I'm pretty sure. I have filtered out the fluid, have smelled it, tasted it and analyzed it. The samples of the slick I gathered today smelled like the same fluid I've been filtering out for weeks only this slick is much stronger. Based on my very preliminary observations, I would say large amounts of fracking fluid are leaching into the lake. I say a large amounts because a smaller dispersion would stay at the bottom. There must be enough fluid seeping into the lake that it is starting to rise to the surface. Again, I must caution you that at this point it is only my opinion not much more than a guess."

Exasperated Colby replied, "A guess based on your professional expertise. Thank you my dear. That wasn't so hard was it? The problem before us is what if anything does this have to do with our pliosaur?"

Dr. Cooper nodded understanding where Lindenhurst was going. "I see two problems we have to solve before we release this information to the public. First, how does an animal this size maintain a breeding population without interacting with humans. Second, why do they start interacting with us now? I would speculate the animal prefers the depths of the lake. They only surface for air and do that at night or early in the morning when the lake is quiet. When they do come to the surface, they try to avoid man. There are certainly enough fish to feed a breeding population."

"As for the human interaction, I bet humans have seen them. The sightings have been dismissed as fish or at least something much less astounding. But you still have to ask why are we seeing them now? I think Gloria has given us the final piece of the puzzle. I think the fracking fluid is pushing them away from the bottom. This new pollution released into their previously pristine home at the bottom of the lake has forced them to the surface. Believe it or not, gas pollution is fracking up dinosaurs."

Colby itched his chin with his thumb and forefinger, "Precisely my boy. A good hypothesis based on the available facts. It provides a practical explanation people can understand. We must think about this and meet again before we release this information. I will get the press to hold off on the story of our fossil. Dr. Cooper, we need to organize our data. Right now, I still find this discovery hard to believe and I've seen the evidence. The press will accuse us of faking this tape so we need copies that we can get verified as authentic. I have a network media contact who can certify that the film has not been photo shopped. Gloria and is it, Steve?"

Steve nodded.

"Right, Steve. You have done something incredible today. You'll get full credit for this video. If we do this right, there will be fame and monetary rewards for all of us. Fame is nice, but you may have found the pot of gold at the end of the rainbow."

Before they left, Steve insisted, "Gloria and I have agreed that before we surrender the tape, we want to share it with Shanty and Annie. For them this will be a spiritual experience. It confirms their legends."

Colby turned to Harold with a quizzical look on his face and then remembered, "Oh yes, the Indian girl and boy. Can they be trusted?"

Harold answered, "Of course. Now before we leave I want you to form a team. Drop your personal claims to the fossil. Now it's only a piece of the puzzle. You need to collaborate."

Colby reluctantly agreed "For the time being, I will relent and share the credit for discovering the fossil, but only to publish this amazing story of prehistoric survival."

Dan challenged him. "You don't deserve any credit for discovering the fossil. You are on record calling it a fake. Credit for finding it belongs to Annie Brandt."

Harold lifted his hand, "The fossil will be extracted and examined by a team of scientists from both universities. You and Colby will lead that team and the fossil will be named "Annie.""

****

Ruth pulled into the short driveway next to Charley Morgan's small bunga-low. There was just enough room to get off the lake road and park behind his pickup. She really wanted to meet him at the restaurant, but he had insisted that picking him up was part of the deal. *Anything to make a...what did he call me? A Suit. Yes that was it.* She thought. *Anything to make a Suit wait on him for a change.*

She knew Charley wanted to take full advantage of her, but didn't mind. After their experience in the mine, she hoped picking him up would show him how much she appreciated his bravery during the quake. She shud-dered when she thought of being down there in that horrid hole when the earth above and below her started shaking. From now on, she would stay on top of the world where it was safe.

Ruth expected him to be waiting outside, but of course he wasn't there. As she walked down the stone pathway to his door, she thought, *I should have brought him flowers and chocolates.*

Looking around, she noticed it was a pretty lot with a line of large pine trees on each side of his house reaching down to the lake. Tied to a short dock was a flat fishing boat with two swivel seats. When she knocked on the door, nothing happened so she knocked again with more force. Prepar-ing to leave, the door finally opened.

Through the storm door, Charley shouted, "Sorry, I nodded-off. Be with you in a second. Please, please c'mon in."

After such a gracious welcome, Hilda pulled open the glass storm door and stepped inside. To the left was a long living room with a large flat screen hanging on the wall across from a couch. At the end of the room sliding doors opened to a deck overlooking the lake. To the right was an office area with a desk leading into a kitchen with a small eating area that also had a great view of the lake.

Small, but efficient, she thought. *Everything was clean and comfortable.* It was spotless. That surprised her.

Charley emerged from a door to her right. As he did, she noticed the bedspread was so tight a drill sergeant would appreciate it. Dressed in kaki Dockers, his light blue knit shirt accentuated his blue eyes. With his hair slicked back, he looked almost, well, handsome. That surprised her.

As they walked to her car, Charley apologized for not being ready. She tried to convince him that she wasn't upset, but he didn't seem to get the message. As they neared her car, he rushed ahead to open the door for her. When she was in, he ran around the car and folded himself into the passenger seat. He seemed quite excited. That surprised her.

Almost with glee, he told her he had always wanted to ride in her car and called it, "A real beauty."

Still parked behind his pickup, she asked, "Do you want to drive it?"

With glee, he answered, "Ya mean it?"

After she nodded, he rocketed out of the car, ran around it and opened her door. After escorting her around to the passenger side, she noticed his eyes lingered on her legs as her skirt hiked up when she swung into the passenger seat. That surprised her.

Then Charley ran around the car again and tried to jump into the driver's seat. With the seat up for a shorter driver, he bumping his knee hard on the steering column, "Mother fa..." but caught himself. Embarrassed he looked at her, "Sorry." He found the seat release and shoved the seat back so he could climb in.

He carefully pulled out of the driveway then accelerated through the twist and turns of the lake road steadily increasing the speed until they were racing down the road. He was surprised Ruth didn't complain and tell him to slow down.

Ruth enjoyed having someone else drive and smiled knowing she normally drove even faster on her way to work. As he rushed down the highway he asked, "Where too?"

"I have reservations at ZaZa's Cucina."

"Is that the one on Cascadilla with the covered arch entry?"

"That's it. Have you been there?"

"I'm more of a pizza and beer kind of guy. But since you're paying, I don't mind moving up in class tonight."

"It's definitely on me. I want to thank you for your brilliant idea to increase production."

"That may be the first time I've been called brilliant in my life."

"Well, you deserve it. And in the mine today. I don't know what I'd done without you."

"Hey tonight is for good food and fun. Forget production and quakes. I've spent half my life in the salty depths of hell. Tonight, I want to enjoy myself on top of the world. I don't date much. I've been looking forward to tonight."

He's treating this like a date, Ruth thought. That surprised her.

When they reached the city limits he slowed down to five miles an hour over the speed limit. Without asking for directions, he went directly to her favorite restaurant. Ruth ate there at least once a week and knew the owners, Lex and Falminia.

Lex met them at the door and personally showed them to a secluded table in the corner near the fireplace away from the bar. Charlie looked around like a school boy eating out for the first time. Surprised the restaurant was so big, he called it elegant at least three times on the way to the table. After they were seated, Lex told Ruth how nice it was to have such a loyal patron back with them.

With a flourish, Lex announced tonight they would start with Semolina Crusted fried calamari with a side of his famous pomodoro sauce. The main course would be a special Saltimbocca. For Charley's benefit, he explained that would be veal cutlets and Prosciutto di Parma sautéed with butter and a white wine sauce finished off with a sprinkle of fresh sage.

At the end of the meal, Lex told them they'd have a special treat. "Bepi Tosolini grappa."

Easy for you to say, Charley thought, as Lex explained a new shipment of this special liquor had just arrived from Italy. Charley didn't understand half of what he said, but it all sounded good. He would have been satisfied with spaghetti and meatballs, but this sounded better. Certainly more elegant.

Before the meal, they shared a bottle of Taurasi merlot straight from Italy. By the time the wheat encrusted squid arrived looking like small onion rings, Charley was feeling relaxed as the wine loosened his tongue. Enjoying the evening, he told Ruth she didn't have to keep thanking him for saving her in the mine and told her to forget the mine. What he wanted to know was how a little girl grew up to be a salt mining exec.

Feeling the effects of the wine, Ruth felt comfortable with this guy and that surprised her. "My father owned a salt mine in Michigan. After college I couldn't find a job so he pulled some strings to get me a job on his staff. I showed my dad and the other men in the organization that I could more than hold my own."

"I've noticed your car parked there when I go to work on the late shift and it's there when I get off. Don't you ever sleep?"

"My life is simple. I work, sleep and go back to work."

After Lex opened another bottle of Merlot, Charley confessed, "I have a much more varied life. I work, sleep, fish and go back to work. I don't drink much. Most of the bars are closed when I leave work. I can't remember the last time I saw stars in the night sky. Occasionally the moon is still there when I drive home in the morning."

"How do you go back down there day after day or should I say night after night. I'll never go down there again if I can avoid it. I'll have nightmares of the lights going out with the whole world shaking around me. I thought I was going to be crushed under tons of salt."

"You were there on a very bad day. Believe me, I don't want to go through that again either. When I concentrate on my job, the environment disappears. It's like your fancy office. After you hang your degrees and awards on the wall, you forget them. The mine is my work space. That's all. After a while you don't give your surroundings a second thought. You just do your job."

"I have windows."

"I have a light on my hat."

"I had one on too, but the bright yellow helmet clashed with my outfit."

"You looked good. I hope the salt dust didn't ruin your expensive suit. Crawling out that elevator couldn't have been good for your clothes."

"A small sacrifice when I thought I was going to die."

Charley was silent and thought a moment, "Until tonight, I thought we were very different. I guess our basics are about the same."

"How so?"

"We work, sleep and go back to work. There are differences. Each night, I throw my Hungary Man frozen dinners in the microwave and grab a beer. You, on the other hand, come to a fancy place like this to have dinner with wine. Don't get me wrong, this is great. I appreciate the experience, but I could never come here alone."

"Why come alone?"

"No family, no friends and an ex-wife who didn't want to be married to a mole."

"Me too. No friends or significant other, but I come here alone."

"I'm too old to learn new tricks. Give me a good frozen dinner and a Bud. I'd starve without my microwave."

"Yuck, frozen dinners. You're not too old to learn. I come here alone once and sometimes twice a week. My waist shows it. Anytime you want to come here just give me a call, but next time we split the check. You can't freeload off me forever."

"Your waist is just fine. No problems there."

Embarrassed, but pleased by his compliment, Ruth blushed. Both the compliment and the heat in her body surprised her. It was the first compliment on her looks that she had received in a long time.

Charley noticed her blush, but didn't say anything. "I'm not freeloading. I earned this dinner doing a *Suit's* job. My suggestions will save the salt mine enough money to pay for this evening and your salary."

"If you're blasting advice works, you'll make me a star." Ruth raised her glass and toasted him, "To the man who may have saved my career."

After their glasses clinked, the Saltimbocca arrived with a flourish. Soon they were both concentrating on this tasty delight without much conversation between bites. Ruth was pleased. An evening she had dreaded was turning out to be pleasant, even fun.

Charley realized his plan to stick the *Suit* with the bill was turning into the human contact he'd missed for a long time. Between gulps, he asked, "You like to fish?"

"Never had the time. Besides, I'm not sure I want to get that close to worms."

"Hey, you could use lures that don't wiggle. I could teach you to pull in the big ones."

Is he asking me out again? Another date? That surprised her.

Near the end of the meal, Lex arrived with the grappa. As Charley tried a sip of the fine wine brandy, Lex assured them it aided digestion and insisted it was the only way to cap off their dining experience.

Charley found the grappa potent. Sort of like a pleasant tasting lighter fluid. When it was gone, he told her, "That was smooth. Would you like some more."

Before Ruth could answer, Lex was at the table filling their glasses. This time he left the bottle.

Enjoying the ambience and conversation, Ruth sipped her refill and suggested, "I know how we could change our lives."

"How's that?"

"One week, I'll take you to one of my favorite places and the next you take me to one of yours."

"Honestly, I don't have a special place to take you. I used to go to Pete's bar downtown, but when they put in new toilets, it became *Yupified*. Too many of the places around here are so full of college kids I feel uncomfortable."

"Even a college place is better than sitting at home."

"That's not a very high bar. How would this diner thing work?"

"I don't know. Maybe we pick a place we've never been to. If we like it we put it on a return list. If we don't like it, we never go back."

"I'd want to come back here."

"Then we put on it on our return list."

"We'd just pick a place?"

"Out of the yellow pages or off the internet."

"Might work. You ever been to a Greek restaurant? I remember drinking ouzo once, but that's all I remember about the evening."

"That's the spirit. Greek it is. The Souvlaki House has been there forever. We could try that and I haven't been to an Indian restaurant in a long time."

"We could eat our way around the world." Charley told her as he reached across the table and held her hand. That surprised her.

In no hurry to end the evening, Charley drove the speed limit on the way back to his place as they chatted about their plan. After parking behind his truck, he hustled around the car to open Ruth's door. As she stood up to get out, he put his strong arms on the top of the small car trapping her between them.

"In the mine during the quake, I made a resolution that if I got out alive, I would change my life. Life is too short to just work and sleep. I want to live while I still have a chance and tonight, I discovered you're my chance. I'm a simple guy, not cultured like you, but I could grow on you. I enjoyed being with you tonight."

Then he bent down and kissed Ruth.

Ruth was so surprised, she was slow to respond. It had been so long since she had been kissed that the whole situation seemed foreign to her. When he pulled back, she realized this was a moment she had been waiting for all her life.

CHAPTER 23

Walking back to Shanty's cabin amazed by the video, Annie suggested to Steve and Gloria that they have an impromptu campfire to celebrate.

"I'm sorry. I've got to ride back with Dr. Lindenhurst."

After Annie volunteered to drive her home after the campfire, Gloria announced, "Sounds good to me. I do like to party."

Shanty winked at Annie, "Maybe Steve could take her back. I'll need you to help me cleanup." As he threw the keys to Steve, he asked, "Would you mind driving her home?"

"Not at all."

"Better drive her over to the hotel and let her tell Lindenhurst she has another way home."

Annie smiled, since Hilda had been driving Shanty had become less protective of his pickup.

Shanty and Billy were building a fire as an old silver jeep pulled up next to his cabin. Harold and Ursula jumped out of the back seat as Dan and Shelley climbed out the front. Surprised, Shanty welcomed his new guests.

Dan led the group to the fire, "I hope you don't mind a few party crashers. When I heard about the fun from Gloria, I gave Shelley a call to join us."

When they were alone, Dan whispered to Shelley, "I've got to convince Harold to rethink donating the fossil to Cornell. I've got to become his best buddy. Use your considerable charms to help me."

Shanty welcomed them as Billy ran to the cooler to get beers for the Director and his wife just as Steve and Gloria showed up in Shanty's pickup. The party was on.

The personal dynamics of the campfire that evening were interesting. Annie and Billy were definitely a couple. They were glued to each other the whole evening. Hilda arrived alone and at first she sat down near Shanty. Little by little, she moved closer to him until she was sitting next to him. As Annie watched her timid moves, she was proud of her girl.

Shelley sat next to Harold being pleasant and charming while Dan sat on the other side of him talking about the fossil. Ursula roamed and talked to every male. Finally she settled down on the other side of Shanty doing her best to enchant him while she glared at Steve who was oblivious to her anger.

Steve was enjoying Gloria and at least for the evening, they were a couple.

When Link showed up with his arm around Lea's waist, Lea was disappointed when Steve didn't seem to notice or care. Annie enjoyed the evil looks sparking across the campfire and told Billy to watch the fun. Billy was the only man there who saw the fangs of jealousy being flashed back and forth between these women. Throughout the evening, Hilda was astounded as Ursula pursued Shanty right in front of her husband. She was upset, but at the same time admired Ursula's brazen confidence.

From the beginning of the campfire, talk of the Cayuga sea monster, or Apotamkon as Shanty and Annie called him, was the only topic of conversation. Gloria passed around her cell phone for everyone to see. When Gloria retrieved her I-phone, Dan cautioned her to be careful with it. It was the only visual proof they had of the lake monster. Gloria assured him that she had already sent text copies to Lindenhurst and him.

Shanty quieted his audience to tell them the Iroquois legend of Tatoskok. As everyone settled back, he explained his ancestors had seen demons in Lake Champlain and always honored them after a good harvest.

When he finished, Dan told everyone that in 1609, Samuel de Champlain, the namesake of the lake, reported seeing a sea monster in it. Since that early sighting, others had seen it too. "Today this sea monster is called "Champ."

Then Dan told them of another lake monster. "In western Canada on Lake Okanagan, a sea demon called "Naitaka" by the Indians is now called "Ogopogo" in the newspapers. Lake Okanagen is long, narrow and deep like Cayuga. All the descriptions I've read of this creature describes a pliosaur. The similarity of these sightings could certainly be a coincidence, but with what we learned today, this creature might be real too."

When Shanty asked why Apotamkon would suddenly be more visible, Dan explained his theory of fracking pollution causing this aquatic reptile to spend more time on the surface.

Dan worked the discussion around to the fate of the fossil and was disappointed when Harold announced, "I'm giving it Cornell. This will ensure it gets the proper academic scrutiny. Besides, it's my alma mater."

Cooper objected, but did it carefully, claiming that since he was part of the discovery, Ithaca College should be the final resting place for this fantastic fossil. "Lindenhurst called it a fraud. He doesn't deserve to have it at his school."

Harold remained firm, "You're a geologist. Lindenhurst is an odd duck, but he is a world renowned paleontologist."

Shelley put her arm around Dan's back and pinched him. When he looked at her, she said under her breath, "Stop. Not the right time or place." Dan understood and surrendered.

Then Annie entered the fight for her fossil. "I found that fossil and without me it would still be sitting out there all alone. I think I should have at least been consulted before you gave it away. You people see it as a bunch of interesting bones. Shanty and I see this as a part of our heritage. It confirms our legends. In many ways, it is a religious artifact for our people. It was my hope this relic from our past would be given to the Mashantucket Pequot Museum. There it would be available to any college or university researcher. And it wouldn't be hidden from the public. This find is too important for one or two professors to hide it in the backroom of their research lab to use for their fame and fortune."

As she begged Harold to reconsider, he was surprised. This was the first time he realized that Annie had a personal interest in the fossil.

Shanty echoed Annie's claim, "My sister's right. What you call a fossil is part of the dust and blood of my ancestors. My forefathers lived with that beast. We would honor it as part of our heritage. I'm not against science, but this find, as you call it, should be respected while it's studied."

Harold was upset with Cooper, but the idea of this fossil being part of the Native American tradition caught him unaware. Shaking his head, he agreed to give his donation more thought.

To relieve the tension, Billy brought out his guitar and started playing. Soon everyone tried their best to sing the old folk songs. Part way through his repertoire, Gloria asked to borrow his guitar and took over the show entertaining them with soulful Country and Western ballads. She finished with a rendition of 'Cherokee Nation' that made them all think of the Native American heritage surrounding the lake.

Dan and Shelley were the first to leave explaining they had a long drive back. Harold invited them to stay in one of the guest rooms in the hotel, but Dan politely declined. In his jeep on the way home, they discussed what home meant to them. They realized that they were a couple now and their home was where their hearts were.

Ursula had been urging Harold to drink the whole evening. When he finished a beer, she was quick to ply him with another. Harold was a bit tipsy and felt completely in tune with the world.

When Annie noticed the cooler was almost empty, she asked Shanty to get a case of beer from his cabin to replenish it. Shanty nodded and headed to the cabin. When Ursula saw him leave, she let Gloria entertain Harold with another song while she followed Shanty.

Ursula carefully opened the screen door to the cabin and quietly tiptoed up behind Shanty before sliding her arms around his waist and kissing the back of his neck. Surprised, he turned around and Ursula pulled him close and kissed him on the lips.

Shanty wondered. *How can a woman sneak up on a Mohawk warrior without me hearing her? My ancestors will be disappointed in me.*

But her touch. Her touch was unwelcome. He pushed her away saying in a firm voice, "No." He wanted nothing to do with the Director's wife. He was about to tell her to leave when another body pushed through the screen door.

Hilda had followed Ursula when she saw her trapesing after Shanty. She witnessed Ursula's attempt to force herself on Shanty and saw Shanty reject the bitch. Joining them in the cabin, she spoke up. "Ursula, you need to get back to Harold. You know your husband. You're not welcome here. Back to my brother, now."

Ursula turned with a sneer, "This guy is all yours. He's as boring as you are."

Suddenly Hilda found herself standing alone in front of Shanty not knowing what to do. How could she explain why she was there? Maybe, she could convince him that she had followed Ursula because she was tired of her cheating on Harold? *That might work.*

Before she could offer an excuse, Shanty grinned. "Thanks for the rescue. I was about to tell her to get lost. Your brother has been good to me and I wouldn't do anything to jeopardize his support."

"I was following her cause…I..,I…"

"You don't have to explain. That's not the first time she's tried that. It's always awkward. Thanks for saving me. Glad that you're here. I'm glad you came to the campfire tonight."

"Happy to be here until I saw Ursula try to seduce you. I just wish my brother could see how she behaves. He needs to get rid of her. With his money, he could buy a dozen like her. He might even find one who didn't love him for his money."

Shanty stepped toward her, "Forget her. I've been wanting to be alone with you all the evening."

As his words rang in her ears, Shanty embraced and kissed her. As he leaned over, Hilda stood on her tiptoes to meet his lips. All thoughts of Ursula vanished as he kissed her. Truly lost in the moment, every part of her was delighted as she hugged him tight. Being close to him was exciting and felt right.

After a moment, she didn't want to end, Shanty pushed her back, "That's been on my mind for a long time."

Hilda didn't say word because she had no idea what to say. Her mind was blank.

Her silence spooked Shanty. When he started to apologize, she threw herself against him and hugged his neck. This time she kissed him as they both learned that at times, words just get in the way.

When they separated again, Shanty looked down into her eyes, "I've wanted to talk to you for a while now. Well, actually more than talk. I don't want to sound condescending, but I'm proud of you. I've been tough on you, but you've met every challenge."

Hilda answered from her heart without thinking. "You are very special, No, no more than that... I...I'm not sure... what...to say."

"Then don't say a thing."

They embraced again for their most passionate kiss yet.

After a moment of sharing, Hilda pushed back not daring to reveal her true feelings, "Thanks to you, I can now do dirty without falling apart."

Shanty laughed. "Dirt happens." Nodding toward the door. "We'd better get back." As he passed her, he added, "You're the surprise. I had written you off as a lost cause. There is much more to you than I expected."

"Thanks, I think." Hilda answered as she followed him out the door.

On the porch, he turned to her again. This time their bodies touched as they kissed. When they started down the steps and their hands met. Shanty laughed, "The beer. I forgot the beer." After he returned for the case, Hilda held the screen door open for him.

When they returned to the campfire, Shanty refilled the ice chest while Hilda stood beside him. Everyone had seen their long kiss on the porch and couldn't help but notice they were holding hands when returned to their seats near the fire.

Harold wasn't sure what it meant, but was excited for his sister. Ursula thought. *He turned me down for that.* Annie was dumbfounded and clapped her hands telling Billy her project was working. It was the first time she had seen her brother make any move toward a woman since Afghanistan.

Steve noticed and was relieved. *Now,* he thought, *maybe you'll stop stalking me.* Passing up Lea tonight, he decided he'd to stick to his creed, *Love the one I'm with.*

As the campfire burned low, the couples filtered off in different directions. Lea watched Steve walk Gloria down the beach after Harold and

Ursula left for the hotel. Then Billy and Annie walked down the beach in a different direction to find a spot to be alone.

Shanty and Hilda were staring at the embers when Lea stood up and yelled, "No way I'm gon'na put up with this."

She went to the cooler and threw off the top. Mad as hell, she threw the beers on the ground next to it. Then she picked up the cooler with icy water sloshing around in the bottom and lugged it off down the shore with Link, Hilda and Shanty following her to the water's edge.

Lea knew where Steve was because he had taken her to the exact the same place on the beach several times. When she spotted Steve with his new country and western star laying on his towel hidden in a slight depression in the beach, she stood above them and poured the icy water over her ex-summer boyfriend and his new partner.

As screams ricocheted off the lake like flat stones skipping across the surface, Steve tried to catch his breath as the bitter cold penetrated his body. With his friends clapping, he rolled away from Gloria.

Gloria jumped up shouting, "What is wrong with you people." Swiping her wet hair out of her eyes, she ran back to the fire shaking the freezing water off her clothes.

Steve grabbed the towel they had been laying on to rub off the cold water and laughed with his friends. "Thanks Lea, I should have seen that coming. After all, this used to be our spot. At least one of them. Don't worry, we're not over. I think Gloria may be rethinking our relationship."

Lea wasn't exactly sure what he meant, but hoped it was an apology or at least an invitation.

Alone on the beach in a space of their own, Billy interrupted a long kiss and embrace when he heard the screams down the beach.

Annie looked up at him, "A little noise is more interesting than me?"

"Sorry, the yells interrupted my concentration. Believe me, you are much more important to me than anything else."

"I should hope so Billy Barton. By the way, I don't want to be your friend."

"What?"

"I don't want you as a friend. Your pledge to be a friend and not a lover is over or I'm going back to Connecticut."

"You mean...."

"Yes, an adult relationship. All or nothing. Your choice."

CHAPTER 24

The next morning, a tired Dan Cooper walked stiffly into his lab carrying a cardboard tray of coffee followed by Shelley with newspapers tucked under her arm. He had spent a sleepless night trying to figure out a way to get Grayson to donate the fossil to Ithaca College and now he was paying the price. After setting the tray down carefully on a lab table, he pulled out his cup hoping the jolt of the dark black brew would give him the energy he needed to make it through the day. After Shelley handed him the *New York Times*, he retired to his office and leaned back in his desk chair to peruse the news.

Sitting in the lab sipping her creamy latté, Shelley opened the *Ithaca Times*. Just below the fold on the front page a picture made her shout, "Oh my God."

As she ran into his office, Dan immediately folded his paper down and looked over the top. "What's up?"

"Your plan to keep the Cayuga monster a secret may need to be revised."

"Why?"

Shelley handed him the paper and pointed, "Look at this."

After Dan took the paper, it didn't take him long to discover the problem. A blurry, but easily recognizable picture of Steve and Gloria's lake monster chomping down on the end of the canoe was on the front page for everyone to see. The article proclaimed, "Sea Monster Attack in Cayuga" and informed the reader that several teenagers had photographed this prehistoric creature attacking people in a canoe. It gave the teenagers credit for scaring it away by running over it in their motorboat. Just before they hit this beast, the article informed the reader, Anna Hogan snapped this shot with her cell phone.

Dan yelled, "Damn it. Get Lindenhurst on the line."

Soon Shelley handed Dan the lab modular phone. "Did you see...yeah, I was surprised too."

"The paper has already called you? You should say something...I'm not sure. Maybe you should tell them you're investigating it."

"Yes, that's good. You'll comment later...Sure, use my name."

A Deal...The Exploration Channel...Great work and fast...How much? Really! TV pays that much? At the camp, great. See you then."

Dan told Shelley the papers were already pestering Lindenhurst for comments on the authenticity of picture and then with a smile, he broke the news that the National Exploration Channel (NEC) wanted to produce a video based on the lake monster. Dan added that they wanted to interview all the people who witnessed the monster and guaranteed everyone would be paid. He didn't mention that as an expert he would get an extra stipend almost equal to his salary.

＊＊＊＊

With some reluctance, Hilda opened the door of the Camp Director's office. Looking up from his laptop, Harold pushed back in his desk chair and waved her in. Deciding to do something she had never done before, Hilda sat down in the chair next to his desk. Before she could start, Harold complimented her on how she had changed and told her he had never been so happy for her. With effusive glee, he expressed how much he appreciated her new interest in the camp.

Glowing from the compliments, Hilda waited politely for him to finish. Finally getting a chance to talk, she gave all the credit for her new outlook on life to Shanty, Annie and Billy Barton. She explained they were all real friends who cared more for others than they cared about themselves.

That brought her to the reason she had come to talk to Harold. "Last night you said you were going to give Annie's fossil to Cornell University. I want you reconsider that donation. For the university, the fossil is only a scientific find. It has no emotional value. To Shanty and Annie it's personal. To their people it's spiritual. If you let Annie's museum have it, it will be open to more researchers than if you give it to Cornell. But more important, it will be treated with respect. It will be revered. That's something we don't think about in today's society. Please give it to the Pequot museum."

Harold didn't respond immediately. For a moment, he thought about how to respond. "You think I made a snap decision to donate the fossil to Cornell. That's not true. Yes, Cornell is my alma mater and I have great respect for the university. That's part of the reason, but it is also a top notch research institution. I know Lindenhurst is a weird old guy, but he is respected throughout the world. He has great contacts everywhere. This find belongs to Cayuga Lake. A discovery this important should remain close to home. However, I never thought of the Indian, pardon me, the

Native American connection. I agree that they perceive it in a totally different manner than we do."

Hilda continued to prod him. "Then change it. Americans have never respected their culture. We can't change history, but you can do the right thing now. You can make a difference and open this important discovery up to more scientists. Cornell is not the only university in the world. In fact, Ithaca College certainly has as much claim to it as Cornell."

"But the Pequot Museum is so close to Yale. I don't want them to dominate this find. Never did have much use for that degree mill. Tell you what, I'll think about it."

"I need to talk to you about something else. I have supported Mr. Brandt and his sister has been a gem this summer, but Ursula just told me that Mr Brandt has approached her on several occasions trying to convince her to have sex with him. I also know Brandt hasn't always been completely truthful with me. He runs a winter camp for young men and women from the Onondaga reservation. I looked the other way because I think it's a good idea to use the camp year round, but he should have asked me first. I'm going to fire him at the end of the summer. That will end his problem with Ursula and end the debate as to where the fossil should go at the same time."

Incensed Hilda wasn't sure where to start. She stood up sputtering, "It's...It's Ursula you can't trust. Not Shanty. At the campfire last night, I followed them into the cabin. I...I saw Ursula approach Shanty, not the other way around..."

Harold held up his hand to shut her off, "I knew you'd say something like that. I saw you and Brandt holding hands last night. Yes and the kiss on his porch. You've always had it in for Ursula. You're emotionally involved. I'm glad you're letting others into your life, but Brandt isn't what you need."

"You have no idea what I need. Shanty is the most honest and...and level headed person I've ever met. You don't get it. Ursula lies to you. All she wants is your money. She doesn't give a damn about you."

"Don't say that about her. If you were nicer to her, you'd discover she's got a good heart."

"No, she's doesn't. Shanty is a good person. You should see the plans he has to expand your camp into a year round retreat. He isn't lying to you. He wants to surprise you. His plans are incredible. You should be paying him a lot more than you are. And...and instead you believe that whore you call your wife."

Now Harold was mad. Standing up, he shouted back, "Don't ever call her that again. She's my wife for God's sake. Don't ever forget that again. Treat her with respect. You disrespect her, you disrespect me. Brandt has been trying to take advantage of her and now he's doing the same to you."

"You just said you're happy that I've changed. Shanty is the reason I've changed. He's a great guy. Certainly a better person than either of us."

"Has he told you I hired him to work with you?"

"What?"

"I told him you needed help. I bribed him to take you under his wing. I told him I'd pay him extra if he helped you."

"You son-of-a-bitch. He wouldn't do something like that."

"Go ask him."

"I will." Hilda charged out of Harold's office with tears flowing down her cheeks.

It was lunchtime. Hilda checked the dining hall, but evidently Shanty wasn't eating with the campers today. Hilda left the hall and stormed off to his cabin. Breathing hard, she rounded the corner of his cabin and found him sharing a salad with Annie on the porch.

In an angry voice with tears streaking down her face, she yelled, "You bastard. My brother paid you to be nice to me. I actually thought you cared for me. How could you do that? "

Feeling guilty and defensive, Shanty shouted back at her, "That's right. Your brother asked me to help you and I did. There's nothing wrong with that. Back then, I thought you were a spoiled mean irritating bitch and you were. Now I know you are much more than that. I don't regret one minute I've spent with you."

Feeling hurt and betrayed, Hilda realized she didn't know how to handle the situation beyond shouting at him again. To add to her confusion, she didn't want to keep crying and reveal how much she cared for him. To get away, she turned and ran down to the lake shore.

When Shanty started after her, Annie grabbed his arm, "No let me go. You've already done enough. Calling her a bitch really helped. You might want to rethink that."

Hilda stopped just beyond the campfire site looking out at the lake crying. When Annie caught up to her, between gasps Hilda told her, "I...I don't...don't want to talk to you. Go...go away."

"You're going to talk to me. You think you know the whole story, but you don't."

"I know your brother lied to me. Let me think he cared. And you, you're not much better. Acting like my friend."

"That's right. If you blame anyone, blame me. It wasn't my brother or Harold that thought up the idea of putting you and my brother together. It was me."

"What do you know about anything?"

"It was all my idea."

"What was your idea?"

"Everything. You may not know it, but you and Shanty are a lot alike."

"That's crazy. I can't think of two more different people."

"Yes, you're different in many ways, but you're also alike in one important way."

"What's that?"

"You're both damaged people."

"Thanks, you're full of compliments just like your brother. Go away. Leave me alone. I don't need either of you." Hilda turned and started to walk away.

Annie firmly pulled her back, "No, you need to hear this. My brother was inelegant, but pretty much on the mark. Compare the fun you had last night at the campfire to the woman you were before you started to working with Joey. Mean and unfriendly are pretty accurate. I apologize for him calling you a bitch, but he's a man. What do they know?"

Hilda gulped a laugh between her sobs as Annie continued, "I would add scared, introverted and shy. You had little or no confidence and you were dedicated to driving away anyone who wanted to get to know you."

"I don't need you to tell me my problems. I'm well aware of them. Your brother was paid to like me by my brother. Now you're trashing me. Great friends you two turned out to be."

"We're better friends than you think. Let me tell you about Shanty. He's the reason I'm here this summer. He's damaged too."

"Shanty damaged? Right. He's the most squared away person I know except of course for being a lying devious bastard. Oh, he's also a stubborn pigheaded know-it-all. No way he's damaged."

"Shanty graduated from college, did you know that."

"What college?"

"You know my brother's camp drawings you marveled at?"

"Yes, I'm sure my brother will be impressed."

"Done by a graduate of architectural design from Dartmouth."

"A caretaker from Dartmouth?"

"Do you remember when you were learning to rappel? He mentioned he was in the army."

"Kind of."

"He was a sergeant who lost three buddies in an attack in Afghanistan. He was wounded three times there. You're only the second person outside our family, I've ever heard him even mention his military service. Even then he dismissed it by telling you he was a grunt. He's been a recluse for four years. He hides in this camp. He only leaves this place for groceries or to go back to the reservation. I know he hasn't had a relationship with a woman for at least four years. Not since he returned from Afghanistan. That's not normal for a stud like him."

"Four years?"

"That's right, four years. Before he left, he was a woman magnet. Right now, Shanty may be the only person I know who has fewer friends than you do. But since you came into his life he's changed. In the morning, he gets up looking forward to the day. When the old mine collapsed under the cabins, his training kicked in and he saved lives. Something your brother seems to have forgotten. Shanty wanted to join the college kids on their run each morning, but wouldn't do it until I got on his case. The campfires were my idea to get him some normal social contact. Now for you."

"Me?"

"Yes you. All summer long I have been watching you. I wanted to reach out to you, but wasn't sure how. Every time I tried to talk to you, you blew me off. Then one day I was thinking about him when I saw you. I started to realize that you and Shanty had the same problem for different reasons. Neither of you have any idea how to reach out to others. Sitting in the bleachers next to Harold watching a soccer game, we started talking about you. Actually, I talked and he listened. He thinks he cooked up the idea of you working for Shanty, but I led him there. No money was involved. Shanty didn't take a dime to work with you. In fact, at first he hated the idea. I forced him to do it. Believe me, he was not easy to convince."

Hilda wiped away some tears and sat down on one of the campfire benches staring out at the lake. Annie sat next to her. "After nagging, I finally got him to try it. Harold also wanted to get you away from his office paperwork. Evidently you really screwed it up."

Wiping her eyes, Hilda smiled, "Yeah, I did."

"When you started working with Shanty, you really pissed him off. Day after day, he came back to the cabin swearing about you. Insisting it wouldn't work, but I convinced him to hang in there. Something about you told me there was a real person lurking in there trying to get out and I convinced him he could make a difference."

"Then I noticed a change. Each day after working with you, he'd start talking about you without any encouragement from me. The swearing stopped. Then he was curious about you and peppered me with questions about what made you tick. Then he started sharing his day with you with me. All this without me saying a word. When I suggested the campfire last night, it was his idea to invite you. That kiss the other night on the porch wasn't paid for. It was inspired by you."

"By me?"

"No one else."

"What do I do now?"

"Would you stay here if I go to the cabin and convince my brother to come down here? Will you promise not yell at him if I send him to you?"

"I'll wait here. How I react depends on him. And...and thank you for helping me...ah...him...us."

Shanty was pacing back and forth on the porch when Annie climbed the steps and made him sit down. When he was calm, she told him what she said to Hilda. Listening to Annie cooled him down and when Annie told him to talk to Hilda, he was ready. When he left the porch, she cautioned him, "No swearing and start by apologizing for calling her a bitch. Listen more than you talk." After he promised to behave, she let him jog to his woman.

Shanty slowed down as he approached Hilda. With his head down kicking some of the flat stone beach pebbles, he let out a weak, "Sorry."

Hilda wasn't impressed with the opening, "For what?"

"Telling the truth, but not all of it."

"So you think I'm a bitch?"

"Not now. What's important is you've changed. And so have I."

"Last night? Was that part of my brother's plan?"

"Last night was a surprise."

"Why."

"Hell, I don't know. I've been thinking about you. Trying to sort it out. You, you snuck up on me. You were a project that turned into a woman. A woman I like. When you rescued me from Ursula, you surprised me."

"Forget Ursula, what do you think of me?"

"You're stubborn, opinionated and funny. You can be a real pain-in-the-ass and I like it. You're tough and not afraid to stand up to me."

"I'm not as stubborn or bull-headed as you are."

"Maybe not, but close." Shanty laughed shaking his head. "At first I hated working with you. It took me awhile to put it together. For all your faults, you're fun to have around."

"Me too."

"Me too what?" Shanty asked.

"You used to make me mad every day and I tried to get back at you, but couldn't make you mad."

Shanty kicked the ground again, "I used to do that. Do things just to piss you off. Now I look forward to working with you. We're sort of a team."

"Why'd you kiss me last night?"

"Jesus, I don't know. It seemed like a good idea. I wanted too."

"Do you want to do it again?"

"Course."

"Well. Do I have to do everything?"

"Not everything, but I'd like you to call me Joseph. I don't mind Shanty, but I'm proud of my name."

For the first time in her life, Hilda stood up and put her arms around the neck of a man she loved. Just before she kissed him, she whispered, "Joseph."

Annie watched them from the porch. After some animated dialogue, she saw them kiss and sighed. Things seemed to be back to normal. At least normal for them.

****

Hilda's first swimming lesson with Steve was successful. After they finished, Hilda sat on the dock with Steve, Annie, and Joseph to soak up some of the beautiful soft sun while they dried on the dock. Worried, Hilda shared with them that Harold was going to fire Joseph because Ursula accused him of making frequent sexual advances toward her. Before Shanty could defend himself, Hilda told them she knew it was the other way around and described what she had seen in the cabin at the campfire. She explained that she had no idea how to convince Harold he was wrong. When it came to Ursula, he was blind.

Annie was incensed and defended her brother. She couldn't believe that Harold could consider firing the most loyal person who had ever worked for him.

All of Shanty's friends volunteered to talk to Harold alone or as a group, but none of them felt that approach would do much good. Shanty was so upset, he stood up and walked to the end of the dock and stared out at the lake with his arms folded across his chest. The others agreed Ursula was the problem. Somehow, they needed to prove she was a liar. The problem was how to expose her without Harold rushing to her defense.

Steve knew how to stop Ursula, but kept quiet. If he turned on Ursula, he might lose his job. When the dinner bell rang, everyone headed to the dining hall vowing to think of a way to save Shanty.

As the women walked up the road, Steve told Shanty he wanted him to look at a leak in his cabin roof. When they got to his cabin, Steve told him there wasn't a leak. He had a plan to expose Ursula.

****

Shanty heard his pickup skid to a stop at the side of his cabin. He didn't like Hilda taking his truck without him, but knew he had to put up with it. The main problem was the way she drove around camp. She went way too fast. One of these days he was afraid she might use a couple of campers as speed bumps. Shanty had changed. He knew he would miss her when the camp closed at the end of the summer, but the army had taught not to think of the future.

Hilda came around the porch bragging she had all the barrels he wanted to paint in the back of his truck. He was amazed she had wrestled the barrels into the bed of his pickup without him. Yes, he thought, she had impressed him in many ways. They hadn't had an opportunity to get together since their fight and he wanted to be close to her again. He just needed to find the right time.

Shanty patted the top step next to him. When Hilda sat down beside him, he handed her a large manila envelope and warned her that he was going to show her some pictures that she had to accept without asking how he got them. With a puzzled look on her face, Hilda pulled the pictures out of the envelope.

The one on top showed Ursula's naked butt in the men's shower room. Everyone in camp could identify that backside. At the end of the room was a pixilated image of a naked man. Surprised at the content, she quickly leafed through the pictures. One shot captured the lower half of the man and Hilda knew immediately it was Steve.

After all, she thought, *I saw him that time I was playing chaperone.* As she slowed to look at each photo, she noted several interesting positions she might like to try. Not with Steve, of course, but with a real man like Joseph.

When Shanty saw her reach the last photo, he told Hilda, "Keep this a secret. I don't want to get anyone in trouble 'cept Ursula. Maybe you can use these to redeem my reputation with your brother."

Nodding her head Hilda agreed, "If these don't convince Harold nothing will. These pictures make it clear she's not being forced to do anything. And there are no scars on the guy's legs so it can't be you. My brother will no longer be able to claim that Ursula is the faithful little wife he thinks she is. I take it these are my copies?"

"They're yours. I'd appreciate it if you could help me with your brother. I value this job." Embarrassed and wanting to change the subject, Shanty asked, "How the hell did you get all those barrels in the truck by yourself?"

"I'm stronger than you think. I wanted to help you. I'm the one who should be thanking you. You have literally changed my life. Given me a life. I am not the pain-in-the-ass my brother saddled you with."

"My sister shares that guilt. You certainly were...are a challenge. Christ, every night I'd come back swearing at you. Annie just told me to relax as she handed me a beer."

Wanting to keep Shanty talking so he might say something about her or even better about them, Hilda responded, "So you've changed your mind about me?"

"Sure. You're a good worker. You aren't nearly as fussy about dirt. Now and then I can see you actually enjoying the outdoors. I even saw you take a sip out of the hose last week when you thought I wasn't looking. And thank God, you stopped putting that white goop on your nose. Now, I can work a whole day with you without swearing when I get home."

"Is that all?"

"No, now you run all over the camp in my pickup. It is mine you know. It belongs to me not the camp."

"I wasn't talking about your damn truck. I was talking about me."

"What about you?"

"Damn it, the kiss at the campfire and the next day. What was that all about?

"I'd like to do it again."

"Then why the hell don't you?" Hilda almost shouted as she stamped her foot on the step. As Shanty leaned forward with a smile, Hilda eagerly threw her arms around his neck. At first, they kissed tentatively. With growing passion, they pressed against each other slowly slumping to the porch floor.

Just as they embraced, Annie came around the corner of the cabin and climbed up the steps, "You two need to get a room."

Carefully stepping over the entangled bodies, she said, "Excuse me", and went through the door with a smile.

CHAPTER 25

Dan followed Shelley back to his apartment and waited in the parking lot while she ran up to change. Looking at the interior of his new ride, he had to admit this new Jeep was a big step up from his old one. If Lindenhurst was right about the payment from the NEC, his assistance with this lake monster story would more than pay for his new ride. He reached out and touched the leather dashboard and sniffed. *Nothing like the smell of a new car.*

Shelley surprised him when she jumped in beside him, "Where are we going?" Dan laughed and drove up the West side of the lake toward the Taughannock Farms Inn. It was a fancy place just right for a proposal and besides, he wanted to test this new Jeep on the road.

Driving up the lake, Dan told Shelley he felt the environmental meeting earlier that day had gone quite well except for that one kid from Cornell. "What's his name?"

Shelley thought a second, "You mean the emaciated one with the scraggly beard?"

"Yeah, him."

"Tom Ellinger. Everybody calls him, Tommy Eee. He's sort of a new comer."

"Well, I don't like him. He tried to convince people to stick to fracking and leave the salt mine alone, but I didn't have to do a thing. Evidently the salt mine has tours and some of the other kids took one. They couldn't believe the caverns and roads under the lake. They immediately saw the potential for disaster and shut Tommy Eee up without me having to say a word."

"You call them kids. I'm not much older than them."

"All I mean is that their undergraduates. You're a graduate I happen to love." Thinking this might be a good time to pop the question, Dan continued, "Is your infatuation with the Barton kid over?"

"Yes and no."

"What does that mean?"

"Seeing him after so long was strange. When I saw him up at the collapsed mine, old feelings kicked in that I didn't even know existed. Since then I've been evaluating the relationship I have with you."

"Well, what do you think about me?"

"I decided I love you." With that Shelley leaned over and kissed his cheek. "Besides, I doubt if any other man could actually make the earth move when we make love. Remember what we were doing during that last earthquake."

"Yes, we were right in rhythm with each tremor that mother earth sent our way. Are you sure you want to eat? We could turn around and consummate that proposal."

"You're not getting out of dinner that easy, Doc. Let's have wine and cheese at the Taughannock Inn. We can consummate later."

"Now that we're engaged will you tell me how you get those ISC memos?"

"We're engaged?"

"What do you think?"

"We're engaged."

"Don't change the subject. What about those memos. Inquiring minds want to know."

"You don't know much about my family do you?"

"No, but right now let's focus on the memos?"

"Do you know who the Vice President of the International Salt Combine is?"

"Can't say that I do?"

"It's Albert Olson."

"And that's important why?"

"Do you know my last name?"

"Olson. Wait. What did you say the Vice President's name was…?"

"Now you're getting it."

"You're his daughter?"

"Can't fool you."

✱✱✱✱

Charley Morgan was tired of chauffeuring engineers around in the lonely twilight of dim electric lights. Of course in the mine that was all you had, there was no night or day. These skilled practitioners of mechanical science had finally deemed it necessary to examine the damage from the second quake and for some reason, they wanted his input. He was surprised they would give up their evening television shows to explore the mine. Insisting that they start at the bottom and work their way up, Charley led the way.

At each level they nodded and took lots of pictures without asking Charley a single question.

They treated him like a chauffeur. Finally, standing in front of the great dome above them on the top level, they turned to Charley. To answer their questions, he assured them that chunks of salt kept falling out of the dome every day and that the miners could hear the falling pieces echo throughout the mine. They were becoming superstitious and shunned the area.

He insisted this was a safety problem, but the engineers concluded it was more of a psychological problem. For the engineers the mine was as safe as ever. As they were talking, a large chunk fell from the ceiling. Charley laughed as they scurried back to the truck ready to call it a night. They had seen enough.

On the way back to the hoist, the engineers assured Charley the collapse had not weakened the overall integrity of the mine. When he kidded them about their reaction to the piece that fell, they admitted they were surprised that the ceiling on the first level kept shedding. *Shedding*, Charley thought. *An educated word to hide the fact the roof was caving in.*

When Charley quizzed the engineers on the pillars, they told him not to be concerned. They were going to increase the size of the thin pillars to withstand a 6.0 quake. There would be no more collapses. They added that a few broken pillars could not affect the overall stability of the mine. They recommended stapling around the dome and declared the problem solved.

They also pointed out to Charley that the lack of visible fractures or water leaks was a good sign. They told Charley to check this area at least once a week for the next couple of months. If he found any leaks or substantial changes, he should contact them immediately. Other than frequent inspections and stapling the ceiling, they insisted nothing else needed to done. They weren't concerned.

Charley knew their visit was a waste of time as he walked back to his desk. These guys had just placed the responsibility for all future problems on his shoulders. If something bad happened, they would blame him for not spotting it or failing to report it in a timely manner. As he started his shift report, Terry Neal sat down in the chair next to his desk.

In a respectful tone, Terry hesitatingly asked, "Do you have a minute? I...I need to talk to you."

"Sure, what's up?"

"It's about that last quake. I was really scared. My mind flashed back to Afghanistan. I've been having nightmares about the war and this mine. I'm not cut out to be a miner."

"Hey, you aren't alone. I've been in the mine over thirty years and thought it was coming down on my head. Hell, being scared isn't supposed be part of this job, but that quake was something I never want to live through again. You stepped up. Saved lives. Prevented a panic. You were calm and sure as hell impressed me. Son, if anyone down here acted like a miner, it was you. If you were scared, you hid it well."

"I got the hoist working because I wanted out of this damned hole. I rode on top to make sure I on the first trip out. I didn't go up on that hoist because I was brave."

"Don't care why you did it. You still did it. Hell, in the military you'd get a medal. Your motives don't matter."

"They matter to me. I was lucky to get out of Afghanistan alive. I'm not sure putting my life on the line again for a job is worth it. I've got a family."

"You should think of your family. I wouldn't have wanted to serve overseas, but you did. Now you're home. This is a good job. Don't judge your time in the mine by these last couple of quakes. I have lived through the exact same number of serious quakes that you have. Quakes are very unusual around here. You shouldn't let them dictate your future as a miner. If you can't stand the claustrophobia of a mine then you aren't a miner. That's not a problem for you. You're a miner and I'm a miner. Both of us were scared. Give it a few months before you leave a job that pays this well."

"For me working in a mine isn't much different than being under a tank or working in a Quonset hut, but the shaking got to me. Reminded me of when an IED blew up under a hummer I was riding in. The ground moved. We were tossed in the air like rag dolls. Felt just like the quake. Two of my buddies were killed and I was sitting between them. Do you believe that? Between them. Except for temporary blindness and ringing in my ears nothing happened to me. Still don't know why I wasn't killed or ripped apart. I got a purple ribbon from Uncle Sam for a cut on my ass, but that doesn't dull my memory. The quake brought it all back."

"Son, I'm not a psychologist or even a bartender. I don't think being a miner is your problem. I don't know much about PTSD, but when you leave here, you should go to the nearest veteran's hospital. I think there's one in Freeville. They may have a clinic in Ithaca. Look it up on the internet. With this job, you have health insurance. Use it. You're a good worker and I'd hate to lose you. Say, why don't you go with me when I inspect the shift tomorrow? It's time for you to see how the whole mine works.

****

Everyone who had seen the lake monsters sat together in the camp dining hall to meet the National Exploration Channel team. Dr. Lindenhurst was there to talk about the fossil. Gloria Snyder sat next to him ready to tell her story of the attack in the canoe. Annie was there to be interviewed for discovering the fossil. Harold and Ursula attended to make sure the camp was presented in a positive manner. The film crew consisted of three people: the producer and spokesperson, a cameraman, and a grip to carry and set up the equipment. The grip was a slim African-American girl who immediately caught Link's eye. When the NEC spokesperson introduced the team, the only name Link heard was Kia Washington.

Jerry James, the NEC producer, explained that they planned to create a two hour show that was based on the discovery of a prehistoric creature in Cayuga Lake. They had already filmed the teenagers who had saved Steve and Gloria with their motorboat and obtained some additional blurry pictures of the monster. The show would speculate that there was a connection between the fossil and the lake creature. To produce the film, Jerry explained, each person who saw the creature would be interviewed separately on camera. The interviews would take place at different locations to take advantage of the natural beauty surrounding the camp. The film would end with an animation of the canoe attack followed by the images captured by Gloria on her I-phone.

Jerry was the face of NEC television and was dressed in his traditional short-sleeved khaki safari shirt and khaki trousers. He guaranteed that this program would break from the traditional searches for *Big Foot* and explained this show had the best evidence he had ever seen for this type of program. He pointed out that most of the people viewing the show would still be very skeptical, but added that he had done three shows on Big Foot and had never once seen the creature or even snapped one new picture of the beast.

As his audience laughed, he continued, "I have also investigated four different ghost stories and have never seen a ghost." After more laughter, he continued, "Most of you have not seen the whole video Ms. Snyder took in the canoe that day, but I have closely examined it and there is some exciting footage you may have missed."

Kia fired up the computer and projected Gloria's video on the white wall at the end of the dining hall. Then she handed the remote control to Jerry as everyone waited in anticipation to see the new pieces of their puzzle. The first shots on the video were a panorama of the waterfront as Steve paddled away from the shore. Then Steve shot a video of Gloria bending over the side of the boat taking a sample of the slick. As a wave rocked the canoe, the camera moved up and to the right. Jerry stopped the video and went up to the image on the wall. With a laser pointer, he drew attention to the upper right hand corner of the frame pointing out three sets of black spots toward the interior of the slick. He told everyone in the audience to "Watch these spots closely."

He explained that these spots were hard to see on the small screen of the phone video, but these spots proved there were three of these creatures watching the canoe not just one. He pointed to a larger one in front and two smaller ones in the background. Again, Jerry told everyone to watch this area as the video continued. He clicked the video forward in slow motion. The images were definitely more than black dots. Three creatures were moving toward the canoe. Then the camera switched back to Gloria putting the sample in her bag.

In the next scene, Gloria was taking the video of Steve ready to dive in the water from the canoe. As the video continued, Steve jumped out of the canoe causing the boat to rock back and forth. Each time the I-phone focused on the right of the canoe you could see the heads of these three creatures coming closer to the canoe. When Steve climbed back into the boat, Gloria reached out to help him. For a few seconds the I-phone in her right hand pointed to the other side of the boat. The three creatures came into focus again before the camera moved back to Steve.

Everyone saw the larger one leave the two smaller ones behind and swim toward the canoe. When the video reached the section of the attack that they'd seen before, Jerry stopped it and everyone applauded. Jerry smiled and held up his hands, "These additional shots of the creatures, especially now that we know there are more than one, really adds to the authenticity of this video and our program will show it all. Soon the nation and the world will realize that not all prehistoric beasts have disappeared from our world."

Jerry explained they wanted to talk to everyone that encountered these creatures and would work with them to decide the most appropriate spot to film each segment. While the witnesses were being interviewed, Link approached Kia and learned she was a media student at Ithaca College working with this film crew as part of a summer training program. He was surprised to learn she already knew who he was. She was an avid basketball fan and had seen him play at Cornell home games. While he listened to this beautiful Black angel describe how impressed she was with his talent, Link knew he'd have to convince Shanty to have another campfire. He wanted a chance to get close to this lady with flames reflecting in her beautiful eyes.

When Jerry and "Mac", the cameraman, talked to Shanty, they were entranced with his boyhood story and the Iroquois legends he told them. Immediately they knew they had a star to pull together the different facets of the story. They also discovered the name for their lake monster; "Apotamkon." Then Mac suggested that it be shortened to just the nickname

"Appy." Jerry agreed that a shorter name would attract more viewers and decided Appy was now the title of their show.

Jerry and Mac told Shanty that he would have to get rid of the old red baseball cap because it shaded his face from the camera. When Shanty told them he didn't want to take off his hat or make repeated appearances on the program, they tried to convince him to change his mind and explained he was very photogenic and would receive a substantial stipend.

When they suggested he should wear a red head band with the ties at the side falling to his shoulders, Shanty told them in a contemptuous tone that he was Mohawk not Apache. Still smarting from what he felt was an insult, Shanty told them he didn't want any part of their program.

Annie had been watching Joey closely during his interview because she felt he might have trouble handling the attention. Shanty surprised her at first when he was quite positive and was comfortable describing his experience with the creature and telling these newcomers the legends of his ancestors. When they focused on his personal appearance, he quickly reverted to his shy introverted self and immediately erected the barriers he used to hold out the world.

When Annie saw Joey pulling into his shell, she stepped forward and took over the conversation. She told the producer that Shanty would love to tell the Iroquois legends for the camera and suggested a campfire would be a good backdrop for his part of the program. She suggested that Shanty could wear his hair drawn back in a ponytail which would let the camera see her brother's rugged, but handsome face. Then Annie turned to Joey and told him he was going to do this for the ancestors. Shanty wasn't pleased, but shook his head as the film crew quickly agreed to Annie's suggestions.

****

Hilda attended the NEC team briefing, but kept to the back. She hadn't seen the lake monster and had some doubts about the stories she'd heard. She also questioned the video. She wasn't sure how it was faked, but she knew kids could do anything with computers these days. The existence of a lake creature was hard to believe, but now there was evidence of more than one of these creatures. As she shook her head, she had to admit what the NEC guy had just pointed out was quite remarkable, but she didn't care about finding a lake monster. Her mission was to protect Joseph from Ursula. *I've got to keep Harold from firing him?*

While the NEC team planned their sessions, Harold returned to his office leaving Ursula deep in conversation with the good-looking and very fit NEC spokesperson. Hilda watched Ursula creep up on her new prey and ingratiate herself to him. While Ursula toyed with her new victim, Hilda waited for her by the door. With the NEC spokesperson drooling over her, Ursula broke off the conversation now that she had him hooked. As Ursula headed for the craft area, Jerry watched every step of her shapely body as she walked away. At the door, Hilda stepped in front of her and begged Ursula to tell Harold that Joseph had been nothing but a gentleman with her.

Ursula laughed at her and asked why she would do that. Hilda pulled the pictures of Ursula's shower room strip out of the large manila envelope and showed the top one to her. When Ursula saw her naked butt, she grabbed the photos out of Hilda's hands and quickly leafed through them. Furious she ripped them in half and threw them across the floor. Then she pushed Hilda aside and stomped out of the dining hall.

As Hilda brushed the pieces together, Lea came into the dining hall to get a cup of coffee after finishing a private tennis lesson. When she saw Hilda picking up the torn photos, she knelt down to help her. Lea quickly identified both subjects in the photos. She couldn't miss Ursula's saggy old ass and immediately knew the pixilated man was Steve. She had seen those same muscular legs up close and personal many times.

Lea asked Hilda how she got these shots and Hilda told her not to ask. After Lea handed the torn photos to Hilda, she headed off toward the waterfront to confront her ex-boyfriend.

Hilda shoved the pieces into the envelope and started toward Harold's office. When she pushed open his office door, she saw Ursula sitting on Harold's desk talking to him. When Ursula looked up and saw Hilda, she stood behind Harold with her hands on his shoulders. With a nasty grin, she nodded a sly greeting to Hilda.

Hilda started to talk, but Harold held up his hand. Pointing his finger at her, he told Hilda, "Don't say it."

Almost shouting, he told Hilda he was sick and tired of her picking on Ursula and insisted it had to stop. In his rant, he told his sister that he thought she had changed, but now it was clear she had reverted to her mean old self.

All the time Harold was attacking Hilda, Ursula stood behind him making faces at Hilda. At one point, she even stuck out her tongue.

When Harold stopped yelling, Hilda took her best shot. First, she defended Joseph. She told Harold he was completely innocent. She described how she saw Joseph reject Ursula advances in the cabin at the campfire and added that Ursula was attacking Joseph because he rejected her.

When Hilda called Ursula a mean vindictive bitch, Harold stood up and yelled at her again. He told her to never call his wife that again. As he tried to cut off Hilda's tirade, Ursula kept smiling behind him. Harold reminded Hilda that she was talking about his wife and told her in no uncertain terms to leave Ursula alone. Then he turned to Ursula and asked her to leave. She smiled sweetly at Harold as he explained he wanted to talk to Hilda alone.

Worried about leaving Harold alone with Hilda, Ursula reluctantly started for the door. As she got close to Hilda with her back turned toward Harold, Ursula stuck out her tongue again at Hilda. Hilda balled her fist and landed a good punch on Ursula's chin knocking her to the floor. When Ursula recovered, she dove at Hilda's legs sending her crashing to the floor.

Biting and scratching as they rolled around, Ursula ended up on Hilda's chest slapping her face. Hilda yelled and grabbed Ursula's hair as Ursula landed a good slap across her cheek. Hilda yanked on Ursula's hair pulling her to the side until Ursula hit her head on the floor. Ursula wildly swung her fists as Hilda climbed on top of her. Hilda grabbed Ursula's hands, but Ursula pulled one hand free and slapped Hilda hard across the face.

Stunned, Harold rushed out from behind his desk and grabbed Hilda under her arms dragging her off Ursula. Left on the floor, Ursula started to cry. Through her tears, she whimpered that this was proof Hilda had always hated her.

Harold pushed Hilda away and told her to stay put. Returning to Ursula, he helped her to her feet. Just as Ursula stood up, she collapsed in Harold's arms. Over his shoulder, Ursula gave Hilda an evil smile and stuck out her tongue again.

Hilda tried to smack Ursula, but instead, clubbed Harold on the back of his head. Harold yelped at her to stop as he helped Ursula out of his office.

After Ursula was gone, Harold turned in the doorway, "How dare you hit my wife and attack me."

Standing next to his desk, Hilda was so mad she stuttered. "Me...me...me, what...what about her. She, she lies. Runs around on you. No, let me make it clear. That woman screws around on you."

Hilda retrieved the manila envelope from the floor and poured the contents out on Harold's desk as Harold retreated behind it. With a sweep of his arm, he brushed the pieces off his desk on to the floor.

Hilda told him, "Spend your afternoon putting that puzzle together. Then maybe, just maybe, you'll understand who you married."

Harold swept a few remaining pieces off his desk, "You can't expect me to accept this photo-shopped crap as evidence."

"That's her. You can't be that dumb. I dare you. Put those pieces together and then tell me how they're photo-shopped. Where does she go every morning? Oh, let me guess, nature walks. Yeah, that must be it. Nature walks with young studs in the men's locker room. When are you going to wake up?"

Harold shouted back, "Did you ever think that the way you treat Ursula drove her to this. Do you ever think of me? You're messing with my life. I don't know why I bother with you."

"I appreciate everything you've done for me, but you've got to wise up to who you married."

"I suppose you're Miss Perfect." Harold shouted back. I know all about Ursula. Have you ever stopped to think I love her? I saw you kissing Brandt on the porch. Surely you must understand something about love?"

Suddenly Hilda felt sorry for Harold. She wasn't sure what falling in love was all about, but knew it blinded you. "I'm not sure what love is, but I'm learning. I don't care one bit about Ursula. You can have her. She's your problem. I'm here to save Joseph. You can't penalize him because you love Ursula. Remember when he saved the girls after the mine collapsed that evening. You promised him a reward. Where is it? What is it? Now you want to punish him for something he didn't do. You should be on his side. He's the one who makes your camp a success."

Harold sighed, "Finally we agree on something. Mr. Brandt is out of my dog house. When I saw him talking to those TV folks, I realized he's the soul of this camp. It took me awhile to understand that. You're right. After he saved those girls, I made a promise to him. He'll get his reward. Let him have the damned fossil. Put it wherever he wants. As for you, I defend Ursula 'cause I don't know what else to do. Just leave her alone and let me deal with her. Now get out of here and let me think."

After Hilda slammed the door, Harold bent down and slowly picked up the pieces of the photographs. When they were all back on his desk, he started putting them together nodding his head in disbelief.

****

Lea picked up a paddle as she walked passed the canoes. Twirling it above her head like a baton, she stomped toward Steve who was standing on the dock watching two of his lifeguards work with intermediate swimmers. He never saw her coming.

Holding the paddle with the flat blade toward him, she swatted him on the butt as hard as she could. Steve half fell and half jumped off the dock. When he surfaced, he wiped the water out of his eyes wondering what had just happened and why his backside was stinging.

When his eyes cleared, he saw Lea standing on the dock twirling a paddle above her head. He smiled at her. Evidently his locker room photos had a wider circulation than he intended.

Lea threw the paddle at him, "You bastard. Really. That old woman."

Steve watched her leave and waded to the paddle. At least she didn't split the blade, he thought, as he climbed back on the dock rubbing his sore butt.

****

Bob Fletcher was concentrating in his office. Just as he pulled back the head of his putter, there was a knock on his door. When his putt went to the left, he yelled, "Damn it, what is it? I'm busy."

Louise opened the door and apologized for disturbing him. After he yelled, "Get on with it", she told him Herm Douglas needed to see him. With a sigh, he separated another ball from the pile at his feet and told her, "All right, get him in here."

When Herm found his boss working hard on his special putting green along the long window overlooking the lake, he found it difficult to keep from smiling. He was about to give his boss bad news and knew it would make him madder than missing a putt. "I just got a call from an engineer at the salt mine. The one, you know, that gets the stipend to keep us informed. They've had an explosion."

Bob looked up from his putting stance, "Good. For once they get the negative press and we look good. About time."

"It's not that, you know, simple."

"But it's got to be good for us."

"No."

Frowning, Bob replied with a quick. "How can it be our fault?'

"They're saying our fracking fluid, you know, is dissolving the bottom of their salt mine and pushing gas into it."

"Is that even possible."

"I've talked to our engineers. If our fracking fluid followed a fissure, you know, a crack under the salt bed it's possible. Our fluid formula is acidic enough to eat through the salt. It could get into the mine. It has a petroleum base so it could explode."

"Can they prove it?"

"It would be difficult, you know, for them to prove it. Evidently they're analyzing the fluid they found in the mine. They could pin it on us now that the researcher at Cornell has discovered our formula."

"Let's do what Chevron did when they had a well explosion in Dunkard, Pennsylvania. Chevron sent the good citizens coupons for pizza to make up for the noise and pollution. Send some pizza over to the salt miners. Tell them that's all they get. Hell, I'll even spring for some extra-large drinks."

"It may not be, you know, that easy."

"Make it that easy. Get our engineers off their butts to invent some reasons why it's not our fault. Tell our lawyers to earn their exorbitant salaries. They need to put the fear of God in that damn salt company before they dare sue us. Hell, sue them first. What about the publicity? Can we keep this quiet?"

"They don't want the public snooping around in their mine any more than we want them around our wells. So, you know, we should be okay on that front. They don't want to, you know, advertise the explosion."

Bob yelled at Herm, "Jesus Christ will you stop saying, you know, you know. If I knew, you wouldn't have to tell me."

Bob stroked a ball toward the cup bending backwards with his putter up in the air guiding the ball into the hole with body language. As the ball rolled slowly passed the cup, he adjusted his grip for the next try. "I don't want this to be like the explosion in Charleston, West Virginia. That blow-up almost killed six or seven contractors at the site. The explosion wasn't even at the well head. The explosion was at a pump where they were recovering the water and the escaping gas blew up. Hell, we can't prevent something like that from happening. You know! You know accidents can happen."

"Are you serious about the pizzas?"

"Not really, but it seems to be an established practice for gas companies reacting to an explosion. What do you think we should do?"

"Pizzas might piss people off. You…Make things worse."

"Counter-sue. Let them find out what big gas money can do." Bob got a devilish smile on his face as he separated another ball from the pile. Quietly he whispered, "Was it us?"

"Probably. No one knows exactly what happens when waste water is pumped into the ground. No one knows for sure what happens down there. We break up the layers with the gas in it and then pump the waste water back down to fill whatever space it finds. You're replacing solid strata with broken wet stuff. There's bound to be settling in the earth when the rock that deep is broken up. In addition, our rebel Ithaca College professor and other scientists insist that our waste water migrates along faults and causes earthquakes."

"Does it?"

"Yeah, I guess. No one can tell exactly what happens that far down. These are, you know, really deep wells."

"What's the company position? Our talking point."

"Our engineers say no one can prove it, so it's not us. Maybe we should stop drilling until we can find out what happened at the salt mine."

"Absolutely not. If we stop injecting here, we'll get lawsuits at every drilling site with a tremor and that's most of them. Ignore the facts. We keep drilling and rake in the money. Get our engineers and lawyers on it. Now get out of here. Tell Louise to give me twenty uninterrupted minutes, I've got a T-time in an hour. My stroke isn't working and I've got some serious work to do before I leave."

CHAPTER 26

At Camp Minnechaug, the film crew was having coffee and sodas in the dining hall discussing the next day's shoot with the camp staff. Tonight, Jerry explained, he and Kia would write the script they wanted to play over the video and then he broke the news to Shanty that they wanted him to read it for the cameras.

Nodding his head no and holding his hands palms up, Shanty told them absolutely not. Again, Annie had to intervene. After Annie got them to agree to call him Joseph on the tape and include a reference to the historic Chief Joseph Brandt, Shanty agreed to narrate their script.

Jerry also wanted Shanty to help them write the script. He wanted to make sure the Iroquois legends concerning the lake serpent were accurate. After Joseph told them that his grandmother kept the legends of the Iroquois alive for him, the NEC crew suggested they could get an older Tribal American woman to do some of the voiceovers using the Mohawk name of his grandmother. Joseph not only agreed to keep helping them, but was thrilled with their suggestion.

Joe was so excited, he told them one of his great grandmother's stories. "When my grandmother was a little girl, her mother told her of a time when her father, my great great grandfather, took her out on the lake with other members of the tribe. The warriors built floating fires on the lake to draw Apotamkon to the surface. After a long wait, Apotamkon's descendants rose out of the water and frightened her."

"The beasts were so scary, she hid in the bottom of the canoe, but after a while, she peeked over the side and saw the creatures devouring the deer carcasses the braves threw to them. The men of our tribe fed these creatures to keep them from devouring their children."

Jerry wondered, "How do you build a fire on the lake? Doesn't water keep things from burning?"

"Making a fire on water is easy. I do it up at the falls at the end of the summer each year. Unfortunately, Apotamkon has never joined us."

"Can you do it the same way your ancestors did?"

"Sure, you lash three logs together into what you would call a triangle. Then I lash branches on this frame and build the fire on top of the branches."

Jerry liked the visuals of a campfire on the water. "Can you make the fire frame and have a fire on the water tonight?"

The idea of recreating his ancestors' celebration for the camera appealed to Shanty. "I can make the fire if you can get the Camp Director's approval."

Jerry didn't think that would be a problem and started for the Director's office.

Before Jerry left, Shanty grabbed his arm, "Don't expect Apotamkon's relatives to actually show up."

"It'd be great if they did, but all I'm hoping for is a great visual. Imagine a fire burning on the lake surrounded by camper's in canoes listening to you tell your grandmother's story to the camera. It doesn't get much better than that."

"I'd like to do it for you,"

"With films like this the viewers never expect to actually see the ghost or monster the show is about. What they are looking for is a good story that will entertain them. With the fossil evidence, I already have more corroboration than most of my stories. With Gloria's video I have a dramatic climax. The addition of your Native American legends enhance an already exciting show. Make a big fire tonight. Maybe two or three of them to make sure I have enough light for the cameras. This fire sequence might turn this show into a mini-series."

Annie followed Jerry to the Director's Office and waited outside. When he came out smiling, he told her, "We can do it if your brother can make it happen tonight."

"Oh he can do it, but you need to know more about my brother. I don't want him presented as an ignorant savage whose head is full of old stories. He is a graduate of Dartmouth and earned bronze and silver stars defending his country. He's a tribal hero. You've got to include his full biography for your viewers."

Jerry hugged Annie and then walked with his arm around her shoulders. "He's our star. We'll include everything you've just told me. More, if there is more. A war hero makes his participation even more believable. He looks great on camera and sounds even better. We'll make him larger than life. Hell, he already is."

****

As darkness squeezed the last rays of sunlight from the sky, Steve led a flotilla of canoes out to Shanty's floating fires on the lake. Steve had them form a semi-circle around the three fires that were arranged in a triangle in the middle of the lake.

To film the lake fire, the cameraman set up on a platform in a whaleboat with Jerry standing next to him with a bull-horn. After dark descended on the lake, Jerry blasted out the directions to the campers as he set the scene. He told them to turn off their flashlights and keep them off during the fires. "The firelight is all we need to capture the images." Jerry didn't realize the fires were very close to where Gloria and Steve were attacked.

He finished by telling them the whale boat would make a half circle behind the canoes to get shots from every angle and asked everyone to focus on the fire and not to look at the boat behind them. "You need to forget the camera and concentrate on Mr. Brandt while he tells you his grandmother's story."

As the whale boat moved behind the canoes, he encouraged them to hold their paddles above their head and shake them like they had rehearsed on the shore. When everyone was ready, he told Shanty to light the fires and begin his story.

The camera captured a blazing torch dancing through the dark touching down on a dark teepee shaped pyre. The dancing torch ignited a fire that exploded into roaring flames illuminating a Mohawk warrior standing in his canoe. Still standing, he paddled his canoe silently to the next pyramid waiting for his torch. As the torch touched the second fire, flames erupted reaching for the sky. As the solitary warrior continued his quiet journey passed that fire he touched the third pyre ablaze. Now the lone tribal figure was silhouetted by the three fires.

Shanty paddled his canoe to the middle of the triangle. With both hands, Shanty held his paddle high above his head and shook his paddle. Following his lead, the campers lifted their paddles and shook them. Slowly the warrior extended one arm and pointed his paddle at the moon. With a descending arc, he hit his flat blade on the water making a slapping sound. Just after his paddle hit, the campers followed his movements slapping their paddles on the dark water.

The camera caught a spectacular silhouette that would be shown at the beginning and end of each segment. Jerry couldn't believe how the camper's actions were perfectly choreographed. The paddles hit the water in unison creating a great splash that echoed across the lake. Jerry smiled. With these great images the documentary was already turning into a three part mini-series.

Shanty felt the presence of his ancestors as he stood in his canoe. Jerry had staged the scene well. Earlier, much to Shanty's horror, Jerry insisted that an ample amount of gasoline be poured on each pile of wood so they would burst into flames. He explained to Shanty that in this case the spectacular outweighed the authentic. Now Shanty understood and approved of the image Jerry was trying to capture.

Still silhouetted by the fires behind him, Shanty recited the story he learned at his grandmother's knees. When he finished, he slapped the water with his paddle again calling on the beasts to appear. In unison, the campers slapped the water hoping the creatures would appear.

The cameras caught close-ups of the white foam from the splashing paddles as the bubbles caught the orange reflection of the fires in the dark water. Jerry was so moved by the ceremony, he actually expected Apotamkon to rise out of the water like a breaching whale. Unfortunately that didn't happen.

Shanty finished the scene by chanting a warrior's song that ended with the words, "The land shall remain and change not."

The camera finished with a close up that caught Shanty's rugged features streaked by the shadows of orange flames. Jerry pressed the trigger on his bullhorn and announced the scene was over and thanked everyone for their great work. As the campers turned toward shore, the cameraman kept the camera focused on the dying fires as the whale boat slowly pulled away back toward the shore.

As the fires receded in the background suddenly the lake exploded into flames. Some of the fiery branches had dropped into the slick setting it afire. From Shanty's fires, the flames spread rapidly up and down the lake stretching for almost a half a mile in each direction. Residents came out of their houses and cottages to see their pristine lake burn.

How could Cayuga Lake burn? Jerry didn't care, but made sure his cameraman kept filming the flames stretching across the water. The burning lake was spectacular. The cameraman zoomed in and out of the flames and then slowly panned the fire from end to end.

Jerry laughed out loud. He could never have imagined such a great finish to this segment of his show. And, even better, Mac caught it all on camera.

Three canoes turned to watch the burning lake. Steve and Lea were in one with Annie, Billy and Hilda next to them. Shanty joined them as they sat in wonder watching their lake burn. Shanty was disturbed that the white man had polluted his beautiful lake, but even he had to admit it was an incredible sight. Orange and yellow flames reached to the heavens from a black sea as far as you could see up and down the lake.

****

Charley and Ruth entered the Sangam Restaurant; Ithaca's first and finest Indian Restaurant. They were eager to share the food and each other's company. To start the evening, Charley went for a Kingfisher beer.

"It's the Budweiser of India," the waiter assured him.

Ruth ordered Lassi, a yogurt shake with mint and masala. Soon they lifted their drinks and toasted to surviving earthquakes. After perusing the menu, they decided to start with Murgh Shorba, a chicken soup with garlic, ginger and Indian spices. They agreed that chicken soup would be a safe way to start their exploration of the Indian subcontinent.

While they waited for their meal, Ruth asked Charley for advice and described how she had discovered that the ISC Vice President was funneling private company memorandums to the environmentalists. "What should I do?"

Charley was quick to point out, "I'm not a *Suit*. I have no idea what you should do. I'm a denizen of the dark and like a mole, I'm confused by sunlight. You people on the surface have always been a mystery to me."

"Except for my father, you have the most common sense I've ever seen in a man. Your lack of experience with business politics is exactly what I want to tap. You don't have to worry about playing corporate games and can give me the unbiased perspective I need."

Ruth knew she had him when he told her, "Do you want to know what's best for the company or what's best for you."

Confused, Ruth asked, "Aren't they the same thing?"

"They could be, but they could be very different. This guy is your boss, right?"

"Yes."

"Then forget the letter and suck up to him?"

"But he's hurting the company."

"Really? I doubt it. Those protesters won't change anything. You think he's sharing the information to hurt the company, but you don't know why he's doing it. That's what's important. Maybe the negative publicity keeps him on the right side of the gas company or your Board of Directors. Sometimes making people mad shows the people above you that you're working hard. He may be creating a problem to show how tough he is. You do that."

"I do not."

"Oh yes you do. Before you discovered I could help you, you pissed me off and didn't care. You did it on purpose. I was beneath you and in your way. You hated to ask me for advice, but you needed me because I had answers that you wanted."

"I rely on my own hard work. I don't like to ask people for help, but you're right, I needed you."

"I knew you wanted to fire me."

"How can you say that?"

"I know people. You were pretty transparent. Admit it, you were planning on firing me."

"It might have crossed my mind, but if you knew that why did you help me?"

"If I told you to go to hell, you would have fired me anyway. If I helped you, I had a chance to change your mind. You're a *Suit*. Above ground you're the boss, but literally beneath your feet the life blood of this company is ticking away without you giving a damn. I wanted to show you that miners are valuable too. To your credit, you listened and learned."

"My experience with you has changed my opinion about a lot of things, but that doesn't help me now. What do I do about these letters and my boss?"

"You just said it. He's your boss. He decides if you keep your job. You don't get anything by attacking him or going over his head to the Board of Directors. Cover his ass. Either shut up and don't say anything or tell him if you found out where the letters came from others can too. Show him you're there to protect him. To support him. Hey, but that's just my fuzzy thinking. It's your choice."

As their soup bowls were removed, they agreed it was a tasty start and decided to order three dishes and share them. They agreed to select one spicy hot dish, one that was mild and one they considered normal just in case they couldn't stomach the spicy ones. They ordered a Tandori Mixed Grill, mild Lamb curry, and hot beef Vindaloo with an order of Nan to help mitigate the spices. As they waited for their meal, Charley broached a topic that had been on his mind since he'd researched the RAG brine spill in the lake on the internet.

"I don't want to get into *Suit* business, but something has been bothering me."

"What?"

"Why is ISC in bed with RAG?"

"What do you mean?"

"ISC is a quality organization. RAG only counts dollars. Those guys don't' care about anything else. The reputation of our salt mine is damned by working with them. I like this lake. I don't want anything to happen to it. They dumped their damn waste water brine in the part of the lake I used to fish. I've been there. Nothin' is alive there now. You should convince our company to dump them. Get as far away from them as possible."

"They're in the same business as we are."

"The hell they are." Charley said with a bit more anger than he intended. Luckily, the waiter showed up with their meals and gave him a chance to calm down. Avoiding the topic, Ruth fussed over her food. Enjoying the taste as they gingerly appreciated each delicacy, they shared them with each other. Ruth held out a large piece of lamb from the curry on her fork waiting for Charley to try it.

"Yeow. That has a bite." Charley took the last swig of beer to cool his throat. "Man, I need another one." He got the waiter's attention by holding up his bottle. The waiter bowed and left for the bar.

As they enjoyed the meal, Charley kept trying to convince Ruth that RealAirGas wasn't a trusted ally. "I couldn't sleep this morning and went on the internet. There's been research. When a gas companies start fracking, you get earthquakes."

"You can't believe anything on the internet."

"But it's my experience too. Before they showed up I never felt a quake in our mine. You were down there for one of the big quakes, but I swear that I feel small ones every day."

"Miners and drillers have the same job. They both get stuff out of the earth to make a profit."

"Yeah, but it's how you do it that counts. I've worked in that mine over twenty years, hell over thirty."

Amazing, he thought, *has it really been that long.* For a moment, Charley stared at his empty beer bottle before he looked into Ruth's eyes. "We have never polluted the lake or started an earthquake. RAG has been here a few years and has already messed up the lake. First, they spilled brine into it. The other day out fishin', I found a slick in the middle of the lake. This lake never had a slick before these guys showed up. RAG started drilling and shoving gunk between the layers under the lake. I'm not surprised that it leaks to the surface. Mark my words, RAG will bring down the whole mining industry around here."

"They're our corporate partners. We have to support them."

"No you don't. You want to impress your boss. Show him there's a potential downside to the relationship."

Charley waved his hand in front of his mouth wondering where his beer was. Ruth insisted he take a sip of her yogurt shake to cool his throat and shut him up. After a sip of Ruth's drink, Charley's beer finally showed up. After a long swig, he started again.

"RAG's fracking fluid is forcing gas into our mine. Dissolving our product and polluting the lake. The salt dome on the first level keeps caving in. Every time I hear a chunk fall, I wonder if the lake is going to come down on us. I'm pretty sure their wells are causing smaller quakes they don't tell us about. I mean I can feel them. Sometimes more than one a shift. None of this ever happened before RAG showed up."

As they left the restaurant after a great meal, Charley grabbed Ruth's hand as they walked to her car. While Charley drove Ruth back to his house, she was the first to see it. "My God, the lake's on fire."

As soon as he could, Charley pulled off the road so they could get a good look. They jumped out of her sports car and stood on a cliff overlooking the lake. Watching it burn, Charley told her, "This lake never burned until RAG showed up. It has to be their slick."

Ruth answered, "Lakes don't burn."

"They do when you pollute them with fracking crap. Remember in the sixties when the Cuyahoga River leading into Lake Erie exploded into flames? I think there were over a dozen fires on that damn river. Why? 'Cause of the oil and gas pollution. It was a dead river. No oxygen, no fish, but plenty of fires. I don't want Cayuga to become the next Cuyahoga."

"That couldn't happen here."

"Look, it already has. The lake is burning right in front of us. The gas has to come from somewhere. When you frack you get flames in your faucets and showers. Why not a lake. Hell, you can watch water burn on *YouTube* for God's sake."

CHAPTER 27

Shanty slowed as he finished the morning run with the young athletes, Annie and Hilda. Hilda had surprised him. She kept up with the group until slowing at the very end. Shanty was impressed, her treadmill workouts had kept her in pretty good shape. After he gave Hilda a quick hug and kiss on the cheek, he told her he wanted to see the video from last night before he cleaned up for breakfast.

Excited, Shanty hoped the camera had captured a scene from his Mohawk past. Entering the dining hall, he saw Jerry bending over Mac's shoulder looking at his computer studying a video. When he heard the door swing shut, Jerry looked up and waved Shanty over.

With excitement in his voice, he announced, "Remember when we were watching the lake burn on the way back to shore. When I was bitch'in about Apotamkon not showing up. Well, guess what, I was wrong. He was there, look at this."

More than surprised, Shanty bent over the cameraman's other shoulder as he played the video. When it started up, Shanty realized he was watching video of the end of last night's campfire.

Jerry explained, "Here we are pulling away from your fires and Mac is zooming his lens back from a close-up on the fire to a wide angle. Did you see it?"

Shanty shook his head, no. "See what?"

Jerry laughed. "I didn't see it the first time either. Mac was the one who spotted it."

Jerry asked Mac to play the video back slower this time. Then he pointed to the upper right hand corner of the screen. "Watch right about here."

As Mac played the video again, Shanty saw three sets of orange dots floating in the water and knew immediately those spots were animal eyes reflecting the flames of the fire.

Jerry told him, "I've filmed gator hunts down South. Alligator eyes shine bright yellow when you shine a flashlight at them at night. My guess is there were three animals out there watching us. This will be great for our program."

Shanty asked, "Play it back one more time."

"Not yet. Now watch the left side of the screen." Circling his finger at the lower left of the screen, he repeated, "Right about here."

As the camera panned to the left suddenly more sets of orange eyes appeared.

Shanty quickly counted them, "My God, there's what, five of them on that side of the fires."

Just as the camera stopped moving to the left, one more set of eyes popped up from under the water. These were further apart and you could just see a dark shadow of a triangular head connecting the dots.

"That's six," Shanty shouted. "You can see him. Look his head. He's a big one."

As the camera panned back across the scene, the five sets of eyes reappeared in slightly different positions. They were moving around. The camera was focused on a close-up of the fire when Mac stopped the video.

Jerry asked, "What do you think."

Shanty nodded his head, "Amazing. Never saw anything like that. Is it possible?"

"Wait. There's more."

Mac fast forwarded the video and stopped it where the lake caught fire. Jerry touched the screen, "Watch right about here."

Mac ran the video again on slow motion. All of a sudden a big black object shot out of the lake like a whale breaching and plunged back into the flaming water. You could see a head, body, and even make out flippers. Then with a splash it disappeared.

Under his breath, Shanty uttered, "My God, what was that?"

"That my dear man is Apotamkon. Your legend was with us last night. Better yet, we caught him and his buddies on film. I think we got the campers out of there just in time."

****

Link's interview for the camera was the last one the NEC team needed to complete the portion of the program dedicated to personal experiences with the lake creatures. Link led them to the rope bridge that still swung across the raging stream. It had been a rainy summer and water roared under the bridge almost spilling over the banks. After his attack on the bridge, Link had vowed never to get on that rope thing-a-ma-gig again, but Jerry wanted to film him climbing up the bridge and wanted Link to tell his story while standing in the middle of the rope bridge just above the rushing water.

Link was more than reluctant to get on the bridge again. He was scared. His experience with the bridge still filled him with terror. The memory of that night was too fresh in his mind for him to climb the rope again and he tried to convince Jerry that standing on the ground at one end of the bridge to tell his story with the bridge behind him would be just as effective.

Jerry told him that wouldn't work and insisted that Link climb out on the bridge. With a smile, Kia Washington encouraged Link to give it a try. Link didn't want this beautiful sister to think he was a coward so he gave in. Carefully, he slid up the rope to the crossed logs holding on to the rope railings that stretched across the stream. He hesitated at the 'V'.

He looked back and shouted, "I don't want to do this. It's all coming back to me. I won't do it."

Sensing a dramatic moment, Jerry whispered to Kia to encourage him.

"Link, you can do it. Be my hero."

Challenged by this beautiful woman, Link gritted his teeth and looked up and down the stream. No monsters in sight. Spurred on by her sexy voice, he finally inched down the rope to the center of the bridge. With him in the middle, the rope bridge sagged almost to the water. Mac adjusted one camera on a tripod to catch the full view of Link standing in the middle of the bridge and used his hand-held gyro-balanced camera to focus on Link's face. When Kia was ready with the directional mike, Mac nodded. Jerry shouted at Link to tell his story.

Link turned sideways to look at the camera, but kept hanging on to both rope hand rails. Before he started, he had to swallow the bile that came up to his mouth. Finally he told the tale of what had happened that fateful evening.

Concentrating on what he was saying, Link's foot slipped and he almost fell off the rope bridge. Swinging wildly back and forth like he did that night, Link tried to regain his balance and stop the damn bridge from swinging.

Jerry loved it. It was great action. If nothing else, it could be used as a blooper segment when the credits rolled up the screen.

Swinging back and forth made images of his encounter with the monsters flood Link's mind. When he was finally able to stop the bridge from swinging, Link began again with a voice stressed with emotion.

The camera caught a man reliving his experience. Looking through the camera and listening to Link's story through earphones, Mac was convinced only a genuine skeptic could reject his story. When Link finished, he bowed his head and stared into the rushing water. Mac caught tears running down Link's face in a close-up.

Jerry demanded, "Did you get that?"

"Got it boss. It's great. It'll be an important part of the story."

Embarrassed by his tears, Link carefully climbed across the bridge to the other side of the creek. Exhausted from reliving his ordeal, Link sat on the ground with his head between his knees and his arms around his legs.

Jerry nodded to Kia, "Go help him. I'll carry your stuff back."

Kia carefully crossed the rope bridge and sat next to Link. First, she put her arm around his shoulders and then gave him a gentile kiss on the cheek. "That was great. Wait 'til you see it. You'll be proud of the way you told your story. I know it hurt, but you'll be glad you did it."

Kia helped him up, "Are the falls you were telling me about around here?"

With little interest, Link held out his left arm, "That way."

Kia put her arm around his waist and led him up the path, "Show me."

As they walked up the path together, they met Shanty coming back from the falls. He stopped and explained, "I just finished tonight's campfire. It's a floating one in the middle of the pool at the bottom of the falls. The flames reflecting off the waterfall will make a great backdrop for the continuing legend of Apotamkon."

Kia smiled, "Is there anybody up there?"

"No, I was alone. Annie and Billy are over on the rappelling cliff stowing gear. I'm going to wash up for dinner. By the way, that's a great place for a swim."

"Great, we don't have our suits." Link added.

"I believe it's a clothing optional pool." Smiling, Shanty continued down the path.

After a short hike, they went around a large boulder leaning against the rock face of the cliff. There in all its majesty were the falls with beautiful sprays of white water splashing eighty feet to the green pool below. Kia walked to the edge of the water to look up at the falls as Link sat on a board bench resting on stones near the edge of the water staring at his feet.

She looked back, "Stop feeling sorry for yourself. You told your story. Get over it."

She pulled off her T-shirt revealing a well-rounded black sports bra hoping to get a response. When there was no reaction from Link, she stood in front of him, "You don't want any of this?"

Link finally looked up at her as Kia slipped off her shorts revealing a red thong. Visons of her fine bronzed bottom drove the memory of horrible monsters from Link's mind as he watched her walk into the pool.

As he watched her slowly wade into the cold water, he stripped off his camp T-shirt and dropped his shorts. Running to catch her, he stubbed his toe on a rock and had to limp to the water's edge. Swearing at his throbbing toe, he watched her dive under the surface of the green pool.

Lea splashed up through the water whipping it out of her braided hair. With smooth strokes she swam to Shanty's fire platform and held on to the platform waving for Link to join her. "C'mon sissy. Afraid to get wet? I won't let the monsters get you."

Link waded slowly into the water until it was up to his thighs getting his boxer shorts wet. Wanting to be close to this beauty in her skimpy outfit, he dove under and came up spiting. He didn't like to swim, but the reward for this dip was too great for him to pass up.

When he got close to her, he dove below the surface hoping to see her beautiful body under the water as he swam up beside her. Gliding below the green water he opened his eyes and looked down. Passing below him was a huge black animal that looked up at him with huge teeth. To the right was a smaller one that was still bigger than Link.

Gulping water, he let out a stream of air bubbles as he kicked toward the surface. As he did, another one passed under him so close that his foot hit its rough skin. Clawing at the water, he broke the surface screaming.

As he kicked toward the safety of the fire platform, Kia laughed, "At last, the great black whale surfaces."

Sputtering, Link brushed passed her climbing up on the fire platform to escape the terror below. Once he was on it, he grabbed Kia's arms and yanked her up on the platform yelling, "They're down there. Down there, under us."

Kia laughed at him. "Don't be scared. I'll protect you."

"No, no, honest I saw them. Three of them. The big one and two smaller ones. They swam right under me. Jesus, they'll eat us. Tear us apart."

Getting tired of his rants, Kia told him, "Relax. You just had a flashback after telling your story."

With that she dove into the water and surfaced. Treading water, she called to him, "C'mon. Get a little of this Black beauty."

Link couldn't overcome his fear. At that moment, survival was more important than sex. Wait what was he thinking? Here was a sexy lady waiting for him in a bra and almost no panties. He tried, but couldn't force himself to dive into the water.

Finally, Kia gave up and swam to the edge of the pool. Link watched her pull her glistening body out of the water and slip on her clothes. She didn't even turn around as she walked away from him down the path.

****

Earlier that day, Ruth looked up as her boss arrived at work. *It's was quarter after ten, he likes to keep banker's hours.* She thought. *This is it.*

She stood up and smoothed her suit. She had taken Charley's advice and altered her wardrobe for this meeting. Today, she had on a light beige suit with a muted yellow blouse topped off with a bright orange and black striped scarf tied around her neck in a loose knot.

Ruth was confident and ready to put Charley's advice into action. She had decided to tell Olson about the memos to demonstrate her loyalty.

Ruth approached the Vice-President's secretary and asked if she could talk to Mr. Olson. Deferring to Ruth's status in the company, his secretary told her, "Of course, I'm sure he'll want to see you. Let me check to see if he's ready for visitors. He just came in."

The secretary went to Albert's door closing it behind her. Inside, she explained that Ruth was waiting to see him.

Albert sighed. Meeting with Ruth usually led to a confrontation. *Starting the day off with a fight sucks.* He thought. *On the other hand, I'd better to solve her problem now and enjoy the rest of the day.* Reluctantly, he told his secretary, "Get her in here."

When Ruth entered his office, Albert was surprised. She actually looked good. *First, time for that,* he thought.

Entranced by her new look, he did something he had never done before with her. He got up from behind his desk and went to an easy chair and invited her to sit across from him on the couch.

At first, Ruth wasn't sure what he wanted. He had never invited her to sit on the couch before. Usually she stood in front of his desk or if she had a presentation they moved to his conference table.

When she hesitated, he motioned for her to join him. As she sat down, Ruth felt this was a good start.

With Olson looking directly into her eyes, Ruth wasn't sure how to begin. Flustered, she rambled on about the university environmental group and how they were expanding their protest to include the salt mine.

Trying to get her to focus, Albert asked, "How do you think we should respond to these protests?"

Finally, Ruth calmed down and told him she had discovered that private intra-office memos were being sent to the environmentalists. She explained how she put out a memo that she could identify to discover who was giving the memos to the protest group.

Ruth watched her boss's face carefully. There was no indication of him flinching or getting nervous. *He's good,* she thought. *Very good.*

Albert found her discovery interesting, but nothing more. "Who sent them out? That's something we need to stop."

Amazed at his reaction, Ruth announced, "Sir, it was you."

As Albert leaned toward her, Ruth pulled back worried that he might hit her.

With a quizzical look on his face, Albert simply asked, "Me?"

"Yes sir. They have your letters."

"There must be some mistake."

"No sir. I'm certain."

Albert leaned back in his chair rubbing his chin obviously thinking. Then he almost shouted, "Damn, it must be Shelley. My daughter. She must be going through my office at home. I often take correspondence home to read. Yes, it has to be her."

Not sure what to do next, Ruth nodded because she couldn't think of anything to say. *Is this guy is a good liar or could he be telling the truth?*

"I appreciate your dedication. Tracing these documents was a good idea. To be quite honest, I'm surprised you brought the results to me. It would have embarrassed me if you went to the Board of Directors and told them I let these private letters get out of the office. Thank you for bringing them to me first. I must admit I've never felt you liked me. Let's say our working relationship has not been the best. At least more formal than personal."

"I'm sorry you feel that way. I've always tried to do what was best for ISC. I assumed that would be best for you, too."

"I must admit that isn't how I perceived your efforts in the past, but coming to me first with these letters forces me to rethink my opinion of you. Suffice it to say, I will end the pilfering of my papers at home. My daughter is like every young person. Eager to right the wrongs of the world by breaking the rules of that world. I will put an end to this problem."

Reevaluating the woman across from him, he added, "Thank you, for this and your hard work. I can't think of anyone who puts in more time than you. I appreciate your loyalty to the company and now to me."

With his first compliment ever spinning wildly in her head, Ruth took a moment to regroup. "I've wanted to talk to you about our relationship with RAG. I'm not sure we should be working so closely with a gas company. In the past, students never protested our salt mine and now we're being condemned with the *frackers*. They're hurting our reputation as a safe clean company. I think we should distance ourselves from them."

Surprised, Albert thought, *I've been thinking the same thing. This woman has more on the ball than I thought. How do I explain it to her?*

"This is a very delicate topic with the Board of Directors. You might be surprised, but several of them agree with you. Unfortunately, the others want to get closer to the gas companies. That gas money is hard to ignore. I've been mediating the debate, but haven't taken a position. I'm not sure if you go with reputation or profit. Profit drives any business, but I'm old fashioned enough to think it's important to stand up for your values. I value this lake more than any environmentalist."

As Ruth listened to him, she found his thinking more like Charley's than hers. However, she was changing. Learning. After discussing both sides, they came to the conclusion they both wanted to take this debate to the Board. Albert told Ruth to set up a meeting with the ISC Board of Directors and the RAG company officials for Saturday afternoon. That would force the RAG executives and ISC Board members to ride through the protest outside the ISC gates that was scheduled for the weekend. He hoped that experience would make all the salt executives think about their reputation in the community now that they were partners with a gas company.

Ruth and Albert agreed to point out to the ISC Board of Directors that this would be the first protest ever held outside their salt mine. That alone should make it clear that an alliance with a gas company comes with a price.

Glowing from this success with her boss, Ruth decided to try one last idea that was actually hers. Ruth hoped to see more of Charley in the daylight so she broached the idea of rotating shifts for the mine workers. Charley had often complained about not living a normal life above ground.

Olson explained that the union had been asking to rotate the shifts for a long time, but management was opposed the idea. His management team had rejected the idea simply because they had never tried rotating shifts before and were afraid production would go down. "Besides", rejecting union demands is what we do."

"I've talked to some of the union leaders and they have assured me that production would increase. You know how hard it has been to meet the new quotas."

When Albert heard the words production and increase in the same sentence, his ears tingled. After considering this idea for a moment, he told her, "You have my permission to rotate shifts on a trial basis for six months. If production increases, the practice will continue. Make it happen."

Then Albert told her that the engineers had told him about her experiment to drill the blasting holes deeper to get more product and complimented her for finding a way to increase production. "It's a great idea. You seem to understand the pulse of the mine."

Delighted by the most successful meeting of her career, Ruth stood up to excuse herself. "I'll set up the meeting for the Board and get the union on board."

As she stood in front of him, Albert stood up to thank her one more time. "I really appreciate you bringing those letters to me first. Being my kid is tough for Shelley. She's rich, spoiled and I love her. Hard for me to see her faults."

Albert sighed and as Ruth started to leave, he added one more compliment, "You look great today. Professional and stylish. Keep it up."

That personal comment was the first one she had ever received at work on any job. Ruth glided out of his office with a big grin on her face.

CHAPTER 28

Back at camp, Kia met with the crew and staff to tell them about Link's breakdown. Concerned for their friend, Shanty led the group to the falls where they found Link still sitting on the platform floating in the middle of the pool below the falls. While the others waited at the edge of the pool, Shanty jumped in the canoe he used to take fire wood to the floating platform and rescued Link. When Link stepped on dry land, they waited for him to put on his clothes and then they all rushed to him.

As his friends tried to cheer him up, Jerry apologized to Link for making him relive his experience with the monsters on the rope bridge. Then Link amazed them by reciting his new story of the creatures swimming under him. He insisted that they were out there in the pool right now.

Jerry was glad he didn't have this footage on tape, Link sounded crazed. He even claimed to have touched one of them. Jerry knew that one crazy could hurt the credibility of the whole project.

When Link finished his story, Billy handed him a beer to calm him down and Kia sat down next to him on the bench and tried to comfort him. When Dan and Shelley came down the path waving, the group left Link and Kia to welcome them as they joined the group. Soon Ursula and Harold showed up with Dr. Lindenhurst in tow.

Jerry arranged the group so they sat on rock and board benches looking at the pool below the falls with the cameras behind them. As the moon crowded out the sun, Jerry waved that he was ready to tape the night's segment. At first he explained they would shoot with just the moonlight and fire. If that didn't work, Mac had set up a bank of lights to provide more light if it was needed.

With just the light of the full moon reflecting off the white water cascading down the falls, Jerry announced it was time to start the ceremony and explained his idea to light the fire out in the pool by shooting a flaming arrow into it. When everyone was quiet, he directed Shanty to begin.

Before Shanty picked up the bow and arrow, he stripped off his T-shirt and jeans too the hoots and hollers of all the women except, of course, for Ursula. Together they clapped for more.

He silenced them by lifting a single finger to his lips with a smile. A polite hush descended on the raucous crowd as they viewed the scarred body of a warrior who had survived many battles.

Shanty stood on the edge of the pool naked except for a loin cloth and one white feather with a black tip suspended behind his head from a black and white wampum headband. Using flint and steel on one knee, he started a small fire. With the fire at his feet, he dipped an arrow in it setting it on fire. When it burst into flames, he placed it on his bow.

The cameras recorded a silhouette of a well-built Iroquois brave dipping an arrow into the small fire with the white water of the falls exploding behind him. The Mohawk warrior stood and drew back his bow sending the glowing arrow high over the full moon.

Jerry couldn't believe the image. As it descended, the path of the flaming arrow chased across the falling white water. The only problem, Shanty missed the platform. With a fizzle, the arrow snuffed out in the pool. Shanty hung his head as his audience clapped with more than a few snickers.

Jerry told Shanty to relax. They had plenty of film. The next arrow would give Mac a chance to catch his arrow from a different camera angle. When Mac was ready, the second arrow reached for the heavens, but it too fell short of the target.

Jerry was still enthusiastic and told Shanty to keep firing until he hit the damn wood.

Shanty told him there was another problem, "I only have one more arrow."

Jerry shouted, "Then you'd better not miss this time."

Billy stood up, "I could swim out to the fire platform with a lighter and hide behind it. If Shanty misses, I can light the fire without anyone noticing."

Jerry nodded, "On film it will look like the arrow hit it if Shanty can shoot it behind the fire."

Billy did share one worry, "I don't want Shanty's last arrow to hit me. I'm not the target."

Shanty guaranteed he could put the arrow behind the fire without hitting Billy in the head.

Annie shouted out, "Just aim at Billy. Then he should be safe."

Jerry liked the idea and told Billy to swim out.

Billy borrowed a lighter from Lindenhurst and just as he entered the water, Link stood up and pleaded, "No. You can't go in there. Honestly, they're out there. I saw them. They'll get you. Eat you. Kill you."

Billy swam on his side behind the platform holding the lighter above the water and yelled, "I'm ready."

Shanty pointed his last arrow toward the moon and let it fly. Billy watched as the arrow arched down toward him. As it fell out of the sky, the flaming shaft seemed to be descending directly at him. With visions of it hitting him right between the eyes, Billy ducked beneath the platform.

When the arrow hit the pyre, the gasoline soaked wood burst into flames. As the flames exploded on the top of the platform climbing toward the sky, Billy surfaced underneath the platform for a quick breath. To keep from spoiling the shot, he swam away from the platform underwater.

As Billy swam through the black water, flames from the burning platform sent ribbons of light shooting through the water in front of him. Looking toward the surface, his knee hit something below him. Thinking that he had hit the bottom, he was surprised that the pool was that shallow. *No, he thought, this pool is deeper than that. It must be something else.*

With the flames reflecting off the water, Billy looked down as a large dark object swam up under him. Then something hit his leg. *Fish,* he thought. *Yes, fish drawn to the firelight.*

He surfaced and swam to the edge of the pool. Climbing out of the pool away from the cameras, Annie rushed to him with a towel and helped dry him off. Taking the towel from her, Billy told her, "I know what Link saw. There's some big fish out there. A couple ran into me."

Link stood up, "I'm telling you, it's not fish. It's them." He insisted again and again that there were creatures, prehistoric monsters, out there waiting to kill them.

Everybody laughed politely, but wished Billy hadn't set Link off again.

To shut him up, Jerry called for everyone to focus on Shanty so they could finish this sequence. The camera caught Shanty standing at the edge of the pond so his silhouette was framed by the fire on the pond on his left, the foamy white water of the falls reflecting the moonlight behind him with the small fire at his feet on his right.

Shanty held up his arms and slowly lowered them. In his deep throated made for TV voice, he began the story of Apotamkon, but just after he started, Shanty's audience gasped.

Their reaction surprised him, but he continued without missing a word.

Suddenly, his audience stood up pointing at the fire. When they gasped again, Shanty stopped and looked over his shoulder. There was a splash next to the fire burning on the platform. What was it?

Jerry stood dumbfounded staring at the fire with his right hand on Mac's shoulder, "Tell me you got that."

Mac was too busy to answer as another black object rocketed out of the water silhouetted by the fire. This one was bigger than the first. Time and time again, black silhouetted creatures exploded from the water and fell back with a triumphant splash. There were two smaller ones and a bigger one. They kept jumping at the fire. One of the smaller creatures landed half on and half off the platform letting them get a good look at its body.

It looked like an escapee from a Natural History Museum or one of Mr. Spielberg's films. Mac smiled as his camera captured every exciting moment of this incredible scene.

Soon everyone was standing in awe of the spectacle unfolding in front of them. Some clapped, others whistled and yelled as they watched the prehistoric animals perform. No one could take their eyes off the show. They were all amazed when one of the smaller ones came to the edge of the pool in front of them and splashed out of the water near the small fire that Shanty used to light his arrows.

Shanty had to jump back from this creature as it landed much too close to his bare feet.

First, the thing looked at the fire and then it looked up at Shanty. The camera caught this creature and an Indian brave contemplating each other. Staring each other, they shared a silent message each amazed at the others existence. After a brief moment, it wriggled backward sliding into the water.

Jerry stood behind Mac yelling, "Tell me you got that. Did you get that? Jesus."

To shut Jerry up, Mac yelled back without taking his eyes off his camera, "I got it. I got it. I got a close up, too. Man, it was right there in front of me. God, I don't believe it."

Annie held on to Billy's hand and grabbed Shanty's arm pulling him back next to her. "He's with us. Apotamkon's children are alive right in front of us. The ancient ones were right. The legend is true."

Shanty put one arm around Hilda's waist and drew her to him. "The ancient ones are with us tonight."

At different intervals, everyone sat down keeping their eyes glued on the pool as the show continued. Suddenly one of the smaller creatures jumped out of the water on the rocks near the small fire only a few yards away from the spectators who were watching his every move. Then Mac decided to flash on his bank of camera lights wanting an even brighter image of this enticing creature.

The monster teen's eyes reflected an iridescent glow. His teeth seemed to be jumping out of his mouth as he snapped his jaws at the fire and then the lights. Surprised by the sudden lights, this teen monster shook his head back and forth at them.

Suddenly another smaller one jumped out of the water beside him hitting her brother in the neck with its head. This new arrival let out a terrifying squeak. Like a giant mad mouse, it called out "Eeecckkk." Then they both sang together. The crowd on the bank sat in awe as they screeched their high pitched duet.

Their loud EEECCCKKK echoed off the cliff walls. They were like dolphins frolicking near shore. They raised their heads in song and then snorted at the lights. The animals were so close, everyone could see spray come out of their nostrils.

Slowly a large ominous black head rose out of the water behind them. Opening its saber-toothed mouth, this adult screamed out a much louder more authoritarian cry, "AAHHCCCKKK."

The two siblings slid back from the small fire and disappeared into the water. In their hearts and minds, every person watching immediately dubbed this new creature "Big Momma." For a moment, *Big Momma's* eyes blazed in the camera lights and then she too, slid back into the dark water.

As the platform fire burned down, the show seemed to be over. Jerry was yelling over and over again at Mac, "Did you get that? Did you get it all?"

While Mac tried to calm his boss, he kept pointing his camera toward the platform fire with his camera lights still blazing. As the others talked in hushed tones sharing what they'd seen, through his camera lens Mac spotted the large Black head emerge to the right of the platform and focused on it for a close-up. The camera caught the image of this creature opening its terrifying mouth again with water dripping down her long glistening saber teeth.

Big Momma wasn't finished. Opening her throat, she sang out one more shriek, "AAAHHHEEECCCAAA." With that parting roar, she ended the night's performance.

The camp staff stared in wonder as they turned just in time to see the creature's head slip under the black water. Shanty recognized the shriek. It was the same one he heard call in the fog as a boy when he was with his dad on the pier.

With the ancient call echoing off the stone walls surrounding the falls, everyone shared excited comments about the miracle they had just witnessed.

Amazed by this ancient aquasaur's visit, Shelley wasn't surprised when Dan hugged Colby and swung him around. Shanty looked up at the moon extending his arms toward it with his hands in fists. Arching his back, he screamed loud doing his best to imitate the monster's roar.

When Dan put Lindenhurst down, he made fists and shook them at the moon echoing his best monster's roar. Soon, Colby was howling at the moon with them. At first, it seemed to be a male thing, but when Billy and Jerry started screeching the prehistoric call, the women soon joined the men mimicking their best aquasaur roar. After all, they had just seen Big Momma, the matriarch of the clan.

As their calls echoed off the surrounding cliffs, much to everyone's surprise, their roars were answered when a dark head poked out of the water just below the falls letting out a screaming..."AAAHHHEEECCCAAA." This call of the wild stopped them all cold. While Momma's echo was still bouncing off the rock cliff high above them, they all laughed and congratulated themselves on their ability to communicate with this ancient dragon.

When Jerry looked at Mac, Mac shouted back at him, "Yeah, I got it all. Screams and everything. Even that last good-bye."

After everyone stopped hugging and celebrating, they turned to Mac who smiled giving them a thumbs-up. He was glad his second camera, the one on the tripod was still pointed at the falls when Big Momma surfaced to let out her final scream. He caught every moment of this incredible evening from two different angles. When Mac turned off his lights, everyone had to wait a few seconds for their eyes to adjust to the moonlight. Slowly they gathered around Mac wanting to see the images he had captured. The camera screen was too small of everyone to see so Jerry invited them to the dining hall to view the raw unedited video.

Flashlights came out and everyone helped Mac carry his equipment down the trail. As they started to leave, Annie spotted Link still sitting alone near the edge of the water and called for everyone to stop. Running to Link, the others followed her. At first, Link didn't want to be touched and pushed Annie away. When his friends surrounded him, Link stood up still shivering from this new visit from his monsters. He tried to explain that what they considered fantastic had frightened him to the core.

They all apologized and told Link, they had been wrong to doubt him. Billy apologized and slapped Link on the back. Shanty gave him a bear hug and lifted him off his feet. After the girls hugged him, Link finally accepted their apologies.

Quietly he trailed after them on the trek back to the dining hall, but Link couldn't shake the image of the beasts swimming under him. Still frightened, he was happy to leave the falls behind. All the way back, he wondered why anyone would want to see the dreadful images of these creatures cavorting across the wall of the dining hall.

Inside the dining hall, everyone waited impatiently for Mac to set up his equipment. When he was finally ready, they sat on the picnic tables to watch Big Momma and her kids dance across the dining hall wall. If anything, the uncut video was more dramatic than real life, especially the close-ups. Even after being there, it was hard to believe the images on the wall were real. It seemed more like science fiction than science fact.

When the last image of "Big Momma" disappeared from the wall, everyone clapped not quite ready to head for their beds at the end of an adrenalin filled evening.

Shaking their heads sharing their thoughts as they headed for the door, when Harold called them back, "We have a problem."

Tired, but obedient, they gathered around the Director to find out what was wrong. When Harold had their attention, he asked, "What about the swim meet tomorrow?"

Steve was the first to respond, "What's wrong with the swim meet?"

Harold explained, "How can we have a swim meet with those creatures swimming about? I mean, is it…would it be safe?"

Shanty nodded, "Hadn't thought of that. It might not be safe. Remember the dead man in the swimming area. He had to be one of their victims."

Worried that he might lose his main event of the season, Steve tried to save it. "We can't cancel the meet. What are you going to tell the parents? There are sea monsters out there. They'll think we're crazy."

Harold hesitated, "We could show them tonight's video."

Jerry jumped in, "No, we need to keep this video secret. With tonight's addition, this show will go national and make us all rich."

Dan Cooper added, "Yeah, you can't just show this to parents. Someone will tell the papers before we're ready."

Flustered, Harold repeated, "But I don't want campers eaten by these things. I mean right in front of their parents."

Steve kept arguing, "These things are scared of motorboats. When that one chased me and Gloria in the canoe, the sound of the motor kept it away. We could station motorboats around the swimming area. That would make it safe."

Harold was puzzled, "That might work. Mr. Brant, what do you think?"

Not sure he wanted to take responsibility for the decision, Shanty responded, "These things seem to hide during the day. I think motorboats with their engines running ought to make the swim meet safe enough. All the parents will be here tomorrow. We need to have something to entertain them."

Harold asked Steve, "Where would you get the motorboats?"

"At least five or six parents come to the swimming meet by boat. They will be happy to watch the activities from their boats. That should protect the swimmers."

Annie wasn't buying Steve's argument. "What are you thinking? We know these things have already killed one man in our swimming area. You need to cancel the swim meet. We need to call in experts to determine what we're dealing with."

Steve and Jerry quickly rejected Annie's idea. Reluctantly, Harold agreed with them, "No, I'll leave it up to Steve to get the motor boats. That should make it safe enough. Okay then, we're still on for tomorrow."

****

Annie, Billy, and Shanty lugged Mac's equipment up the narrow forest trail with Mac lagging behind. Mac was out of shape and could barely drag himself up the steep climb. Wheezing up the mountain, Mac wished he had stayed on the waterfront and sent Jerry up this mountainous trek. When they reached the clearing above the falls, Mac flopped on his back staring at the cloud sprinkled bright blue sky trying to catch his breath. When the others offered to help him, Mac waved them away.

Worried about him, Annie took a bandana from her neck and wet it in the stream. Hurrying to him, she wiped Mac's face and neck. After Annie's care and a couple swigs of cold bottled water, Mac recovered enough to set up his computer and cameras. He directed his new crew to place cameras on tripods around the site so they looked out on the lake. He wanted lake shots that included a long distance view of the water meet. Then he decided he wanted one camera out on a branch hanging over the edge of the falls to catch images of Big Momma and her kids if they came out to play in the pool during the day.

Billy volunteered and with Shanty holding a safety line as he braced against the tree, Billy edged out on the branch over the cliff. When Mac announced the computer image was just right, Billy fastened the camera to the limb with duct tape.

Sitting in front of his computer that was on the ground in front of him, Mac focused one camera on the people gathering at the waterfront for the competition and another one on the lake stretching out from the dock. The top of the falls was the perfect place to view the lake and the water meet. With his assortment of lenses, Mac bragged he could pick up the freckles on any girl at the beach. After checking the Wi-Fi connections on his computer, Mac declared he was ready.

When he focused one camera on a huge yacht in the middle of the lake, he saw two good-looking young females sunning themselves on the front of the boat without their tops. As he panned along the large vessel, he saw an older guy walking a bikini clad beauty along the side of the yacht and disappear through a cabin door.

Annie stood at the edge of the cliff soaking in the beautiful vista. Today the blue lake with its collar of green was more radiant than ever. Leaving the cliff, she told her friends, she was still worried that Big Momma and her children might show up at the swim meet.

When Shanty suggested that would get the competitors to set new speed records, they all laughed.

Mac demonstrated how his computer could pick up the images from Jerry's camera at the waterfront and was able to catch and record every image from each camera on his hard drive. He added that he didn't expect much from Jerry's shots. Jerry was a real dog. The most you could expect from him would be close-ups of the best looking girls in swim suits. He told them that Jerry had already hit on the Camp Director's wife last night in the hotel and insisted that Jerry claimed that she had made a pass at him in the hallway.

Billy laughed as he glanced at Shanty who told Mac that was no surprise.

When Mac brought up the computer image from Jerry's camera, sure enough Jerry was focusing on an attractive young counselor that filled out her tank suit rather well. Mac told his attentive new friends that Kia was his only hope. With her down there directing Jerry to different scenes, they might get a few good shots once the action started.

****

As his water meet ticked along smoothly, Steve was proud of his organization. Motor boats were stationed around the swimming area with their engines running to keep the monsters at bay. A large enthusiastic group of parents, brothers, sisters and grandparents lined the shore cheering on the campers racing for ribbons. The competition was awesome. Steve couldn't believe some of the times his kids were turning in. To set up a canoe race, he was about to lead a group of campers out to the middle of the lake for a race back to shore.

Unfortunately, the next event was the backstroke. He hated to miss this competition because it pitted two of his favorite campers against each other. *Preston Wilder will probably win,* he thought. Preston was tall with the lean body a swimmer needs, but still needed to develop a bit more muscle to power this long arms and legs. Robert Maxwell, or "Bobby Max" as the campers called him, would be his main challenger. Bobby Max didn't have a swimmer's build, but he was the best athlete in the camp. He had the strength and coordination to do everything well.

Preston would be in the outside lane and Bobby Max would be in the lane just inside him. As he passed them on his jet ski, Steve shook his fist at both swimmers as he shouted at them to do their best. To keep the meet on schedule, Steve waved to his canoers who followed him out into the lake.

Lea and Link stayed behind to run the backstroke competition. When Link announced, "Get ready." The swimmers hoisted themselves up on the backstroke bars on the side of the dock to get ready for Link's whistle. Preston and Bobby Max pulled their upper bodies out of the water and leaned back ready to spring into action. When everyone was set, Link's loud whistle sent the swimmers splashing off.

Link looked down the course and was the first one to see it. A large black ominous triangular head surfaced just outside the swimming area. For a moment, Link froze. He hated these dreadful monsters and wasn't sure what to do. A father in the nearest boat spotted it too and gunned his motor to drive his boat toward the creature to frighten it off. Instead of being scared out into the lake, the aquasaur dove under the buoyed rope and came up in the swimming area.

The two outside swimmers, Preston and Bobby Max, were heading directly toward the dark monster's snapping jaws. Now, the parents on the shore saw it and screamed for the swimmers to stop. The swimmers heard the parents yelling, but dismissed the noise as applause. Encouraged by the screaming crowd, each boy dug deeper on each stroke to go faster.

The roar of the parents shook Link out of his daze. He repeatedly blew his whistle to get the swimmers to stop. The four swimmers nearest the shore finally stopped and looked back at Link wondering why he stopped the race. When they noticed the new entry in this race had very large teeth, they set records getting to shore. Filming from the beach, Jerry and Kia captured the terror on each camper's face as they ran out of the water with the monster framed behind them.

Preston and Bobby Max didn't stop for Link's whistle or the screaming crowd on the shore. Instead, they just swam harder in the outside lanes thinking the noise was part of the excitement. Next to the rope, Preston was in the lead. The monster had surfaced in the next inside lane just waiting for Bobby Max to swim right into his open jaws.

With the Bobby Max only a few feet from the monsters teeth, the crowd on the beach let out an anguished roar. Leading Bobby Max by half a body length in the outside lane, Preston crashed into the monster's side. The creature turned his head to find out what had hit him just as Bobby Max ran into its neck. Both boys wondered what they had hit and pushed away from the object spitting out the water they swallowed from their sudden stop. After they cleared the water from their eyes, they found themselves staring into the jaws of a huge prehistoric dinosaur with incredible teeth.

As the frightened boys splashed away from this monster, the creature let out a scream and backed away despite its size advantage. Finally it dove below the surface and disappeared. The scared racers set records swimming as fast as they could back to the dock. Lea and Link grabbed the boys and swung them up on the dock the moment their hands touched.

With the two racers safe, everyone on the beach, the dock and in the boats held their breath as they surveyed the water waiting for the creature to surface. Link pointed to the end of the dock shouting, "There it is."

The large black beast broke the surface just before it swam under the dock. With Lea and the boys, Link ran to the other side of the dock to see the creature swim out from under it. Emerging from under the dock, they were amazed by the huge black body that swam through the swimming area. When it reached the buoyed rope, it shot out of the water up and over it more like a performing dolphin than a retreating prehistoric beast. Everyone in the crowd got a good look at its large head and body as it took to the air. Jerry and Kia caught this dramatic exit from the perfect angle as a mixture of screams of fright and astonishment bid the creature good-bye.

CHAPTER 29

Washington Irving wrote a story about a man in New York who went into a wood to escape his nagging wife. After meeting another man on his wander and assisting him with his liquor, a young Rip Van Winkle fell asleep. Waking up many years later with a long white beard, the old Mr. Winkle wondered how long he'd been asleep. The Clarendon-Linden Fault in upstate New York turned out to be the Rip Van Winkle of faults. Long ago after moving the earth as a young fault when the earth was forming, Mr. Linden Fault escaped his labors by falling asleep content with his work. Just as the smell of coffee brewing in the kitchen can wake up a young man growing old, RealAirGas had been intravenously pumping a stimulating beverage into this sleeping giant. Blinking his eyes, Rip Van Linden was getting ready to announce to the world he was awake and lethal. Tugging on his fault plates, he wondered who dug this big hole in his beautiful salt bed. He didn't like the work of man and decided to stop it. *A good shake or two might do the trick*, he thought.

****

The friction holding the Clarendon-Linden fault together was rapidly decreasing as waste water from the fracking process lubricated its plates. The old fault was ready to move the earth like it had many years ago. Like the good old days before dreams had quieted his land for so long.

Running along an unknown crack in the strata leading from Cayuga Lake to the Linden fault, fracking fluid and waste water under high pressure let the fault below Batavia, New York suddenly slip. The two plates of the Linden fault crunched over each other creating the initial quake. This movement measured 7.47 on the Richter Scale and would be called the *Jumbo Quake* named after the *747 Jumbo Jet*. The land along the fault was ripped apart for over 23 miles. The vertical displacement was just under 10 feet forming ridges and cliffs all along the fault. The actual fault rupture lasted just over four minutes, not quite matching the duration of The Great Alaska Quake in '64 that set the North American record lasting four minutes and thirty-eight seconds.

The fault plates far below the earth tore the earth apart sending out tremors that ripped apart the land all the way to the surface. As the surfaces of the geologic plates crawled and bumped over each other, they generated tremor after tremor. When the movement stopped, the shaking still continued as the plates tried to secure a new grip on each other as they settled together. The quake radiated out from an epicenter just west of Dale, New York and was the big one that no one thought would happen or wanted to happen. This tremendous release of energy literally shook apart upstate New York.

Just over two minutes after the initial quake, an aftershock measuring 6.3 kept the land shaking as it ripped apart structures on the surface and below the ground that had been weakened by the initial quake. Just as residents started to recover from the first two earthquakes, five minutes later a second aftershock shook the earth registering 5.7 making sure the damage was complete.

Each movement of the fault plates created a quake that people felt above and below the ground. These shakes forced the residents of the state to hang on as cracks appeared in their homes and roads. Each foot that the fault plates crunched over each other released tremendous amounts of energy that radiated out in every direction. Cars going east crashed into ridges and cars going west flew over low cliffs as the roads were ripped apart. As the soil liquefied, houses and stores sunk while others were pushed up as one plate rolled over the other pushing up the land. Gas, water and sewer lines were broken starting fires and floods. Disaster falls short of describing the destruction.

****

On the cliff above the falls overlooking the lake, the trees started to whip back and forth. As the earth began to shake, Billy, Annie and Shanty looked up at the sky. The movement of the earth became so intense Mac didn't even notice the monster that had joined the swim meet. The rippling earth sent one of Mac's cameras plunging into the pool below the falls and others tipped over. Only one rode out the quake still upright on its tripod.

As the tremors generated by the quake traveled toward the lake, a camera landed on its side, but still caught the action of quake as it rolled through the camp and out to the lake. Big waves tossed around the boats on the lake and even moved a big yacht violently up and down. The camera that stayed upright caught the panic of the people at the water meet as the trembling earth knocked them off their feet. Mac leaned over to protect his computers and sitting right next to him, Annie braced herself as the ancient ones moved the earth beneath her.

Standing at the cliff near the falls when 747 struck, Billy was knocked him off his feet and tossed forward. Thrown on his chest, his shoulders slipped over the edge of the cliff as the earth still trembled beneath him. With his hands and arms already dangling in air, he had no way to stop his slide. Slowly the moving earth carried his body over the edge.

As Billy's head and chest dangled over the cliff above the falls, he yelled and tried to stick his fingers in a small crack on the face of the cliff to stop his fall. His fingers held for a moment, but then slipped out. As death dragged him toward the rocks below, he realized he was at nature's mercy and couldn't save himself.

Shanty rode out the big shake on one knee with his hands braced on the ground to keep his balance. When he saw Billy falling into the abyss, he dove for his leg. As Shanty's hand clamped over Billy's ankle, Billy wondered why he was no longer falling. Hanging over the cliff without a rope was terrifying. In his panic, he didn't notice the firm hand on his ankle. Billy let out a long scream that he thought was his last.

Refusing to acknowledge the strain on his fingers as gravity pulled Billy's body toward the rocks, Shanty slapped his other hand on Billy's leg just above the ankle. Slowly Shanty pulled his legs up under him and leaned back pulling hard on Billy's leg. Ever so slowly, he inched Billy back from the edge.

Literally dangling over the cliff, Billy stared at the deadly rocks below. Then he felt his body jerk back toward safety. As Shanty heaved again and again, Billy scooted back another couple of inches. As the tremors kept increasing, Billy swung wildly praying that Shanty had the strength to hold on.

Shanty's hands were slipping. He didn't know how much longer he could hold Billy's body as it swung back and forth as the quake continued. The energy released by each tremor was ripping Billy's ankle from his hands. He was losing his grip.

Suddenly Annie appeared next to Shanty and grabbed hold of Billy's other leg. She put Billy's ankle under her arm and gripped her hands just below his knee. Pulling back with all her might, she was able to stop Billy's body from swinging.

Annie's arrival gave Shanty a chance to reset his grip one hand at a time. With his hands firmly planted on Billy's ankle, Shanty nodded to Annie. Together they leaned back and heaved. Slowly, Annie and Shanty dragged

Billy back over the edge, but Annie couldn't match Shanty's strength. Another tremor, loosened Annie's grip on Billy's leg and he slipped back toward the rocks. Through gritted teeth, Shanty shouted, "Grab it again. Help me."

Annie's fingers closed in a death grip on Billy's denim pant leg as she leaned back to help Shanty pull Billy back from the cliff. Feeling weak, Annie wasn't sure she had enough strength left to save him. She pleaded with her eyes as she looked at Shanty.

Shanty saw the strain on her face and knew this was the moment. They could drop him or save him. Their physical strength was gone. Billy was a big load. Shanty pressed his lips together as he tapped his inner warrior. Shanty knew only the strength of their ancestors could save Billy now. He nodded at Annie with grim determination streaking across his strained face. She understood and gritted her teeth. Their minds took command as their bodies failed. Somehow they managed one final tug. This final surge dragged Billy's shoulders to solid ground. Without their help, breathing hard, Billy inched carefully back from the cliff.

With Billy safe, Shanty let go of his leg and moved his fingers to bring blood back to his hands. Staring at his hands, Shanty realized his strength helped Billy survive, but his mental discipline had saved him. His mind forced him to keep his grip long after every muscle and fiber of his body cried out for him to let go.

Annie helped Billy crawl back from the cliff. When Billy was safe, he rolled over on his back gasping for life's breath. Annie threw herself on his chest with tears streaming down her face yelling, "You...you almost died."

As Billy gasped for air, he shouted, I...I...I thought I was dead." Between breaths, Billy tried to make sense of his ordeal finally mustering enough energy to speak, "You, you saved me."

Shanty fell on his back looking at the sky as a Golden Eagle glided out of a frothy cloud. The messenger of the *Great Spirit* cried once before flying off as the ancestors kept shaking the earth below him. Looking up at the trees still swaying from the quake, Shanty laughed as Annie shouted at Billy.

"Damn you. Why did you do that?" Annie pounded Billy's chest and he was too exhausted to stop her. Finally, he started to laugh. Annie hit his chest one more time crying out, "I thought you were gone."

"Me too, me too."

Annie kissed Billy's cheeks to make sure he was really there. Convinced he was still with the living, Annie rolled off him. After a moment of deep breathing, they crawled to Shanty. Still on his back staring at the sky while the earth rolled beneath him, Shanty pushed up on one elbow as Annie kissed his cheek, "You are amazing. Thank you."

"Couldn't have done it without you." Shanty whispered in her ear, "I like him too." Then he turned to Billy, "If you're going to fall off cliffs go on a damn diet."

As Shanty sat up, Billy laughed as he threw his arms around their shoulders. The three of them rocked back and forth together in an adrenalin draining hug as the ground finally stopped rolling beneath them.

Monitoring his computer screens oblivious of the life and death drama he had just missed, Mac called to them, "Man oh man. Get over here. You've got to see this."

Annie, Billy and Shanty forced themselves to get up as the shaking subsided. They had to force their exhausted bodies to make the short trek to Mac's computers and found him pointing at the screen. The images from the camera that was tied to the branch overlooking the pool at the bottom of the falls were flashing across his screen. Even with the camera bouncing up and down, you could still see three dark shadows swimming in the churning water below the falls. These shadow creatures swam across the pool and headed down the creek that emptied into the lake.

Mac yelled at them, "They came out from under the falls. There must be a cave or old mine down there for them to hide in."

While the men rushed to the edge of the falls to catch a glimpse of these prehistoric creatures, Mac grabbed Annie's arm and pointed to his gyro camera. After grabbing it, she left him running to the cliff. At the edge, she arrived just in time to capture the images of the creatures swimming under the same rope bridge where they scared Link.

After the creatures had disappeared down the stream, Billy and Shanty set up the other cameras. Billy pointed one on the big yacht that was being slowly pulled into a circle of swirling white water at the center of the lake. Shanty focused his camera on the panic of the crowd at the water meet as they dealt with the quakes.

CHAPTER 30

The first tremors of the Jumbo Quake made the crowd at the water meet forget their dinosaur watch and look up the hill. As this huge quake rolled toward them, they could see the large maple, oak and pine trees whip back and forth. Many of these stalwart sentinels lost their tops while others were uprooted crashing to the ground. At the beach, the crowd could see the old hotel sway back and forth as it rode out the tremors.

In the hotel, Harold leaned over his desk trying to ride out the quake in his desk chair. The building leaned one way then back the other. After swaying back and forth several times, the rafters above him broke just as the big quake finished with a jerk. The roof crashed down on Harold with one rafter glancing off his head and another stabbing him through the back.

When the first tremors hit, Ursula was in their apartment trying on the new bikini she planned to wear at the water meet. She ran to the doorway to brace against the quake. When the shaking finally stopped, she heard the roof crash down at the end of the hall and stumbled out into the hallway to find out what had happened. The building kept shaking as energy from the quake kept radiating through the ground. Ursula was just able to stay on her feet as she staggered down the hall.

At first, the door to Harold's office wouldn't open. She grabbed the handle and hit the door with her shoulder, but it still didn't open. Wondering why it was so easy to open locked doors on TV and why it was so hard to do it in real life, she hit it again harder with her shoulder with no luck. It was frozen in place. As the building swayed again, the door popped open by itself. *That's better*, she thought.

With his desk buried under fallen rafters, Ursula couldn't see Harold. When she heard a moan, she climbed over the rubble to find him. Making her way to his desk, Ursula spotted Harold on the floor with the broken end of a rafter stabbing through his side just above his hip. Another jagged piece of timber was sticking out of his back. His head was bleeding and he was groaning in pain.

Thank God you're alive, she thought as she climbed over a rafter and under another to kneel by his side. Realizing that he was dying, Harold blurted out, "I always loved you."

Caressing his head and pushing back a tuft of hair on his forehead, she told him, "You were always special." As those words drifted off her tongue, the first shake of the aftershock brought the rest of the hotel roof down on them.

****

When the ground started to shake beneath their feet, the crowd on the beach forgot the dinosaur and wondered what was happening. 747 threw the spectators to the ground making them fall every which way. For the longest four minutes of their lives, everyone hugged the ground praying for the shaking to stop. Parents held their children tight trying to protect them. The boat shed shook and collapsed. Steve's cabin leaned one way and slammed back the other collapsing in a roar of dust. The storage building at the end of the dock tipped back and forth before it fell on members of the crowd. Two trees along the road fell into the spectators huddled on the ground under them. The dock twisted from side to side and then rolled up and down. Lea and Link were thrown off the dock into the water. At the same time, the high lifeguard chairs tipped over spilling the lifeguards into the lake.

As Lea and Link surfaced, they looked at the shore and were amazed by the destruction. Fear was etched on every face in the crowd. The dock was wrecked with planks thrown in every direction. Most of the spectators seemed to be in shock. Not sure if Big Mama's relative was still around, Lea and Link hustled out of the water.

As they splashed out, they organized the rescue efforts. They ran to the storage building and started pulling trapped parents and kids out from under the smashed boards. After climbing to their feet, Jerry and Kia were able to capture every detail of the rescue through their camera lens. In a collective daze, the crowd began to recover as they tried to comprehend what had just happened. The members of the crowd who weren't hurt helped the others trapped under the trees.

Leading the canoes out into the lake on his jet ski, Steve was pleased to hear the cheering behind him. He had never heard a crowd yell so loud. Steve peeled off to one side and motioned for his canoers to turn around to face the beach. As the campers maneuvered their canoes, on his perch on his jet ski, he saw the trees all over the camp waving with some even tipping over and crashing down. He was amazed when the crowd of parents and children were suddenly knocked off their feet. Confused, he wondered what was happening.

Then Steve saw waves that started at the beach and grew larger as they moved toward him reversing the normal flow of wind on the lake. Still puzzled, he forced himself to remain calm for the sake of the campers. Now the rolling waves had white caps as they grew bigger and faster. He pointed his jet ski toward the waves and quietly told his campers, "Point your canoes into these waves and hold on. This is going to be fun."

When the quake induced waves struck, the canoes were pointed at the shore ready to ride over them.

****

At the RAG site protest, the jumbo quake threw the protestors to the ground. Cars parked nearby bounced up and down with their alarms squealing out a cacophony of discordant sounds. 747 flipped cars over rupturing their gas tanks when they landed. Sparks from metal hitting the pavement ignited the gas. Car after car exploded in a burst of flames. Whips of orange lashed out and set more cars aflame. The cars in the lot took flight as they blew up. Gas flowed under a propane tanker truck parked just inside the fence not far from the protesters. The car fires set this spill under the propane truck ablaze.

The burning gas scorched the propane tanker truck with searing heat until it suddenly blew up shooting jagged pieces of metal and flames in every direction. The red hot pieces of glowing metal flew through the chain link fence slicing through the protesters hanging on to the fence to ride out the quake. The protesters who escaped these glowing shards were burned alive by the flaming propane that followed the flying death. Shrapnel laced blackened bodies blew through the air across the road. Horrible pieces of torn human flesh flew just above the other protesters who, luckily, had been slammed to the ground by the quake.

Inside the RAG compound, one well-head snapped off and two others were knocked loose. Sparks flew as metal was driven into the concrete. One after another, the three wells exploded shooting orange flames and black smoke high into the sky. It was fortunate that most of the weekend shift had been told to stay home due to the protest. Only five workers had made the trek through the demonstrators. These workers were knocked to the ground as 747 rolled though the site, but there was no escaping the orange death that enveloped their bodies. None of these workers escaped the torrent of twisted metal and fire.

****

On the other side of the lake at the ISC protest, the Jumbo Quake wasn't quite as strong due to the different strata under the site and the increased distance from the epicenter. When it hit, most of the demonstrators fall down on the macadam road near the entrance while others grabbed the tall fences topped with razor wire to ride out the quake. With the fences swinging, the protestors laced their fingers through the chain links hoping not to fall. The traffic poles blocking the entrance and exit to the salt mine flew up and down as the guard shack whipped back and forth. The big quake was too much for the poor shack to endure. It collapsed crushing the guard braced in the doorway trying to ride out the quake.

Shelley was enjoying a cup of coffee under the break tent when the first quake hit. She ducked under the picnic table to ride out the quake as the ground moved beneath her. The tent tarp flapped violently as that quake rolled through. This massive movement of the earth ripped up the stakes holding up the tent frame. As the ropes flew loose, the tarp frame above the coffee area crashed down on the picnic tables. The metal beams hit two protesters sitting together near the corner of the tent slicing off the boy's head and gouging deep into his girlfriend's back. Under her table, Shelley was smashed to the ground by the intensity of the quake. One pole and part of the frame slammed down on the table above her, but Shelley was lucky. The table cracked, but did not break.

The cars and trucks in this parking lot bounced up and down setting off the alarms, but they didn't flip over. Unfortunately, the quake was strong enough to rip the razor wire off the top of the fence. As it flew through the air, it whipped to the ground slicing huge cuts in the backs, legs and heads of the demonstrators clinging to the fence. Then the fence toppled over trapping the bleeding victims on the ground under it. With each tremor, the razor wire sawed deeper into the bodies of the protestors as screams of pain escaped their lips.

When the earth stopped shaking, Shelley crawled from under the picnic table. At first, she found it hard to stand up. Her legs were weak and her head was spinning. She flopped down on the bench attached to the broken table. Putting her head between her legs, it took her a moment to recover. Not five feet from her, friends were trapped and bleeding under the fallen fence. When she tried to stand again, this time she felt better. Stumbling to the fence, she reached through the razor wire to help a friend as a sharp blade of wire sliced a deep cut in her arm. In shock, Shelley just wiped the blood off on her jeans and tried to lift a section of fence, but couldn't move it. It was too heavy.

As she stepped back from the fence, her ankle scrapped against another piece of the razor sharp fence cutting open a wide gash. Ignoring her injuries, she reached into her jeans pocket and pulled out her I-phone. She tapped in 911, but there was no answer. Then the first aftershock knocked to her knees. When the earth stopped shaking, she struggled to her feet still bleeding and hit the number again, but still no answer.

Looking around, she saw her friends trying to stand. Others were wandering around like zombies. As the protesters trapped under the fence at her feet begged for help, she called to others to help her lift up the fence. Two guys and a girl joined her.

"On three." Shelley shouted and they heaved with all their might. The fence came up, but as it did, the razor wire slashed new cuts into the flesh of many of the protectors trapped under the fence. As the victims screamed with pain, one boy tried to crawl out, but Shelley and her small team couldn't hold the fence up. It was just too heavy. As it slipped from their grasps, it came crashing down on the boy crushing him to the ground as a coil of razor wire ripped across his face.

As Shelley and her friends stepped back, she tried her phone again. Still no answer. Looking around for help, she spotted a garbage barrel and ran to it. After tipping it over, she rolled it to the fence as the contents spilled out.

Calling for more people to help her, Shelley told a girl to push the barrel under the fence after they picked it up. With a team of college boys and girls, they pulled the fence just high to slip the barrel under it. With the fence resting on the barrel, one by one the rescuers pulled the trapped protestors out from under the bloody chain link.

After Shelley dragged out one girl, another girl grabbed her, "You need to sit down. Your arm and leg are bleeding. You need help."

Sitting on the picnic table bench while the girl wrapped torn pieces of her blouse around Shelley's cuts, Shelley tried 911 again and listened to it ring. Finally, there was an answer. She told the operator to send as many ambulances as possible to the gate of the ISC salt mine. Fifty or sixty people had been injured and desperately needed help.

****

Just before the quake hit, Herm Douglas, R.A.G. Vice President, was standing at one end of the ISC conference table. Angry because this "Salt Bitch" had accused his gas company of causing the small seismic disturbances near their end of the lake, he found it hard to keep his temper. This female miner dared to suggest that the gas company had dissolved the bottom of her mine with their fracking fluid and that threatened to destroy their whole operation. She'd claimed their fracking fluid let gas into the mine that had exploded on the bottom level. She guaranteed that if their mine was damaged again, she would personally shut down their wells forever.

He wanted to shout and, you know, cuss at her.

Slowly, he surveyed the gas and salt officials gathered around the large conference table staring at him. "You, you salt folks sound like the...the crazy environmentalists at the gate. Disposing of waste water in wells is good for the environment. It just puts water back into the ground. Hydro-injection to remove gas does not cause earthquakes."

Just as the word earthquake rolled off his tongue, 747 hit. To remain standing, he leaned over the table as he tried stay upright. The next tremor knocked him back into his chair. Flopped in his chair, a big tremor flipped his chair somersaulting him heels over head to the floor.

The other gas and salt executives grabbed the table trying to hold on as their swivel chairs rolled around from the force of each tremor. Some were able to stay in their chairs while others fell to the floor as their chairs rolled out from under them. When the main blows of 747 hit, Ruth Hager ducked under the table and rode out the quake on her hands and knees. Slammed to the floor, her face hit the carpet, but not before she saw the RAG vice-president turn a full flip in the air as the quake sent him flying out of his chair. The look on his face was priceless. *No, quakes,* she thought. *You bastard, what have you done to us?*

Ruth saw Albert Olson on the floor next to her and was able to roll him under the table before the ceiling tiles began to fall. While the table bounced around, it protected them from the falling debris. As 747 ripped apart the metal frame holding up the ceiling tiles, bent twisted metal rained down on the executives spilled on the floor. As the ceiling frame fell on him, Herm put up his hands up to ward off the falling death. One piece sliced through his hand and another impaled his chest.

Sequestered in a restroom smoking weed, Louise sat in a dark granite stall on her throne as she rode out the quake thinking. *This is some damn good shit. Rocks my world.*

****

Professor Lindenhurst was typing on his computer at his desk. *Yes,* he thought, *I still call it typing not keyboarding.* He loved his computer. It made it so much easier to organize and publish articles. This afternoon, he was working on an article to co-author with Dr. Cooper. He didn't like calling Cooper, doctor. Cooper didn't have one degree from an Ivy League institution. No, he was a California surfer who attended that Stanford pretender.

He swiveled his chair around to look at the photos and certificates that highlighted his professional life. This fossil find and the discovery of living fossils in the lake would be the perfect ending for his distinguished career. It was the big discovery that every scientist hoped for, but few actually achieved. He might even earn a bronze plaque in the *Cornell Circle of Honor.*

Colby sighed a good sigh when he felt the first tremor. *What's happening,* he wondered. *Is this an earthquake?*

As 747 reached its peak, he was scared as the building actually rocked. He loved this old Ivy covered building. Married to his work, Cornell had been his real home for so long. Now his lovely home was seriously shaking. As tremor after tremor forced it back and forth, he thought of standing in the door or going under his desk, but decided to ride out the quake in his chair. The shaking was so bad his oversized desk started to dance across the floor as the tokens of his career dropped off the walls. First one by one, then all of his photos and awards came crashing to the floor. Next his collection of books cascaded to the floor from his heavy eight foot oak bookshelves. Then with a final burst of energy, 747 brought those beautiful antique shelves down on Colby crushing him to his desk. As bricks fell outside, the glass in his windows shattered. Pinned under the bookshelves, a ceiling tile glanced off his head. It hurt. He screamed with pain and was scared.

CHAPTER 31

Far underneath the lake, the tremors from seven-forty seven hit the crack below the salt mine that the fracking fluid had opened in the bottom of the mine. The energy released by the quake radiated up through the weakened strata enlarging the crack that had pierced the mine. Each tremor pulled the earth under the mine further and further apart and the crack grew larger and larger. With the bottom of the mine ripping open, the energy released by the quake weakened all the levels of the salt mine above it. Thin pedestals designed to survive a 6.0 quake snapped when 7.47 hit. Chunks of salt fell from the ceiling throughout the mine. The floors at each level sagged as more pedestals broke below them. The miners were scared. They knew the mine was coming down on their heads and they wondered why they weren't getting the signal to evacuate.

Larger pedestals surrounding the broken dome above the first level were stressed. Cracks appeared, but at first they didn't break waiting for the aftershocks to pull them apart. From 747, the ceiling sagged above the first level of the mine and the aftershocks split the layers of salt above the dome. When the pedestals finally broke, the salt bed and the earth above it sagged. The strata above the mine just below the lake was pulled apart. Gravity pulled each level of the mine down as the energy from the quake pushed up. Jumping from fissure to fissure, a crack split the strata between the lake and the mine. The lake bottom was breached. At first, the sediment from the lake settled into the crack and plugged it, but this was only a momentary delay. Soon the pressure of the water pushing down coupled with the shaking from quake below flushed out the dirt plug opening the crack.

At the beginning the water seeped in, but soon with increasing speed it poured down through the crack eroding the sides of the breach enlarging the size of the growing hole. When this torrent of water reached the interior of the salt mine, it fell through the hole created by earlier quakes spewing water out on each level.

The rushing water ripped off chunks of salt expanding the hole. It was a repeat of the Lake Peigneur disaster only this time it was Cayuga. The forces of nature coupled with a manmade catalyst were too much for the mine and lake to endure. The fracking lubricated the fault plates and initiated the quake that ripped the salt mine apart causing it to collapse. On the surface of the lake, the falling water created a whirlpool as the water poured and roared into the miles of tunnels and caverns in the salt mine. Cayuga Lake began its death rattle.

****

Steve felt proud as he watched his campers ride out the quake-induced waves in their canoes. He had trained them to handle rough water and they were doing a fine job. Riding out the waves, he signaled his kids to paddle in to shore. The race was no longer important. As the boy closest to him dipped in his paddle, his canoe turned its side to the last big wave. This whitecap flipped over the boy's canoe and swamped it throwing the camper into the churning water. Steve threw his jet ski into action and powered over to the boy. When he reached him, Steve jumped off and pushed the camper up on the ski and told him to ride it slowly to shore promising to empty his canoe and follow him in. Pleased to see the little guy safely away, Steve pushed down one end of the canoe making the other end shoot up in the air as he started the process of emptying it.

Suddenly there was a roar behind him. Turning to the noise, he was surprised to see a huge yacht surrounded by a sea of white foam that seemed to be bubbling up from the bottom of the lake. Before he could escape, the white foaming water surrounded him. Holding on to the canoe, he was swept around in a large growing circle of swirling white water. Looking over his shoulder, he saw a terrifying funnel of water swirling below him drawing him into its vortex. He held on to the side of the canoe hoping that would slow his descent while he searched for a way to escape.

The big yacht was also caught in the whirlpool above him and was racing toward him. With the yacht bearing down on him, he had no choice. He pushed himself away from the canoe and dove into the swirling waters disappearing into the deadly whirlpool.

****

Bob Fletcher lay on the bed in his stateroom trying to recover from Doris's visit to his cabin. Through a drunken haze, he noticed his yacht was rolling in the waves and wondered why the lake was suddenly so choppy. *The wind must have picked-up*, he thought.

He noticed the boat seemed to be gaining speed. Suddenly, he heard the girls yelling on deck and smiled as he visualized their bikinied bottoms jumping up and down. When their shouts turned to shrieks, he decided to join the fun.

As Bob staggered toward the cabin door another big wave hit knocking him flat on the deck. With a tangle of oaths falling from his tongue, he pushed himself and stumbled out of his cabin. Having trouble navigating the rolling deck, he noticed the young women were standing at the railing pointing and screaming at something in the water.

Curious, Bob weaved across the deck just able to keep his balance as he banged into the railing and looked over the side. A huge whirlpool was drawing his beautiful yacht down into it. Then he heard his yacht hit something. Looking toward the bow, he saw half of a crushed canoe float by. As he leaned over the railing watching the broken canoe float passed him, another big wave hit that made him lose his balance and flip over the railing into the angry dark green water.

When the girls saw him fall, they screamed. Doris ran down the railing and grabbed a life-saving buoy with a rope attached to it. She drew her arm back and tossed it just beyond Bob. She shouted, "Yes." It was a good throw. As she pulled the buoy toward Bob, it bumped his head.

Bob Fletcher found the water pleasant and enjoyed the white foam swirling around him. Startled when this floating thing hit him, Bob just stared at it as it floated passed him. *God, that girl almost hit me. Won't ask her to come out with me next time,* he thought.

He looked around wondering how he got into this raging water park. *Where are my kids? Wow, this is great,* he thought, as he sank below the waves with a curious drunken smile on his face.

When she saw Bob go under, Doris stopped her efforts to save him and climbed the ladder to the top deck to save the yacht. After she pushed the start button kicking on the engine, the yacht's large screws pushed against the strong current. Hoping the powerful engines of this behemoth would save her and her friends, Doris thrust the throttle forward and prayed. Slowly the big yacht lumbered out of the vortex.

Steve surfaced and saw a guy fall from the yacht. He wanted to help, but had problems of his own. As he spun around in the whirlpool funnel, he realized he was gone. He worked hard to stay on the surface, but wasn't strong enough to swim out of the spinning water sucking him down. White water whipped around him drawing him lower and lower into the lake.

As he disappeared into the bottom of the funnel, he took a long breath with the faint hope that he might swim out of the funnel once he was under water.

****

Under a broken front end loader, Terry felt *Jumbo's* first tremor as it rattled through the mine and immediately slid out from under the machine towering above him literally saving his life. The front end loader dropped off the lift crashing just inches from his head ripping off a three inch chunk of flesh from his shoulder. Terry screamed with pain as the salt bed moved violently beneath him. Jumping up, he dodged the salty hail raining down from above and dove under a steel bench for protection.

747 was turning the miner's workplace into their tomb. Trapped underground, the miners stopped what they were doing knowing something bad was happening to the mine. Most were knocked off their feet while conveyor belts flipped over and machinery was tossed around at each level of the mine. Chunks of salt started falling from the walls and the ceiling. Smaller vehicles were tipped over and larger ones were thrown in every direction. Broken conveyor belts spewed chunks of salt in all directions.

One operator was killed by a flying piece of salt and others were severely cut. Big front-end loaders crushed through the small pillars slicing through them like toothpicks. Miners were killed as these giant machines rolled over them out of control. Product buckets swung back and forth spilling the salt they had been carrying to the surface. Luckily the human hoist was at the bottom. The cables rattled with each surge of energy, but didn't break.

Charley was in the break area and tried to ride out the quake in his desk chair, but 747 flipped him out of his chair throwing him to the mine floor. As he landed, the rusty refrigerator toppled down on top of him crushing his right arm and leg. He yelled out in pain and then kept yelling for someone to help him. While he screamed, he tried to get the emergency remote out of his right pants pocket with his left hand, but couldn't reach under the refrigerator to get it.

Miners weren't sure what to do. They waited in place hoping and praying for the lights to go off signaling an evacuation. Some hesitated while others refused to wait and ran to escape. As the mine started to collapse around them, panic drove the miners toward the hoist. The sound of salt beds crashing and tunnels breaking triggered their primal need to survive and ended any need for a signal.

Still pinned under the refrigerator, Charley struggled to get to his remote while strong tremors rolled beneath him and salt crashed down from above. Charley yelled again and again for help. With one arm crushed by the *fridge*, he couldn't push out from under it.

Terry heard Charley's call, but didn't want to leave the safety of the steel tool bench as larger chunks of salt crashed down from the ceiling. Then his military training kicked in. A buddy was down. He summoned the courage he needed to make a run to the break room. As he moved out, a chunk of salt hit his thigh throwing him to the ground. With a yelp of pain, he fell forward and broke his fall with his hands. Another sharp piece glanced off his shoulder as he popped up running. His thigh ached, but the adrenalin coursing through his system let him ignore the pain. As he ran, he heard loud breaking and snapping noises all around him that were soon joined by the sound of roaring water. This didn't make sense. There is no water in a salt mine.

Finding Charley pinned under the refrigerator still screaming for help, Terry braced his legs and lifted the 'fridge trying not to hurt Charley's arm and leg. Charley let out a groan of pain as he pushed himself out from under the refrigerator. Immediately, he tried to use his right arm to get his emergency remote out of his right pocket, but his arm didn't respond. His crushed arm just hung at his side as pain shot through his body.

Charley yelled, "Get the remote out of my pocket."

As Terry finished shoving the refrigerator aside, he yelled back, "What?"

"My right pocket. The remote. Get it. For God's sake evacuate. Push the damn button."

Terry patted down Charley's pants pocket and felt the remote. With some difficulty, he slipped it out and pushed down the red button. Any miners that weren't already running to escape began sprinting to the hoist as the lights went out while the mine collapsed around them.

****

Steve was afraid to open his eyes as he sunk below the lake and surrendered to the green death dragging him down. Battered from side to side, he was cut and bruised as he fell through the crack at the bottom of the lake. With his lungs about to burst, a calm quieted his fearful mind. He accepted his fate and prepared for death. Suddenly, the falling water spit him out as he fell through the dome at level one of the salt mine.

His body slammed hard into the mine floor knocking out the small amount of air left in his lungs. He rolled on his back gasping for air engulfed in the dark with only a ghostly green glow filtering down through the water falling from above. He wondered where he was. *Is this hell? It certainly isn't heaven.*

He sucked hard for air to fill his lungs wondering if he was dead. *Can you feel pain when you die?* His body was racked with pain. Every part of him hurt. As glorious air filled his lungs, he was sure he was still alive, but had no clue where he was.

Water sprayed over his body from the column of water falling through the chasm at his feet. His primal instincts forced him to move away from the rushing water afraid it would drag him back into the torrent. It was so dark he couldn't see his hand or anything around him.

A piece of the ledge broke off behind him forcing himself to move faster. As he scurried away on his hands and knees into the darkness, suddenly there was a faint light bouncing in the air off in a distance. He forced himself to his feet and ran toward the light. Now it was gone. He slowed down and tripped over the rough surface just as he saw another light. Suddenly other dancing lights appeared in front of him. *Are these angels? Maybe I am dead.*

Steve tripped and landed hard on the ground smashing his face into the surface. Climbing to his feet, he could taste blood and salt in his mouth. Moving again, the faint lights lured him on. Suddenly, a man with a light on his helmet appeared and ran passed him. Other men with more lights were running toward him. Bleeding and clad only in the skimpy racing briefs he wore at the swim meet, the men glanced at him strangely as they ran by. Dazed from his fall, Steve wondered. *Are these demons from hell?*

Charley leaned against a truck as he monitored the miners cramming into the hoist. His arm ached and he couldn't move his fingers. He was pretty sure his shoulder was dislocated and tried to move to get it to pop back in. His arm was smashed or broken. It was difficult to stand up and if he moved, shooting pains shot up his leg, hip and back. When the hoist was full, Charley nodded to Terry to take it up.

Nodding his head, no, Terry told Charley, "You get in. You're hurting. I'll wait for the next ride up."

With his good arm, Charley pushed Terry back into the elevator just as a naked man, well almost naked, pushed his way into the elevator.

Wondering where this tall skinny apparition came from, Terry pushed the button sending the hoist to the top. As the man cage clattered toward the surface, he looked up praying for the elevator to make it safely to the top and promised God that if he made it out of this damned mine, he would never go back. When the elevators doors finally opened, a bright sunny day welcomed him to the surface. The tall almost naked guy with the blood striped body stepped out next to him as they both shaded their eyes from the sun.

Terry headed to the parking lot. Swinging into his truck cab, he vowed never to return. Before he started his engine, he leaned on the steering wheel with a bowed head thanking God for delivering him from hell. Revving his motor, he threw his pickup in reverse and squealed backwards.

Throwing his baby into gear, he spun his tires heading home to join his wife and Mighty Mite.

Down in the mine, the elevator doors opened after descending from the last trip to the surface. A foreman rushed up to Charley and told him the bottom levels of the mine were filling with water and he didn't know where it was coming from. Without another word, they both knew water in a salt mine was trouble. Charley wasn't sure what was happening. *Could the quake have opened the bottom of the lake? I've got to get my people to the top before we all die.*

✱✱✱✱

Ruth Hager rode out the quake under the conference table. When one end of the table collapsed, she huddled with Olson at the other end. When the shaking from 747 stopped, Ruth crawled out from under the table and helped Albert to his feet. When she turned toward the window, she saw a sharp metal shard sticking out of Herm Douglas's chest as he cowered on the floor at her feet. She thought about pulling it out, but remembered from her first aid training that might make the bleeding worse. Leaving Olson, she struggled over the fallen ceiling frame to Herm after grabbing a cushion from a nearby couch. She ripped the pillow out of the case and threw the pillow to Albert. When she reached Herm, she wrapped the pillow case around Herm's wound to slow the bleeding and Albert put the pillow under his head.

Then she stroked Herm's head trying to calm his fears. As her fingers ran over his bushy head, every hair fell back into place. She told Herm that it was best to leave the spike in until the first responders arrived.

Still smiling in her restroom hideaway, the big quake knocked Louise off her throne. She laughed at her predicament. She was wedged between the toilet and the stall wall. As water slopped out of her throne, she held her joint high to save it.

She wasn't scared as she took a long drag. When the shaking finally stopped, she slid out and regained her seat of honor. She flipped the butt of her fag in the water at her feet and took another hand-rolled cigarette out of her purse and lit up. *To hell with going back to that stupid meeting looking wet and bedraggled*, she thought as she inhaled and held her breath.

When the building stopped moving, the gas and salt executives tried to recover from quake. Dazed from the violent shaking, they weren't sure what had happened. First they moved Herm to the couch. Carefully lifting him up on it, Herm moaned when his back hit the soft cushions. Ruth put the pillow back under his head and tried to comfort him.

With weeping eyes, Herm looked up at her, "*You know?*"

She smiled down, "I know."

Then Ruth led these *Captains of Industry* over the ceiling frame and fallen lights to the window to inspect the damage to the site. The corrugated sides of the warehouse surrounding the elevator had been fallen off exposing the building frame that was still shaking, but standing.

Ruth saw the elevator doors open and spew out miners. Watching for Charley, she was surprised to see a tall naked man streaked with blood walk out of the elevator and look around. *That's no miner,* she thought.

Steve stepped out of the elevator and felt like he had entered heaven. On the way up, he learned from the miners he was leaving a salt mine. The miners didn't believe him when he insisted he was in a canoe on top of the lake when a whirlpool sucked him down into the mine.

Slowly the impact of the quake sank in on all of them. The mine had collapsed and the lake was emptying into it. As they rode up in the elevator, all the miners touched Steve just to make sure he was real. They wanted to share his luck. It was hard for Steve to imagine that fate had spared him. Just as he had accepted death, he had been thrown from its grip.

As he walked out of the elevator, miners slapped him on the back and congratulated him. Blinking from the bright sunlight, Steve waved to the miners as he left them and walked across the parking lot through the vehicles that had been tossed around by the quake. At the exit, he saw the body of the sentry crushed under the guard shack. Over to his left, people were pulling others out from under a fallen fence resting on barrels. In his state of shock, it didn't occur to him to help these people. He just wanted to return to camp.

As he was trying to figure out how to get back, a big black Ford F-150 pickup pulled up beside him. The passenger window slid down as the driver asked, "Came up with you in the hoist. Need a ride?"

"Can you get me back to Camp Minnechaug?"

"Going that way. Climb in."

As Steve opened the door and jumped into the cab, Terry looked Steve up and down, "Heard you in the hoist. That's quite a story. Hard to believe."

Steve simply answered, "I'm not sure I believe it. Let's get out of here." Then he noticed the blood on Terry's t-shirt and arm, "What happened to your shoulder?"

Looking down at his bloody arm for the first time, Terry simply told him, "Must have cut it in the mine. Too excited to notice. Not as bad as you though."

For the first time, Steve looked at his body. He was covered with blood and was still bleeding from cuts torn open during his descent. Every cut smarted as if salt had been rubbed into them.

As Terry drove over the broken exit pole, Steve slipped deeper into shock trying to understand what had just happened to him. As they drove carefully through the protestors trying to recover from the quake, one pounded on Terry's window and begged for help.

Terry yelled back, "Sorry, got to get to my wife and kid." As soon as he was free from the crowd, Terry hit the accelerator spinning the tires leaving the protestors behind. "They wouldn't let you down there in the mine dressed like that. What really happened?"

Still shaken from his brush with death and running on adrenalin, Steve answered, "You'll never believe me."

"Try me."

"I'm really not sure. Honestly, I was starting a canoe race on the lake out from Minnechaug. Then this whirlpool swallowed me up. I fell into this funnel in the lake. Thought for sure I was dead. Then I ended up in this completely black place with water falling behind me. Saw helmet lights and followed you guys into the elevator."

"Bullshit."

"Believe it or not."

"That would mean the quake punctured the mine and flooded it. If that happened, the mine's gone."

CHAPTER 32

The water plummeted from the bottom of the lake into the crack leading into the salt mine ripping open the crack until it was a full breach. A tremendous volume of water hit the salt floor on the first level, but didn't rupture that level immediately. The rush of water snapped the remaining pedestal supports that had survived 747 on each level of the mine. As the thin pillars buckled and broke, the first level sagged, shook and finally collapsed when the second aftershock hit. Like a house of cards, each level of the mine fell down upon the other. The Jinga Tower had fallen. The complete collapse of the largest salt mine in North America created an enormous empty vessel waiting to be filled and Cayuga Lake had to respond.

A column of water didn't just pour into the mine, instead a cylinder of lake water dropped from the lake into the hole created by the collapse of miles of roads and caverns. This huge displacement of water generated great energy when it smashed into the bottom of the mine. The water surged up with tremendous force trying to escape the confines of the mine. More energy was produced as water poured in behind the cylinder of water that had already dropped into the mine. The massive movement of water energy rising up from the bottom of the mine collided with the water crashing down into this great hole in the earth. This collision generated an incredible amount of energy that reached up for the surface of the lake creating great waves.

A loud roar coming from the middle of the lake caused everyone recovering at the water meet to stop and turn toward the sound. Link saw frothy white water explode and shoot up hundreds of feet in the center of the lake. As this wet energy generated waves radiating out in every direction, Link was first to spot the drawback. Water receded from the shore exposing the bottom of the lake. Soon there was no water under the broken dock. Link had spent a vacation in Hawaii with Steve and was well schooled in what happened when a Tsunami was imminent. Not questioning what caused this act of nature, he knew what was happening in the lake. Link yelled to Lea and told her they had to get everyone away from the lake to higher ground and pointed to a hill off to the left.

As the water receded toward the middle of the lake, Jerry and Lea filmed the drawback and transmitted the images to Mac.

Link and Lea started shouting for everyone to follow them. The already stunned crowd on the beach was slow to comprehend what these counselors wanted and even slower to react. Yelling and waving his arms, Link ran backwards through the crowd trying to get people to follow him.

Lea picked up two small children and carried them away from their parents. Upset that this girl had kidnapped their children, the parents ran after her. As the people on the beach witnessed this chase, they finally ran after this small group running up the hill not sure what danger they were eluding.

As Lea continued to carry the young kids up the hill, other parents grabbed their children and dragged them after her. It was clear that this young man and woman were frightened by some unknown danger. Then panic set in. Trampling some of the campers as panic turned to fear, the crowd rushed away from the shore.

Burdened by his camera, Jerry started to run with his battery pack bouncing on his hip when Kia grabbed his arm and quickly convinced him that he had to document this scene.

Kia yelled, "These images will make national TV and be shown thousands of times. This is our chance to break into the national media."

Jerry smiled. *You're right.* He stopped running and started shooting the images of the panic as Kia pointed out the most dramatic scenes. The shots of the stampeding crowd looked like an old horror movie with everyone running from the monster except this monster was *Mother Nature,* and she was very angry and right behind them.

****

Charlie stood next to the elevator counting miners as they entered. *This load won't get everybody in,* he thought. *I'll need at least one more trip.* As he was about to push the button to send the elevator up, he heard the loud collapse as the walls and ceilings of the mine were torn apart by roaring crashing water. The stark sound was so loud, he and the other miners ducked and braced against the noise.

Down the tunnels stretching out from the elevator, he could see the levels caving in followed by a torrent of water falling to the bottom of the mine. Without thinking, he shoved the rest of the miners into the elevator. Everyone crowded into hoist to escape the foaming death that was chasing them. Charley knew the hoist was over capacity, but this was their only chance. *If it breaks down, it breaks down.* He doubted the elevator would make it to the surface before the water hit anyway. *We are about to die.*

At first, not a miner spoke as the man cage soared toward heaven. Listening to the deafening roar that was following them up the shaft, many were mouthing silent prayers and others were thinking them. Charlie prayed the cable wouldn't snap and wished the damned old cage would move faster.

When millions of gallons of water reached the bottom of the ruptured mine, the water searched for a way out. Other than the hole it had just fallen through, the product, ventilation and elevator shafts were the only other outlets the water could find. The falling water was squeezed into these narrow escape routes creating tremendous pressure as the water drove toward the surface. The pressurized water pushed everything it encountered in front of it. When the energy packed water hit the elevator, Charlie no longer had to worry about the cable snapping or the elevator going too slow.

With a shudder, the water rushing up the shaft pushed the elevator faster and faster toward the surface. At first the miners gave a collective sigh. The water was sent by God to rescue them. Then the water began to fill the cage. The miners didn't know what was going to happen first. Drowning or being smashed against the sides of the shaft seemed to be the only options.

In a brief flash of optimism, Charley thought. *At least we don't have to worry about falling.*

The speed of the ascent increased as the water propelled the old cage bumping and rattling toward the surface. With a chorus of guttural moans, the miners stood on their toes as the water reached their shoulders. One short man started choking out of breath as the water went over his head. His friends tried to lift him up.

****

Above ground, the gas and salt industry executives were standing at the window recovering from 747 and the aftershocks when they heard a boom. The building rattled and shook again. At first, they thought it was another aftershock and then stared in disbelief as foaming white water shot up like a fountain erupting in the center of the lake. Ruth immediately knew something bad had happened far underground. Charley was in danger. She knew he would be the last one up and prayed for him to make it out.

She went to Herm Douglas on the couch as one of his engineers kept pressing the pillow case around the piece of metal in his chest to stop the bleeding. Ruth put her face in Herm's and yelled, "You gas bastards did this."

As the building continued to sway and rattle from the underground turbulence, she worked her way back to the window looking for Charley.

Enjoying another round of shaking, Louise held the fag between her ruby lips and held on to the toilet seat with both hands. She wasn't going to fall off again. *Man, this is fun.*

****

Steve slouched against the door of the pickup trying to make sense of his ordeal. Suddenly they both heard it. Steve snapped out of his stupor and sat up as Terry pulled off the road with his truck pointing toward the lake. They both saw an explosion of white water reaching into the sky from the middle of the lake. Steve was the first to notice the water sliding back from the shore. From his surfing experience, he knew what was happening and yelled, "Drawback, a Tsunami, get out of here."

Not sure what a Tsunami was, but reacting to the terror in his new companion's voice, Terry slammed his truck in reverse and pulled back on the road before jerking it back into drive.

As the tires spun, they roared down the highway with Steve yelling, "No, No. Got to get higher." Pointing to the bank on the other side of the road, he yelled, "Off road man, up the hill."

Now you're talking, Terry thought. He pulled across the road and rammed his 4-wheel drive Ford up the bank snapping through a barb wire fence with ease and into a field climbing away from the lake. After bouncing across the field scaring cattle out of the way, he slammed on the brakes of his chariot. As it lurched to a stop at the edge of the woods framing the field, Terry looked at Steve, "This high enough?"

Steve glanced back at the lake. "Jesus no. Higher. As high as you can go."

Terry yelled, "Hold on" as he tromped down on the accelerator. With his tires throwing mud, he entered the woods dodging trees and bouncing over logs. He got air when they hit a rock shelf. Terry was in his element. Fighting to control his steering wheel, Terry charged up the hill over leaves, moss, rocks and the occasional small tree.

****

Link and Lea kept running up the hill with the panicked parents following them. Lea stopped and set the children down for a moment. Their parents were out of shape and had fallen behind. Trying to catch her breath, she waved and yelled at the people to keep running. Some of the parents ran passed her with their children. As Lea encouraged the crowd to go faster, Jerry got good a great shot of her picking up the small kids again and running up the hill again.

As a rather small wave ran across the lake, it hit shallow water multiplying the energy it was carrying. The water of this horrible wave climbed higher and higher. As it grew in size, it revealed the monster it was. The dragon had exited the underworld ready to gobble up the people around the lake.

As the crowd ran passed him, Link looked over his shoulder at the lake and saw the devil wave rising above him. Then he spotted it. A huge black beast captured by the wave was coming right at him. The lake monster had returned to get him. Driven by fear, Link left Lea and sprinted toward a large pine tree. He leaped skyward grabbing a big branch that could support his weight. Like an experienced gymnast he swung up on the branch and started climbing the tree in a panic. Glancing over his shoulder as he climbed, he saw the wave pushing the horrible lake monster straight at him. His foot slipped. To keep from falling, he grabbed a branch with one hand.

Kia pointed to Link swinging above them by one hand and Jerry captured the moment.

Dangling from a branch above his head, Link swung back to the trunk and scrambled higher. At the very top, he hung both legs over two large branches and wrapped his arms around the trunk.

Jerry held his camera on Link and hoped his link to Mac's computer at the top of the falls was working. This shot was sure to make the national news.

****

Worrying about the rumbling and shaking below them, the executives on the surface in the shaking headquarters building continued to stare out at the lake and mine complex. Holding tight to the window sill to remain standing, they saw the gigantic product buckets spit out of the earth like watermelon seeds. A geyser of white water at least a hundred and fifty feet high spewed out of the ventilator shaft. This was followed by the launch of the elevator high into the air followed by a stream of water that would have made any European fountain proud.

Ruth watched in horror as the hoist shot out of the personnel shaft. Slowly it reached the apex of its ascent. For a moment it seemed to stop in the air only to finally fall back to earth with a crash. When it smashed to the ground, three men shoved in the back of the elevator were immediately crushed. Others had drowned and most were broken and hurting. Luckily the welds on the cage split when it hit the ground and the sides fell off letting the wet tangled mass of humanity squirm over each other to escape. Miners desperately crawled out of the cage to get away from the fountain of water pouring down on them.

Charley's broken arm was caught under a dead miner next to him and his legs were pinned down by another. He couldn't move until one of his foremen rolled the body off Charley's legs and pulled on his good arm to drag him out of the mess. As his buddy pulled him out, Charley discovered the true meaning of pain as the man tugged him over bloody bodies while he grimaced and groaned.

The pain had one redeeming feature, Charley thought. *I made it to the surface and I'm still alive. I'll heal. I've survived a mine collapse.* As other miners grabbed him under the arms, he thought, *I'll see Ruth again.*

Ruth realized Charley might be in the elevator that had just been ejected from the earth. If he was in it, he was probably hurt. She turned and ran out of the conference room trying to stay on her feet as the hallway swayed beneath her still shaking from the turbulence below in the mine.

She had to find him. Protect him. *What if he's still in the mine? By now, anyone down there is gone. Dead.*

No, she had to get out on the tarmac to find him. She knew he was out there alive. He had to be there. Ruth ran out the double glass doors toward the smashed elevator with medical attendants running close behind her. By now, the miners were staggering away from the crushed hoist. Others had collapsed on the ground next to the cage with the water still raining over them as they tried to recover from their ordeal.

Ruth didn't pay attention to the water. She ran through the bodies glancing at each man trying to find Charley. *My Charley. Where are you?*

When she reached the remains of the elevator, she saw some miners dragging another guy along the ground off to her left. It was Charley. She jumped over a dead man to reach him and shoved away the others away as she fell to her knees beside her man.

His eyes beautiful blue eyes opened as he groaned from the pain radiating through his body. After she grabbed both of his arms to pull him to his feet, his scream told her he was alive, but in pain. She realized she was doing something wrong. Carefully, she laid Charley back down on the tarmac and spoke to him, "How can I help? What's wrong?"

Charley whispered, "Think my right arm is broken. Something's wrong with that shoulder too. And my hip really hurts."

He lifted up his left arm, "Pull on this one." He gasped, "Need your help."

Ruth carefully helped him to his feet and together they dodged withering bodies as they stumbled away from the smashed cage.

Ruth told him, "Lean on me, I won't break. I'm strong."

When they were free from the others, Charley told her he felt sick and needed to sit down. As he crumpled to his knees, she supported him as he fell to the pavement. On his back, he started to breathe rapidly. After a moment, his breathing slowed and he was able to speak, "I know you're strong. On the ride up I thought of you. You are my life. The only good thing in it."

Ruth bent over and kissed him on the lips and then his cheek. "I saw the hoist shoot out of the shaft and hoped you were on it. No, no. I didn't want you hurt. I wanted you out of that damn mine. I didn't want you down there all alone. You're so stubborn. I knew you'd be the last man out. All that matters is that you're alive. No more mines for us. From now on we live on top of the earth."

"Us?"

"It's about time one of us said it. I want to spend the rest of my life with you."

Ruth tenderly hugged her man as he wrapped his one good arm around her waist and pulled her to him. As they kissed, suddenly they heard a roar behind them. Celebrating their love, they didn't look up as the terrible Tsunami wave towered above them. They had just enough time for one last hug before it crashed over them.

The tsunami didn't pause or even notice the lives it had just robbed from the lovers. It crashed into the headquarters building as the executives frozen in place just stood and watched in awe as the wave descended on them. Albert Olson was picked up and slammed through the door and washed down the hall. Herm lived a bit longer as the water picked up his couch and used it as a battering ram to break through the window at the end of the hall. Herm rode his soft chariot as it was launched out of the building into the water rapidly flowing around the building. The couch floated in this torrent of water as Herm held on for dear life.

The building shuddered, but even this powerful wall of water couldn't pull down the steel reinforced concrete building. After slamming through the windows, inundating the conference room and killing all the men and women who had worked so hard to create this catastrophe, the rushing water slammed through the corridors of the building and flowed outside where it found Herm still clinging to his couch. Holding on as he rode this wild thrill park ride, the couch was ripped from his grasp. As it floated away, the swift water pulled him, you know, under the hungry wave.

When Louise had gone into the restroom to smoke pot, she had locked the door not realizing that in the fifties, the restrooms in this building were built as bomb proof shelters with heavy metal doors that would save her. The steel hardened gate to her kingdom held up. Sitting on her throne as the water rampaged through the halls, she enjoyed her hand rolled fag. Some water squeezed under the door, but no more than a foot or two.

As the water rose in her granite palace, she slipped off her expensive shoes to save them. Other than wet stockings, she was okay. As she toked on her joint, Albert Olson's body floated by just outside her restroom door. Louise didn't know or care what was happening outside her castle hide-away. She just leaned back dreaming pleasant thoughts.

The horrible wave streaked across the parking lot outside the salt mine carrying cars toward the protestors outside the gate. It ripped through the fallen chain link fence just as Shelley was freeing a girl snarled in the razor wire. She looked up and saw the wall of water crashing down on her. There was no time to run as the wave crushed over her and her friends as it moved on with no regrets.

The protesters never had a chance. The lake they were trying to save had just killed them. Only three survived. Two were making out in a car that was swept away and floated away on the frightening killer wave. The third was inside a port-a-potty that tipped over and swirled around covering him with unspeakable filth. His foul blue chariot was deposited on the roof of a fast food franchise miles down the road where he climbed out stinking, but alive.

★★★★

As Kia and Jerry filmed the crowd running up the hill, they heard the roar behind them. Jerry turned and caught the image of a wall of water growing tall above them. The cameras captured a ribbon of light of wet green crowned by deadly foaming white water. The shroud of deadly dark water roared over these two journalists erasing their lives. Even though they both knew it was the end, they spent their last seconds making sure Mac would have a great video for the national media. Kia's last thought as the wave crashed over her, *I hope Jerry doesn't get all the credit. I want someone to remember me.*

Lea didn't think she could run faster. The two children she was carrying were slowing her down. Her back felt like it was going to break and her lungs were bursting. She knew the terrible harbor wave was right behind her and didn't dare glance back. She kept running while the kids hugged her neck. One little boy looked behind them and pointed at the wave screaming for her ear to go faster.

The morning runs with her friends and Shanty had prepared Lea for this race for life. Every muscle in her body ached, but she lengthened her stride for a final burst of speed. If she dropped the kids, she knew she could beat the death looming behind her, but that was not an option. Her passengers cried as they watched the wave crash over their parents. She wouldn't abandon them. *Not possible. Wasn't going to happen,* she thought, as she kicked for her final sprint.

All she had to do is reach some unknown point up the hill where the Tsunami would crash and die behind her. She pressed her body beyond all limits. Exhausted, fear drove her up the hill. She marveled at the depths of strength within her as she flew up the hill. The pain was gone. She didn't know how she kept running, but she did. She passed others who had given up accepting their fate. *Not me. Not this time, not ever.* She had just perfected her serve. She would be the Number One tennis player at Cornell this year.

She pushed forward with her feet barely touching the ground. Thank God for those morning runs. With adrenalin surging through her body and the proximity of death so close behind, she drove forward as the terrible wave swept over the people right behind her. She was next.

The deadly wave swept over Lea and the children. She was lost. They were lost. Others were lost. Thanks to her leadership thirty-seven people out of the hundreds of spectators at the water meet made it high enough up the slope to escape the watery death. That was her gift, her reason for living. The video of her magnificent final sprint was captured from the cliff-side camera and would be shown time after time by the national media. The Cornell tennis team would miss her serve and wear black arm bands on their uniforms to commemorate her existence.

Link couldn't go higher. The top of the tree was broken off from an old lightning strike. That's all there was. He glanced down before the water hit. He had to be sixty feet in the air. He plastered his chest to the tree trunk with his back to the water. Just as his legs hooked over two branches and his arms wrapped around the trunk, the top of the wave broke just below him.

The water bent his tree over as it rushed under him. He was sure it would break and dump his body into the deadly wave. He prayed as smashing water passed the tree wetting him with foam. The wave was strong, but couldn't pry him from his perch. It flowed by just below him.

Suddenly it was gone. The tree snapped back throwing Link off like a bucking bull getting rid of an unwanted cowboy. He flew through the air and landed in the wash as the water slid back down the hill. He surfaced sucking for air trying to find a way to survive in the debris sloshing around him.

Then he saw it, one of them. A huge lake dinosaur, bigger than Big Momma, was coming directly at him. He wondered how fate could be so cruel. How could he survive a Tsunami only to be eaten by a prehistoric dinosaur? With jaws snapping wildly open and shut it was so close, he could smell its foul breath.

Could its teeth be any bigger? Just right to rip me apart, he thought. He prayed a quick prayer hoping it would be a quick easy death. Grabbing a broken log floating by, he prepared to die. As the creature closed in on him, he looked into its eyes as the monster stared back at him.

Link thought of Little Red Riding Hood and understood how she felt when the wolf smacked his lips making ready for the coup-de-grace. He wondered how he could survive two attacks from these creatures and a Tsunami only to be subjected to a terrible death in the jaws of a monster.

Suddenly, their eyes met and they shared an unspoken message. This aquasaur was just as scared as Link. Both were wondering what had happened to their beautiful lake. The creature half floated and half swam passed Link as he rode this terrifying Tsunami back into the lake. After he was rescued, Link would insist the monster winked at him as he went by. Both Link and his creepy new buddy survived.

****

Ursula shook her head and surveyed the debris the quake had dumped on her. Her leg was pinned under a rafter and was hurting. She couldn't get away from Harold's body that was resting quietly next to her. *Finally,* she thought. *I've outlived the bastard.*

Now it's mine, she thought, *all mine. Well, not all of it. That bitch, Hilda will get this stupid camp and some of his money, but not enough to care about.*

She would have more than enough. She would keep the Central Park apartment and the mansion in California, but the London apartment had to go. She wanted one in Paris.

To enjoy her new riches, she had to get out of here. Or she could just wait. Someone would notice the hotel roof had collapsed from the earthquake and rescue her, but her leg hurt. She looked for a way to get it out from under the rafter that was pinning it down. Near her head was a dangling piece of a broken 2 X 4. She twisted it and pulled on it until it broke off and then used it as a pry bar. She heaved the rafter up, but it just slid down an inch or so pinching her leg even tighter. She yelled out in pain and took a moment to recover.

With the pain in her leg growing, she had to try again. This time she braced the piece of 2 X 4 over one rafter and like a teeter-totter, she slipped the rafter up off her leg just enough to pull her leg out from under it. When she was free, she let the rafter slam back to the floor. Rubbing her leg, she discovered it hurt, but was not broken.

Slowly, she climbed over and under the debris to the office door wondering where her rescuers were. *I'm a rich woman now, they should be trying to find me.*

Ursula stumbled down the broken hallway to the front door of the hotel. After forcing it open, she stepped out on the porch and looked up just in time to see a great dark green wave crash down on her washing away her dreams.

CHAPTER 33

ilda stayed to clean up the rappelling site while the others hiked to the top of the falls to video tape the lake and water meet. She had learned the clean-up routine and was proud of her new role in the camp. She amazed herself by taking the filthy garbage bag out of the trash can and putting in a new one. Dirt, yes dirt and even garbage. Thanks to Shanty's training she could now handle icky things. As she tossed the old bag into the back of Shanty's pickup, she realized he had given her the keys without her asking for them. *That was a good sign. Maybe, he cares as much for me as he does his pickup.*

Parked on a rise above the rappelling cliff, the first tremor dislodged the emergency brake on Shanty's old pickup. As 747 grew in intensity, his truck started to roll slowly toward the cliff. Hilda saw it creeping toward the edge and run after it. As she sprinted toward it, a strong shock knocked her flat. She crawled and scrambled off the ground horrified to see Shanty's beautiful old truck getting perilously close to the cliff. Finally, she grabbed the back bumper digging in her heels. The truck didn't stop and dragged her forward. When it started over the cliff, she had to let go. Shanty would never forgive her.

Hilda almost fell over the cliff as the shaking ground pushed her toward the edge. Falling and crawling back, she watched Joseph's pickup crash head first into the hard ground below and flip over. When Shanty's family treasure finally smashed between a large boulder and big tree, it blew up in a cloud of orange flames wrapped in a cocoon of black smoke. The explosion surprised her as she held on to the ground as more tremors raced through the site. After 747 passed through, Hilda struggled up and cried as his smashed pickup burned below her.

Hilda started back toward the climbing gear when the first aftershock hit. The chunk of the cliff she had been standing on was torn from the edge and dropped into the abyss. She ran away from the cliff and held on to a small tree to remain on her feet. When it was done, she had to pause and wonder. *What is happening to my world?*

The second aftershock frightened her more than the first two quakes. *Will this ever stop,* she wondered. After the shaking stopped, Hilda went across the site to inspect the damage to Billy's rappelling cliff. As she peered over the edge, Hilda heard a noise out on the lake and spotted a foaming white water plume shoot up in the center of the lake. From her vantage point, she saw a funnel develop with waves radiating out from it in every direction.

After watching a big yacht chug out of the whirlpool, Hilda was entranced by nature's spectacle. When she saw the water draw back from the shore, she wasn't sure what was happening. When a small wave came closer to the shore, it suddenly grew into a great wave that rose high above the people already running from it. She tried to will the scared people to safety, but just couldn't do it. She shuddered as the great wall of water swallowed them up. Only a few managed to out run the terrible killer as the water surrounded the hill and ran below them as they stared down in awe as it flowed by.

Horrified by the terrible wave rushing up the valley toward her, suddenly she realized that she was next. The huge wall of water was streaming toward her and it was higher than the cliff. She ran for her life grabbing a rappelling line as she crossed the site. Threading it around her waist again and again, she ran toward the nearest big tree. Hiding behind the tree, she threw the rope around it tying off the line with a bowline, a knot Shanty had taught her. Just as she pulled the knot tight, the Tsunami roared over her.

The Tsunami hit the cliff wall below the falls splashing white foam up over the edge. For the crew at the top of the falls, watching it roll in had been terrifying. When the massive wall of water crashed into the wall below them, Annie, Billy and Shanty were frightened and Mac even looked up from his computers.

As the water receded, the giant wave revealed the devastation it had wrought on the lake and surroundings. Mac turned back to his computer screen staring at the video of the terrible wave rolling over the people at the water meet. He was amazed by the shots he'd gotten of the quake and its aftermath. He was drawn to the brutal moment when the wave engulfed Jerry and Kia.

Tears ran down his cheeks as he rolled the final images from Jerry and Kia across his computer screen. Drawn by the terror of the video images, he couldn't stop watching them. He told Annie who was sitting next to him, "Jerry and Kia got it all. But what does it matter? Who cares? How could that happen? They got great images of people running for their lives, but it cost them their own."

He nodded in despair as the final images of Lea running up the hill with the two kids wrapped around her neck flashed across his high-definition screen. The cameras on the cliff also caught the devastation of the wave as it raced toward the falls demonstrating its terrible power. It was all there. The hotel and cabins going under. Any tree left standing, stood as a stark sentinel with its leaves stripped off. People were just gone. Swallowed up. Yes, he had it all, but at a terrible price.

As the crew watched the water run back to the lake, Shanty yelled and started to run down the path, "Hilda. My God, she's down at the rappelling site."

Rushing down the hill, he was soon slipping and sliding over the mud and debris left by the Tsunami. Grabbing a line he had carried with him, Billy followed Shanty down the path. In some places where the trail was washed out, Shanty and Billy used the rappelling line to get across breaches in the trail. Their slow progress down the mountain infuriated Shanty, but Billy convinced him that they gained nothing by risking their lives.

When Billy and Shanty reached the area where the path widened, they ran through the debris. The skills they had developed during their morning training runs served them well. Jumping over fallen trees and ducking under tangled branches, they finally reached the clearing at the rappelling site. Trees and even large rocks were strewn across it. They looked for Hilda, but couldn't find any evidence of her. They rushed to the cliff and looked over searching for her body in the tangled mess below them. They didn't expect to find her alive, but hoped to at least spot her remains.

Shanty pointed out the burned wreckage of his truck lodged between a large boulder and a tree. It was almost buried in the debris left from the wave. Depressed, they turned from the cliff and surveyed the area again. Nothing on the site spoke of human use. Everything seemed to be gone.

Then Billy spotted some blue rappelling line tangled in a fallen tree and raced to it. When he saw her body, he shouted to Shanty. She was tied to a tree that had been uprooted and fallen over. Her body was suspended between the tree trunk and the ground with her head, arms and legs dangling down from the rope tied around her waist. She hung limply without moving.

Trying to be a brave warrior, Shanty fought back the tears clouding his eyes. With a quick wipe of his nose and eyes with his arm, he joined Billy as they worked their way through the tangled branches to reach her body. Their approach was complicated by another tree that had fallen on top of the tree where she was tied. When they finally reached her, Shanty took a knife out of his pocket and cut the line.

Billy caught Hilda's body as the final piece of line was severed and carefully laid her down under the broken tree trunk trying to find the pressure point in her neck with his fingers. He looked up at Shanty shaking his head, "Can't feel a thing."

Shanty grabbed her wrist desperately probing for a pulse, but found nothing.

Billy was surprised when Shanty hit Hilda hard in the chest with the flat of his hand. He hit her once, twice and a third time. Then he pushed on her chest with a steady rhythm stopping every couple thrusts to use mouth to mouth to breathe air into her lungs.

After a few minutes, Shanty nodded as he kept pushing on her chest. Billy grabbed Hilda's wrist and shook his head. Still nothing.

Shanty hit her again with the bottom of his fist and put his finger in her mouth to hold back her tongue that had fallen to the back of her mouth. He gave her mouth to mouth hoping to revive her. Billy could see her chest rise and pushed it down to help her exhale between breaths. After several minutes, Shanty stopped, breathing hard, he nodded for Billy to check again.

Billy pushed his fingers deep into her neck, "Something's there. I think."

Shanty grabbed her wrist, "I feel it, too."

Billy shouted, "Is she alive?"

"She is."

Shanty gently brushed her cheek, but she didn't respond. He didn't want to shake her or move her afraid she might be hurt. He didn't want to make it worse. Her chest was barely moving up and down, but it was moving. He stroked her head and held his hand to her mouth and felt a faint breath. Then her chest stopped. If she was breathing, she wasn't breathing very deeply. He bent down and started mouth to mouth again.

Suddenly she coughed and jerked her face away from his. Then she thrashed and waved her arms.

Shanty gently grabbed her arms and told her in a gentile soothing voice, "You're okay. You're alright, I'm here." Finally Hilda opened her eyes without speaking. Shanty held her shoulders firmly, "It's over. You're okay. I'm here, you're safe."

Hilda whispered in a very weak voice, "What happened."

Shanty explained, "A large wave from the earthquake crashed over you."

Hilda nodded, "I...I saw it. Coming right at me. Used your knot to tie the rope."

"You're a quick learner."

Hilda breathlessly confessed, "Your pickup's gone. Over the cliff. I tried to stop it, but couldn't. I'm so sorry."

"Don't worry about it. Everything's gone, but you're still here. That's all that counts. Everything's going to be okay."

He lifted her up and hugged her, but she protested telling him her chest hurt. He gently laid her back down and told Billy, "Use your scouting skills and put together a stretcher so we can carry her out of here."

At the top of the falls, Mac's keys clicked to the camera tied to the limb over-looking the pool at the bottom of the falls. When Mac noticed a big black object had washed up next to the pool below the falls, he pointed to the screen and asked Annie, "What's that? Is it one of them?"

Looking at the screen, Annie answered, "Yeah, I think it is."

Annie slowly walked to the edge of the cliff and looked over, "Yep, it's one of them."

Mac shouted at her, "Is it dead?"

Annie stared at the creature's body and finally answered, "It's not moving. I doubt anything could live through that."

****

Dan Cooper sat with Rahul watching the data explode on their computer screens and yelled, "What the hell is happening?"

Rahul answered, "Another earthquake?"

"Under the lake?"

Confused Raul shot back, "I'm not sure."

"How strong?"

"7.47."

"No, not that one. The one happening right now. What just happened under the lake? How strong was it?"

"Probably an aftershock."

"It can't be an aftershock from the Linden fault. The epicenter is under the lake. Maybe there's a fault running from the gas drilling site to the center of the lake."

"How do we pin it down?"

Cooper wasn't sure. "Maybe the Linden quake set off a response under the lake. Keep searching the data, the answer's in there somewhere. I'm calling Shelley, maybe she knows what happened."

Dan pulled out his I-phone and touched Shelly's number. After letting it ring and ring, his call went to voice mail. Dan said more to himself than Rahul, "She must be busy with the protest. Can't believe she's not answering. After an event this big, I expected her to call to find out what we know."

****

Doris, Bob Fletcher's favorite administrative assistant, couldn't believe the devastation around the lake. Houses had collapsed and cars had been thrown into the lake. As she steered the LuvGas to the north end of the lake, she was horrified to discover that the RAG complex was a burning mess. The roof of the administrative building had caved in and the whole site was tangled with debris. A catastrophe of twisted pipes and smashed vehicles were strewn across every inch.

By far, the worse damage was to the wells. All the gas wells at the drilling site were burning with great orange flames licking up and staining the bright blue sky with their tongues lashing out of the dense black smoke. Trees all around the sight were ablaze and the administrative building was burning. Seeing Bob go under was bad, but this. This could end gas exploration on the lake forever. *Do I still have a job? God, I don't want to go back to Texas.*

As questions flashed through her mind, Doris glided the "LuvGas" up beside the dock and two girls jumped off to tie it up. Not sure what to do, she surveyed the site. She didn't think she could get through the fire to her car in the parking lot and doubted it would be in one piece if she did. Wondering what to do, she turned off the motor and climbed down to the main deck. When the other girls ran up to her, she had an idea. They would have a party on the boat until someone came to rescue them. It would be the last party at RAG for a long time.

As they poured the drinks and raided the refrigerators, suddenly the "LuvGas" seemed to float on air. They couldn't believe what was happening. Angry water slashed up on each side of their beautiful floating palace as the giant wave lifted the yacht into the air and carried it passed the burning buildings.

As the wave poured down on the flaming wells snuffing them out, the LuvGas slid back from the crest and fell into the trough behind it and was impaled on the well heads. Water smashed through the yacht portholes and doors ending the last voyage of the LuvGas and her crew.

★★★★

Terry spotted a rock promontory overlooking the lake. He effortlessly guided his muddy 4-wheel drive as it bounced over bumpy logs and slammed on the brakes. Stopping far above the lake, they watched the Tsunami grow to what Steve estimated to be about forty or fifty feet. It was a terrifying sight. Cabins, homes and cars lining the lake were swept across the roads. Only the biggest trees remained standing. A mini-van was swept away and two ambulances rushing down the road toward the ISC salt mine disappeared in the wave. Two cars tried to out run the wave, but were swept away. Lydia, Bob Fletcher's wife, was returning from a soccer match with her kids when the wave washed her mini-van high into the air and deposited it in the top of a giant oak. Her children were terrified, but they all survived as the wave washed passed them.

Terry pounded his steering wheel and cried between sobs, "Do you believe that? My family, my family. God, no one could live through that. My house is just a few miles down the road. God, my parents live right next to the lake. My...my wife. My son, all gone."

"Are you sure?"

"Of course I'm sure. It's just down the road. Look at it. Nothing around the lake survived. Everything is gone. Christ, what was that? How did you know? Never seen anything like that on the lake before. Not in my life."

Steve shook his head, "I'm not sure. I guess it was a Tsunami."

"A what?"

"A big wave the Japanese call a Tsunami. I saw one after an earthquake near Hawaii. An earthquake under the ocean causes them. When they get near land they suck the water out from the shore. That's how I knew. Never knew they could happen in a lake."

"My Mom and dad, gone. My kid. My wife. Why do I survive when my friends and family die? God, why did you save me?"

Terry pounded his steering and suddenly looked up yelling, "Hold on, I've got to find them."

Terry drove wildly along the line where the wave had ended. With wild abandon, he raced passed the devastation. In and out, he weaved his way around cars, homes and the dead. Some of the mangled bodies half buried in mud had arms sticking up toward the sky that seemed to be beckoning them to stop. Terry kept pointing his pickup toward his parent's house as his tires slipped through the muck.

Steve put on his seat belt and held on to the dashboard as they bounced over and around debris. Nothing could stop Terry as his four wheel drive spun and drifted through the mud looking for his parents' house. Finally he spotted it crushed and half buried about a hundred yards into the debris left by the terrible wave.

There was the broken empty shell of his family home. He slid to a stop and jumped out of his truck. Climbing over the clutter of trees, cars, and crushed boards all mired in sticky black and brown goo, he fell down. As he tried to get up, a brown lab coated with mud suddenly appeared at his side and licked his face. Terry couldn't believe it and hugged his good 'ole dog thinking *if Kona is alive maybe my family made it.*

With his dog beside him, Terry trekked over and around the mess left by the killer wave finally making it to his home or at least what was left of it. Kona pulled on his pant leg trying to pull him back, but Terry brushed him away.

Barefoot and almost naked, Steve sat in the car and watched him go. Hell, from the cab, he could see two bodies. He knew his new friend wouldn't find anyone alive in that muck and mess. He watched the dog barking behind Terry and wondered how he survived. Then he thought of his own improbable survival and knew that anything was possible.

Terry worked his way over the mud, bushes and a broken fence to what had been his home. It was half buried in a pile of debris. Toppled over on its side, he climbed up one slanting wall and looked down through the broken living room window. He couldn't spot anyone in the mud filled room. Pretty sure no was one there, he crawled around a corner to the back of the house. Carefully climbing over the splintered siding of the house, he worked his way to a broken kitchen window. His first glance revealed what he had been praying not to see. There they were. They had been in the kitchen. Why hadn't God let them go on an errand somewhere far away from the house? That might have saved them.

Below him were three broken bodies shoved into the corner partially buried in the mud. His father was face down. All he could see of him was his dad's head and one arm. His mother's body was slammed upside down against the wall with just part of her body exposed. He could tell it was her by what was left of her dress. Next to her, he could see the right side of his wife's beautiful face now streaked with mud. His boy, his precious son, where was he? He couldn't see Tommy, but knew he would've been close to mom. Probably buried deep under the muck near her.

Terry broke down and cried. After a moment or two, he wiped away his tears. Could he get down to them? He could jump down to them, but looking around he realized he wouldn't be able to get back out. He swore silently. Even if he did jump down, what could he do? He didn't have anything he could use to dig them out. He couldn't get them up and out of the house if he did dig them out. Best to get help and come back. Besides, they didn't need him now. After Afghanistan, he knew that the dead were just dead.

Through his grief, he wondered why he was always the one to survive. He'd rather be down there with them. He said a silent prayer and opened his eyes for one last look at what was left of his wife and parents. His family was gone and covered with filth. He turned away. He couldn't keep looking at them. The guilt of living was just too much. And his son. Yes, he didn't want to see his boy dead. Images of Mighty Mite's smile and touch ran through Terry's head. *Gone, all gone.*

Terry pushed away from the house and slid down the side. When he landed, his barking dog ran up to him. Terry yelled at Kona to shut-up. His dog backed away and ran back over the debris barking again. Mindlessly, Terry followed his dog over the mess toward his truck. When they reached the mud at the high point of the wave, Kona ran up the hill and stood barking next to some bushes.

Mad that only his dog had survived, he picked up a clump of mud and threw it at him. As he followed the flight of the mud, he noticed two chubby legs sticking out from beneath the bushes where Kona was barking. When the mud hit the bush, he heard a cry. The most beautiful sound he would ever hear.

Terry fell down in the muck as he raced toward his dog. Crawling and stumbling toward the bushes, Kona barked louder. Finally Terry reached down and pushed the branches back. There was Mighty Mite, his son Tommy, crying and looking up at him with tears streaming down his beautiful chubby mud covered cheeks. When Terry carefully picked up his son, Tommy recognized his dad and stopped crying. He rewarded his dad with a mud smeared smile.

Little Tommy had on his little life vest. *Mama was going to take you swimming,* Terry thought. *She didn't know she was saving your life, did she?*

Terry cradled his boy on his chest and swayed from side to side to calm him. Carefully wiping away Tommy's tears, he made streaks of mud down his boy's face. He laughed and hugged his son as Kona nipped at his hand. Terry went down on one knee sitting his son on the other. Kona licked Mighty's mud covered face and the boy gave his dog a big smile. Terry grabbed Kona's neck crushing them both to his chest as his eyes filled with tears. After glancing skyward in a moment of thanks, Terry pulled off Tommy's vest and threw it in the muck.

Steve joined his friend standing quietly next to him. He couldn't believe anything could survive that terrible wave let alone a small kid and a dog. With a sigh, he realized sometimes you beat the odds. He had done it, why not this kid. Then he noticed a trail leading from the mud up to the bushes. It was a single smooth path with deep dog prints on each side of it.

After Steve helped Terry up, he pointed to the ground. Terry looked down, but wasn't sure what he was supposed to see.

"The trail, the trail with the dog prints on each side. I think your dog dragged your boy up here to save him."

Terry knelt down again and looked at the prints. Sure enough that's what must have happened. As he wondered how that could happen, Kona nuzzled his nose under Terry's arm. Terry put one arm around his dog's neck and kissed him. With his tail wagging, Kona gave him a big slurp across his face. As Terry hugged his mud covered dog and son, he thought. *This time, I'm not the only one to survive.*

CHAPTER 34

Good afternoon, I'm Rob Ross and this is *Ithaca Today*. With me today is Dr. Daniel Cooper from the Ithaca College Seismic Center. We're here to talk about who killed Cayuga Lake and how they did it. Dr. Cooper, may I call you Doc?"

"I'd prefer Dan."

"All right, Doc. First we need to talk about the human cost. It's been a month. How many were killed in this disaster?"

"The death toll is pretty firm now, but a number can't possibly represent the true impact of this disaster. No number can describe the suffering inflicted on the citizens of this community and their environment."

"Certainly the true impact can't be measured, but for our viewers, what's the final death toll, Doc?"

"That's Dan. The number stands at just over 7,000, but there are still missing persons. That death toll makes this one of the worst natural disasters in American history."

"Describe the worst of it for us."

"Ithaca was hit hardest. The Tsunami surge at the southern end of the lake wiped out almost half of the town. A little over 3,400 people died downtown. That included three public schools having summer activities. Around the lake there were pockets of disaster. Two places that were hit hard were Camp Minnechaug and the Taughannock Falls State Park. At the camp, they were having a year-end swim meet where over 400 hundred spectators, campers and camp staff died. I knew many of the staff and feel a personal loss."

Feeling the impact of what he had just said, Dan looked at his feet nodding his head. Then he looked up and continued. "There was a rock concert at the state park. Over a thousand died there. Oh, and Wells College. It was completely inundated by the Tsunami. Another 700 died there. The Tompkins County Airport lost planes and people. One plane filled with people was washed away, but everyone in it survived."

"Almost all the people living around the lake were wiped out. People in cars were swept off the roads and lost. Others enjoying the lake in small cabins and homes all died. Let's see, who am I forgetting? Oh, of course. The environmental protesters at the RealAirGas site and the International Salt Combine mine were killed. Almost 700 died at the RAG and ISC sites. My fiancée was one of them. It's a terrible list that just goes on and on."

Thinking of Shelley's golden hair and exquisite smile, Dan sighed and looked at the floor again wondering if he was ready to do an interview like this.

"What about the economic impact, Doc?"

Finding it hard to concentrate, Dan answered, "Please call me Dan. The list is long, but I'll highlight some of the worst damage. It will take a long time for downtown Ithaca to recover. The ISC salt mine is gone. Completely filled with water. The collapsed mine is now the bottom of the lake. The RealAirGas drilling site was wiped out. Hopefully that will end fracking around here for a long time. Too bad it takes a disaster of this magnitude to eliminate fracking."

"Let's see, businesses, gas stations and most of the homes along the lake are just gone. Roads are washed out. They can be fixed, but no one can bring back the people we lost. The head of RealAirGas was lost in the lake, but his family survived. The wave hit their mini-van. Miracle of miracles, they rode it out ending up in the top of a tree."

"Doc, the personal cost can't be measured, but what about our institutions?"

"Cornell University lost almost half of its buildings from the initial quake. The one the media is calling "747." Almost 200 students were lost as buildings fell on them. Others were hit by falling trees and some died from other accidents caused by the quake. A good friend and colleague of mine, Dr. Colby Lindenhurst, died when his building collapsed. Many of Cornell's buildings were built before building codes were established and the quake decimated them. My college, Ithaca College, only lost about 2% of our buildings and 71 students. Our buildings are newer and meet today's stricter building codes. Modern construction standards saved lives.

"Doc, shift to the ecology of the lake."

"Call me Dr. Cooper or Dan, please. The ecology of the lake and its environment has completely changed. Let's see, where do I start? The lake has lost approximately one-third of its volume. Not lost really, but one third of the lake is now in what used to be the salt mine. The water in the lake is slowly dissolving the salt beds at the bottom of the lake and is getting saltier all the time. It will remain a salt water lake far into the future. Probably forever. Fish are dead or dying. Vegetation in the lake is dead. Due to the salt content, Cayuga can no longer be used as a source of drinking water for the area. Now water has to be shipped in from surrounding communities. Simply put, the lake will never regain its former glory in our lifetime. Man has ruined a national treasure."

"Doc, let's turn to your specialty. How did this happen."

"Rob, please call me Dan or Dr. Cooper. I consider Doc sort of insulting."

"Sorry Dr. Cooper. Let me try again. Doc, what caused this disaster?"

Wanting to slap this guy, Dan wondered why he had agreed to come on this show. The disaster was still too raw for his mind to handle. "The death of Cayuga Lake was a combination of natural and human factors. It started with the salt mine. This was a big dangerous hole in the ground just waiting for a collapse. It was dangerous for two reasons. The pedestals that supported the mine floors were designed to withstand an earthquake between 4 or 5 on the Richter scale. This quake is being called the 'Jumbo Quake' because it was 7.47 on the Richter scale."

Rob looked puzzled so Dan added, "You know, like the 747 Jumbo Jet. The quake snapped many of the pedestals that held up the mine floors. This made each level of the mine weaker, but if it was just the quake, the mine might have survived."

"What made the mine collapse, Dr. Dan?"

Annoyed by the moderator's continued attempts to corrupt his name and piss him off with his insolent tone, Dan decided to ignore him and concentrated on the question. "Now RealAirGas enters the picture. When RAG started drilling at the northern end of the lake, the injection of fracking fluid and the disposal of wastewater under great pressure into the strata deep below the surface started what is called a 'Swarm' of small earthquakes around the drilling site."

"Dr. Dan, our audience is now viewing a map you brought with you with red circles on it. Describe what those circles represent."

Still recovering from the shock of this disaster, Dan got mad at what he considered the moderator's demeaning alterations of his name. In a sarcastic tone, he answered, "Well Robby, each circle represents a small earthquake between 1.0 and 4.0 on the Richter Scale. These quakes were too small for most people to notice and by themselves would not have caused a disaster. Now look at that line of circles leading to the west. The gas company forced waste water under high pressure into the ground and this vile salt-laden crap flowed along a fissure to the Clarendon-Linden fault. This is a major fault not much different from the well-known San Andreas Fault in California."

Feeling emotional and wondering if he was strong enough to continue, Dan struggled on. "When the fracking fluid reached the Linden fault, this fluid lubricated the fault plates. The friction holding these fault plates together was reduced letting them slide over each other. When fault plates shift like that you get earthquakes. In this case, a jumbo quake. Today we are concentrating on the impact of the quake on Cayuga Lake and Ithaca, but the damage to the cities around us was also devastating. From Buffalo to Albany, people had to be rescued from collapsed buildings and roads were torn apart. Businesses were ruined. It took them over a week to put out the fires from ruptured gas lines. Water and sewer lines are still broken. People are finding it difficult to recover from this quake. The quake has ended what we consider normal life in upstate New York for a long time."

Rob didn't like the tone Dan used when he called him Robby. Now he felt he was the injured party and fired back, "Doctor Danny, so you're saying that RealAirGas is responsible for the quake."

Ignoring Robby's attempt to provoke him, Dan answered, "That's exactly what I'm saying. If it wasn't for their fracking fluid, this quake would never have happened."

Disappointed that Doctor Dan didn't react to his insult, Robby decided to call out this expert. "You're contradicting what you just said. You just told us the salt company caused the quake by not having strong enough supports."

"That's right." Dan wondered when this had become an adversarial interview. He had been asked to come on this show to describe the geology of the quake. He decided to ignore Robby's attack. "You're missing the sequence of events."

In a bored tone, Robby interrupted him, "My viewing audience is waiting for you to describe that sequence. Can you get to the point?"

Dan answered, "I'm trying to do just that if you give me a chance."

"What's stopping you?"

"At the moment, you are."

Hearing the need for a commercial break through his earpiece, Rob announced, "Hold that thought Doc. We need a short break to pay for the show."

As soon they were off the air, Dan asked, "What the hell are you trying to do. I'm here to describe the quake and you're attacking me?"

"My we are a little touchy aren't we Doc?"

"There you go again. Why do you insist on calling me Doc? Why can't you just call me by my name, Dan?"

"Doc, it's my show. I get to call the guests whatever I want."

"Well, you can call me gone. I'm out of here. I don't need you or your show."

Through his earpiece his producer pleaded with Robby, "Apologize and keep this guy here. We don't have much time."

Robby swallowed his pride and begged Dan to stop as he was pulling off his microphone. "Dr. Cooper, Dan I'm sorry. Don't leave, you're doing great. The people out there need to hear what you have to say. They're trying to figure out this mess and you know what happened."

"You'll call me Dan?"

"Yes, yes or Dr. Cooper anything you want. I didn't mean to insult you. I was just concentrating on the questions and Doc rolled off my tongue."

"Okay, I'll stay. But it's Dan or I walk."

When the red camera light changed to green after the commercial, all the viewers saw was Dr. Cooper adjusting his clip-on microphone.

Robby began carefully, "Dan, when we left, you were about to describe the sequence of events for this disaster. Would you please do that for us now?"

Pleased with Rob's respect, Dan continued. "First, the salt company digs a big hole in the ground they call a mine. A really big hole. Then the gas company pumps fracking fluid between the layers of strata deep below their wells. This fluid flows through a crack under the lake and weakens the bottom of the mine. This fluid also runs west to the Linden Fault and lubricates the fault plates. This lubricant on the plates caused a big earthquake that broke open a crack in the strata under the lake. The lake drained into this crack causing a whirlpool of water. This water ripped open the crack. The water running down the crack collapsed all the layers of the mine. When the mine caved in, the water from the lake literally fell into the mine. When this falling water hit the bottom of the mine, it released a tremendous amount of energy. This energy shoots up and hits the water now flowing into the mine. The energy from this collision initiates a large wave or Tsunami that devastates everything around the lake. This sequence of events resulted in the destruction of the infrastructure, an environmental disaster and a human catastrophe almost beyond measure.

"How can a mine collapse generate a Tsunami? Isn't that an ocean thing?"

"The mine collapse displaced a massive amount of the water in the lake."

"What do you mean displaced?"

"Let's see, how can I explain it? Say you had a bucket of water. When you tip it to one side the water pours out. Now imagine a bucket with a trap door in the bottom of it. When you open the trap door on the bottom, the water doesn't just pour out, it actually drops out. With the lake, the mine collapse created a huge hole under the water and the water actually dropped into the mine to fill that hole."

"It gets worse. When the falling water hit the floor of the mine, it splashes back up with great energy. The combination of the water falling into the hole and the water splashing up from the bottom crashing together produced an incredible amount of energy. This energy came to the surface creating a wave the Japanese call a Tsunami."

Still confused Rob asked, "Wait, wait, a Tsunami? They only happens in Japan or Hawaii out in the ocean. We're talking about a lake in the middle of New York State. How can Tsunami happen in a lake?"

"You're right, Tsunamis are usually ocean events. Fault plates under the ocean shift and displace water. When the water smashes back together it produces the energy to create a powerful wave or Tsunami. Scientists have known for a long time that lake Tsunamis are possible. Lake Tahoe residents are living with this danger right now. There are fault plates under that lake. If they shift and displace a sufficient amount of water, it could produce a Tsunami on Lake Tahoe just like the one we had here."

"Did a fault open up under what's left of Cayuga Lake?"

"No. The key feature in this Tsunami is the displacement of the water. When the salt mine collapsed, it displaced a large amount of water. This falling water created the energy to generate a Tsunami on the lake."

"Wow, I did not know that. People say they didn't see a big wave until it suddenly appeared. Does that make any sense?"

"That's typical Tsunami action. The Japanese called the waves Tsunamis or harbor waves. Fishermen go out in the ocean and never see a big wave. Then they come back to find their harbor and everything around it destroyed. Out in the ocean, or in this case the lake, the Tsunami is not a large wave. It becomes dangerous when it gets to shallow water. The energy in the wave is concentrated when it hits the lake bottom and suddenly grew into the terrifying destroyer we saw all around the lake. Many of the survivors reported the classic Tsunami feature of drawback before it hit."

"Drawback? What's that?"

"Before a Tsunami, the water on the shore recedes or draws back. You've heard of people walking out on the ocean beach when the water is being pulled away from the shoreline. They walk out into the ocean looking for shells or to explore the area that was under water. When the Tsunami hits, they all die because they have no chance to escape the fast moving wave. The water drew back the same way in the Cayuga Lake. Many of the survivors reported seeing this phenomenon. It was even caught on film."

"A lake Tsunami, amazing. So if I'm following you. The salt mine provided the hole under the lake. Then the fracking fluid set off the quake that collapsed the mine. The water in the lake fell into the mine generating the Tsunami. Is that it?"

"Now you've got it. Man and nature combining to destroy the lake and people around it."

"We don't have much time left. Let me turn to another topic. Tonight I understand that you are going to appear in a documentary that is supposed to prove beyond a shadow of a doubt that prehistoric dinosaurs are living in Cayuga Lake. Would you care to comment and try to convince us?"

"Not dinosaurs. If you will aquasaurs. Most scientists identify them as aquatic carnivores that are called Pliosaurs. These ancient animals have lived since prehistoric time in the lake. The video evidence in tonight's show will convince you. We found that there is a breeding population living in the lake."

"Wait, wait. How could a bunch of aquasaurs, as you call them, exist in Cayuga Lake without people seeing them?"

"Tonight's special will answer that question. The team researched the history of the lake. In the past, there have been sightings, but they were dismissed as fakes or falsely identified as something else. The Native Americans saw them and honored them in their ceremonies and legends."

"Okay, we may have seen them before. Why do they all of a sudden show up for you to photograph them now?"

"I can't really tell you for sure, but I have a theory."

"I bet you do. What is it?"

"The fracking fluid from RealAirGas polluted the lake. Remember the night when the lake caught fire."

"Of course, our On-the-Spot News Team got footage of that horrible environmental disaster and shared it with our viewers."

"R.A.G.'s operation forced gasoline into the lake. I think the aquasaurs like to stay deep in the lake and the pollution drove them to the surface. The team that caught them on tape happened to be in the right place at the right time. They had come to the lake to film some fossil ancestors of these aquasaurs. Annie Brandt from the Mashantucket Pequot Museum found a fossil of them."

"None of us thought the film crew would end up recording real lake creatures or the destruction of the lake from the quake. This is the same crew that filmed the quake and tsunami that has been broadcast over and over on national television. They lost two of their crew to the Tsunami. All the followers of the NEC channel will miss Jerry James and his assistant, Kia Washington. Sorry, I digress. Tonight's show will prove these creatures exist up close and personal."

"You certainly have caught my attention. I'll be watching tonight, but won't this be like every other *Big Foot* program on TV? You know fuzzy images of something disappearing in the distance. I'll believe you when I actually see one of these things."

"I guarantee this won't be one of those shows with a cloudy image disappearing in the water."

Dan looked directly into the camera. "I'm not supposed to tell you, but tonight you'll see a real live lake monster smiling for the camera."

"What do you mean alive?"

"I mean just that, alive. After the Tsunami, the camp caretaker found a juvenile aquasaur at the bottom of the falls at Camp Minnechaug. Joseph Brandt, the narrator of tonight's premiere, thought this creature was dead. When he approached it, he discovered it was still alive. Evidently, it was caught by the Tsunami and knocked out when it was rammed into the cliff face at the camp. With the help of other members of the camp staff they corralled it. Well, they confined it to the pool below the falls at the camp and fed it. It's alive and well. More than fossils and films, tonight, you'll get to meet the actual creature. Wait until you see this guy, you won't believe him. This prehistoric animal is truly amazing."

Getting the notice to wrap up the show, Rob decided to tease his guest one final time. "Doc, I'm sorry to say that's all the time we have. You've been great. I can guarantee I'll be watching tonight. Until then I'll wait to make up my mind about your lake monster. A lake Tsunami and a live dinosaur. We are living in amazing times in Ithaca. Next week, I will interview a man with the most astounding story of survival that you will ever hear. He was boating on the lake when he was sucked to the bottom of the lake and flushed into the salt mine. Then had to out run the Tsunami in a Ford pickup. This is Rob Ross signing off for *Ithaca Today*."

****

Standing above the falls, Hilda shook the container of Harold's ashes into the water. After she said a short prayer, Shanty and Annie blessed the ceremony with a short chant. After the flakes of sand floated over the falls, she did the same with Ursula's. As the last bits of ash fell, Shanty put his arm around Hilda's waist and embraced her carefully. He knew her bruised ribs were still hurting from being slammed into the tree by the wave and probably from him hitting her in the chest. He hadn't mentioned that to her.

Billy kissed Hilda on the cheek and Annie held her hand. Slowly they walked away from the water rushing over the falls to the vista overlooking the new salt lake. It was still blue, but had visibly shrunk in size. A brown strip now ringed the lake between the blue water and green land. It looked like a dirty ring around a bathtub.

They walked to where Shanty had unrolled a long sheet of paper that he held down with stones at each corner. On one knee, he gathered the others around him.

"This camp can survive. People swim in salt water all the time. Here is my vision for the camp. We get rid of all evidence of the old hotel and build a modern dining hall and infirmary over here."

Pointing at his drawing. "We build a steel structured administration building and year round hotel down by the shore. On the other side of the camp, we build a year round lodge for boys and girls. We will still have cabins during the summer, but now the camp can be used all year long. Over here, we'll build a double gym with shower rooms in the middle."

Hilda interrupted, "I want to keep Harold's vision of selecting needy campers alive, but the winter session will only be for Tribal Americans from across the country. Shanty you will be in charge of the physical fitness program. Annie, after you deliver Apotamkon's fossil to your museum, I want you to come back and take charge of the culture program. We will all work on recruiting Native American girls and boys for the fall and winter sessions. Billy, after you graduate, you will be in charge of the outdoor education program. Until then you will help me select the people who will implement the program. As a team, we will breathe life into this camp again. Make it better than ever."

Communicate at: daltonmire@yahoo.com

ABOUT THE AUTHOR

As a boy, Dalton Mire learned of a way of life long gone as he walked through plowed fields picking up arrowheads and broken pottery with his father. He enjoyed the cool waters of Cayuga Lake after collecting fossils along its shores. Once after reading a book about Nessie of Loch Ness, he was sure he saw an ancient dinosaur disappear in a bank of fog hovering over the shimmering waves. Dalton Mire spent his adult life working around the world and was shocked when he returned to Cayuga shores to find this beautiful lake threatened by fracking. *Fracking Dinosaurs* dramatizes the need to preserve this delicate ecosystem from the industries that threaten it.

CPSIA information can be obtained
at www.ICGtesting.com
Printed in the USA
FFOW02n0212050417
34210FF

9 781460 221495